Florey, Kitty
Burns.

Duet

NOV 3 0 1987

$16.45

DATE		

DUET

Also by Kitty Burns Florey

Real Life
Family Matters
Chez Cordelia
The Garden Path

DUET

Kitty Burns Florey

William Morrow and Company, Inc.
New York

Library of Congress Cataloging-in-Publication Data

Florey, Kitty Burns.
  Duet.
  I. Title.
PS3556.L588D8   1987   813'.54   87-11166
ISBN 0-688-07222-4

Printed in the United States of America

First Edition

1 2 3 4 5 6 7 8 9 10

BOOK DESIGN BY PHILLIP REDISCH

This book is affectionately dedicated to
La Groupe

Author's Note

I have lived at various times in Syracuse, Boston, and New Haven. The cities and their neighborhoods are real, but all the inhabitants who appear in this book are fictional characters.

I am grateful to the Center for Independent Study in New Haven, Connecticut, and to the National Endowment for the Arts, for their support during the writing of this book. And thanks to Leander Bien, Amy M. Davis, Frank Dineen, Jim Hadler, Carolyn Kone, and Martha Bennett Oneppo for invaluable assistance.

KITTY BURNS FLOREY

First of all, love is a joint experience between two persons—but the fact that it is a joint experience does not mean that it is a similar experience to the two people involved. There are the lover and the beloved, but these two come from different countries. . . .

—CARSON MCCULLERS
The Ballad of the Sad Café

If love is a thorn, they show no wit
Who foolishly hug and foster it.

—W. S. GILBERT
Patience

All you need is love, love,
Love is all you need.

—THE BEATLES

ANNA

EARLY WINTER

1

My grandmother, Mamie Nolan, was a singer—an untrained, instinctive, domestic, noisy contralto. She came to live with us when I was sixteen, after my mother died, and when she got going on "Danny Boy" or "Come Back to Erin" in our tiny living room, playing chords by ear on the piano, with the pedal permanently down, I used to grit my teeth with embarrassment. If it was summer and the windows were open, I imagined the neighbors cursing us while they tried to listen to a ball game or eat dinner in peace or get the baby off to sleep. Even in the winter, coming home from school on twilit afternoons, I could hear Mamie's voice escaping through our flimsy storm windows like warm air, and I used to get inside fast, before anyone could stop me to complain.

And yet I knew she had a beautiful voice, one that all through my childhood had lulled and comforted me in my bad moments. It wasn't that I didn't love hearing it. Even as I seethed and squirmed and wished she would shut up, the warmth and depth of it, the mysterious huskiness of the top notes, the lovely old sad songs she favored, could invade me if I let it, could unclench my teeth and smooth my brow and loosen the various knots that bound me.

I might not have minded a certain amount of visibility, even notoriety, for myself; I had my reasons for wanting to be singled out. But all I asked of my family was inconspicuousness, a quality Mamie stubbornly refused to cultivate. Her speaking voice was almost as fortissimo as her singing. She was tall and broad and she wore outrageous hats—her one extravagance. She was demonstrative and nosy and fussy. I loved her fiercely and she drove me crazy. I suppose she felt the same; I was certainly not an easy teenager to have around the place.

13

My father taught English at the public high school. I attended, from age six, St. Joseph's Catholic Academy. My father's place of employment gave me status with my fellow students; the nuns, however, didn't like it at all. Northside High was forbidden territory. We were given periodic pep talks on the dangers of dating, or even befriending, the kids from Northside. They might be "non-Catholics" or—almost worse—"lapsed Catholics." The point was, there was no sure way of knowing *what* they were. If we stuck to parochial-school kids, we could be sure they were securely within the fold. "It just makes sense, doesn't it?" Sister Marguerite, our senior-year homeroom teacher, used to ask us, looking smilingly over her Ben Franklin glasses, clasping her hands before a starched bib that was as spotless as she hoped our souls were. "It just makes your life that much easier."

That these cautions acknowledged some precariousness in our adolescent Catholicism, a certain inclination of our souls to smudge, never seemed to occur to her. Before I realized I was some species of lapsed Catholic myself, I couldn't help feeling that the oppressive burden of faith I carried around was, paradoxically, light as a leaf, able to be blown away by the merest heathen breeze, and in constant need of tending.

On Tuesday afternoons, as we filed out of school by the west door—obediently silent and segregated by sex, uniformed, and carrying armloads of books—the wilder Catholics from Northside High would be entering by the east door for religious instruction: bookless, in mixed couples, in jeans and bright skirts and leather jackets, and laughing—no doubt at us. Because my father came into daily contact with these blithe fringes of the Church, the nuns saw me as vaguely suspect, possibly subversive. I know they blamed my modest rebellious impulses (I talked in class, I wore my skirts too short and tried to get away with eye makeup, I was once caught cutting benediction on a Friday afternoon during Lent) at least partly on my father's teaching job and its dangerous influences. It made me someone to be watched.

They watched harder than ever after my mother died. Once, I was stopped in the hall by a nun I barely knew, Sister Veronica from downstairs in the elementary school. She said, "You're the girl who lost her mother, aren't you?" I admitted it. "I hope you pray for her every day," she went on. "And *we*—" She nodded her head thoughtfully, fixing me with a look I could only interpret as threatening. "*We* are praying for *you*, my girl."

14

I needed prayers, though not for the reasons the nuns supposed. They expected me, motherless, to burst loose in some unspecific but probably sexual way. Girls without a mother to control them wouldn't know any better than to give in to what nuns called the baser passions. What the nuns didn't know was that I was kept from transgressions of that sort by my pure love for Will Westenberg, the thin, poor, unfriendly boy whom no one liked but me. It was the kind of love that maybe only lonely, romantic teenage girls are capable of: unrequited and thorough. It absorbed most of my waking moments, and many of my dreams. For years, since the day in third grade when he stood by me waiting for a turn at the pencil sharpener and smiled at me his shy smile, nothing else interested me much. The baser passions attracted me only in terms of Will. I would have become his mistress, stolen for him, thrown bombs, smoked dope, gone on the streets, if he'd asked me to. He didn't, of course. The only things he'd ever asked me for were the loan of my homework, or of the odd dime so he could play Elvis singing "My Baby Left Me" on the jukebox at Smitty's. I used to gaze at the back of his head in Latin class and think: *Moriar propter te. I would die for you.*

I needed prayers not because of my sex life, which was minimal, but because of my father, who was also minimal. I mean by this that when my mother died my father withdrew from life. He stopped talking. He lost weight and forgot to get his hair cut. He went to school, where presumably he stirred himself enough to teach the leather-jacketed heathens about Shakespeare and Milton. He came home, ate dinner in silence, read the *Herald-Journal*, took a long walk, graded papers, and went to bed early—to meet who knows what demons that still inhabited the room he used to share with my mother. Sometimes he asked me how school was going and forgot to finish listening to my answer. Often he smiled vaguely in my direction as if he thought I were some stranger he'd remembered it was his duty to be polite to. Once, he didn't say a word to me or acknowledge my presence for two days.

His behavior went on so long that I wondered after a while whether grief was the cause, or if this seed of eccentric detachment had always been a part of my father that only my mother's presence had kept from flowering. I wondered what there was of him in me, if the days when I came straight home from school and sat dry-eyed and angry and miserable on my bed until dinnertime, with only Charlotte the cat for company, was the first stage of a life like the cold and lonely one my father had begun to lead.

I don't know how it was arranged that Mamie came to live with us; I doubt my father asked her. I expect she just came, and my father was too apathetic to ask her to go.

It helped to have her there. I suffered horribly from my father's remote sorrow; it was like losing two parents. Before my mother left for the hospital, while I was helping her pack into the pink overnight case a matching lace-trimmed nightgown and bed jacket, her cosmetic case, a bottle of My Sin, and the new *Ladies' Home Journal,* she said to me, "Take care of Daddy while I'm gone." I lay awake at night for months after that terrible Christmas when she died, listening to my father pacing the floor while her words banged in my head. How could I take care of Daddy when he barely noticed I was there? And was I destined always to love those to whom I was nothing?

The three of us lived crammed into the little house on Spring Street that my parents had rented ever since I could remember. Mamie slept in the alcove off the living room. My bedroom was the small room behind the kitchen—meant to be a pantry, I suppose, but large enough for a single bed and a dresser with a mirror over it. Daddy built a long shelf high up on one wall where I arranged my sparse hoard of books, my miniature animals, various school mementos, a crystal vase filled with dusty silk violets, a wooden box containing my mother's costume jewelry, four years' worth of locked diaries, and a picture of Will Westenberg and me in costume for a fifth-grade Thanksgiving pageant.

I spent long stretches of time in that room. Years later, I can recall every detail of it. I can see the wallpaper, its background darkened to beige by the years, and the pale-pink nosegays tied with faded-blue ribbon that ran up and down it in rows. I could probably draw with accuracy the exact slope of the wall over my bed where the dormer cut in, and the mountainous configuration of the crack that diagonally bisected one pane of glass in the window.

My voluntary solitary confinement there, with the door firmly closed, worried Mamie. Whether she suspected me of reading dirty books, or of dancing naked in front of the mirror, or simply of dangerous antisociality, I don't know. She was not someone you could pin down. "I just don't like it, it's not good," she would say— *not good* was her all-purpose condemnation. I would hear her muttering in the kitchen, to herself or my father or her boss friend, Mrs. Schweid. Mrs. Schweid would make a fat, satisfied *tsk* noise and say, "My Mary Rebecca sits with us in the kitchen, praise God." If my father was there he would say, "Leave the girl alone, Mamie." "Well, what's she doing in there, is what I'd like to know," Mamie would mutter.

Mostly what I did in my room was meditate on Will Westenberg. He was more real to me than my family, my school, my friends, my mother's grave, the writing bump on my third finger, the cold that penetrated my room when the winter wind blew from the north. I wasn't seriously antisocial. I hung around Smitty's after school with my girlfriends. I went to the Friday night dances. I spent long hours on the phone with Martha Finch and Marie Barshak. I even had dates, now and then, with a boy named George Sullivan. I was good at my schoolwork and I sang in the glee club; in my sophomore year, during a rehearsal of a medley of Negro spirituals, I broke down in the middle of "Sometimes I Feel Like a Motherless Child" and had to be led over to the convent by Sister Cecilia for a cup of tea, some unconvincing talk about God's wisdom, and the startling compliment, "Be thankful to God that you've inherited your grandmother's blessed voice," that pointed a direction for me.

But Will was the important fact in my life, as vital as the running of the blood in my veins. There was never a moment of any day when, in some corner of my brain, he wasn't present in all his excellence: his sulky mouth, his lean wrists and golden-downed forearms, his broad and bony back, the splotches of rose-red that appeared on his cheekbones when he was called on in school. If I did my homework with care, it was mostly so that if he asked to borrow it I would be ready for him. When I won the New York State Dental Health Essay Contest, and the All-City Latin Competition, and the oratorical contests at school, I cared only that he might notice me. Singing in the glee club at the Winter Concert and the Spring Musicale, I sang directly to him. If I couldn't be near him, what I liked best was to huddle under the blanket on my bed, staring at the wallpaper flowers and thinking of him.

Once, during Lent, Sister Josephina passed out a leaflet entitled "A Meditation Manual" which gave instructions for meditating on the suffering, crucifixion, and death of Christ. It said the keys to successful meditation were concentration (on, for example, the five wounds of Jesus), knowledge (of the subject of one's

17

meditation), imagination (of the blissful reunion with God in heaven), and devotion (to same).

Joey McCoy, class clown, changed the tall blue letters on the cover, in heavy ballpoint, to "A Masturbation Manual," passed it around the room, and was betrayed by our laughter, as he almost always was. He was sent to the office, and Sister Josephina gave us a short lecture on reverence and nastiness. When the fuss was over and the class settled down to read the manual, I realized I spent a large part of my time doing what could only be called meditating—on Will. Concentration, knowledge, imagination, and devotion: where Will was concerned, I was master of them all. It came to me, as I sat there in Sister Josephina's classroom, with crucified Jesus hanging sadly on the wall over the blackboard, and Will Westenberg sitting in a front seat two rows over, that I was an idolator. "I am the Lord thy God, thou shalt not have strange gods before me": that was the rhythmic and awe-inspiring first commandment, the one the nuns had always told us was the foundation for the others. Unless we loved God above all else we couldn't properly keep holy the Lord's day or honor our fathers and our mothers or refrain from stealing, murder, and adultery. I looked at suffering Jesus and at the back of Will's neck where the rough light hair was clipped short, and I knew my choice was made. I didn't, at that moment, like a reverse St. Paul, lose my faith in one blinding stroke, but I began to see that it had been quietly deteriorating since that day at the pencil sharpener. I saw that Will was my golden calf.

I wrote in my diary that night (March 5, 1959), "Vivam pro amore," not knowing exactly what I meant but feeling it had greater validity as an idea than living for a faith I had lost somewhere without even realizing it—as I had, over the years, lost pocket handkerchiefs and mittens and my birthstone ring.

My devotion was remarkably unrewarded. Until our last year at St. Joseph's, I couldn't even claim Will as a friend. I hoarded any contact I had with him—silver moments I banked and counted over in my bedroom: every borrowed math paper, every smile and kind word, every accidental touching of hands or shoulders. These were few, not only because of his indifference to me but because Will just wasn't around much. He was a chronic school-cutter, he didn't go to dances, and if he stopped in at Smitty's after school he stood leaning against the jukebox in silence, speaking if he was spoken to, occasionally borrowing a dime or laughing at someone's joke. Marie called him "Rebel Without a Cause," and everyone deplored his shabby clothes and home-cut hair, but I loved his shy aloofness and what I thought of as the clean poverty that set him apart: I could fancy that, living in his drab little house on Danforth Street with his pale and saintly mother, his dour German-speaking father, his two tall, horsey-looking older sisters, he was saving himself for me. Any day he would become aware of the affinity between us, he would stroll over to me at Smitty's, he would raise his voice over the sound of Elvis and the Everly Brothers, take my arm, and say, "Let's get out of here."

There was a late afternoon around Christmastime the year before my mother died. I was fourteen. We had company at our house: Mamie was there, and Uncle Ralph and Aunt Nancy, Uncle Phil and Aunt Gert and my cousin Roseanne, the Schweids (including pudgy, prim Mary Rebecca and her two fiendish little sisters), and the principal of my father's school and his wife. We had crowded into our living room to hear Mamie sing, as we often did when there was company. She would eventually belt out her Christmas specialties, in particular "O Holy Night" and "When Flowers Blossomed in the Snow," but it was the old, romantic, sentimental songs she liked best, and at the moment I am recalling she was singing "I Dreamt I Dwelt in Marble Halls."

I remember this because in the middle of it the doorbell rang. My mother frowned at me to answer it, and at the door was Will Westenberg.

"Oh," I said when I saw him there. He was wearing a brown knitted hat. Two spots of rose-red colored his cheekbones. He was carrying a paper bag.

"Hi," Will said, and looked past me into the house. Mamie's voice carried out to the porch and beyond, out to the snowy streets:

> *I had riches too great to count,*
> *Could boast of a high ancestral name.*

He has come to see me, I thought. He has come to give me something. He has come because it's Christmas, because he has loved me secretly all these years, because I love him so much I called him to me, because he is Will, he is my Will.

Will rummaged in the bag. "I'm delivering the prizes for the Christmas-card sale." He pulled out a tissue-wrapped package. "This is yours."

Why Will, who was usually on the wrong side of the nuns, had been deputized to trek out in the cold to deliver the plastic angels and holy-water fonts and rosaries we had won by brow-beating our parents and neighbors into buying cards on behalf of the African missions, I never knew.

I took the package from him, my fingers touched his glove, I said thanks.

"Feels like an angel," he said.

"Right." I had a mad impulse to kneel and lay it at his feet: *You are my angel, take it, I love you.* "Big fat deal," I said.

He smiled at me suddenly, and we looked at each other in silence for a moment. Some kind of alliance hovered between us, based on the absurd fact of the plastic angel and all it implied: Will's perennial troubles at school, my own small reputation as a rebel, various unspoken shared hells.

My heart turned over; my eyes misted. I thought, correctly, I'll remember this moment all my life. Behind me, in the warm room, Mamie sang,

> *But I also dreamt which pleased me most,*
> *That you loved me still the same,*
> *That you loved me,*
> *You loved me still the same . . .*

Then it was gone. He shrugged. "So Merry Christmas, Anna."

"Merry Christmas, Will," I said.

I watched him go down the porch steps: brown hat, red jacket, battered leather gloves, unfastened rubber galoshes.

> *That you loved me,*
> *You loved me still the same.*

There was a florid run on the piano and a burst of applause. "And Happy New Year," I called.

He turned. It was freezing out. The tip of his nose was red. He said, "Same to you, kid."

I went back inside and, company or no company, retreated to my cold room and unwrapped the plastic angel. It was blue and white, with a baby face and furled feather-textured wings tipped in gold. It gazed down at its hands, which were joined in prayer. I smoothed the tissue paper—he had touched it—and stood on my bed to put it on my shelf; I set the angel on top of the tissue paper.

Mamie was taking a break; I heard everyone talking, my mother offering plates of cookies and candied fruit. Little Patty Schweid screamed, "No, no, no!" The song whirled in my brain, and the memory of Will's smile, his words, his beloved face, his breath in the cold like a white cloud, the brief complicity between us.

I sat on my bed and banged my head on the wall behind me. I will die of this, I thought. Will, my angel, my trap, my life. "Kid," he had called me: What did it mean? what did he know? how could he not know? "So Merry Christmas," he had said, and spoken my name. I put my hands over my mouth and bit the flesh of my palm to keep from crying out.

In the other room, loud enough to reach heaven, Mamie began on "O Holy Night." I hardly noticed. "That you loved me, you loved me still the same," echoed in my head, and Will and I were in a great hall somewhere, running toward each other down a vast open corridor. We met, his arms went around me, we kissed, we sank to the floor and pulled at each other's clothes. I stroked his hair and murmured, "Will, Will, my angel, my love."

When he began dating my friend Martha Finch in the fall of senior year, my face broke out for the first time in my life—angry red welts on my chin and, when things were especially bad (like the time I was forced to watch them kissing on Martha's porch), on the end of my nose. I used to join the crowd at Smitty's, flirting with George Sullivan and Johnny Tenaro, talking to Marie, drinking Cokes, and fingering the pimples on my chin, while Will and Martha stood over in a corner talking quietly, hand in hand or with his arm around her shoulder. Once I saw him lift her hand to his lips and kiss it, and I had to leave. I made George drive me home, kissed him passionately in broad daylight, burst into tears, and ran inside, leaving him there to puzzle over my behavior. When he called me, I refused to come to the phone. "Are you still using that Clearasil?" Mamie asked me.

The worst agony, and the most complicated, was listening to Martha talk about Will. Not that she said much, not nearly as much as she had said about other boys she had dated. I wondered if she guessed my feelings for him and so spared me—though I think not, probably. What I think is that Martha was discovering the delights of secrecy that I had been familiar with for so long.

Still, I knew a lot. I knew they double-dated with Arlene Nuncio and Art Brewer, who were known to be sex maniacs. I knew they went to the drive-in a lot that fall. "Will is crazy about movies," Martha said—a fact about him I immediately stored away in my small bank account, knowing of course that people didn't go to drive-ins to watch movies. I saw the two of them at parties, and at the Friday night dances. Will had never been so sociable; it was generally agreed that Martha had brought him out—that and the money he was making at his job as a delivery boy for the Victory Market. "From Rebel Without a Cause to the Reluctant Debutante," Marie said, and Martha laughed and said, "God, wasn't that an awful movie? Will and I hated it," and I imagined Sandra Dee on the huge screen at the Starlite Drive-in pouting down at Martha and Will necking in the backseat of Art Brewer's '54 Chevy.

Another time she said to me, "He's really strange. You know— wild. He scares me a little."

"Oh, really?" I spoke cautiously, not too interested. My heart pounded. Strange, wild, scary: the passionate Will of my fantasy life. "Like how?"

"Oh, I don't know," Martha sighed. I could tell she wasn't going to say more. "Sometimes I don't know what I see in him."

"Well, he's kind of good-looking."

"Do you think so?" We were talking on the phone, and I knew Martha was on the extension in her bedroom—her birthday present—and looking over at the enlargement of Will's school picture in a frame on her dresser, a photograph I would have killed for. "I can't decide," she said. "Sometimes he looks sort of— I don't know—scrawny to me. I keep telling him he should eat more. But his family is so *poor*. I feel so sorry for him."

"I guess he is a little thin," I said, thinking of the perfect beauty of his bony fingers, with their delicate tangles of blond hair, and the sharp points of his jawbones beneath his ears. I imagined nuzzling his bones with my tongue.

"Still, you're right," Martha said. "He is kind of cute. But that's not why I like him. There's just something about him, I can't explain it." There was a pause. "I suppose it's the same with you and George."

"Oh, Wilbur," I said. "There's something about Wilbur, all right—his money."

Martha laughed; it was a joke between us, that she was going with the poorest boy in the class and I was hooked up with the wealthiest. We called George "Wilbur" after the rich kid in the *Little Lulu* comics.

"Even aside from his money, I think he's better-looking than Will," Martha said. I cried silently: *You can have him, take him.* "Don't you? Be honest."

"Oh, definitely," I said. Before the cock crows twice, thou shalt deny me thrice.

"George looks a little like John Gavin, I think. Tall, dark, and handsome."

"I really like dark hair," I lied. "Much better than blond." Cock-a-doodle-doo.

Martha giggled. "Speaking of dark hair, Will says I look like a gypsy."

It was that kind of revelation, those insights into their intimacy, that drove me into my room to stare at the pink flowers on the wallpaper and pound my fist on the bed. I would try to imagine the possible context of a remark like that:

1. Martha tossing her black hair—at Smitty's, say—and Will smiling at her: "You look like a gypsy."

2. Will and Martha kissing on the porch, Will whispering into her neck: "My wild, beautiful gypsy."

3. Martha opening the door to Will on Saturday morning with her hair scraggling down unwashed, and Will surveying her with distaste: "God, you look like a gypsy."

I tried to decide if looking like a gypsy was good or bad. Martha was pretty, probably prettier than I was, but she wasn't pretty all the time. She had bad days, and when she parted her hair on the side and let it hang in her eyes she looked awful. (God forgive me, I told her I liked it that way.) And I knew that she sweated like a pig and had a B.O. problem; so did her brother Trevor; they had to use a special deodorant. And she had stubby little fingers: her school ring reached nearly to the knuckle.

I saw her and Will kissing good-night on her porch the one time George and I double-dated with them. We all went out for pizza, and it wasn't a success. Martha liked George, but Will didn't, and the two boys had nothing to say to each other. While we ate, Martha and I did all the talking while Will sat in stubborn silence and George kept putting his hand on my leg under the table. We all drove home in George's huge new Impala. Will walked Martha to the door, and, sitting in the front seat with George's arm around me, I stared into the dimness, unable not to watch. She put her arms around his neck. Will wasn't very tall, but Martha was short, and he had to bend to kiss her.

It was a long kiss. Watching, I remembered the time—a memory that always shamed and confused me—when Martha and I at age eleven or so had tried French kissing. We had giggled at first, and then got to like it, so we stopped. Neither of us ever referred to it. I could still remember the peculiarly musky taste of Martha's mouth, the smooth elasticity of her thin lips. I thought of the old idea that everyone in the world was probably a handshake or two away from everyone else. My uncle Phil, for instance, had shaken the hand of Jack Dempsey once when he made an appearance at the War Memorial, and I had seen a newspaper photograph of Jack Dempsey shaking hands with Jack Kennedy. (I told this to my uncle, and after that he made a point of letting me shake his hand whenever he came over: "this sacred hand," he called it, and claimed he never washed it.) I sat there one kiss away from Will Westenberg, listening to George talk about the American League pennant race with tears welling up in my eyes. They looked so right together, up on that porch. They looked so happy to be kissing each other. I thought of George's wet mouth, and the melodramatic way he moaned between kisses.

George said, "Hey, relax. God, are you tense."

"I can't sit here all night, George. I told Mamie I'd be in early."

George leaned on the horn and yelled "Hey! Lovebirds!" out the window; Will and Martha broke apart and Will came running down to the car.

"I'm going to walk home," he said. "You don't have to wait."

George nudged me and said, "Okay, pal—see you around," and we pulled away. "What an operator," George commented.

"I don't see that it makes him an operator," I replied coldly. "Just because he wants to kiss his date good-night and then walk four lousy blocks home. I don't know why you always think people have to be hauled around in your stupid car, George. I mean, it's a beautiful night, it only makes sense to get out and walk."

George's mouth tightened; I had hurt his feelings. He pulled the car over sharply to the curb and parked. "You're right," he said. "I'll walk you home."

Which meant I had to walk six blocks holding hands with George while he finished giving me his views about the Baltimore Orioles. On the other hand, he could only kiss me a couple of times on my front step instead of trying to take my clothes off for half an hour in the front seat.

DUET

"I'm sorry for yelling at you," I said at the door.

"You going to be home tomorrow?"

"I have to write a book report."

"On what?"

"Oh, I don't know. Some damn thing. I guess on *Wuthering Heights*."

"Good. I'll call you. We can talk about it."

"That would be just stupendously wonderful, George."

It used to amuse George to pretend that irony was lost on him, to take literally every word I uttered. "I'm glad you think so," he said, and he grabbed me and kissed me again. I hated his wet lips and fat tongue, and I disliked the way he smelled—some soap or hair tonic he used that smelled to me like laundry soap. He put a hand on my breast. "You know I really like you, Anna."

Mamie clicked the porch light off and on. "I've got to go in," I said, and broke away, knowing my quick exit was being interpreted as tantalizing maidenly shyness. I brushed past Mamie and shut myself in my room, where I opened my diary and wrote Will's name over and over, like a spell that would exorcise what I had seen, eliminate George and Martha from the evening, and leave only Will's beautiful, tense face sitting across from me at Tino's.

George was devoted to me, pimples and all, and I couldn't stand him. He drove me crazy. George liked to talk about issues, to have intense and serious discussions—about anything: politics, world events, sports, books we read in English, stuff we learned in biology. If he wasn't handsome and rich, if he didn't drive a big convertible, he would have been considered a finky bore like Hanky Wheeler, who talked about his stamp collection and wore ear muffs.

George was always trying to goad me into arguing with him. He insisted, for instance, that Jack Kennedy was a pinko—that was the way George put it. "Pink as a carnation," he said. "Pink as a newborn baby pig." He said that we needed Joe McCarthy to come back and keep our politicians honest. One of his favorite topics was the injustice done to McCarthy back in 1954.

"I saw those hearings on television," he said. "I saw the way they made a fool of him."

I said, "George, you were a little kid. You were eleven years old!"

"I was precocious. I know a bunch of Commies when I see them."

25

"Oh, George, it was McCarthy who was no better than a Communist—spying on people like the secret police. How can he be your hero, George?"

He looked at me with approval and said slowly, "Annie, you are one—warped—cookie." He put his arm around my shoulders and poked one finger into the neck of my sweater. Argument excited George sexually. I pulled away from him. He smiled at me. "I'll bet you think Castro is cute. With that stupid beard."

"Yes, I do, actually," I said, and George pulled me to him and began kissing me, calling me his little Commie, his beatnik. I submitted, trying to pretend he was Will. But I knew Will would never kiss like that.

I did get some benefit from Martha's relationship with Will. He and I, after a fashion, became friends. He talked to me sometimes at school. Once he called me up to get a chemistry assignment. We shared a well-known pecularity: we both thought the whiny, obscure "My Baby Left Me" was Elvis's best song. And we could both sing: his soft true tenor became public knowledge when Martha got him to join the glee club. For a while, the idea was tossed around that Will and I should sing a duet at the Christmas Concert, but nothing ever came of it. Sister Cecilia apparently thought it was too great an honor for someone like Will, who was low on school spirit and had, in fact, just gotten around to joining. I sang a solo as planned, the inevitable "O Holy Night." But because of our shared ability, Will and I were considered, from time to time, as a sort of pair. At parties, people sang old songs that were easy to harmonize—not the showstoppers Mamie favored, but easy ones like "Shine On Harvest Moon" and "Heart of My Heart." Will began coming to parties that autumn with Martha, and he and I always led the harmonies. Sometimes we would smile at each other across the heads of the others, acknowledging how easy it was for us, how good we sounded.

My secret hoard of Will mementos grew into a respectable collection because he was going with Martha—so that, finally, the way I felt about the two of them was not jealousy but sad, irritable gratitude. Part of it was the hope, of course, that I could win him away from her.

I danced with him only once. It was at a Friday night school dance; it was, in fact, November 18, 1960. Will always came to the dances now, with Martha. They always danced together, usually not especially close and often not talking at all, just staring past each other into the crowd with the impatient, vaguely unhappy look that meant they would have preferred to be alone together—or so I interpreted it at the time. A couple of months later, I realized that it might have been plain, uncomplicated misery on their faces.

On this particular night, I was dancing with George—by then I was officially his girlfriend. Martha and Will were next to us on the dance floor, and Martha said, "Quick! Switch partners!"—for some reason, no reason, just fooling around. She grabbed George, and I found myself in Will's arms. It was Oldies-but-Goodies Night; the song was "Mr. Blue." I was so stunned I couldn't speak; it was as if someone I had made up had come to life and touched me. Behind me I could hear George chattering to Martha. Will's arm was around my waist. He held me closer than I would have expected, and he danced well. I was searching desperately for something to say, all the inane teen-magazine conversation starters running through my head (*How do you like your job? What do you think of this song? Wasn't Sister Cecilia being a real bitch at rehearsal today?*) when he surprised me. He put his cheek against my hair and began, softly, to sing. My voice trembled at first, but I sang along with him. With my lips, I could feel his collarbone through his shirt. We moved dreamily around the dance floor, singing. I remember that I was conscious only of Will: I could see only the blue-and-green plaid of his shirt, the rest of the room was nothing but light, the only sound was our blended voices. The song seemed both to go on forever and to stop almost immediately. This is it, I thought. This is where he falls in love with me. This is the beginning of my life, November 18, 1960. Will—my God—Will.

When it was over, we looked at each other and laughed, and then Martha and George came up and claimed us.

"You two should cut a record," said Martha.

"Mickey and Sylvia here," George said, putting his arm around me as if I were his prize ewe.

Will stood smiling, looking down at his feet. I leaned hard against George's arm; I thought I might faint. Martha and Will danced away to "The Great Pretender." Will looked at me blankly over Martha's head, the smile half dying on his face, and then he bent his head to hers and closed his eyes.

I kept thinking my passion for him would diminish. I didn't want it to: who would I be if I didn't love Will? But I was sure that, like it or not, I'd wake up some morning with something to look forward to besides the sight of Will Westenberg coming, late as usual, through the door of Room 12. Things, people, were supposed to change. After that day at the pencil sharpener, that first shy smile, the externals of my life did change: I grew taller and got breasts, my mother went to the hospital and died, my grandmother moved in with us, I learned trigonometry and French and chemistry, my uncle Phil shook hands with Jack Dempsey who shook hands with Jack Kennedy, I wrote away for college catalogs and sang "O Holy Night" at the Christmas Concert and shocked everyone by going to the Mistletoe Dance with Johnny Tenaro instead of George Sullivan—and still my wasted, hopeful, violent love for Will went on, changeless.

2

The winter of our senior year in high school, Martha drove her brother Trevor's car off a bridge into the Fayette River.

It happened after a New Year's Eve party at Johnny Tenaro's house, and it was all chance, as these tragedies often are. Normally she wouldn't have had a car to drive, but Trevor had hitched a ride with a college buddy up to Rochester to see his girlfriend, leaving his ancient Chevy for whoever wanted to use it. Normally Will would have driven Martha home in Trevor's car, but they had a fight at the party because Will got drunk, and then he passed out and ended up having to spend the night at Johnny's. Martha drove four other people home. It was chance that two of them lived way across town and over the river. It was chance that the guard rails were down at the icy approach to the bridge, so that on Martha's way back there was nothing between the car and the cold river but a hard dirt bank.

She apparently died by drowning. If she hadn't drowned, she would have frozen to death: Did it matter? Maybe it mattered to Martha, though probably not. Trapped in that car at the bottom of the river, she knew nothing. Everyone agreed that she lost consciousness immediately. That was what people kept saying: At least she didn't suffer.

It was the rest of us who suffered.

My grief over Martha's death brought my father near to me for the first time in the two years since my mother died. It was Mamie who held me tight and dried my tears and rocked me in her arms that New Year's morning when we got the news, but it was my father who talked to me, long and quietly, in my room where I lay with a cold cloth on my forehead.

He said, "I thought I wouldn't be able to bear your mother's

29

death, and for a long time I couldn't, and I wanted to die, too. But I came to realize that as long as I'm here to remember her she'll never be really dead."

Mamie came in with a fresh washcloth; I could hardly see her in the dim room—darkened as if I were an invalid—but I could imagine the disapproving look she cast on my father: to talk of death, to drag in poor Elinor at a time like this! My grandmother was all for keeping your chin up and thinking positive. She'd come into my room and find me in tears again and say, "Don't think about it, Anna, love, for heaven's sake. Don't keep brooding about it!" At which Daddy would raise his hand to shush her, sit beside me and light a cigarette, and talk about my mother as he never had before. "You say it's not fair, Annie. You say that Martha was so young. Your mother was young, too. She was thirty-nine. That may seem old to you but to me your mother was just a girl." His voice was odd, strained. I realized he was making an effort not to cry, and my own tears flowed faster. "I don't suppose death ever seems fair," he said.

I hung on to his voice, and to his solid presence on the chair beside my bed, and as our talks went on all that cold weekend, into my awful, shocked mourning there came a gleam, like a match struck in a dark room, that was the resumption of my father's old reliable love for me—so that the nonsense my grandmother kept babbling was perhaps true, I thought, that the good Lord knows what he's doing.

I found out, though, that Martha hadn't been struck down by the Lord's wise hand. Her death was a premeditated suicide, and she did it because she was four months pregnant.

I discovered this the day after the funeral. My father wouldn't let me go. My grandmother said, "She should go, Michael, she's got to get over this." ("Wallowing in it," I heard her say to Daddy in the kitchen.) "You'll never forgive yourself if you don't go and pay your respects to the family," she said to me. But my father said no, and Mamie, in her black fake-fur toque that made her look like Khrushchev, flounced off to church with the Schweids. I stayed home with my father, lying in my dark room listening to his gentle voice and trying not to think of the icy river closing over Martha's silver party shoes, her red velvet dress, her raccoon-collared coat, the rhinestone barrettes in her black hair, Martha.

It was the tail end of Christmas vacation, and school would begin in two more days. That night, after dinner, I got a phone call from Will. "I need to see you," he said. "I need to talk to you."

I began to cry into the phone. Will's voice did that to me: he sounded so young and devastated and changed. It seemed a year since I had heard his voice. It had been, in fact, four nights ago, at Johnny's party. One of the things I had been thinking about during those terrible days was that Will must be blaming himself. If he hadn't gotten drunk, hadn't quarreled with Martha, had insisted on driving Trevor's car . . .

"Oh, Will," I wept. "Oh, God, oh, God, Will."

"Take it easy, Annie," he said. "Easy now."

I told him to come right over, we would go for a walk and talk. "A walk!" Mamie said. "It's ten degrees out there and pitch dark." Again my father raised his hand, and I washed my face and brushed my hair and put on lipstick. Just as well it would be pitch dark: my face was blotchy and swollen, my hair greasy, I was wearing baggy slacks and my father's old brown sweater. I leaned my forehead against the mirror over the bathroom sink and thought, before I could prevent myself, *I'll take care of you, my darling Will,* and then stepped back and frowned at my face, and watched in fascination as it distorted into grief and the tears began to run down my cheeks again.

The doorbell rang. Red-eyed, I went to meet him. He and Mamie were in the living room; she was in her filthy apron, talking to him about the weather. There was a moment, a fraction of time when I first saw him standing there by the piano, his head bowed, his blond hair falling down nearly to his nose—Will, so familiar, so tragic, so beloved for so long—when I experienced, in spite of everything, the same perfect happiness that came to me whenever I saw him.

My grandmother handed me a scarf. "Bundle up," she said. "And don't be out long, you'll freeze to death." She didn't notice what she had said, but Will's face was stricken in the hall light, and then the door closed behind us.

We walked fast up Spring Street, without speaking. He took my hand and put it into his jacket pocket with his own. The cold air dried my tears and froze the inside of my nose. I thought I should say something but could think only of the unsayable words of love that were always with me in his presence. Even then, as we hustled along in the snow, with between us *Martha Martha Martha,* the sensation of his warm hand firmly around mine set up the usual painful throb of desire: even then, I would have allowed

him to ravish me on the icy sidewalk in front of the Nelsons'
house. I let myself picture this: the cold snow under me, the black
starless sky above, and Will tearing off my old slacks and plunging
between my thighs, my arms locked around the back of his school
jacket where it said *St. Joseph's* in gold embroidery.

My hand tightened around his. I couldn't believe he didn't
feel the force of my lust, and that it didn't vanquish him, but he
said nothing, made no sign. The only sounds were our hard
breathing and the crunch of our boots in the snow.

We turned right on Court Street and crossed at Park to the
church. We went inside. In those days, the church was left open
until nine every night, on the chance that someone might want to
step in to pray or light a candle: making a visit, it was called. When
Will and I entered, there were two old women kneeling in a front
pew. One of them got up slowly, made her way over to the side
altar where the bank of votive lights was, clanked a coin into the
box, picked up the wax taper, and lit a candle: one more red
gleam. Then she went to the altar rail, knelt, prayed, genuflected,
and finally the two of them left and we were alone.

We sat in back. The church was warm. The altar, far off
down the long row of pews, was draped in red, studded with pots
of poinsettias, and there were wreaths of holly on all the pillars.
Christmas lingered, the Epiphany was coming up; it was the li-
turgical high season. And yet here, that morning, the priests had
donned black and purple and the gloomy smell of incense and the
drone of the Requiem mass had filled the place.

It was time to speak. I sensed it would help him out if I said
something first—anything. "My father wouldn't let me go to the
funeral."

"You didn't miss much."

Our low voices boomed in the emptiness, a daring sound:
talking in church was some minor species of sacrilege. I looked at
him. We had disentangled our hands. He sat slumped and listless.
For the first time I wondered why he'd needed to see me. I had
assumed it was so the two of us, who had been closest to Martha,
could pour out our grief together. But he had something else on
his mind. I had observed him closely for years, and I could read
the signs: the false nonchalance, and a way he had of looking at
me and then quickly away. There was a bar of tension between us
that needed to be crossed. I touched his arm. "What is it, Will?"

He reached inside his jacket and under his sweater and

removed something from his shirt pocket. "Open it," he said. "Read it."

It was an envelope addressed to him in Martha's handwriting. I stared at him.

"It came this morning," he said. His voice was even, emotionless. "She must have mailed it just before she died. Open it."

Inside were five twenty-dollar bills and a note that said, "I'm sorry, I can't do it. Love, M." I sat looking at the rounded blue letters on the pink paper, the crisp bills cool in my hand, the inexplicable words. Then I heard a sound: it was a hard, wailing animal sound, and it turned into a sob—it was Will. He reached for me, and his face was against my neck, his rough hair against my cheek. He cried and cried, harshly and horribly, and I held on to him. Almost all I could think was: Oh, God, what if Father Wallace comes in, what if Mr. Decker comes in to lock up, what if another old lady comes in. The sound of Will's sobbing echoed through the church.

No one came in. Gradually, he quieted. He leaned against me and breathed raggedly, trembling. I kept my arms around him, I stroked his hair, I whispered, "Will, Willie, Will." I could smell his hair and his skin.

For a long while we didn't move. Then he pushed away and sat back, inhaling deeply through his mouth, wiping his face with his fingers. His profile in the dusky light was drawn down with sadness. He pulled out a handkerchief and blew his nose, and then he said, "She killed herself, Annie. She was pregnant. I wanted her to have an abortion, I gave her the money. She wanted to get married. I wouldn't marry her." He sobbed once more, a quick double gasp, and leaned his forehead into the palm of his hand. "I know she drove off that goddamn bridge on purpose. I don't know what to do. I wanted to tell someone."

Home in bed later that night, I was able to examine my feelings about Will's revelation. I identified shock (Martha was pregnant), shameful joy (he didn't want to marry her), hatred (he'd abandoned her), envy (God, she'd slept with him), resentment (she'd never told me), a new dimension to the sorrow I felt for Martha, and, somewhere toward morning, the hope that Will was wrong and that Martha hadn't driven deliberately into that cold river.

But at that moment, sitting there with Will in the back pew, with the odor of the incense they'd burned for Martha still faintly present in the close air of the church, all that was clear to me was my love for him, and his need for some kind of comfort.

I touched the back of his neck with my fingers, I put my lips to his ear and said, urgently, "Will, do you want to go someplace and—you know—do it? We could find a car or something. Or here, now, down on the floor." My lust for him was undiminished. I felt strong and vital, I was an ancient female force that would restore him, I would worship him back to sanity. I kissed the stubby underside of his jaw and cupped my hand to his cheek. "Will? Would that help? Would it make you feel any better?"

I felt his body stiffen and draw a little away from me. Then he gave a cry and collapsed against me. I took this for assent, and held his head against my breast. It was a few seconds before I realized he was laughing. I pushed him off but he held me to him and laughed into my neck as he had wept just a few minutes before.

"Oh—oh, Annie," he got out finally, gasping, trying to stop. "Oh—God—Annie, honey!" He lay back in the pew, with his eyes scrunched shut and his crooked teeth gleaming, and giggled like a mad person. I just looked at him. The eternal tears overflowed my eyes, and I prayed he would rot in the dankest pits of hell.

He took my hand. "Have I ever told you how great you are? Oh, God, oh, God." He bent his head and kissed my knuckles, and I felt his lips tremble as the laughter returned.

"Shit," I said, and began to laugh with him. The two of us sat there holding our stomachs and filling the church with our noise until we heard Mr. Decker shuffling in to lock up. Then Will gathered up the letter and the cash, and we wound our scarves around our necks and walked back to my house in silence, our hands linked in his pocket.

At the door he kissed my cheek. I would have gladly died there, in that tiny second when his cold lips met my cold skin.

"I meant it, Will," I said.

He closed his eyes. I looked at his face: the ivory eyelids, the light lashes, the mole on his cheek, his full red bottom lip. He opened his eyes: his eyes were full of pain.

"Don't," he said, and left me there in the porch light.

3

I couldn't settle it in my mind whether or not Martha commit-ted suicide. Long after I got used to her being gone, when her death was, like my mother's, a small mended rip in the fabric of my life, I was still trying to figure it out.

The eulogies from her funeral were printed in the newspa-per. Father Wallace said, "She was a girl who loved life." Maureen Roesch, the president of the Student Council, called her "a spirit of affirmation who was an inspiration to us all." Her brother, Trevor (who "broke down in sobs," the *Herald-Journal* reported), said, "My sister should have lived a long life. There were so many things she wanted to do. She wanted to get married and have children, she wanted to go to college, she talked about becoming a doctor." All of this was true—except for her wanting to become a doctor, which I suspect Trevor invented out of some temporary daydream of Martha's. But she did love life—if anything, she was a little frantic in her pursuit of it, and I suppose that's what made me wonder: was Martha's daredevil vitality some reversible force that, in her predicament, pushed her in the other direction?

I wondered, too, if loving Will did the kinds of things to her that it did to me, if Will made her a little crazy. If she, like me, lived mostly inside herself. If she dreamed of Will saying to her, "Of course I love you, of course I want to marry you, my gypsy, my beautiful gypsy." So that when reality was five twenties and Will blind drunk on New Year's Eve, she couldn't see any reason not to swerve the car at the turn onto the bridge.

I knew I could never be sure, and that it didn't, as Mamie might say, bear thinking about, but I thought about it compul-sively just the same. I kept remembering Martha at Johnny's party, doing the twist with everyone but Will while Will sat morosely on a cushion on the floor, watching Martha's silver shoes and drinking beer. There was always plenty of beer at Johnny's parties. I tried afterward to decide whether Martha had seemed depressed, or merely angry with Will and determined to have a good time in spite of him. "He seems to be trying to drink himself to death tonight," was one of the things she said to me, with a shrug. And later, "I think people who can't hold their booze are disgusting"—this within earshot of Will. He made no reply, just kept staring gloomily at the floor. At midnight she was kissing Joey McCoy—by that time Will was very drunk—and shortly after that they had their argument, outside in Trevor's car. This was unwitnessed, but everyone knew she had dragged him out there to tell him what she thought of his condition—though, after Will's confession to me, I was pretty sure it was her condition they were fighting about. And then Will came in and went to sleep on the plastic sofa down in the rec room, and Martha drove some people home. And then she was dead, and no one ever saw her again except for the still body at Ryan's Funeral Home that Marie told me looked "hauntingly beautiful." I doubted it. I doubted that a dead body could be beautiful. My mother, laid out on pink velvet, had looked like a stranger—a faded doll with my mother's hair and wedding ring and good blue dress.

I missed Martha more than I could have predicted. She had been in my life since I was six. We had jumped rope and learned to ice-skate together, practiced kissing on each other, eaten lunch together at school for twelve years. She was my partner in chem lab. For Christmas she had given me a red leather wallet; I gave her the stationery she wrote to Will on. I dreamed about her after she died—trivial little dreams in which she asked me about a math problem, or stood at her kitchen sink washing dishes, or tied her hair back with a ribbon. I woke from them in tears.

One day when she had been dead a week I went to see her family. Mamie had been nagging me to do it, and I had resisted, until one day I saw, suddenly, that it was thoughtless, even cruel of me, not to have done it before. There were rituals that tagged along with death. When my mother died, Mrs. Finch kept us so well supplied with food that I had to throw most of it away: a three-layer coconut cake, Parker House rolls, huge noodle casseroles, a meat loaf decorated with green-pepper rings and ketchup ribbons. Into the trash it all went, untouched, or out for the birds, but the misguided abundance of it did, in some odd way, provide a little comfort. I was Martha's best friend. When Mamie said my sympathy might help, I figured that was probably true.

The Finches either approved or disapproved of things; they liked me, maybe because Mrs. Finch and my mother had been friends. Mr. Finch was a mailman, tall and heavy and freckled, who told jokes and coughed terribly from smoking. Mrs. Finch had one of those ruddy, high-cheekboned Irish faces that look almost American Indian. Somewhere in its harsh planes you could see Martha's features, roughened. She was overweight, always in an apron over a housedress—two opposing sets of flowers pulled tight over her big belly and breasts.

I had never seen Mrs. Finch when she wasn't perfectly serene. I knew Martha had found her rigid and judgmental and insanely religious—she went to mass every single morning as long as I knew her—but to me she seemed a sympathizer, a dispenser of good advice, a mother to confide in. Maybe it was just that she was fat; my mother had been slender and self-absorbed. For years I had a mild urge to tell Mrs. Finch about my passion for Will, to see what she might say. The urge intensified when Martha began dating him, because I knew the Finches didn't approve. They didn't like Will's parents—his out-of-work father, his shabby mother—or the fact that Will got bad grades and had no college plans. I thought, on my most desperate days, that I might get Mrs. Finch to help me remove her daughter from Will's clutches.

In my rational moments, thank God, I entertained no such hope. And I knew, of course, that Martha's parents' opposition was probably one of the complex of factors that kept Martha and Will together.

I thought: if they knew he'd knocked her up, they would tear him apart. It excited me to think of Mr. Finch's huge red fists slamming against Will's delicate bones. The temptation that came to me as I walked to their house was to tell what I knew.

They lived half a mile or so from us, at the extreme end of St. Joseph's parish—a nicer part of town than ours. They owned their house, a newish ranch style that seemed luxurious to me then. It was always very clean, with a spotless front room, never used, where the furniture was sheathed in plastic. When I stayed overnight with Martha, they made a great production of wheeling a folding cot into her bedroom, zipping off its plastic cover, and making it up with heavy white sheets. Martha and Trevor cleaned their rooms every Saturday morning; after Trevor left for college,

Martha had to clean his room when she was done with hers, even though the only mess was an invisible layer of dust. And she had to iron her bras and underpants. "My mother is a maniac," Martha used to say. "She should be locked up in a home." But all that cleaning seemed to me a cheap price to pay for such cheerful parents, a house full of good food, a big television, a phone extension in your room.

I walked over there after school. It was Trevor who let me in. I had forgotten that he'd still be home on semester break. "Intersession," he called it, and once said, in front of his mother, "Sounds like some Catholic holiday." She said that wasn't funny, and if the University of Rochester was going to turn him into a heathen he just might find himself transferring to Le Moyne, the local Jesuit college.

"Oh," he said when he answered the door. "Anna. What's up?"

I didn't know what to say, he was so unwelcoming. "I guess I've come to see your mother. Your parents. If they're home."

Grudgingly, he opened the door wider. "All right. Come on in, my mother's in the kitchen," he said, dubious and frowning, as if he couldn't imagine why I would come to see her, as if his sister hadn't just died and I hadn't been her best friend who'd known her all her life. As if he hadn't tried to pull off my bathing suit one time when I was sunbathing in their backyard.

I never liked Trevor much, at least not since we were twelve and he was fourteen and he lent Martha and me a copy of *Peyton Place* and then told his parents we were reading it. He thought that was hilarious. He was the kind of kid who'd snatch the cookie you were eating out of your hand, who'd dance around the room with the mustard if you needed it for your hot dog, saying "Try and get it, try and get it." Then, the summer before he left for college, he'd sneaked up behind me when I was lying on a beach towel out back, and before I knew what was happening he was on top of me and pulling down my straps, ogling my breasts. I screamed and hit him hard, and then he heard Martha coming out from the house and ran away laughing and saying I couldn't take a joke.

"Anna Nolan is here," he called out to his mother, and she came to the kitchen door with her arms held wide.

"Annie, Annie, I'm so glad you came. Mamie told us you were just prostrate over it, honey. Your best friend, I know how

it must hurt." On and on she went, and yes, I let her bury me in
her hot embrace, and I wept on the shoulder of her apron.

"I'm so sorry," I kept saying, marveling at how soft she was
all over, like a giant beach toy. "I'm so sorry, oh, God, I'm so
sorry."

Eventually I stopped crying, and she released me and made
tea. We sat at the kitchen table with the Kleenex box between us.
Mr. Finch wasn't home from the post office yet. Their arthritic old
dog, Sandy, lay under the table with his chin on my shoe. "The
poor old thing hasn't been the same since that day," Mrs. Finch
said, taking a tissue. "He just doesn't understand why she isn't
here."

"I don't either," I said, and began to cry again.

"It's the will of God," said Martha's mother.

"Then the will of God stinks," I couldn't keep from saying. I
had my face buried in a tissue, but I could feel the shock waves
from Mrs. Finch coming at me across the table. Then she put her
hand over mine and patted it.

"These things take time. You'll come to understand it. Be
patient, Anna."

I think now that the worst thing about Martha's death was
those platitudes that accompanied it, those inane declarations that
it was all for the best, it was the Lord's will. I heard them from
everyone—but not my father, thank God: he admitted it wasn't
fair. But Mamie, the nuns and the priests, the sermons in church,
and now Martha's own mother—all of them were telling me it was
for the best that Martha died a grisly and terrifying death at the
age of seventeen and a half.

"Truly, Anna, things like this are a test for the living. A trial
we have to pass through. Of course we miss her, we wish she was
still with us—" She paused, gave a little moan, and blew her nose
again. "But we have to accept this, we have to believe in God's
mercy."

I shook my head without speaking and glanced over at
Trevor, hard-eyed on his stool by the door. I heard him say "For
Christ's sake" under his breath. Mrs. Finch either didn't hear him
or refused to acknowledge him. She said, "If we don't believe in
that, then where are we, Annie?" She looked me in the eye, and I
saw in that moment that her tears were tears of terror, that her
faith was indeed being tested and was beginning to fail. I wondered if she still went to church every morning. I thought to

myself that if I hadn't already lost my religion over Will, I would have over Martha. *Don't worry,* I wanted to say to Martha's mother. *These things take time, you'll get used to it, you'll hardly miss it.* How cheap it was, I thought. Religion. How thin and sleazy and unsatisfying, like powdered milk.

We drank our tea, and then she told me to go into Martha's room and choose something for a keepsake. Her room had remained untouched since the tragedy. "I haven't had the heart to clean it," Mrs. Finch said, and I imagined Martha looking down from heaven with approval. "You go in there and take whatever's meaningful to you. Whatever—clothes or jewelry or books, anything."

I didn't want to do it, but I went down the narrow hall to Martha's room at the end of it. The door was closed. I took a deep breath before I turned the knob. I'm not sure what made me hesitate—maybe the sense that Martha's ghost was lingering there and would witness the sneaky, perverse, dishonest act I was inspired to perform.

I went in. The room was warm, and smelled of the perfume Martha wore. It was like a heaven, that room that was so full of her—all the pieces death had blown apart. If they could only be put together, like a jigsaw, or like the scattered fragments of something broken, there she would be: Martha restored. On a chair was her brown shoulder bag. Inside it, I knew, was her wallet crammed with pictures, and her allowance probably still intact. I imagined Mrs. Finch, when more time had passed, removing the two dollars and pocketing them. How funny: would she just throw them in with the grocery money? And her schoolbooks piled neatly on the desk: what would become of them? Would they go back to the nuns? Be used by some future student who would see Martha's name and know they were a dead girl's books? And her blue looseleaf notebook, the green plastic zip-up thing that held pencils, the paper she was writing on the hidden causes of the Civil War, the perfume bottles and tubes of lipstick, her stuffed animals, her pearl necklace and silver charm bracelet and gold circle pin? Would they offer her monogrammed sweaters to Mary Fannicelli?

And Will's school picture in its frame on her dresser. It was a beautiful photograph, exactly like him, with his hair falling in his face and the glitter in his eyes that made me light-headed to look at him. I went to it immediately and stuck it into the waistband of my skirt, under my sweater. The glass was cold against my skin. My cheeks burned. I closed my eyes and whispered, "Forgive me." Then I picked up Martha's silver charm bracelet from the dresser tray and clasped it on my wrist.

I turned and there was Trevor. I held up my arm and jingled the charms at him. He nodded approvingly. Across the room I studied his narrow eyes: what had they seen? "I gave her the dog charm," he said. "It's supposed to be Sandy."

"I always liked it. And the little bottle of Coke. And the suitcase."

"She got that when we went to New York City."

"I know." I touched it with my finger.

Trevor moved farther into the room. "My mother hasn't been able to come in here yet." He picked up a stuffed cat from the bed, put it down, picked up a copy of *Seventeen* magazine and threw it back on the bedside table. He said, "Does it give you the creeps, being in this room?"

I tried for an honest answer—not for Trevor, but for me. I stared behind him into the mirror where Martha's things were reflected. In a way, there in her room, among all the ordinary junk of her busy life, it seemed that, if I had let it, a great weight would have rolled back from my mind. Surely this room wasn't *tragic*. This handbag, this half-written school paper, this hairbrush full of Martha's black hairs . . . If I had tried, if I had wanted to, if I had been crazy enough, I could have stood there and convinced myself Martha wasn't dead. I thought it was probably a good thing Mrs. Finch didn't enter the room. "I feel better in here, actually," I said. "I mean, it just reminds me of her so much." I fingered the cold little silver charms, one by one. My father had said that as long as you remember them they're not dead, but I didn't feel like saying that to Trevor.

"Why in hell weren't you with her?" he burst out. He had picked up the stuffed cat again, and he was holding it in one fist and punching it softly with the other.

"With her when?" I asked him, though I knew. That night, in the car. Marie had said that, too, and Johnny Tenaro: if only you'd gone with her, Anna . . . "If I'd gone with her I'd be dead too," I said to Marie. "What could I have done? Grabbed the wheel when she skidded? Jumped out and sprinkled sand on the road?" Marie just shook her head—as if the mere fact of my friendship would have been a charm to keep her on the road and out of the river.

"*With* her," Trevor said, punching the cat.

Will's picture dug into my stomach. "I don't see what earthly good that would have done," I said to Trevor. "But for the record, I wasn't with her because I went home with my date. Obviously."

"Who? George Sullivan?"

"Yes. What of it?"

"You're still going out with that jerk?"

"Oh, Trevor, what does it matter?" I went toward the door. I was tired of talking to him, tired of his greasy black curls and the acne scars on his cheeks and his stupid hostility, tired of waiting for him to discover Will's picture was gone.

He grabbed my arm. "She drove off that bridge because she was in a rage," he said. "You could have calmed her down. Martha was a good driver, but she was pushed to the wall, Anna." His voice was a whisper, hissing. "Pushed to the fucking wall."

I pulled out of his grip. "She wasn't pushed to any damn wall, Trevor. You're just feeling guilty because it was your car, so you're trying to blame someone else." Will, I thought: he blamed Will. Not me, for deserting her in her hour of need, but Will, for pushing her to the wall. Little did Trevor know.

"Someday I'm going to kill that little shit," Trevor hissed.

I fled down the hall and got my coat from the closet. I saw Trevor's skinny fingers around Will's throat, and I stood there shaking and crying. Sandy the dog shuffled out from the kitchen and nudged my leg with his nose. I knelt down and cried silently into his patchy fur. I remembered him as a puppy, jumping on everyone. He breathed in short rasps and licked my face. I breathed in his doggy smell until I calmed down. Then I tied my coat tightly around the picture stuck in my waist and went to the kitchen where Mrs. Finch still sat over her cold cup of tea. "I took the charm bracelet, Mrs. Finch," I said, holding up my wrist. "Is that okay? I didn't know if it was too valuable."

She clasped her hands before her face, lips against knuckles, and the tears leaked from her eyes. "It's what I hoped you'd take, Annie honey. And her rosary, her good one—I'd like you to have that, too. Go and get it like a good girl, the crystal one that always hung from her bed, with the silver cross."

I had to go back down the hall. Trevor was sitting on Martha's bed. "Your mother told me to take this, too," I said, and plucked the rosary from the bedpost fast, as if Trevor were some vicious species of monkey, crouching there ready to grab me again. Then

I remembered that he had broken down at the funeral, and I said, "I wish she hadn't died, Trevor."

"Go fuck yourself," Trevor said.

"Same to you, you jerk," I said, and I kicked him, hard, in the shins before I left.

Oh, God, everything was different after Martha's death. All the joy went out of senior year and life seemed nothing but schoolwork all of a sudden, the massive tedium of Virgil and chemistry and *Macbeth*. The cold weather, the dull white skies of that winter, dragged on into April. Plans for the senior play were abandoned; the nuns decided we wouldn't be able to get into the proper lighthearted mood for *Cheaper by the Dozen*.

My solo at the Spring Musicale ("You'll Never Walk Alone") could have been a disaster. Rehearsals were all right; there was always so much fooling around and flirting, so many pauses while Sister Cecilia banged her baton on her music stand and screamed at us, that the impact of the song didn't get to us. But on the night of the performance, the soprano chorus, backing me up with hums at the reprise, faltered badly and faded to a wobble, and I was left alone to carry the soaring rise to high G that Sister Cecilia had programmed into the finale. I called up all the simple love of the sound of my own voice that I'd inherited from Mamie, and all the concentration and musicianship I was still learning, and I got through it. The applause was tremendous, half the audience honking into handkerchiefs, and, backstage afterward, Marie and I wept together as if it were January again and Martha had just died.

Her death changed my relationship with Will. A bond had been created between us, a weightier one than the bond forged by my long adoration or our matching musical talents. I knew a terrible truth about him, and he depended on my knowing it and absolving him, and at the same time I think he hated me for knowing. I could see that in the way he was friendly to me— attentive, almost: I recognized that he was placating his jailer, and who has ever not hated his jailer?

I didn't stop loving him of course. But my love for him darkened, became a grim, hateful thing. Before, I had hoped to convert him through love, as Martha had—to change him, settle him down, domesticate his alien streak. My absurd visions of happily ever after, though sex-crazed, had always been essentially tame

and sunny. Now it was his wildness I loved. I stopped imagining
Will coming to his senses and declaring his love before tenderly
ravishing me in some idyllic scene. After that night in the church,
I could imagine nothing but scenes of degradation and pain, brutal couplings that culminated in our hurting each other physically.
I used to gaze in school at the beloved back of his head, and
dream of pounding at him with my fists, scratching his face, drawing blood, grappling with him in furious combat until we sank to
the floor and et cetera, et cetera, the usual.

I used to think, with horror, What would I be if I didn't love
Will? Now I prayed for deliverance. If I didn't love him, I would
be free to despise him.

He never came to Smitty's anymore, or to the dances, but he
used to sit next to me in the lunchroom once in a while, or walk
the two blocks home with me before he had to turn off for the
Victory Market. We didn't talk about Martha again. We talked
about school. He was afraid he was going to flunk chemistry, and
I lent him my notes. One of his sisters got married and moved to
Albany; he told me that. Once, we sang for those two blocks, tenor
and soprano, one of the songs we were practicing in glee club:
"Oh, What a Beautiful Mornin'."

Every time he talked to me, was nice to me, smiled at me in
the hall—every time something occurred between us that, in happier days, I would have added to my rosary of special moments—
I went home to my cold, silent room and stared at the faded
wallpaper. I thought sometimes that I should make him talk about
Martha. I should convince him somehow that it wasn't his fault, or
that if it was his fault I understood and forgave; I should over-
power him with my love and faith. If he makes a move, I told
myself. If he gives me one sign. But it was all phony smiles, all
small talk about chem lab. I clutched him once when, for some
reason, he walked me to my door: I put my arms around him and
said, "Will," and he held me at arm's length and said, "Cheer up,
kid, things are tough all over." I went inside and sat on my bed
with Charlotte, and imagined, quite seriously, telling Trevor Finch
what I knew.

Even my father was changed by Martha's death—or, I suppose, by those hours at my bedside when he talked about my
mother while I cried for Martha. By a process I couldn't explain,
he rose out of his long depression—as if some ransom had been
paid, a death for a death, a sorrow for a sorrow.

He told me that before they wheeled her into the operating room, that last time, my mother had said to him, "If I die, be happy, and make sure Anna grows up happy, too." He smiled at me when he said this—I was soggy with tears—and added, "I guess we're not doing too well, either of us."

I sobbed, "I will be happy, Daddy, I promise I will," and I clung to him miserably. At that moment I was convinced my prospects for happiness were bleak. I knew I never would be loved by anyone as my mother had been by my father. And, listening to him talk, trying not to think of Martha in the frozen river, wishing, as I always was, every minute, for Will to love me, I couldn't help believing that nothing else was worth anything—nothing but that kind of devotion. It never occurred to me that an adult could indulge in romantic fantasies every bit as powerful as my own—and certainly not that my father would betray the memory of my mother by marrying again.

He did, though. He started dating Jean Eckhart on Valentine's Day that year. Mrs. Eckhart taught home economics at Northside. For years, she was one of the cast of characters that populated my father's job. I knew her slightly from an after-school knitting class I took in sixth grade. I made a skinny, crooked muffler for my father and some ugly little potholders for my mother. Mrs. Eckhart's tact and encouragement had been unfailing.

My father began calling her Jean, and on Valentine's Day he took her out to dinner. Soon after that, she came home from school with him for a cup of coffee. She was tall and bosomy, her heavy blond hair was teased and twisted into a knot, and she wore the pale whitish lipstick that was in fashion then—that the nuns had forbidden us to wear at St. Joseph's.

"I remember that poor scarf, Anna," she said. "I'll bet your father still wears it. Or aren't you sentimental, Michael?"

I hated the way she called him Michael in front of me; I considered it brazen. I said, "My father is very sentimental. Aren't you, Daddy?" I glared at him across the kitchen table, challenging him to contradict me. Sentimental about your poor dead wife was what I meant—too sentimental to care for this silly knitting woman.

But my father laughed, and reached across the table to ruffle my hair. "Not that sentimental, honey," he said. "I'm sorry to tell you I got rid of that awful scarf a long time ago."

I was hurt, but I smoothed down my hair and laughed. Everyone laughed, even Mamie, who wouldn't sit at the table with us but stood leaning against the sink looking put-upon, as if she were waiting for Mrs. Eckhart to go—the way she'd wait for the milkman to go if he inexplicably sat down at her kitchen table for a cup of coffee.

"I'll help you knit another one," Mrs. Eckhart said.

"I'm not very good at things like that," I replied with a polite smile, hoping she'd get my meaning: that I was too intelligent, too special and gifted and busy with important things to waste my time making mufflers.

"It'd be good for you to do something constructive," my father said. "When you're hanging around in your bedroom doing nothing."

"Well, of course, teenagers need their hanging-around time, too," Mrs. Eckhart said with another laugh.

Mamie poured more coffee, as if it killed her. My father didn't look at Mrs. Eckhart unless she spoke directly to him; that's how I could tell he really liked her. I knew all about how he'd had to win my mother's hand, how he'd had to overcome her doubts and the disapproval of her family, the Parretts. It was during the Depression. He was two years younger than she, a poor Irish boy with a widowed mother and no prospects. My mother, Elinor, was the daughter of an established businessman, and her mother had inherited some money; her brothers, Phil and Ralph, were on their way up. My father put himself through the university by means of a series of bizarre jobs: he sold butter and eggs and live chickens door to door, he cleaned cages at the city zoo, he taught ice-skating at the Parretts' country club, he swept chimneys. All this to win my mother. And—I could see it—this divorced muffler-maker would drop into his hands like a volleyball. The more he didn't look at her, the more she couldn't keep her eyes off him. When he lit her cigarette, she cupped her hand around his the way girls my age did, and then gazed into his eyes, blowing out the smoke. He looked away from her, into the sugar bowl, and I knew it was practically all set; I might as well go down to Chappell's and pick out my bridesmaid's dress.

It was nearly a year before they got married, though. And I did knit my father a muffler—a red one, finished during a June heat wave and presented to him for Father's Day. Mrs. Eckhart laughed a long time when he opened the package. By then I was reconciled to her—we became quite friendly during the knitting of the muffler—and didn't mind the way she laughed so hard at everything. But I had trouble calling her Jean; it took years before I could say that name without feeling resentful and forced into things.

Mamie was another story. From the time Jean entered our lives, Mamie began to decline. She stopped prying into my life, stopped waiting up for me on Saturday nights so she could click the porch light on and off, stopped keeping track of how often I went to confession. She became devoted to Charlotte, our old tiger cat, and was devastated when one night Charlotte lay down on the rug, heaved a contented sigh, and died. Mamie began to live for the piano and the old songs. On those wet, dusky evenings of early spring, I used to come home late from Smitty's or glee-club rehearsal to find dinner not even started and Mamie sitting at the piano crashing out chords and singing "Danny Boy."

I spoke to my father about it. "She's not herself," I said, but he just shook his head and smiled in that new way he had—his I-love-the-world smile. "You're never satisfied," he said to me with a chuckle. "First you complain that she nags you all the time, next thing I know you're upset because she stops."

"Are you okay, Mamie?" I asked her once when she came into the kitchen from her stint at the piano, looking like she'd just run a mile and then seen ghosts—fagged out and pale and glassy-eyed. "Do you feel all right?"

"Mind your beeswax," she said.

Another time, I asked her what she thought of Mrs. Eckhart. She smiled wickedly. "Mrs. Home Ec-hart?" she said, surprising me: Mamie seldom made jokes, and certainly not puns. I laughed immoderately. "What do I think of her?" Mamie repeated. "I'll tell you what I think of her. I think she dyes her hair." Once, when Daddy and Mrs. Eckhart were drinking coffee in the kitchen after school, Mamie played and sang "Black Is the Color of My True Love's Hair" on the piano; from my room I could hear her harsh laugh during the crashing chords between verses.

I had a new boyfriend to distract me from the anxieties of home. His name was Roger Gable, and he used to sign his name "Roger Gable, C.D."—meaning "Clark's Double." He had deep-set brown eyes, slick dark hair, and a smart-aleck smile to sub-stantiate this claim, though no moustache. He wore a black leather jacket, he drove a car that could be heard for half a mile, and, needless to say, he went to Northside High.

We met at a Friday night dance. Every once in a while the tame, predictable, priest-infested St. Joseph's dances would be invaded by outlanders on the prowl—usually our counterparts from another parochial school, crew-cut boys in clean chinos and button-down shirts, but once in a while a few thuggy public-school boys who stood uneasily in a corner and laughed among themselves in a jeering sort of way. Sometimes they were boys we knew. A kid named Ed Kuminsky, who had been thrown out of St. Joseph's for smoking in the hall and general insubordination, came sometimes and brought his new seedy friends. There were others who lived near us, or who had dated someone from St. Joseph's. Usually they just watched for a while and then left, presumably for wilder pastures, though sometimes one of them would ask a girl to jitterbug—somebody like Janice Delporte, of what George called the padded-bra/pack-a-day crowd. Never me, certainly, until Roger Gable showed up.

He came with Ed Kuminsky. Johnny Tenaro and I danced by them, and Johnny raised a hand and said, "How's it going, Ed?" Ed saluted Johnny, and Roger smiled at me. The next time they played a slow song, he asked me to dance.

He looked like a hoodlum, but he was a very straight boy, very clean-cut, as dull as anyone in a crew cut and pressed chinos. Duller. Roger was the most boring person I ever met, and possibly the stupidest. At first I mistook his taciturnity for depth, blamed his failure to laugh at my jokes on the silliness of the jokes, assumed he never did schoolwork because he was too cool for such goody-goody nonsense. But the longer I knew him, the more convinced I became that, as George Sullivan used to say, Roger's porch light was out.

I liked him, though. He was always nice to me, and he had that quality the nuns always told us was number one: he respected me. He used to take me to a beer joint downtown near the train station called The Track, a hangout for railroad men, where they didn't ask for proof of age. It was dark in there, and we used to sit at a corner table drinking beer and listening to the jukebox. I used to talk. It was like a psychiatrist skit I saw on the Jackie Gleason show: the patient rambles on and on to a shrink who never speaks; later on the shrink, who has been napping all this time, presents the patient with a whopping bill which he pays gladly. "You've been great, doc," he says. "I feel a lot better." It was the same with Roger, though he never actually went to sleep.

In fact, he looked into my eyes intently while I talked about my mother, my father, my cat, my grandmother, Martha, my friends, school, my life story, but he never commented, never asked a question, never interrupted. Sometimes he would smile, or signal to the bartender for another round. I suppose he must have been bored, but he never let on. I did try, from time to time, to "draw him out," the way you're supposed to with quiet boys, but it was wasted effort. He just wouldn't talk, and so I kept on with my biography while he kept on with his patient listening—or not listening, it didn't matter.

And his bland receptive presence did make me feel a lot better, so much so that eventually I told him about Will. Not by name—I kept the details vague, and I didn't mention Will and Martha, but I told him about my ancient passion, my sorrows, my humiliations. The relief was immense: God, how trivial it all sounded, what a fool I'd spent my life being. Parts of the story were even funny, in a sick sort of way. As I talked, of course, my fantasy life with Will, which was so omnipresent and long-practiced that I could invoke it without even trying, was weaving a new drama: I told Will of my long love for him, told him it was over at last, that I saw it for the pathetic crutch it was, and he grabbed me and threw me down and kissed me brutally and said, "Don't say that, don't say you don't love me anymore, I can't bear it," and we would struggle and et cetera, et cetera . . .

When I was done, Roger actually spoke. He took my hand and said, "He must have been crazy not to fall in love with you, Anna."

That was the night I decided to let Roger deflower me. He was gentle, good-looking, and discreet, he apparently loved me, and, unlike George and Johnny, Roger had never put any pressure on me. It took several dates before he did more than kiss me quickly on the doorstep, and it had been a slow, gentlemanly progression to breathless gropings in his car. What the hell, I thought. Let's get it over with.

We were parked at the reservoir in his rattly old Rambler. It was late April, I think—a night that was almost warm. We necked for a long time, on his side of the front seat with the steering wheel pressed into my back. I whispered, "Roger," and took his hand and put it on my breast. He was shocked, and pulled away. "Roger, I think we should get in the backseat."

"What? You're kidding," he said, but he was already fumbling for the door handle. I hurried out after him. He pushed the front seat forward and we got in back. Roger twisted around to close the door, and then we squeezed together on the backseat. "Oh, Jesus," he said. "I don't believe this, Annie, are you sure you want to do it?"

"Yes," I whispered, trying to sound passionate. By this time I regretted everything. I was scared to death. He was unzipping his pants and pulling them down. There was just enough light to see his white underpants. I closed my eyes, but when I opened them he still had them on. He was fishing around on the floor for his wallet. "What are you doing?"

"Shh," he said. "It's all right." He pulled out a little white packet and opened it. I was so naïve I thought it was going to be a pill, maybe some drug he was going to force on me. When he took out a condom I didn't know what it was. He pulled down his underpants and fitted it on: I couldn't believe what I was seeing. I closed my eyes again, and he laid himself gently on top of me and began kissing me and unbuttoning my blouse. "Annie, Annie, oh, baby," he said.

I don't know why I assumed we were both virgins. Maybe because George so obviously was, Johnny was, maybe because Roger's pursuit of my virtue had been so measured. I should have realized that his lack of haste meant he was an old hand, and was maybe even getting it elsewhere. But it was obvious, as he unhooked my bra and took the tips of my breasts, one by one, gently between his lips, moving his tongue over them, and then slowly, slowly, pulled down my skirt and underpants, caressing my stomach as he went—it was obvious that he knew what he was doing.

He was, in fact, a master deflowerer. By the time he put his swollen, condom-covered penis into me I wasn't even afraid of it anymore. I had taken it into my hand and felt its hotness, felt it throb. I had run my hands over his muscular, hairy chest and his hard little buttocks. He had knelt on the floor beside me and stroked me with his fingers, and put his lips in strange and delicious places: under my arms, in my navel, on my tensed thighs. When he climbed back on top of me and gently, by stages, kissing me all the while, pushed himself in, I was ready, and I clutched his naked back hard, and panted, and opened my lips to his slippery tongue.

But I wasn't prepared for it to be painful, or I'd forgotten it was supposed to be. When he started battering at me I let out a scream, and he put his hand over my mouth. I wrenched away. "It hurts, you're hurting me." He kept murmuring, "Shh, it's all right, Annie, almost there, shh, don't," but I flung my head from side to side and tried to push him off. I knew I was acting like a baby, but when the sharp pain of it came, it was as if I was jolted awake, and I knew I didn't want to lose my virginity to this dumb, inarticulate boy whom I didn't love. I thought of Will, I thought of his cold lips on my cheek that night. He was the only one I wanted to do this with. I said, "Stop it, Roger, stop it, get off of me, damn you. Roger, you're hurting me." I quit trying to be reasonable, or polite, or considerate. I didn't care if he called me a cock-teaser afterward, if he never spoke to me again, if he hated me. I squirmed frantically under him, and I hit him with my fists as I'd imagined doing to Will, and with tears running down my face I begged him to stop.

It didn't do any good; he held me down and kept battering until he got in. The pain wasn't much, really—just that first quick shock. I stopped complaining and lay there, letting him rise and sink and rise and sink back into me until he moaned and collapsed, a dead weight on my chest with his lips at my ear. "Oh, baby," he said. "Oh, Annie, baby, you're wonderful, you're so wonderful."

I saw Will's face in the picture I'd stolen from Martha's room, looking at me with sad reproach. "How could you do this to me?" he asked. "Didn't you know I loved you all along?" The tears trickled from the corners of my eyes and collected at the boundary of Roger's cheek and mine, but he never said a word about them, and eventually we pulled our clothes back on and he drove me home in silence.

When we stopped in front of my house, I could hear Mamie. It was nearly one in the morning, but she was playing the piano and singing "Danny Boy."

"You don't have to walk me to the door," I said to Roger, but he insisted, and at the door he said, "It'll be better for you next time." He put his arms around me and kissed my neck, ran his fingers down to my breast. In spite of myself I was stirred, but I wanted nothing more from Roger. I would never willingly see his Clark Gableish face again. I kissed him on the cheek and said a civil good-night and opened the front door. Roger looked startled; Mamie was singing loud and clear:

But come ye back when summer's in the meadow,
Or when the valley's hushed and white with snow . . .

"What's that? The television?"
"It's just my grandmother."
"Oh, yeah, I guess you told me about her." He peered over my shoulder into the living room. There was Mamie, oblivious to us:

It's I'll be there in sunshine or in shadow,
Oh, Danny boy . . .

"Holy Christ, what a voice on an old lady," Roger said, and nodded. "Yeah, you did tell me about her."

I thought of all I had told him: whether he remembered it or not, whether he even wanted it, the whole story of my life belonged to him. Somewhere in Roger's gray matter lived Will's adored face, my dark fantasies, my clandestine love. God, how I hated him. I wanted only to be alone, to rid myself of the evening.

"I've got to go in now, Roger," I said firmly. "Good-night." I closed the door on his amiable face, his hand reaching for me.

Inside, Mamie finished her song with the usual florid run, and everything was quiet. My father was out with Mrs. Eckhart. "Is that you, Anna?" Mamie called. I was in the bathroom inspecting my bloody underpants. I would have to soak them in cold water and Clorox. She came and knocked on the door. "Is that you? Are you going to be up a while?"

"Yes, a while," I said. "I think I'll take a bath."

"At this hour?"

"Yes." It was all I could think of, to bathe away Roger's touch and ease my sore crotch in warm water.

"Will it bother you if I play the piano a little more?"

I opened the door. She stood there anxiously—a tall, stooping old lady with a blunt-featured face and double chins. Her bright blue eyes looked cloudy behind her glasses; they had lost some of their life. All her energy lately went into her voice and her strong fat hands on the piano keys.

"I'll try to play softly," she said. "I know I get carried away."

I stepped forward and surprised her with a hug. She leaned against me and patted my back, as if she knew I needed consoling. Her gray curls were wiry against my face. She smelled of the Muguet des Bois talc she always wore and of something else sweet and stale. I wanted to beg her not to get old, not to change, not to die. I said, "I love to hear you play, Mamie."

She drew away, smiling at me, and said, "You're a dear girl, Anna." I thought of how, when she was dead, I'd remember the night I lost my virginity and Mamie hugged me and said I was a dear girl and played "Danny Boy" and "Believe Me If All These Endearing Young Charms" and "When Irish Eyes Are Smiling" on the piano.

I soaked in the tub, and then I went to my room and sat up in bed. I missed Charlotte. Mamie had stopped playing by then and was snoring softly in her alcove. I heard my father's car, and his tiptoeing footsteps at the back door. He went into the bathroom and then to his room. The light clicked, the bed squeaked. I wondered if he and Mrs. Eckhart had done it; I imagined him sliding his penis into a condom while Mrs. Eckhart panted beside him. He would fall asleep smiling, thinking of her breasts and thighs and her bleached blond hair let down from its knot.

I retrieved the photograph of Will from the hiding place on my closet shelf. I looked at it for a long time. When Martha died, I had prayed to be released from the long, crazy spell I was under. I had prayed not to love him. Now I was glad of it again. *Vivam pro amore.* There were worse things than hopeless love—and of course, in my soul, I still refused to believe it was hopeless. The proper fantasy created itself as it always did. "Little did I know, Anna," he whispered. "I must have been crazy all those years. I can only be thankful that you never stopped loving me, never stopped waiting for me. . . ."

I touched the glass covering his cheek, I pressed my lips to his cold lips, I thought of Roger's hands on me, and then my teeth began to chatter, and I began to sweat and tremble all over. I wanted, suddenly, to go to my father's room and blurt out to him what had happened, or to run up Spring Street to Marie's house on the corner of Danforth, to bang on her bedroom window and tell her that I had brought tragedy upon myself. I looked into Will's eyes and said to him, blasphemously, the words of the sacrament of confession, "Bless me, Will, for I have sinned." I put the pillow over my head to keep my sobbing from rousing the house.

Eventually, I became calmer, but I couldn't sleep. If Charlotte had been there, I would have petted her until she purred and dug her claws into my leg through the blanket. I would have to get a new cat: something to love. I picked up my book—*Pride and Prejudice*—and tried to read, but that polite minueting seemed to be taking place in a world other than mine. I dragged out my diary. Nothing would come to me but Will's name, and I wrote it compulsively, over and over, with the date, as if it had been Will with me in that backseat: and, toward morning, I almost began to believe it.

4

Spring finally arrived and settled in. The lilacs in our backyard had never been pruned, and the flowers waved like purple clouds far above my head, scenting the neighborhood. I broke up with Roger and went to the prom with good old George. He wore a light-blue dinner jacket; I wore a long white gown trimmed in the same blue. I still have the picture we had taken at the prom. We look very handsome together, very stiff, not particularly happy. I remember how pointless the whole evening seemed to me. Will wasn't there, Martha wasn't there. Why was I there? What did it matter if my dress was blue and white, or screaming green, or black?

After the prom, George and I drove out to Skaneateles Lake with Johnny and Marie. We sat in the car, necking and drinking beer until the sky began to lighten, and then George and I walked along the beach. I ruined my white satin shoes in the damp, pebbled earth. The lake was gold where the sun hit it, with deep black shadows along the shore. Gradually, the gold spread over its surface. We walked in silence, holding hands, but after a while George said to me, "Hey, Annie—I wonder if we'll stay friends after graduation."

"I don't see why not, George." I spoke carelessly. I hadn't been thinking of him at all, and I didn't care if we stayed friends or not. George was going, unbelievably, to Yale; I was going, thanks to Uncle Phil and a scholarship, to the New England Conservatory of Music. Our college plans set the two of us apart from the rest of our schoolmates, who were going to Le Moyne or Syracuse or the state colleges or business school. No one from St. Joseph's ever went to such exotic, distant, pagan places.

"I'll always consider myself your friend," he said, and stopped walking so he could look at me. "Do me a favor and remember that. Promise? If you ever need a friend, you got me. Okay?"

"Oh, Wilbur, such melodrama." I squeezed his hand and walked on.

"I mean it, Anna. Remember what I said."

"I will," I said, to make him happy. "And the same goes for you." We promised to write to each other. When we got back to the car, Johnny and Marie were sitting on a bench in the sun. Marie's pink formal looked bedraggled, her hair had come down from its French twist, and she was crying.

"She's upset," Johnny said.

Marie jumped up and flung her arms around George and me. "I don't want to graduate," she said. "I don't want to never see you guys again." We put our arms around her and made room for Johnny, and we stood there by the golden lake, the four of us, crying and laughing in the sunrise.

That whole last month of school was like that—awash in emotion. There were a dozen parties, too much drinking, more backseat activity than you'd imagine from a bunch of repressed Catholics. The yearbooks came, dedicated to the memory of Martha Finch, with her picture in a black border and Maureen Roesch's now-famous eulogy printed beneath.

Under my own simpering picture, it said:

Witty . . . talented . . . Miss Blue Eyes
"The hills are alive with the sound of music"
Student Council 1,2   Debating Club 2,3,4
Glee Club 1,2,3,4   Honor Roll 1,2,3,4
NYS Dental Health Essay Contest Winner 3
All-City Latin Competition Winner 3,4
C.S.M.C. Oratorical Contest Winner 2,3

and beneath Will's:

Reserved . . . independent . . . musical
"Lonely Boy"
Basketball 1   Glee Club 4

Graduation night was hotter than blazes. Under our heavy robes, we sweated. "Man, are these things going to stink when they send them back," Jerry Nelligan said. He was next to me alphabetically. Will was at the end of the line. I watched him march up onstage to get his diploma. Bishop O'Keefe was giving them out, and we were supposed to kneel and kiss his ring. "William John Westenberg," the bishop said. Will didn't kneel, and there was an awkward pause before the bishop handed over his diploma. "Hey—good old Willie," Jerry Nelligan whispered, and clapped softly a couple of times as Will marched back down, expressionless, the auditorium lights glinting off his sweaty forehead. The nuns would have killed Will for that if school hadn't been over forever. His diploma, I knew, was hard won. He never would have passed chemistry without my lab notes, and he got a D in Latin 4. He told me that Sister Marguerite had said to him, "Anyone who's acquired as little school spirit as you have in four years, Mr. Westenberg, shouldn't be allowed to graduate from high school at all."

There was a reception for parents and friends after the ceremony. Trevor Finch was there, talking to the Barshaks and the Tenaros. He waved at me; I ignored him. Ed Kuminsky turned up, too, showing off his greased ducktail haircut. Maureen Roesch brought her hulking crew-cut boyfriend from Niagara, and they announced their engagement. Joey McCoy's twin sister, Kathy, was going into the convent, and Hanky Wheeler into the seminary.

George whispered in my ear, "Ditch the parents and let's hit the road. Pass it on." We were going to a party at Johnny's, the first one he'd had since New Year's Eve. It wasn't easy to get away. My newly gregarious father, with Mrs. Eckhart on his arm, had to talk to everyone, get the congratulations of people he hadn't talked to since my mother died. I had won the Latin award, the French award, and a plaque that they gave every year to the glee-club soloist. Mamie took charge of them, hugging them to her bosom. She wore a green satin turban, its edge darkened with sweat. "Her mother should be here to see her," she said, weeping, to everyone she knew. She was a little drunk. We had had wine at dinner— courtesy of Mrs. Eckhart, who kept squeezing my hand and beaming maternally at me. I heard Mamie say to Sister Cecilia, "I want her to do everything I never did—everything. I want our Anna to go as high as you can go." Her voice carried to the far corners of the room, and she had Sister's arm in her tight grip. I went over and said, "Mamie, I have no intention of becoming an astronaut," and everyone laughed and then Daddy and Mrs. Eckhart took her home.

Will's parents also left early. I had only a glimpse of them. I saw his pale little mother embrace him, and his father in earnest conversation with Sister Josephina, who was smiling. Apparently Will was to be forgiven for his failure to kiss the bishop's ring. When Will's mother hugged him, he looked embarrassed and then, a moment later, he leaned over and kissed her cheek.

I didn't expect him to go to Johnny's party, but when I arrived with George he was already there, leaning against the wall in the kitchen and drinking whiskey from a flat pint bottle.

George greeted him, "Whaddya say, Will?"

"Sure is good to be out of that hellhole forever. That's what I say."

George laughed and steered me ahead of him toward the stairs to the rec room. "What a character," he said in my ear.

I turned around and gave him a dirty look. "Why does that make him a character? Just because he's glad to be out. I'm glad, too. Does that make me a character in your weird scheme of things?"

George jumped back from me in mock alarm. "Hey—sorry. I forgot about your tendency to defend old Willie-boy to the death. Hell, no, excuse me for living, he's no character, he's just Mr. Supernormal. Mr. Pat Boone."

"Oh, drop dead, George," I said, and we went downstairs to dance.

The basement rec room at Johnny Tenaro's opened out to a concrete patio. The sliding doors, that night, were open to the heat, the yard was lit with lanterns, the music drifted out and mixed with the distant buzz of insects. There was a moon above it all—nearly full, pregnant-looking. People were dancing on the grass.

George got me a beer and then swung me into a jitterbug. We danced and drank, spilling beer on our shoes. George got me laughing again. Everyone, in fact, was noisy and exuberant, all the kids we'd gone to school with for so many years, full of the relief of being done with it, and of the same nostalgia George and Marie and Johnny and I had felt on prom night by the lake—unmentionable now on this night of celebration. We weren't schoolkids anymore. We were adults. We drank a good deal of beer, and Will wasn't the only one with a small flat bottle in his back pocket.

I danced with George, and Johnny, and Joey McCoy, and Bobby Horgan. Bobby Horgan, the science whiz, was fat and good-natured; he had written on the back of the graduation picture he gave me, "You'll always be number one with me." When he got me in his clutches he danced me over to the dark side of the yard and tried to kiss me, but I pretended to be shocked, called him a sex fiend, and pulled him back into the light. He laughed and handed me over to George, but I could see that he was hurt, and I thought: have I been Bobby's Will Westenberg all these years?

I kept thinking of Will upstairs in the kitchen, alone. I expected him any minute to come down but he didn't appear. I wondered if he'd left. The more I danced, and joked with George and Bobby and Marie and the rest of them, and drank beer and changed the records and ate potato chips and dip, the sadder it seemed that Will was up there alone in this house, the more urgent it seemed that he not leave without my seeing him.

As soon as I could, I headed back upstairs. "Little girls' room, my sweet?" Johnny leered at me. "Just to the left at the top of the stairs." He goosed me as I went up, and made lip-smacking noises which I pretended to find funny. I went down the hall to the bathroom and wiped the sweat off my face. Then I stood close to the mirror and whispered, "Will." My breath fogged the glass. I drew a *W* and watched it fade. There was a bottle of Arpège on the sink. I dabbed a little behind each ear, and then I went to find him.

There was no one in the kitchen. In the living room, a couple was stretched out on the rug: Arlene Nuncio and Art Brewer. As I passed through I heard one of them inhale, a quick passionate gasp that sent a chill through me. On the front porch I found Will sitting on a wicker settee and drinking whiskey. He held up the bottle.

"Cheers. Want some?"

"What is it?"

"Rotgut."

I sat beside him and put it to my lips because his lips had been there. I took a drink; it tasted like what Mamie gave me for menstrual cramps. I began to sweat again. "I'd rather have a cold beer," I said.

Will took another drink, capped it, and sat in silence, his feet up on the porch railing. I looked at his shoes: brown and scuffed. From the backyard I heard a scream, and crazy laughter. Near us, in the bushes, a cricket chirped with mindless regularity.

I asked, "Are you going downstairs?"

"Eventually, I suppose."

I said, "Come on down and dance with me."

I didn't intend much by this. I half-expected him to throw my arm off and say, "Leave me alone." All I wanted was for him to stop drinking his vile whiskey, to join the party and forget whatever being at Johnny's house again had made him remember. And I wanted, as I always did, to touch him. I didn't expect that my timid touch on his arm would change my life.

The moon was rising across the street just over the Grangers' roof. There was a smell of whiskey and roses and the hot tar of the street. Inside, Elvis sang, "Are You Lonesome Tonight?"

"Come on down and dance with me," I said to Will, and touched his arm. He turned to me and smiled in the dark and pulled me to my feet.

"Let's dance right here."

In a dream I got up and we fitted our bodies together. We hardly moved. His lips were in my hair, touched my neck. I took his head between my hands. We looked at each other, and then we kissed.

We kissed through "Are You Lonesome Tonight?" and "Let It Be Me" and "Summertime Blues" and "Save the Last Dance For Me." Then we heard voices behind us in the living room, Arlene Nuncio's braying laugh, and Will whispered what he had said so many times in my dreams: "Let's get out of here."

Clinging together, we went down the front walk and up Park Street. At the end of a block was a dark house, I didn't know whose—nobody home, a black expanse of lawn behind a line of pine trees. "Here," Will said softly, and we turned down the driveway, our arms around each other's waists, and past the trees to the end of the yard where a fence bordered a flower bed.

"Here," he said again. We knelt face to face on the grass. It was dry and cool, the ground hard. We looked at each other, smiling, and then he reached behind me and pulled down the zipper of my white graduation dress, and then it was off, and I unhooked my garter belt and pulled it down with my stockings, and I knelt there in my underwear, and then that was gone, too, and I lay back with no modesty on the prickly grass watching Will take off his shirt, shoes and socks, pants, underwear—watching him fumble, exactly as Roger had, for the condom in his wallet, watching him rip it open with his teeth and smooth it on. And then we were locked together.

Even now, thinking of it, I am hit hard with the frightening perfection of that night: making love with Will, my Will, whom I had longed for nearly all my life—Will with his fine bones, his small crooked teeth, his smooth chest and hard stomach and frizzy blond pubic hair and long skinny legs. Everything that night was slow, dreamy, deliberate, intense. It was very hot. We were tender with each other. I no longer wanted to hurt him. He made no comment on my unvirginal state. Neither of us said anything at all. Sweat ran from us; we were slippery with it, and we tasted it on our lips. From down at Johnny's we could hear the music, hours and hours, it seemed, of the Shirelles singing:

> *Tonight the light of love is in your eyes,*
> *But will you love me tomorrow?*

I will love you forever, I said to him silently. His face was above me, and he bent, smiling, to kiss me again and again.

We were lying on the grass afterward, my head on his chest, his lips in my hair, when whoever lived in that house came home. We tensed and clutched each other, poised to grab our clothes. The smooth twin beams of headlights came toward us, stopped in the driveway, were turned off, and a man and a woman got out. They slammed their doors and went inside without speaking, without looking out at their flower bed at the two of us, naked and giggling, with our hands over each other's mouths. Whomever they were, I pitied them—so old, so unloving and separate. Will and I kissed again, but the spell was broken, and we stood up and put our clothes back on. Will zipped my dress and held each of my shoes for me to step into, like the Prince and Cinderella; I buttoned his shirt and smoothed down his hair. These domestic acts brought tears to my eyes. I put my arms around him once more; his heart beat in rhythm with the pulse in my temple.

Across the backyards came the music:

> *So tell me now, and I won't ask again:*
> *Will you still love me tomorrow?*

I murmured yes into his shirt. His shirt smelled of grass, and beneath it I could smell his skin where his sweat and mine were mingled.

We sneaked out past the house to the front sidewalk, and blinked at each other under the streetlight. "What should we do?" he asked me. "Do you want to go back to Johnny's?"

"I don't care," I said, but I didn't want to go back. I looked at Will's face, glowing in the yellow light, I stood close to his wiry body—mine now—and looked into his narrow eyes, and it was as if I had been dead all those years and Will had resurrected me with a touch, as if until that night my whole life had been lived in a wintry shade. I didn't want to go back to the party. I wanted to find some other dark place, to take off my clothes again and draw him down on top of me. I wondered how many condoms he carried in his wallet.

He took my hand and said, "I guess we should. It's early. We could dance."

"Okay, if you want to."

"What about George?"

"George."

"Your date. George."

"Oh—*that* George."

This got us laughing so hard we had to lean against the lamp-post and hold on to each other. Then we walked back down Park Street to Johnny's. It was only eleven o'clock; we had spent less than two hours on that anonymous back lawn. If that silent couple had come home half an hour later, if I had insisted that we skip the party and go somewhere, anywhere, to make love again, if Johnny's party had been raided by the police and everyone arrested for disorderly conduct and disturbance of the peace: if only, for whatever reason, we hadn't been at that party at that particular time. But chance was hard at work, as it was the night Martha died. Our return to Johnny's house, like my touch on Will's arm on the porch, put another kink in our lives, bent them forever.

The party had divided into two groups: people dancing and necking down in the rec room and out on the lawn, and people drinking beer and fooling around upstairs in the kitchen. Will and I went around the back, heading for the patio, and George called to us from the kitchen door. "Well, well, well—look what the cat dragged in."

I said, "Hi, George," and Will said, "Whaddya say, George?" Something about the moment reminded me of Will at the graduation ceremonies refusing, for whatever reason, to kneel and kiss Bishop O'Keefe's ring. It was what I had loved in him all these years—his arrogant apartness. I moved closer to him, and he put his arm around me.

We were standing in the light from the house, the lanterns,

the moon. I suppose our clothes were wrinkled and grass-stained, I suppose we had the dazed, otherworldly look of lovers.

"Well, well, well," George said again. I looked at him through the screen door and couldn't tell if the emotion on his face was anger, amusement, disgust, admiration. I didn't care. Will's arm was around me. George was of no importance whatsoever, he had ceased to exist.

Johnny came to the door behind him. "Trevor was here before, Anna, looking for you."

"Trevor? What did he want?"

"Who knows?" He opened the door and peered at us. I could see that he was drunk. "Who's that? Willie? Hey—what have we got here? An item?"

Will and I went down the lawn to the patio. Behind us came Johnny's wolf whistle. We were a scandal, we would be what everyone talked about next day: Anna and Will, do you believe it? The song was going around for the hundredth time on the automatic turntable:

> So tell me now, and I won't ask again:
> Will you still love me tomorrow?

I went over to it, took the arm off, and pulled up the stack of records to start again. Elvis sang:

> Hold me close, hold me tight,
> Make me thrill with delight . . .

The dancers, sunk in each other's arms, didn't notice. Will smiled at me and put his cheek against my hair. There was a shout from the patio: "Hey! Shithead!" Trevor Finch lurched through the door and came toward us. "Hey! Fucker!"

"Watch it, Trevor," someone said. Joey McCoy was behind him. He tried to hold Trevor, but Trevor marched straight up to Will and me and said, "There you are, you fucker. What the hell do you think you're doing?"

I said, "Get out of here, Trevor."

"Who asked you?" he said. He pushed Will hard in the chest, and Will fell back. "What the hell do you think you're doing, fucker? Hmmm?" He pushed Will again, and Will recovered and grabbed the front of Trevor's shirt.

"None of your goddamn business," Will said. "Just beat it, Trevor. Get the hell out of here."

Johnny Tenaro came running down the stairs. "What in hell is going on here? Cut it out, you guys."

"It's just stupid Trevor, making trouble," Joey said.

Trevor turned around and pushed Joey into the record player. Elvis was silenced, the needle made a scratching noise. Johnny went over and turned it off. "Come on, you guys," he said. "Let's just forget it. Whaddya say?"

But Trevor and Will were facing each other. Trevor was obviously very drunk. He held his hands in front of him like claws, opening them and closing them. His small, pinched face—ugly, nothing like Martha's—twisted up so his teeth showed. I remembered turning, that day on the beach towel, to see his vicious mouth grinning horribly at me. "You little shit," he said to Will. He panted in and out through his teeth. "I could kill you, you shit. I could knock you in the goddamn river and drown you, motherfucker. Asshole."

His language, if nothing else, shocked us all. No one used those words. It was as if a Martian had burst in on us, or an obscene, jabbering monkey.

Johnny tried again. He pulled at Trevor's arm, but Trevor shook him off and in the same motion he hit Will in the face. Will staggered, and Trevor hit him again. Will's nose began to bleed. He went for Trevor and got his hands around his throat, but Trevor broke free and hit Will once more with the cracking sound of fist against bone. Will cried out, holding his nose. Then everyone was on Trevor, pulling him away. Trevor said, "Let go of me, I'm going to kill that fucker," but they got him out the door, out to the road. There was shouting, and then I heard someone get into a car and peel away.

Johnny came back in. "He's gone. Jesus Christ, what a maniac." His words broke the stunned silence. I knelt by Will. He was sitting on the floor with his head in his hands. Blood was dripping from his nose. It was all over his shirt. "Get some towels," I said. "Someone. Please, some cold water."

There was a rush of activity. Lights went on, Johnny went running upstairs, and Marie came down with a pan of cold water and a dish towel. "Oh, Christ," she kept saying. "Oh, Jesus Christ, I do not believe this." I heard Bobby Horgan say, "Well, hell, you can't blame the guy, can you?"

Will just sat there. I touched his cheek. "Will? Will? Are you all right?" He raised his head and looked at me without answering. "Will? Just let me get the blood off so I can see if you're okay." The blood was dark on his face, and there was a red bruise below one eye. I thought his nose must be broken. I wondered if he had a concussion. It was the worst sight I had ever seen, Will's face covered with blood. I dabbed at it, and he closed his eyes and endured the water and the towel in silence.

I heard George's voice saying to the circle of people behind us, "He's all right, leave him—come on, he'll be okay, we don't all need to stand around and watch." Then George came and knelt beside us and put his hand on my shoulder. "Hey, Will?" he said. "I think we should take you over to the emergency room. Somebody ought to look at you."

Will opened his eyes and slowly, gingerly shook his head. "His nose has stopped bleeding," I said. I wrung the cloth out in the water. The water turned red. I wiped Will's chin, and the blood around his mouth. There was a cut on his lip. I was filled with tenderness for him. I wanted to take care of him, to hold him in my arms and cradle his bloody head on my breast.

George said, "Better be safe than sorry."

Will pushed the towel away. "No," he said, and stood up. I put an arm around him on one side, George on the other. He moved out of our grip. "It's nothing. I'm all right."

"Listen, I'm serious," George said. He was a doctor's son, going into premed at Yale. "Let me just drive you over to St. Mary's, the emergency room."

"I said forget it." Will waved his hands vaguely at us—a dismissing gesture. His hands were bloody-palmed. His shirtfront was soaked.

George stood hesitantly in front of him. "Well, what are you going to do? You can't just—"

"Leave me alone," Will said. "Everybody. Just leave me alone."

"Will—"

He waved his hand at me. "I'm all right, Anna. Just leave me alone."

He didn't look at me. Everyone made way for him, and he went out the back door and down the street. No one spoke. I looked down: Will's blood was on my hands and my white dress and on the tile floor where he had been sitting. I felt faint. I said, "Oh, God," and George was beside me.

"Anna? You all right?"

"Oh, God, it's just so hot," I said.

George led me outside, and we walked around to the front and sat on the porch steps. "Put your head down," George said, and I lowered it to my knees, George's hand on the back of my neck. "There," he said. "That's better, honey."

I suppose it was the endearment that did it—the first kind word spoken since Trevor burst into the rec room. I began to cry, the tears soaking into my dress with the blood.

"Oh, God," I wept. "Oh, Jesus, Jesus."

"Shh," George said. "Shh, Annie, it's all right."

I pressed my forehead into my knees and said, "You wouldn't believe how I love him, George. I love him so much I wish I could die."

"Shh," he said. His hand was cool on my neck. "I know that, Annie. You come here to me now." I sat up. George put his arms around me and stroked my hair, and I cried on his shoulder for a while until I became sleepy with grief, and then he took me home in his car.

It was years before I saw Will again. The day after graduation, he hitchhiked down Route 20 to Albany, where his sister lived. He got a job there, first as a busboy in a pizza joint, then doing maintenance work in a cemetery.

I saw his mother in the drugstore. I asked her, "When's Will coming back?"

"Oh, I don't suppose he'll ever come back," she said. She had a tired smile and a trace of a German accent. She had Will's sharp bones and pale skin.

"Never?"

She shrugged. "There's nothing to keep him here."

Late that summer, my father and Mrs. Eckhart drove Mamie up to the Catholic Home in Watertown. She had had a slight stroke, and then another, and was left confused and silent, her right side paralyzed. She became very placid. She didn't mind going to the home. My father took it hard, though. Mrs. Eckhart said to me, "I don't mind telling you, Anna, Michael cried like a baby when we left her. Just like a baby." She wept quietly into a lace-edged handkerchief. On her finger she wore my father's present to her, an engagement ring whose tiny diamond was flanked by two even tinier emeralds. She brought me a kitten, a black male I named Fred. He was nothing like Charlotte, though. What Fred liked was sunning himself in the backyard, not purring on my lap. He came inside to eat, then meowed at the door again. I would look out my bedroom window and see him curled up in the birdbath.

The house was quiet with Mamie gone. I missed her fierce face, her noise, her hats. I remembered the day Will came to the door and she sang "I Dreamt I Dwelt in Marble Halls," and the night she sang "Danny Boy" while I sat in the tub. Sometimes late at night, when I was in the house alone, I fancied that I heard her music echoing in the walls.

I hated to play her old piano, and I asked Sister Cecilia if I could come over to the convent in the evenings after dinner to practice my solfège. I was taking singing lessons from her. I spent a good deal of time in the convent that summer. It was cool and empty, and smelled of floor wax and cooking. I used to sit at the Steinway in the nuns' living room, looking out over their neat back garden, thinking of nothing, humming a tune, waiting for George to come and pick me up.

George and I were going steady. I wore his huge school ring, taped, a dead weight on the middle finger of my left hand. I warned him I'd be giving it back in the fall. He said, "That's a long way off."

It wasn't, though. It was August before we knew it, then September. I packed up my music, my typewriter, the sweaters Mrs. Eckhart knitted for me, warm clothes for the New England winter, the photograph of Will, my old diaries. My trunk went off to Boston. The night before I was to follow it I let George make love to me at his parents' summer place on the lake, and afterward I gave him back his ring. Sadly, he unwound the adhesive tape and put it back on his finger.

He said, "Goddamn Westenberg." I didn't reply. I was brushing my hair. It had grown long, and I parted it in back and began to braid it. "Goddamn that guy," George repeated, twisting his ring on his finger.

"Don't, George," I said. "Please."

He gripped the end of my braid, and pulled my hair so that I had to face him. "You're crazy," he said. "Do you know that? You're out of your mind. Are you going to carry the torch for that jerk all your goddamn life, Anna?"

Gently, I pried his fingers loose from my hair and began braiding it again. "I don't know, George," I said. "Probably."

AN ALBUM OF LOVE SONGS

1

My grandmother died when I was in my last year at the conservatory. It was a hard year. I was twenty-one, just coming to terms with the knowledge that I would never be a great singer. I shared an apartment on Gainesborough Street with three other girls, and I was sick of our crowded messy rooms, sick of being in school—and at the same time filled with dread at the imminent end of my life as a student.

Mamie had been at the Catholic Home for over three years. Whenever I was home on vacation, my father and I drove up to Watertown to visit her. She no longer recognized us and had begun calling me Bridget; she thought I was her daughter, my aunt, dead since 1948. The last time I saw Mamie, at the end of August, I told her I had been playing Yum-Yum in *The Mikado* that summer. She looked at me with a silent, suspicious smile, and said, in her thick, shaky voice, "If you ever see that yellow apron, tell them I'd like it back." I asked a nun once if my grandmother ever sang, and the nun said, "And what has she got to sing about, may I ask?"

The night before she died, I was at a Halloween party, a costume party I'd been dragged to by my roommate Carolyn, whose current boyfriend, Mark, was an art student. Everyone had to dress like a famous artist or a famous work of art. Carolyn was dressed in a beige body stocking. A sign on her back read: WANTED, ONE STAIRCASE. I couldn't think of a costume, and at the last minute I put on jeans and a flannel shirt and bound up my right ear in a gauze bandage. I was Van Gogh. I dabbled ketchup on the gauze. Carolyn told me it looked like a used Kotex.

She won the prizes for both Wittiest Costume and Sexiest Costume. I got a prize for Most Original. Aside from that, it was a terrible evening. I knew hardly anyone at the party but Carolyn, and she was occupied with Mark. Once the prizes were awarded and my bandage had fallen off, I was just a dowdy girl in her old clothes. No one paid me any attention.

I watched Carolyn and Mark disappear into a bedroom. I watched three girls and a boy squeezed together on a broken-down sofa passing a joint back and forth and laughing. I made a fool of myself trying to join an intense discussion of the war in Vietnam, about which I knew nothing. I stared at a bullfight poster on the wall until the enraged face of the bull, the evil smile of the toreador, the red swirl of his cape were seared into my soul. I sat on the floor drinking beer and listening to the music—Joan Baez records, mostly. I thought if I heard "All My Trials" once more I would lose my mind. I wondered if Joan Baez had ever faced a moment of truth about her shrill, beautiful soprano—that she would never sing Mimì at the Met. I wondered if she had ever just gotten weary of the sound of it.

I considered leaving and finding my way home alone, but rumors of the Boston Strangler lingered in Back Bay, and I was afraid of the dark streets. My mind wandered aimlessly, to the work I had to do the next day, to a fabulous witch costume my mother made me when I was eight, to a hole in the knee of my jeans. I thought of the letter I'd received that morning from George Sullivan. He wrote on stationery from the Yale Young Republican Club, of which he was president. Happy Halloween, he said. When would I come to New Haven for a weekend? Had he persuaded me to vote for Goldwater?

I got up from time to time and refilled my paper cup from the keg. Eventually, I noticed I was getting drunk. And all that time my grandmother was dying at the Catholic Home.

I flew to Syracuse on All Saints' Day with a hangover. It snowed at the cemetery, a few freak flurries, too early, that didn't survive long. They whitened the spray of pink roses on the casket, and fell like petals on the polished wood, but by the time the service was over they'd melted to spots of wet that dripped down the sides.

My relatives were all there, and the old neighbors from Spring Street, a contingent of teachers from Northside, a couple of priests, two nuns from the home—a shivering, huddled group in the brutal autumn damp. My father was holding Patty, my new sister, age eleven months. While the snow was falling Patty raised her face to it, and when a snowflake landed in her open mouth she laughed and waved her mittened fist, just as Father McNulty was asking God, once again, to grant Mamie *requiem aeternam*. Smiles broke out all around and, when the mourners dispersed, everyone said things like, "Life goes on," meaning Patty.

At the edge of the group, far off to one side by a gray mausoleum splotched black with damp, was Will Westenberg. I didn't notice him until we were leaving. He was wearing a dark suit and a tie—no overcoat. His face at that distance looked dead white. He made no sign that he saw me, or that he even knew anyone there. As I looked at him, unsure of what to do, he turned abruptly and walked down the hill behind the mausoleum, away from us. Overhead, an arrow of geese flew south with a sound like rusty gates. I watched Will go. I couldn't very well run after him. I got into the black car with my father and Jean and Patty, and we drove home.

When I got back to Boston after the funeral, I cut classes, slept late, hung around the apartment drinking coffee and playing records. I felt as if I were harboring some diffident germ—coming down with something that never quite emerged. When I thought of Ravel's Greek songs I was supposed to be working on for my degree recital, it was in a mildly regretful way, as if the notes were distant friends who had gone away to join the Peace Corps or something. Even to talk was an effort, or to smile. The bones and muscles in my head seemed hard and glassy; to make them work was too difficult. I kept clenching my teeth, and didn't realize I was doing it until I got a pain in my jaw.

It became a well-known fact that I was depressed, and that I wasn't singing. When people came over, my roommates whispered things like, "She was really, really, unbelievably close to her grandma," and everyone said, "Oh, gee, poor Annie, that's a shame." My friend Hal Jacobs came over. He was a pianist, and we were supposed to be putting together a cabaret act that would make our fortunes. Hal snarled at me, called me a spoiled brat, a prima donna in the worst sense, and told me to pull myself together. My voice teacher said she understood I was having a rough time but I should remember that certain things were expected of me, that if I didn't get control of myself I would be letting a lot of people down.

Carolyn made an appointment for me at the guidance office, where I talked about my problem with a bone-thin young woman wearing a green corduroy shirtwaist dress and, around her neck, a jeweled crucifix on a chain. I told her my grandmother had died and taken with her my will to sing.

She listened with interest to what I said, and complimented me on my sensitivity and self-awareness. She said grief was a natural process that can take strange forms. She said I would have to go through it; it would be like a walk through a dense forest into light. I must have faith. When she said that, I looked at the twinkling red jewels on her crucifix and braced myself for a religious lecture, but it was faith in myself she meant. At one point she reached across the desk and patted my hot hand with her cold one.

"Of course you can sing, Anna," she said as if she'd been following my progress for years. "Believe it."

"It's not a question of faith," I said. "I just don't want to sing. I wouldn't care if I never sang another note."

She looked at me in a kind, puzzled way. "You're having a crisis of confidence. Listen. Everyone isn't Maria Callas." She laughed knowingly. "After all, just because I'm not Sigmund Freud it doesn't mean I'm going to give up psychiatry!"—which was the first time I realized I'd been sent to a shrink.

"I don't think that's my problem," I said.

"Give it time," she told me as I left. "Time and space."

When I left, the wind was blowing hard from the river, smelling of snow. Soft snow petals began to fall, like the snow at the cemetery. I remembered how my father had kept me from going to Martha Finch's funeral, how Mamie had tried to persuade him, how relieved I was not to have to make the effort. I remembered my father's long solitary sadness after my mother's death. It's a family tradition, I thought, this frozen feeling deep in the bones. Trudging home, I hated winter, music, death, life, myself. The way I felt terrified me. When I got back to the apartment I made myself a cup of tea and sat in the kitchen watching the gray light leave the sky above Gainesborough Street until I could no longer see the tops of the trees, and the lights went on in the building across the street, and my roommates came home chattering and laughing and trying to get me to eat some dinner.

Thanksgiving break came, and I took the late train home the night before. I was exhausted, but I drank a cup of coffee with my father, listening to his stories of turmoil at school, Patty's genius, Mamie's modest financial leavings. When he asked, I told him everything was fine with me, everything was great, I was just a little

DUET

tired. By the time I went to bed, I could hardly climb the stairs.

My father and Jean had fixed up a room for me in the attic of the new house they had bought when they got married. It was a long, narrow, comfortable room with sloping ceilings, blue walls, the bed I'd slept in all my life, my old junk in the closet. I'd spent the previous summer there, the first one at home since I left for the conservatory. That was the summer I sang Yum-Yum with the light-opera group at the university, and I also had a part-time job in the office of a department store downtown, stuffing envelopes and filing. I was amazed, every day, at how boring this was; my amazement kept me from quitting.

When I wasn't working or singing, I stayed home. It was years since I had spent any time in Syracuse, and I was afraid of what ghosts might be walking the dull streets of my hometown— creatures more dangerous than the Boston Strangler. In the evenings, after Patty was put to bed, I played Scrabble with my father and Jean, or watched ball games on TV. Under Jean's guidance I began knitting a sweater, but never finished it. I read my father's collection of Russian novels. I wrote long letters to Carolyn and short ones to Hal Jacobs, and I kept up a flirtatious and energetic correspondence with a boy from New York named Nick; I wasn't really interested in him, but he wrote good letters. Sometimes an old friend from high school, Johnny or Marie or Mary Rebecca, came over and we sat around drinking beer, but those evenings were strained. Too many years had gone by, we'd lived too much life without each other, and we had to search madly for topics of conversation. Marie was going with a boy from Oneonta State, and he was all she could talk about. I wouldn't have minded seeing George, but he was spending the summer as an exchange student in France. "Tu dois vivre, Anna," he wrote to me. "Vive ta vie! Viens à la France avec moi, chérie!"

When I woke up in my attic on Thanksgiving morning, it was from a dream in which I was in my old room, in the house on Spring Street, searching for something, pulling everything out of my closet and out of the dresser drawers. The middle of the floor was full of junk, but whatever I was looking for refused to reveal itself. In my dream, I kept saying "It's *not good*," just as Mamie used to. I woke up with the nagging feeling that there was something I had to find, or remember, and I lay there a long time trying to reconstruct the dream, trying to figure out what I'd lost that was so important.

73

Finally I gave up, feeling irritable and bereft, and slept again, heavily, dreaming of nothing. When I woke, I didn't feel well—I was definitely coming down with something—but I dressed quickly and went downstairs. I could smell the turkey roasting in the oven. It was so late that Patty was already in for her morning nap. Jean was in the kitchen peeling squash, Fred the cat was underfoot, my father was out trying to find a store open that sold whipping cream.

I refused breakfast and asked Jean if I could borrow her car. "You don't look so good," she said, and gazed at me with concern. She had become plumper since the baby was born, more motherly. I wondered if my own mother had looked at me like that when I was ill, with all those frown lines. I couldn't remember. The only illnesses I could remember from my childhood were hers. As time passed, I could recall her only as she was on the last day I saw her, in the hospital, giving me instructions, looking white and weak and determined.

"I'm all right," I said. "I'll be back in ten minutes."

I drove down Court Street to my old neighborhood, and up Danforth Street to the Westenbergs' place. I parked the car in front and sat looking at the house. It needed painting—it had always needed painting, always been stained with rust from the gutters, always needed the porch roof shingled and the front steps repaired. There was no activity. He'll be home for the holiday, I thought. Home for the holiday, home for the holiday: it went over and over through my mind until the words became meaningless. *Hol for the homiday, hay for the homidol.* I leaned my forehead against the steering wheel and remembered my dream of searching and searching through my old room. I wondered what had become of Will's photograph. Was it up there somewhere in the attic room with my school notebooks and Martha's charm bracelet and my collection of miniature animals?

My head began to ache, and I forgot where I was for a moment. When I looked up, finally, I saw Will coming down the steps.

I went to meet him. He wore a brown leather jacket with a fur collar, and khakis, and the same kind of scuffed brown shoes he had always worn. His hair was longer. He seemed older, worn down, thinner and tougher.

He smiled when he recognized me—though before the smile I saw a split second of hesitation, even alarm. "Hey, Annie," he said. "Long time no see."

"Three years and five months," I said. "Almost to the day."

We stood there staring at each other. I thought for a second that I would faint and fall into his arms, and he would catch me, and I would be cuddled against the brown leather jacket, his chin against my hair. I remembered the first time he ever danced with me, when we sang together.

"You were at Mamie's grave," I said finally.

"Yeah. I was." He turned his head, and the shadows fell differently on his face, changing it. He looked, all of a sudden, beautiful and delicate and sad, exactly as I remembered him.

I said, "I just came over to ask you why."

He kept his head turned from me, and he flushed slightly—those two spots of red. "She was a nice old lady. I had good memories of her."

"You hardly knew her."

"Hell, Annie, everyone knew your grandmother. I just felt like it, I felt like going."

We were standing on the walk in front of the house. I stepped closer to him, close enough to see the sleep in the corners of his eyes and a tiny shaving cut on his neck. If I fainted, would he catch me, or would he let me fall at his feet? I asked him, "Did you go because you wanted to see me?"

"Annie—"

I reached out and grabbed his sleeve. "Will. I'm in town for the weekend. Could we get together? I mean—are you here for a visit or what? Do you live back here now? Could we see each other? Tomorrow night, maybe?" He looked down at my hand, and then he closed his eyes and covered it with his. I turned my palm to meet his, and our hands locked warmly together. His eyes opened. I smiled at him. "Mr. Blue," I said.

He tried to pull his hand away but I raised it to my lips, holding tight. He inhaled sharply and said, "I can't see you, Annie. I'm living in Schenectady. I'm going back after dinner today." He looked away again. "I'm involved with someone. It's complicated."

"Listen, Will," I said. "Listen." I heard the desperation in my voice. I sounded like someone in a movie. If I had been watching myself on the screen I would have thought, *Give up, kid.* I tried out a little laugh; it was ghastly. "I'm involved with someone, too." I laughed again. "Obviously. But he's back in Boston, and I'm on vacation."

Back in Boston: I hated the big-city sound of it, as if I were mocking him. Schenectady, for Christ's sake. And it was a lie, what I told him so flippantly; I had no involvement.

"I don't know, Annie, I don't think so."

"We could go for a drive or something," I said. "Just to talk about old times. Don't you miss them? The old days, Will?"

He dropped my hand, deliberately—disentangled his fingers from mine and put his hands in his pockets. "Yeah," he said. He shrugged, and spoke with careful casualness. "I guess so. But there's no way we can get together this weekend."

A voice came from the house. "Will?"

He looked straight at me, his face lost all its expression, and he said, "I've got to go. It was really good seeing you, Annie."

I said, "Will?" as if in echo. "Will? Who's that? What's the trouble?"

"There's no trouble," he said.

The voice came again. "Will?" A young voice, female.

"Got to go, Annie," he said. "I'll see you around." He spoke coolly, but his eyes looked desperate—or did I imagine that? He touched his forehead in a salute—the jaunty kind of salute they give in movies before they face the firing squad. I reached out to hold him, but he moved away fast and leapt up the rickety porch steps to the front door. He opened and closed it so softly that I couldn't even hear it.

I headed home, and didn't realize until I was halfway there that I was shaking, the tears were running down my face, and there was an uneven moaning sound in the car that was my own voice.

I drove around until I could stop crying. The neighborhood had been spruced up. On Spring Street, our old house had been painted yellow, and someone had put up window boxes: nothing grew in them in November. When I drove by St. Joseph's I saw that they had sandblasted away the grime, and the school building was pale gray, silvery in the cold light. On the corner, Smitty's had a new brick front and a new sign; the beauty shop next door where I had my hair done for the senior prom was now a gift shop called the Oz Boutique. My life was being erased, blown to bits by time. I told myself that was as it should be. I didn't let myself think about Will. He was there somewhere in my mind—a dull black presence behind my headache—but I wouldn't think about him again, ever. I wouldn't look for his picture, I would assume it had been lost in the move. I would scratch away his memory, tear it finally from my life. The voice from Will's old house, and the new Smitty's, and the empty yellow window boxes—all of them were messages to me to get on with things, to do what George had instructed me to do from France: live my life.

I stopped crying and turned on the radio. The Beatles sang "Love Me Do." The harmonica solo made my headache worse. I sang along for a couple of bars—"So plee-yee-yee-yeez love me do." My voice was harsh from tears, from disuse, from whatever I was coming down with, but I sang anyway, doggedly, all the way home.

The family was already assembling when I got there: Uncle Phil and Aunt Gert and my cousin Roseanne, Uncle Ralph and Aunt Nancy, Jean's brother Don and his wife. Little Patty, in a pink nylon dress and ruffled pink socks, crawled over to me and said, "Nammie!"

"Annie," I said, reaching for her. "Say Annie, Patty."

"Nammie!"

I carried her around the room while we all exclaimed over her. She was a fat, pretty, laughing baby with astonishingly large blue eyes, and she was an amazing talker for her age. When I set her down, she crawled over to Fred the cat, poked him with a finger, and said, "Tee-tat." Fred ran under a chair, and everyone laughed.

"She's so good," I said to Jean. She raised one eyebrow at me: Patty was not a notoriously good baby. But she was so *pure*, I meant—so clean, all promise, untouched by life. If I could just keep her in my mind, I thought, I could—what? what? live my life? be saved? saved from what? "So good for us all," I said.

Jean smiled, misunderstanding me. "For me, she certainly is. Patty and you and your dad. I'm a lucky woman, Anna," she said, and we stood together, thinking our separate thoughts, while the dull black ache pounded at my brain and Patty lay on her stomach babbling to poor Fred under the chair.

I helped Jean set the table—first the hinged pad, then a lace cloth, then a clear plastic cover, then china (my mother's flowered Johnson Bros.) and pale-green wine glasses. Jean had made little Thanksgiving favors—paper nut cups turned into turkeys with construction paper and Magic Marker, a name lettered carefully across each turkey's gut.

Patty's high chair was placed next to me. "Anna's her favorite," my father said. He and Jean were always claiming things like that—the baby's so great with Anna, she adores her big sister, doesn't she look just like her, those blue eyes, that coloring. I always thought they overdid it, and that all the fuss was meant to offset any potential sibling rivalry on my part. Sometimes I resented this, but I was touched by it, too, that they were so concerned about me even though I was twenty-one years old and hardly ever home, and not always very pleasant to them when I was. But it was true that Patty liked me, and that she did resemble me, though she was more vivid, somehow, more polished and clearer cut, even as a baby. Looking at pictures of myself, from babyhood onward, I always saw myself as a vague presence, amorphous and unfinished. In different pictures I appeared to be completely different people. But Patty was always Patty, unmistakable.

Halfway through Thanksgiving dinner, when second helpings of turkey were being handed around, I had a very clear impression that the mournful, maddening dream I'd awakened with and tried to shake off was still clinging to me, like a cobweb or a shroud, that while I fed Patty mashed potatoes and talked school with Roseanne and drank the sweet pink champagne Uncle Phil always brought, my dream was present, my frustrating search was continuing in some world alongside the real one.

I put down my fork and wiped my mouth with a napkin. I thought of the shrink saying that grief is a healing process that can do strange things. It has put me in a dream, I thought. In a cobweb. I thought of the petals of snow falling on Mamie's casket, I thought of the black screaming geese pointing south across the sky. I looked at the paper turkey bearing my name in Jean's elegant calligraphy—*Anna*—and from the other side of the table, Aunt Gert startled me by speaking it. "Anna?" she said. "Anna? Everything okay?"

It was like those first days back at school after Mamie's death, when my head was made of glass and it was so hard for me to talk. I tried to smile at my aunt.

Jean said, "Annie?"

Patty reached out her hand to me and said, "Nammie?" and I turned to her. "Patty?" I heard myself say. "Patty? Patty?" The shrill voice from the house called, "Will?" Loud laughter rang out: mine.

My father was at my side. "What's wrong, honey?"

I looked at my father. He had aged, his blue eyes were fading, becoming grayer; their drooping-down corners drooped further and made him look sad—though I knew that in spite of Mamie's death he was happy. But he seemed too old to have such an energetic little girl. I thought, when Patty's a teenager, my father will be nearly sixty. She'll run rings around him. I said, "Daddy."

"What is it, Anna?"

I began to cry, and said, wildly, "Oh, God, everything is so awful." It wasn't what I had meant to say; I had meant to be cheerful and to look forward. With shame, I heard myself go on, "I had this dream where I was looking for Mamie and she wasn't there. I couldn't find her anywhere."

As I spoke, sobbing into my napkin, I knew it wasn't true, it wasn't Mamie I'd been searching for in my old room. But I couldn't take it back, and it was true enough that I missed my grandmother.

"And my head aches," I sobbed.

I heard a sniffling murmur go around the table, I heard the worried affection in it, the sorrow for my sorrows, and everyone still feeling bad about Mamie. "Annie, honey," my father said.

I wiped my eyes and stood up. "I'm really sorry," I said. "I'm not feeling so great. I think I'll go lie down." I succeeded in smiling, and looked apologetically around the table at their worried faces. Patty began to whimper. "God, I feel like a fool," I said.

My father put his hand on my head. The dream clung to me tight; it was a band around my head, and on my wrists. I swayed toward my father's hand. I saw Will in his brown leather jacket.

My father said, "Jean, she's burning up."

"I think I've got something wrong with me," I said.

From miles away, my uncle Ralph said, "Catch her, Mike!" I fell into my chair, and when I came to Jean was wiping mashed potatoes and gravy off my face.

2

I t was mononucleosis. I was in bed for two weeks with a high
fever and swollen glands, too weak even to walk to the bathroom without help. I spent the first few days in a haze of relief: it
wasn't me, I wasn't a mental case or a hypochondriac. It was a
virus. I would be all right. Thanksgiving Day was like a dream, no
more real than the dream of my hopeless search, and it was over.
I would have to rest, build myself up, take care of myself.

My father and Jean each got a week off from school to tend
me in turns. My throat hurt and my head ached, and when the
fever was high I felt awful. But it was not, on the whole, an
unpleasant experience. The house was very peaceful. I lay in the
second-floor guest room. Patty was next door all day, at Mrs.
Neal's, so she wouldn't disturb me or be infected. My father read
to me, I listened to the radio, I slept.

Very little happened. Once, I was awakened during the night
by the sound of my father and Jean making love in the bedroom
next door. Once, Patty crawled up the stairs and pulled herself
upright in my doorway; Jean came running to retrieve her and
led her away screaming. George Sullivan, home from France,
called up and talked to me for a couple of minutes in rapid,
unintelligible French.

Those were the memories I kept of those first two weeks.
When they were over, and I was feeling better and was no longer
contagious, George visited me in the afternoons. It was Christmas
vacation. He brought me a bottle of Joy from Paris, a stack of
romance magazines, and a recording of *Manon* that we listened to
over and over on George's new portable stereo, which he carted
over for the purpose. He seemed to think I needed cheering up.
He put on an apron and a wig of Jean's, padded his chest with a

80

sofa pillow, and lip-synced "Adieu, notre petite table." He played his Bob Newhart records for me. For my first outing, he took me to a Saturday matinee of *A Hard Day's Night* in a movie theater full of screaming teenagers.

When he insisted on coming over for New Year's Eve, I made him a little speech. "I certainly appreciate all this, George," I told him. "But honestly, you don't have to devote yourself to me. Don't you have a girlfriend in town that you could take out on New Year's Eve? Don't you want to *vivre ta vie* this vacation?"

He looked hurt. "You're my girlfriend in town, Annie."

"You know what I mean," I said.

"That's what I mean." My father and Jean had gone to a party. Patty was asleep upstairs. George had made dinner for us, something he had learned in France: steaks cooked with mushrooms and wine. The mushrooms were very burned. We were sitting at the kitchen table eating them and drinking New York State champagne. I wore a sweater Jean had knitted for me—fuzzy pink, with a collar like a ruffle. George wore a blazer with the Yale crest on the pocket. He had a new haircut—short, with long bangs. He looked at me across the table, lovesick, his tongue hanging out, his eyes crossed, making me laugh.

"If I thought you were serious, I'd feel sorry for you," I said.

"It ain't your pity I want, baby." He spoke in his Humphrey Bogart voice, and then in his own he added, "Speaking of pity, I assume you've heard about Willie."

"Don't tell me."

"Are you kidding?"

I finished chewing a piece of dried-out meat, drank from my glass, and sat back in my chair. I said, trying to joke, "Spare me the anguish. I'm not a well woman," and coughed.

"Be serious. You haven't heard anything?"

"George, who am I going to hear anything from? Patty? The mailman? Tell me, damn it. No, don't."

"Do you want me to or not?"

"Tell me."

"He knocked up some girl named Cindy and they had to get married."

"That's what I thought you were going to say." It was true, I had expected something like that, but all the same it was like being slammed with a bowling ball.

"So," George said. "Are you all right?"

81

"Yeah. I'm all right." I smiled at him. "I'm over it, George. It's past history. I won't say I'm thrilled to hear he got married, but I'm not going to slash my wrists."

"That's good." He reached over and took my wrists in his hands. "I wanna hold your wrists. You have nice ones. Let's get married."

"George, please."

"I'm perfectly serious. Why won't you ever take me seriously?" He gazed into my eyes. I looked away, at the crest on his blazer. It read "Lux et veritas" in metallic thread. *"Ma femme,"* George said. *"Mon amour."*

I should do it, I thought. I should do something—marry George, marry anyone. "I'll marry you the day you graduate from med school," I said.

"That's five years from now. I'll be old."

"And you have to register as a Democrat."

"Christ!"

"Take it or leave it."

He pressed his lips to my left wrist. "I'll take it," he said. *"Mon petit chou."*

The doctor said I couldn't return to school until the next semester. After New Year's George went back to New Haven, my father and Jean returned to their classes at the high school, Patty spent her days at Mrs. Neal's. I was bored and irritable, and at times a sourceless anger would grip me, my hands would lock into fists and my whole body would tense up, and I would walk around the house kicking things and swearing and yelling at poor Fred. When I sat down, I was so restless my arms and legs twitched.

I read *War and Peace* and watched television and wrote letters and looked out the window to see the snow fall. Everything reminded me of Will and his horrible Cindy. Everything made me want to cry. When Prince Andrei died I wept and was still crying when everyone got home. "Oh, God, it's such a sad book," I said, wiping my eyes, feeling like a fool. I could see my father and Jean looking at each other. I blew my nose and went into the kitchen to help with dinner, but that night when we were all watching *Casablanca* on television, the tears started again, unstoppable, and I had to go up to my room.

When Jean yelled upstairs one night that there was a call for me, I ran down to the phone thinking of Will, forcing the thought away. I didn't care who it was—anyone, anything, life, air! Out of breath, I said, "Yes, hello, whatever it is I'll do it."

It was Hal Jacobs, my pianist friend, calling from Boston. "I hope you mean that," he said. "Because you've got to get back here right away, this minute."

"Hal, I'm sick!" I was glad to hear his voice; we hadn't parted on good terms. "Have you heard that I'm not a spoiled brat with mental problems? That I've been sick as hell?"

"Get better fast. I've got us a job," Hal said. "I played our tapes for this guy Eric Silver at the Café Cantabile—down at Kenmore Square? that basement place? And he wants us for a two-week gig."

"Oh, God. Starting when?"

"Valentine's Day. So we've got to get going *now*. The bit is, we do a bunch of love songs—anything we want, he leaves it up to us, the sappier the better. 'An Album of Love Songs,' they're going to call it, and if they like us we'll come back periodically for things like 'An Album of Irish Songs,' 'An Album of Gilbert and Sullivan,' stuff like that. Big bucks, Annie. We're on from nine to ten, and he's paying us fifteen a night each, plus dinner."

It sounded fantastic, it was what we had hoped for. But it seemed a long time ago that I had leaned against Hal's old Steinway and belted out Gershwin and Jerome Kern and Stephen Foster. Hal and that music seemed much farther away than the three hundred miles between Syracuse and Boston.

I wailed into the phone. "Hal, I've got mono."

"I know you've got mono. But Jesus, Annie, you've had mono forever. When are you going to get better?"

"The doctor says I can't go back until the end of this month."

"Screw the doctor. Get back here now, Nolan."

I imagined Hal talking on the phone in his studio apartment, frowning through his thick glasses and pulling at his wild, wiry black hair. He was brilliant, excitable, and madly ambitious. He was sure we would become famous: Nolan & Jacobs—a handle that screamed fame and fortune, Hal said.

I was fond of Hal, but I wasn't feeling at ease with him. It wasn't only that during my depressed days he had called me names and yelled at me. I was used to his lack of sympathy, his belief that singers were the most pampered creatures on earth. But there was something else: one night in October, just before Mamie died, we were rehearsing at his place, and after a long session at the

piano, we shared half a bottle of whiskey and fell into bed together. I woke up at dawn feeling foul, threw up quietly in the
bathroom, and sneaked out the front door. Neither of us spoke of
the incident; I was embarrassed by the whole thing, and I hoped
he had forgotten it, though I wasn't sure. For over a year we had
been friends, partners, Nolan & Jacobs, rehearsing together,
working up an act, looking for gigs. We were proud to be living
proof that a male-female friendship without sex was possible. I
knew that he didn't want to mess things up any more than I did.

I said, "Hal, I don't know what to do."

He stopped shouting at me. His voice became tender and
affectionate. He said, "Annie, I need you." Briefly, vaguely, I
recalled being in bed with him: we had been wild together, drunk
as skunks. I felt the first flimsy stirrings of desire. Hal said, "Listen, honey, they don't want Nobody and Jacobs, they want Nolan
and Jacobs. I need your goddamn gorgeous voice, damn it."

"It's tempting," I said. I looked in the mirror over the phone.
I needed a haircut. I was pale and there were circles under my
eyes. But I had lost some weight and my cheekbones were visible.
I thought I looked pretty good. "I must admit I'd love to get back
to work."

"I'll give you a choice," said Hal. "Okay? Don't ever say I'm
not Mr. Nice Guy. Either you get back here right now and start
singing or I come down there and drag you back by the hair."

The next day I left a note for my father, called a cab, and got
on the noon train. Hal met me at South Station. His eyes glittered,
his frizzy hair snapped with electricity. He threw his arms around
me and said, "I'm so glad you're back, Annie, I'm so goddamn
glad to see you. Let's go over to my place and go to bed, and then
we can start rehearsing."

3

Sex and music: Hal and I became lovers, and on Valentine's Day we became regulars at the Café Cantabile. The audience loved us. Hal analyzed our success: "Half of them are plastered, and three quarters of them are so horny by the time we finish that they'd give anything a standing ovation if it meant they could get out of there and go make it with their dates." But we were good, and Hal knew it, and Eric Silver knew it, and I knew it, too, and I asked myself why I had ever thought I wanted to play Mimì at the Met, or even Yum-Yum with the D'Oyly Carte. It was enough for me to stand on that little stage in a long red halter dress and dangling rhinestone earrings and sing songs that made people want to go home and make love.

Hal asked me to move in with him, but I had a commitment to Carolyn and Liz and Laurie at the apartment. And I wanted to hold some of myself back from Hal; I didn't know why.

Carolyn said, "Don't you love him?" It was the kind of conversation she adored. Carolyn was never really animated unless she was with a man or talking about one. I said that I liked him a lot, I was growing fonder of him all the time. Who wouldn't love Hal, I said, he was so cute and nutty and talented and smart.

Carolyn groaned. "Another George," she said. "Just what you need. Why don't you find someone exciting?"

"Hal is much sexier than George," I told her.

Carolyn looked more interested. "He really turns you on?"

"He's great," I said. "Imaginative."

"Tell me more."

I blushed. "He makes love the way he plays the piano."

"Details, sweetie! Details!"

I could have given her plenty of details, but to say any more would have embarrassed me horribly. Hal and I did crazy things in bed, things I'd never heard of before, that seemed to me perverse, even sick. Our sex life puzzled me, I didn't know what to think of it; it seemed shameful, somehow, to enjoy it so much. And I did enjoy it—God, what lust! If I was singing or riding the MTA or sitting around with my roommates and the memory of what had happened between us the night before flooded into my mind, my knees would wobble, my voice would break, I would lose my concentration, and I would think only of going over to Hal's apartment and ripping his clothes off.

When I tried to figure it out, all I could come up with was that it was bound up with the music we made. When he played and I sang, the music wove its net around us and drew us together in a frightening, exhilarating intimacy—something like what I used to feel with Will when we led the singing at parties, but it was oddly more real than that, more urgent. No one enjoyed our music as much as Hal and I did: it was like the visible skin of our lovemaking, the part we could show the world, and what we did to each other in bed was the dark heart of our music.

We were both still in school—that hectic, exhausting final year at the conservatory—so, after our initial two-week engagement, we appeared at the Cantabile on Saturdays only, at nine and at midnight. We had put together four shows—love songs, Irish songs, Gilbert and Sullivan, and show tunes—and we did them in rotation. Eric was generous with us. He raised our pay to twenty, and in between sets he gave us good dinners in the back room or let us sit out front with a group of friends, drinks on the house for everyone except Hal and me. He didn't allow us to drink when we were working. He also didn't let us smoke, talk to customers, give more than one encore, or eat anything garlicky. He was a paunchy, beak-nosed guy, garrulous and emotional. He took his work seriously; he wanted the Cantabile to be a great club—famous, like the Village Gate, or the old 47 in Cambridge. He used to give us little orations. "I'm taking a chance on you kids," he would say. "I want to be able to say I knew you when. Don't let me down. You be good to me and I'll be good to you. I love you kids like I was your dad"—though he couldn't have been more than thirty-five.

In May, I gave my degree recital—the Ravel songs, some Handel, some Schubert, a few Charles Ives songs, a little Dowland—and in June Hal and I graduated. A week later he stunned me by announcing that he was taking a job at IBM, in a management-training program. "Hell, I'm not Van fucking Cliburn," he said. "I've got this measly little talent. What am I going to do with it? Teach? I hate teaching, I've got no patience. Be an accompanist in some dinky ballet school? Join the army and play the piano at the USO in Saigon?"

He was always cheerful, always upbeat, and I never knew if he was disappointed that his life in music, his dreams of winning competitions and playing the piano all over the world and cutting records and becoming the definitive interpreter of Schubert—dreams he had talked about when I first met him—had dwindled to pop tunes at the Cantabile on Saturday nights.

As for me, I had shed that kind of ambition long ago. I got a job at the Paperback Booksmith in Copley Square, not far from the IBM building where Hal worked. Three times a week we met for lunch, Hal in the IBM uniform (white shirt, sober tie, dark suit), me in the unbecoming fashion of the times (miniskirt, tights, boots). We had other rituals: rehearsals on Sunday afternoons and Thursday evenings, symphony on Fridays, Greek food on payday. And our hot, kinky nights in the sack.

I think of those months with Hal as a time of perfect happiness. No—not happiness, but intensity. It was like a front-row seat at the movies, everything keyed up and brilliant and loud. My life distracted me from my life: I never thought of Will and Cindy, I stopped imagining him in bed with her or trying to figure the age of their baby or plotting to rescue him from his tangled domestic hell. I seized the day, I let bygones be bygones, and if I felt my brain slipping into dangerous waters I went over to Hal's place.

It was a beautiful summer in Boston. The bike paths along the Charles were lined with flowers, there were always white sailboats on the blue water, the sun shone all the time. My roommates moved away; Laurie left to study in Rome, Carolyn and Liz went to New York. I gave up the apartment and moved my plant collection, my records, and my junky old wooden furniture to one large top-floor room on Marlborough Street. I hung white cotton curtains at the four windows. There was a view of the new Prudential building rearing up over the shabby old Boston rooftops. Hal called it the penis in the sky; he said it inspired him.

Every Thursday after work I took the MTA out to Brookline for a voice lesson with my new teacher, Lydia Zeidenberg. She had sung in the Met chorus for twenty years, and done Gilbert and Sullivan with a touring company in England, and had a small local career as a lieder singer, and she also loved musical comedy and folk songs. She let me sing anything, whatever I fancied, as long as I learned to sing it well, and she pushed dramatic interpretation as well as voice. That summer, I was working on "Musetta's Waltz" from *Bohème* and "My Man's Gone Now" from *Porgy and Bess.* On the way home after my lesson, the rattles and squeals of the MTA were part of the music in my head, and I was a *cocotte* in a Paris café or a bereaved black woman in Louisiana.

When I got home one night in August, George Sullivan was waiting for me, leaning against the railing in front of my apartment building. He said, "I'm here," looking pleased with himself.

I said, "You're early," then realized it didn't sound very friendly. I knew George was going to medical school at Harvard, but I hadn't expected him to hit town for a couple of weeks. "This is wonderful," I said, and when I saw the way he smiled and straightened up suddenly to reach out and grab my hand and kiss my cheek, I meant it. I asked him where he was staying.

"I'm at the Y in Cambridge, and I came early so you could show me the city."

I laughed at him. "George, you've been here a zillion times!"

He stood there smiling at me. "I want to see the hidden byways the tourists never see, the fascinating places only Bostonians know."

"Well, come on upstairs for starters," I said. "I'll show you my new apartment."

"And then I'll take you out for dinner. Someplace posh."

"Great," I said, but I didn't really know what to do. I was supposed to eat dinner and rehearse with Hal. I didn't think Hal would mind if I begged off; he was far too confident to have problems with jealousy. It was George I worried about. I'd never told him Hal and I were anything but a piano-soprano duo, and I didn't know how seriously George had taken our New Year's Eve pledge to get married when he got out of medical school. Sometimes I suspected he did have an attachment to me that went deeper than jokes and friendship—something like my ancient, crazy passion for Will. I thought he probably would have gone through with a marriage if I wanted to. And though I was pretty sure he knew it had all been a joke, I wasn't positive. I'd seen him only once since that night—I was home for a couple of days on spring break, and he took me to a movie—and I'd hardly given a thought to his coming to Harvard that fall. I felt guilty: George had barely been in my consciousness all those months, and when I first saw him on my doorstep I had a disoriented moment of wondering who he was and what he was doing there.

I gave George a beer, phoned Hal, and went into the bathroom to change while George flipped through my record collection. He put on *Manon,* and my heart sank: was "Adieu, notre petite table" our song? Oh, God, I thought, he's going to spring a ring on me at the Top of the Pru.

But he didn't. Instead, he sprang his news: he had enlisted in the army, he was on his way to Fort Benning, Georgia, and he had asked to be posted to Vietnam.

He smiled while I sat there in shock. He smiled, and forked up some food and shoveled it in, and smiled again. Then he began to laugh. "Hey—pinko," he said. He snapped his fingers before my face. "Speak to me. Go ahead. Tell me what's wrong with the war. Tell me I'm a stupid, misguided tool of the establishment for going over there. Then I can tell you that your precious Lyndon B. got us into it and somebody's got to get us out."

"Don't get hostile, George," I said. "I just can't believe it. I'm having trouble taking this in. You *enlisted?*"

"Yup. And you think I'm a damn fool. Right?"

I said, "I think you're insane."

George said, "I don't like communism."

"Oh, God, George. *Communism.*"

"Well? That's what it comes down to, doesn't it? We stop it now or else the whole world's going to get as pink as you and your draft-dodging friends."

"It's not our business. It's this little tiny country in Southeast Asia."

"Tell that to your precious Lyndon B."

"He's not mine, George, and he's not particularly precious, and I think it's moderately inaccurate to say he got us into it."

"Your precious Kennedy, then. It doesn't matter. I'm going, anyway."

We sat looking at each other, and then George resumed forking in his dinner. I couldn't eat. I felt sick. Six months ago I knew almost nothing about the war; now it was all anyone talked about. Hal was thinking about graduate school. He was hoping, not very realistically, that his bad eyesight would get him a 4-F. "A 4-F classification means we'd have to fuck four times to celebrate," he had said. "It's a federal law."

I said to George, "I don't understand this. I just don't get it."

He told me how his father and all his uncles had been in World War II, one grandfather in the Spanish-American War, the other in World War I. "That's as far back as I know," he said. "But I obviously come from a family of hawks. I don't want to be a blot on the escutcheon."

"George, this isn't exactly World War I."

"It comes down to the same thing."

"You really believe that, don't you?"

"If I didn't, I wouldn't be going."

I said, "What about med school?"

"I won't be in the army forever. I'll go to med school when I get out. I'm going over as a medic." He sipped from his water glass, still smiling. "I expect it to be a slightly more educational experience than Harvard."

"I'm sure." I was furious with him. No one—no one sane, no one normal—did this sort of thing. I would have liked to get up and walk out. "At Harvard you don't get to be a hero," I said. "You just get to be a doctor. You don't get to dress up in a uniform and be a smug, brainless jerk."

He looked at me for a minute, and then he slammed his water glass down and said, "Hey. Annie." The water sloshed onto the tablecloth. "Do me a favor. I've given this a lot of thought, and I'm committed to it, but I don't mind admitting I'm scared shitless. I took a rather large detour to come up here and say good-bye to you. So could you just do me a favor and quit sitting there disapproving of me, damn it." I stared down at the rosy stain on the pink tablecloth. All I could see was George in a uniform, clutching his chest and toppling over with a cry, his face contorted—like someone in an old Audie Murphy movie. "Annie?" he said. "Can't we just say good-bye peacefully, like friends?"

I reached out for his hand, and I began, of course, to cry. "George—Wilbur—I'm sorry. I don't give a damn about your crackpot ideas. You've always had crackpot ideas. Just please don't go over there. I don't want to lose you, you're my oldest friend."

By this time we were both crying, and we dropped hands and reached for our napkins to wipe our eyes, laughing a little. The people at the next table looked at us, pretending not to. We were seated by the window; the tiny lights of the city twinkled below us and far away. I felt dizzy, and I gripped George's hand again. He said, "Oh, Christ, Annie. Christ Almighty."

"Don't do it, Wilbur," I said. It was all selfishness; I'd known him since I was eight, he was a vital bit of my life, and I'd already lost too many bits. I was so sorry—for him, for my own selfishness, my own losses—that I squeezed his hand tight, and the tears kept running down my face. "Please, please don't go," I said. "As a favor to me? Can't you—I don't know—take it back or something? Say you didn't mean it? False alarm? Just kidding, guys?"

He laughed. "Run away with me. We'll go to Sweden."

"I'd do it, if it would keep you out of the army." He looked at me, as if considering the idea. "Seriously," I said. I was mentally counting my money: how much would two tickets to Sweden cost? "Let's do it, Wilbur. Please?"

I could tell I was making him happy. My reaction was what he had wanted, tears and supplications, but I meant it. I'd do anything to save him. That was how I thought of it: he needed saving, as if he were a sinner. I'd save him from the pits of hell if I could.

"Naah," George said. "Too many pinkos over in Sweden. But I appreciate the offer."

After dinner, we walked down Boylston to the Public Garden and the Common, and then up Beacon Street. We stopped on a corner while George lit a cigarette. The lights were on inside a particularly lovely old townhouse. The curtains were not yet drawn, and inside were walls lined with books, a painting over the mantel of a bird in flight, a doorway into a room where a white staircase ascended.

George and I looked in. Peace, I thought. I remembered the part in *War and Peace* where Prince Andrei, wounded at the battle of Borodino, thinks of how he loves life—grass, earth, air—and asks only not to die and leave it, for nothing. And then he died. Coming from the room, we could hear music, faintly, through the closed windows: a Mozart horn concerto.

George took my arm and said, "Lookee there, little lady." It was his John Wayne voice. He pointed with his cigarette at the lit window. "That there's what ah'm fightin' fer. That and all it represents. Ah'm fightin' fer yer freedom, little lady. And ah'm fightin' fer yer purty blue eyes."

I said, "Oh, George, stop it, for heaven's sake, you're not

funny because you're serious, you really believe all that crap." I put my arms around him. He was wearing a tweed jacket, scratchy against my cheek. We stood there on Beacon Street hugging each other.

"Will you miss me?"

"I'll worry about you every minute. I'll write to you constantly."

"But will you miss me?"

I said yes, and we looked at each other in the twilight, and I thought I should kiss him, but I didn't. We drew apart and walked back to Marlborough Street.

He didn't even come in. He had to leave at seven in the morning—he was getting a ride with someone; he had only two days left before he had to be in Georgia—and he wanted to get home to bed. I hugged him and watched him out of sight. At the corner, he looked back and waved. I waved back. He turned toward the MTA station and I went inside and upstairs.

I was glad to be alone, relieved that George hadn't mentioned our mock engagement or asked too many questions about Hal. On the eleven o'clock news, I watched President Johnson make a speech about Vietnam that sounded insincere, and then I read an article in *Opera News* about a new German production of *Die Zauberflöte*. Hal called me at midnight, and I told him George was going to Vietnam.

"Can you believe it? He enlisted."

"My God," Hal said. "And you used to go with this guy?"

"That was before Vietnam, Hal. It was practically Korea when I used to date George."

"But he must have had tendencies, even then."

"He had tendencies, all right," I said. "He was pro–Joe McCarthy and he said Kennedy was a Commie. But he also had a great big Chevy. You know how girls were in the fifties. Who could resist a man with a car?" I smiled, remembering George's pride in his car, and the absurd, ignorant arguments we used to have about politics, and that evening at the lake when we swore to be friends forever. "We used to call him Wilbur," I told Hal, "because he had money. Remember the rich kid in the *Little Lulu* comics?"

When my father phoned, seven months later, to say he'd read in the paper that George had been killed in Vietnam, I felt first sorrow and then shame, and I wished with all my heart that

I hadn't talked about George with Hal and made fun of him. I wished that I had tried harder, that George and I had left for Sweden that night, that I had at least kissed him good-bye, that he was still alive, that I had saved him. I still have the four letters he wrote me from Fort Benning and then from someplace in Texas. The last one says, "We leave for Nam in three days, and the only thing I regret about going is that it'll postpone our wedding. I'm counting on your kind heart to take pity on a poor veteran and change the timetable and marry me when I get home." These two sentences made me depressed and anxious—was he serious, or was he kidding?—and I kept putting off a reply. When I finally wrote, it was a flippant letter full of dumb jokes that made no reference at all to what he had said, but he probably never received it. He was killed, the newspaper said, twenty-three days after he got there, on a Medevac mission, whatever that was, in a town on the Saigon River whose name I couldn't even pronounce.

4

George died in March, and gradually, in the year following, Hal and I lost whatever it was we'd had together. I'm still not sure whose fault that was. George's death upset me, and the war in general was upsetting everyone. Hal's future was up in the air. By some fortunate quirk, he still had his student deferment, but it couldn't last, and if he was reclassified 1-A he had no idea what he would do. I tried to imagine Hal shooting a rifle or dropping bombs from a plane, Hal in army fatigues smoking dope in some Asian jungle. It was difficult.

Every month, IBM sent Hal to New Jersey for management-training seminars, at which he was learning his end of the business from the bottom up: the punched cards that made the computers run were his *spécialité de la maison*. He insisted these sessions were, as he put it, "a little quaint, a little stuffy, a lot of fun," and he went into raptures about the musical din a room full of computers could make. In fact, he liked his trips to New Jersey so much that I suspected him of carrying on with some female fellow management trainee, but as time went on and he was as ardent as ever, I concluded that it was the world of junior management that he had fallen in love with.

That June, he alienated Eric Silver, and things were never the same again at the Cantabile. He managed to alienate me at the same time. On a weekend when we were scheduled to introduce our new act, "An Album of Music-Hall Songs," Hal was being sent by IBM to Bermuda for four days. The good part was that I could go with him; the dreary part was that we were going to attend a series of talks on what IBM called "Goal-Exploration and Life-style Decisions for Management Trainees."

"It's important," Hal told Eric.

94

Eric was hostile from the beginning. He had invested in a lot of advertising for the music-hall thing. He said, "It doesn't sound important. It sounds like crap."

Hal said, "Look, Eric, I know this was going to be a big weekend, but it's not as if Annie and I are Barbra Streisand and Liberace. I mean, get Butch Malone or Wanda or somebody in here and postpone us a week, for Christ's sake. Nobody's going to care."

Butch was a jazz trumpeter, and Wanda was a singer and stand-up comic, and either of them would have killed for our regular Saturday night spot at the Cantabile. I glared at Hal—I would rather sing than go to Bermuda, personally—but he paid me no attention. Eric smoothed the front of his suit down over his stomach. He fancied exaggerated bell-bottoms and jackets that nipped in and then flared out at the waist—his gigolo costumes, Hal called them. He said, "I don't like it, Hal. I discovered you guys, and I'd like to keep you, but this is a major event, this new act, and it's going to piss a lot of people off if I have to reschedule."

I thought that if Eric fired us I would scream, I would have hysterics, I would kill myself. I loved singing at the Cantabile. Saturday nights in that poky, smoky little den were the high points of my life. I shelved books at the Booksmith, I met Hal for lunches and dinners and sex and practice, I went out to Lydia's for my lessons. I took long walks on my days off, to Chinatown and the North End and across the bridge to the used bookstores in Cambridge. I rode my bike along the river. I went to the Sunday afternoon concerts in the Gardner Museum courtyard, and I went window-shopping in the antique shops on Beacon Hill. I wrote letters and talked to people and read books and practiced the piano and watched the news and listened to records and bitched about Lyndon Johnson, and what I looked forward to most all week was its culmination, on Saturday night, when I put on my red dress or my black dress, and Hal put on his plaid blazer or his white dinner jacket, and we stepped into the spotlight at the Cantabile and made music.

I wish I could explain why this made me so happy. It wasn't only that we were so popular, that the audience loved the old songs we sang, that people listened to us sometimes with tears rolling down their cheeks. Nor was it the electricity between Hal and me, the way we could connect up there onstage, dressed up

95

and elegant and always simpatico, no matter how he'd been boring me with his IBM stories or I'd been irritating him with my need for privacy. The satisfaction I got from our performances came from something more than the various relationships between Hal and me and the audience and the beautiful old songs I sang.

I try to figure it out, and the only way I can put it is to say that I was truly myself then, when I was singing and people were listening: I was truly myself in the way I was when I had someone to love. Whether the song was "Poor Wand'ring One" or "Someone to Watch Over Me" or "I Dreamt I Dwelt in Marble Halls," it was always my life I sang about—my mother's death and my father's sadness, Mamie's music the night I lost my virginity, Will Westenberg's voice singing "Mr. Blue," Martha Finch's plunge into the river, George Sullivan's letter, Fred the cat and little Patty, Hal's thick black-rimmed glasses—the last thing he took off before we got into bed together. All that was there when I sang on the stage of the Cantabile. It was completely true that when I sang I poured out my soul.

I cared about the music more than I cared about Hal. This became clear to me when we left Eric's office that day—he didn't fire us, but he sure was mad—and I said to Hal, "Well, at least we get a free trip to Bermuda."

Hal said, "No, we don't."

"What? We're not going? After all that?"

He took my hand. We were walking from Massachusetts Avenue down Newbury Street on a crowded Saturday afternoon. It wasn't like Hal to take my hand in public. He was the most undemonstrative person I'd ever met.

I said, "What's going on, Hal?" and I pulled my hand away. "Why did we just go through that scene with Eric if we're not going to be in Bermuda next weekend?"

"You're not invited." He tried to take my hand again but I wouldn't let him. I stopped in front of Erewhon and faced him.

"Since when?" I had further visions of the female management trainee, some blond seductress who lived for punched cards, who responded body and soul to the music of a room full of computers. "You mean you prefer to go without me."

"I mean you're not a spouse."

"You said it would be all right."

"I checked with Al and he said he was sorry, he really was,

but they couldn't have us sharing a room and they won't pay for a separate room for you. I'm really sorry, Annie, but I thought I'd better be honest with them. I mean, I can't see us faking being a married couple for four days."

I was looking into the window of Erewhon, at a rough wooden barrel spilling dried legumes like rabbit turds onto a piece of burlap, but when Hal stopped talking I turned to face him. "And what did you say to Al? 'Oh, certainly, sir, whatever you say, sir?' Like a good corporation man?"

"I said, 'Okay, Al, you rat fink, if my paramour can't accompany me I'm not going.' And then I told him I quit. I told him a corporation that doesn't allow premarital fornication during lifestyle weekend is not the corporation for me."

We stood there looking at each other. I disliked him at that moment, and I hated disliking him—Hal, whom I had been with for so long, whom I made music with and loved—but I couldn't help it. "Have a good time," I said, and went into Erewhon, fast, before I started to cry. Hal didn't follow me. I bought some yogurt and a half a pound of the beans in the window. When I came out, Hal was gone.

I went back to the Cantabile and talked to Eric. I asked him if I could do the act solo while Hal was away. I could play the piano myself. I knew it wouldn't be the same, but I could make it good. He looked dubious, but we went over to the piano and I played "Someone to Watch Over Me" and sang it through, and Eric sat there alternately compressing his lips into a line, then pursing them and nodding. I had no idea what he was thinking, but when I finished he said, "It would be different. More of a cocktail-music kind of thing. Not as showy as you and Hal."

"It's just one weekend, Eric."

He leaned back and patted the flowered vest that strained over his stomach. "Show me a list of songs."

"It obviously can't be music-hall stuff. I'd do the standards, the old tried and true."

"A little patter, too. Not much."

"Of course, sure."

"Show me something by tomorrow night," he said.

I walked home terrified and went straight to the piano. I played and sang and talked to myself until I was too tired to think. The next day I called in sick to work and spent the day polishing. I would do some of the songs I'd sung with Hal, but I wanted to add new ones, songs that would be all mine. I dug up a Noël Coward cat song called "Chase Me, Charlie," and I put in a little Kurt Weill—"September Song" and "It Never Was You" and "Surabaya Johnny"—because Hal hated Weill and refused to touch it. I left out all Mamie's songs but "Danny Boy": I wanted the chance to do it simply, the way I'd sung it all my life, without Hal's florid piano accompaniment.

By the time I got over to Eric's I was exhausted. He looked at my list and made me sing "Chase Me, Charlie" and "Surabaya Johnny," and then he leaned over the piano and patted my cheek. "You're cute," he said. "I like it. You don't need that jerk."

I have to say it was a hit. On Saturday night when I walked onstage alone, I was terrified, and it took me a while to relax. Even when I was scared, I could always count on my voice, but the piano gave me trouble at first. My fingers trembled on the keys, and at times I was reduced to playing nothing but simple right-hand chords, but the audience was wonderful, the applause was immense, and by the time I got to "Chase Me, Charlie," my assurance was back and I was enjoying myself enough to tell a couple of Fred stories as an introduction to the song. People actually laughed, and they loved the song, and I got a standing ovation for "It Never Was You." When the set was over, Eric came out and held up my hand as if I were a winning prizefighter, and said, "Isn't she wonderful, folks? Our own Anna Nolan!"

I went backstage and burst into tears, and as a special concession Eric let me have a glass of sherry between sets to calm my nerves. The second set was even better. Afterward, I treated myself to a cab home and fell into bed, but I couldn't sleep. I felt exhilarated and guilty in equal parts, as if I'd cheated on Hal—had an affair with myself.

He came to see me the next day, directly from the airport, told me the weekend was idiotic, the company was full of jerks, his job was stupid and he was only sticking it out because of the money and would I ever forgive him. We were in bed before I could answer.

But at the Cantabile everything changed. Eric was permanently pissed at Hal. He called us into his office after our next show and said we could forget the music-hall evening.

"I'm soured on it," Eric said. "I think it's a lousy idea. Its time is passed."

We had worked hard researching the songs and putting the

act together. I had gone to Goodwill and bought a new dress—
long and, I hoped, Edwardian-looking—and a picture hat with a
plume; Hal had a straw boater and a striped jacket. He said to
Eric, "You mean two weeks ago it would have been terrific and
now it's a bomb and nobody's going to like it?"

"It's me who's not going to like it," Eric said. "With me it's a
bomb."

"I can't believe you're canceling it, just like that."

"It's not just the music-hall routine," Eric said. "I didn't like
your little international jaunt. I'm looking for commitment here,
not some company boy who's going to jet around the world every
Saturday night when he's supposed to be onstage."

"I think you're exaggerating just a little bit, Eric. We're talking about one lousy Saturday."

Eric leaned back in his chair, straightened the crease in his
pale-blue bell-bottoms, and said, "We're talking no lousy Saturdays, Hal. You finish out the summer and then you're gone. No
hard feelings. I won't say I'm not going to miss you guys. But I've
got to have a little commitment here."

I knew Hal was about to quit on the spot, but I gave him a
pleading look and he contented himself with walking out and
slamming the door.

Hal brooded all week. He refused to go out and refused to
rehearse, just sat in front of the television after work drinking
beer and eating Fritos. I couldn't stand to sit there with him. I
stayed home by myself reading *Middlemarch* for the fourth time
and eating Oreo cookies. Every couple of nights he came over to
my place around ten to complain about Eric. Finally I said, "I
think you're getting a little peculiar on the subject, Hal. Can't you
just forget it?" I was feeling bad enough without listening to Hal.

"I can't forget injustice so easily," Hal said. "That guy makes
my blood boil. 'A little commitment,' he says. Haven't we been
committed to him and his seedy dump for over a year? Christ,
that little asshole pisses me off. He's making me *impotent,* for
Christ's sake." It was true. Our sex life was terrible.

"It will pass," I said. It did, of course. We resumed our
Thursday night practice sessions and our wild evenings in bed,
and the summer dragged by—not pleasantly. Hal and I were
jittery in each other's company, unsure of each other, more silent
together than we used to be. I used to catch him watching me with
a considering look in his eyes—the look he probably wore during

management-training sessions. I kept remembering the preceding summer, when Nolan & Jacobs were at their peak, Boston was a beautiful dream city, everything was new and exciting. Now the city looked faded and dusty and old. Even the Cantabile crowd had changed: they seemed drunker and noisier and less enthusiastic, as if they sensed that Hal and I were a dying concern.

Our last performance was in mid-August on a hot, muggy night that seemed to be holding back a thunderstorm out of spite. Eric had advertised our departure ("that fat, calculating, opportunistic sleazeball," Hal said), and "An Album of Show Tunes" was on the schedule, but the midnight show was full of fans who kept requesting their favorites. I sang a lot of Gershwin—I had become moderately famous for "Summertime" and "The Man I Love"—and "Poor Wand'ring One" from *Pirates,* with its coloratura embroidery that always got me a round of applause. I sang "Just One of Those Things" and "Make Believe" and "Till There Was You" and "You Made Me Love You"—all the tried-and-true crowd-pleasers.

The audience was drunk and happy and in love with us. It was like the old days. When I looked over at Hal once I saw that he had tears in his eyes. We closed with a short medley of goodbye songs for the occasion: "Let's Call the Whole Thing Off," "The Party's Over," "I'll Be Seeing You," a set that was both jazzy and emotional, and that was calculated to make the citizens of Boston pine for our return—"just in case that motherfucking Eric ever came to his senses and begged us on his fat knees to come back," Hal said. We got a standing ovation and shouts for an encore. We let that go on for a while, and finally I held up my hand and said, "I think we have time for one more, so we'll end with a song my grandmother used to sing," and before I could continue the crowd began to clap and chant "Marble Halls," because I always introduced it that way on Irish nights, and it was a favorite.

They were very quiet as I sang, as if we were all in church, and while I was singing, the words and the tune so familiar that I hardly had to think, it really came to me what our breakup meant, that it wasn't just the end of Saturday nights at the Cantabile, and the hot times in bed, and the IBM jokes, and the intense Thursday night rehearsals. I listened to myself sing, I listened to the beautiful sound Hal coaxed from Eric's horrible old Baldwin, I saw the audience looking up at us with love, and I realized that what the end of our Cantabile gig meant was the thing that I had been searching for, whatever it was, and that I had found a piece of in the music Hal and I created together, would be lost to me again, more lost to me than ever.

When the set was over, we hugged and kissed for our fans while everyone cheered. Eric surprised us by coming out and making a nice little speech, and then Hal and I walked back to my place. We hardly spoke. It was as if we'd spent the evening at a funeral instead of onstage in a nightclub. The thunderstorm had come and gone, leaving the night humid and dank, the city hotter than ever and smelling of gasoline. We fell into an exhausted sleep without touching each other.

A week or two later, Eric called me up and asked me to come back to the Cantabile, solo, starting in October.

Hal laughed when I told him. "I just wish I'd been there to hear you tell him off."

I said, "I didn't tell him off, Hal. I told him I'd think about it. He says to let him know in a week."

He stared at me. "You'd do it without me?" His voice was a stricken whisper.

We were having lunch at a cheap French restaurant on Newbury Street. I looked away from Hal—his intensity could be so theatrical—and out the window at the lunchtime crowd passing by. Hundreds of people I didn't know, but some of them had probably heard me sing. At the thought, a reckless excitement rose in me. I would be singing again at the Cantabile; I wouldn't have to give it up, I could keep singing.

"Without me, Annie? How could you even consider it?"

I looked over at him. He was holding a forkful of *coq au vin*, ready to shovel it in, glaring at me. I said, "I don't know what you're accusing me of, Hal."

"Sucking up to Eric."

"I wasn't sucking up to Eric. I didn't know he was going to offer me this." I had suspected it, though, and the hope of it was what had kept me from utter dejection when we were fired. I said to Hal, "Well, maybe it didn't exactly come out of the blue. But I didn't ask him for it."

He ate, drank wine, wiped his mouth with a napkin—slowly, watching me, saying nothing. "Okay then," he said finally. "You tell me. What's your motivation for this little betrayal?"

I said, "I need this job more than you do. I work part time in a bookstore, you're a junior executive or whatever you call it. You can call it betrayal or whatever nonsense you like, Hal, but I've got to pay my rent, pay for my voice lessons—"

"That's not it," he said, and it was true. I shut up. If there was one thing I didn't sing for, it was money.

"Well?"

I looked at him helplessly. "I just want to sing." I reached over and touched his hand. "You're so involved with your job, Hal. It comes first with you, it has to, I understand that. But singing is all I've got. It's everything to me."

"And I'm nothing."

I wanted to hit him. I said, "Of course you're not nothing. How can you say that? My singing at the Cantabile has nothing to do with our relationship, Hal."

"God—anyplace but the fucking Cantabile. That slimy little son of a bitch Eric."

My head began to ache, a dull throb behind my eyebrows. How long was I supposed to hate Eric, to participate in Hal's grudge? I didn't mind Eric Silver—he'd been good to me—and I loved the Cantabile, with its nest of wooden tables, the bentwood chairs, the candles and the potted palms, the tiny stage with its bank of lights, the tricky old rosewood piano, the smell of garlic and booze and humanity.

I said, "I'm comfortable there, Hal. I'm too shy to start all over someplace else. There aren't that many clubs anyway. I have my niche at the Cantabile."

He took his hand away. "I'm the one who got you the niche. Remember that?"

I said, "That was a long time ago. And I did just fine on my own while you were gone."

He nodded at me slitty-eyed—a series of condescending little nods accompanied by a tiny smile. "I'm sure you did. I'm sure you were just too frightfully marvelous. I'm sure not a soul in the place missed good old Jacobs. Not with Nolan up there on the stage with her dress cut down to her belly button and her boobs hanging out."

I stood up and said, "Oh, go to hell. Go back to your stinking office. Go back to Bermuda. I'm leaving." I rummaged through my purse for money for the meal; Hal and I always went strictly dutch.

"I see," he said. "I get it. I'm going to suffer for the Bermuda thing for the next fifty years."

The words hung oddly between us: who ever said we'd be together for fifty years? I ignored the implication. I said, "I'm not saying Eric was right to hold a grudge, but I have to agree with him that walking out like that was a pretty crummy thing to do. I mean, you never even apologized, Hal." I put a five-dollar bill on the table. Hal picked it up and pocketed it. He looked at me, still nodding, pursing his lips in a sort of sneer, as if he were listening to inferior music played on an out-of-tune piano. "I've got change coming from that five," I said.

He yanked the bill out of his pocket and threw it at me. "Take it, this delightful lunch is on me." I left it on the table, and he jumped up and tried to jam it into my hand, then down the front of my dress. I slapped his hand hard and threw the money at him. People were watching us. I turned to leave. My face was burning and I could feel the sweat trickling down my back.

Hal called after me, "Are you going to do it, Annie?" I imagined everyone in our vicinity wondering, Do what, do what? Hal said, "Because if you are, you can forget about us. I mean it. Forget about me."

I was halfway to the door. I turned to look at him. He was standing by the table holding his napkin in one clenched fist. His Groucho Marx eyebrows were pulled into a massive frown. All of a sudden I wanted to laugh. I wanted to run back to him—the other customers would love it—and throw my arms around him and say, "Let's not fight, let's make peace." But I knew he wouldn't accept peace unless I gave up the Cantabile job, so I turned my back on him and continued out the door to the August heat of Newbury Street.

But we made up. Hal surprised me: he sent me flowers— white roses that I knew he couldn't afford—with a card that said, "Forgive me, I'm a shit. Do it. I'll still love you." It was signed, "Magic Fingers." I pinned one of the roses in my hair and met him after work as he was coming out the door at IBM. He set down his briefcase, picked me up, and whirled me around right there on Boylston Street. Then we went over to his apartment and did what we always did: went to bed and performed what Hal called unspeakable acts.

Afterward, we lay there together, hot and sweaty, listening to a recording of Gershwin's Second Rhapsody. Hal's noisy old electric fan revolved on a table, and we had the record turned up loud. The setting sun slanted into the room. I thought, I could lie here like this forever. Then Hal said, "You know that I love you, Annie. Don't you? Don't you know that?"

"Yes, I do, Hal."

His lips were against my breast, and I could feel his smile against my bare skin. "I don't say it much," he said. That was true; the word *love* on the card that came with my flowers was a rarity. "I guess I figured it always came out in the music."

I said, "I suppose it did."

He raised himself on one elbow and peered at me. Without his glasses, he looked like an eccentric, sincere twelve-year-old. He said, "Let's get married, Annie. Let's do it. I want to marry you, I really do."

I pulled him against me again so I wouldn't have to answer. His tongue flicked out over my breast, and he moved his hand down my thigh. I felt no desire, only a faint revulsion and panic.

"Marry me," he said again.

"I don't know, Hal. I'd have to think."

He moved away from me and got his glasses from the table. We stared at each other. His face was crazily happy when he was smiling, frozen into sternness when he wasn't. "Don't look so judgmental," I said. "God, Hal, give me a chance to catch my breath."

"You're turning me down," he said. "Jesus Christ."

I had never in my life wanted so much not to talk. I said, with effort, "I'm not turning you down, Hal. I just don't know."

"Jesus Christ," he said. "I don't believe this."

I said, "Hal, you're so extreme. This isn't an opera, for heaven's sake. You've just got to give me some time." I pulled the sheet up and turned my back to him.

I heard him get out of bed. "Time. What the hell has time got to do with it?" I didn't answer. He went over to the hi-fi and clicked the record off in the middle of the last section. "This is really a rotten piece of music," he said. "It's nothing but a tedious little exercise, and it doesn't know how to end."

I thought that was unfair to Gershwin, but maybe an accurate description of what my relationship with Hal was becoming.

We took separate showers—Hal first, while I lay there staring at the fan's invisible blade going around and around, trying to make my mind a perfect blank. I closed my eyes and dozed for a second and dreamed about a teacup my mother used to drink from—her favorite cup, pink with a gold rim. I dreamed that I broke it. When I woke I remembered that it was my father who had broken it, and my mother had cried, and in the world of my childhood it had seemed a shocking tragedy. It seemed tragic still.

When I came out of the bathroom, Hal called to me from the balcony. He lived in one small second-floor room with an alcove for the piano, a kitchenette, and a tiny, absurd balcony overlooking Huntington Avenue. We sat there on ancient canvas folding chairs, our feet up on the iron railing. We had sat like this dozens of times. Hal brought out a bottle of vodka and two glasses and a melting tray of ice cubes. When I drank, I could taste grit.

He spoke suddenly. "Okay," he said. "You've had some time to think. So what about it? Are you going to marry me, or what?"

I laughed, trying to sound fond and carefree. "It takes more than ten minutes to make life decisions."

"Annie." I looked over at him. He was hunched down in his chair, holding his glass with both hands. "Annie," he said again, and then he took a deep breath and said, "I'm suffering. You're making me suffer. Maybe this isn't an opera, but I feel like Don José or someone. Pagliaccio. Jack fucking Point. Some poor slob who's losing his girl. I didn't ever think you'd say no, or that you'd think about it. I assumed you loved me and we'd get married. I thought it was a settled thing. I don't understand this."

I had hoped he wouldn't say any more about it, that he'd think about it and change his mind, or decide that the time wasn't right or that his ego couldn't take my indecision. But in the shower I had decided what I would say if he persisted. "I'm not ready to get married, Hal," I said. "Don't think I don't love you. I just don't think I can settle down yet." He didn't answer. "Hal?"

His voice came after a moment. He said, "I don't get it, Annie. We've been going together almost two years. We care about each other. And it's not as if we're teenagers. I'm ready to settle down. Why aren't you?"

I sighed and said, truthfully, "I don't know," but he was still talking. He said, "Unless you've got somebody else that I don't know about."

A horn honked from the street below, and there was a burst of music from a radio, then silence, then the traffic again. Some indecipherable combination of these elements brought a picture to my mind of Will Westenberg in his brown leather jacket, the cold wind reddening his cheeks, his voice saying yes, he did miss the old days, his eyes sliding away from mine, then back. Our hot hands palm to palm.

I said, "I suppose I do, Hal. In a way. I mean, there is some unfinished business in my life. I guess you could call it that."

He turned in his chair to stare at me, and I told him about Will: *about Will,* what a ridiculous phrase, there was nothing to tell. And yet there he was, as vivid in my mind as Hal. More vivid, always, unless I kept him away by force. Will in his brown jacket, Will pulling me close to dance, his long pale body naked against mine, his breath on my cheek, his blood on my white dress. Will. I hadn't talked about him in so many years—when had I ever, except a few jokes with George and that one night with Roger Gable? Telling Hal about him was like speaking my own language after years in a foreign country. I closed my eyes, drank vodka, listened to my voice grow shaky with emotion.

Hal interrupted. He said, "Wait a minute. Just one lousy minute. When did you see this guy last?"

"I don't know. A year, year and a half ago." A year and ten months, I thought. November 1964, Thanksgiving morning. I had mono and thought I was going crazy.

"And he's married? Got a kid?"

"That's what I hear."

"And you went with him in high school."

"Sort of. Not exactly."

"This isn't the guy with the car?"

"Hal, that's George. I told you about George. George is dead, he was killed in Vietnam." No matter how many times I said it, it was still a shock to remember that George was dead, blown to bits halfway across the world. I swallowed the rest of my vodka and poured myself a little more. My hand was not quite steady. After this drink I'll go, I thought. Take a cab home. I didn't want to talk about it anymore—George, Will, my old, gone life.

"What do you mean, not exactly. Did you have an affair with this guy, or what?"

"Once," I said, and Hal said, "What? *What* once? You *did* it once? And you haven't seen him in over a year? And you're still so nuts about him that you can't even think about marrying anyone else? Me?"

I didn't answer right away. There was nothing I wanted to

say. What I wanted was to work a miracle and whisk myself away from Hal's balcony and home to my cool, quiet, solitary bed. But obviously I had to speak. I said, "I can't explain it, Hal. He just— he gets to me. And I always have the feeling that he needs me, somehow. Please don't laugh. This goes back a long way."

"I'm not laughing. Is he in love with you?"

Is he in love with you. I'd never really thought about it. He had been at Mamie's funeral; I had that fact, nothing could change it. On the other hand, he was married to some Cindy. But he'd been forced into it. But he'd never tried to get in touch with me. But he didn't know where I was. But he could have found out. But he was saddled with a wife and baby. But the way he'd looked at me that Thanksgiving morning. But—

"Is he? In love with you?"

I sighed, and drank. "I doubt it, Hal."

He lectured me. He told me it was sick, that years and years of unrequited love is madness, a neurotic fantasy I had devised to keep myself from reality. He said that my mother's death and my father's remarriage had been hard on me, and I'd stuck at this adolescent level. I was a case of arrested development. I'd better snap out of it if I ever expected to have a normal life. I should see a therapist. He must be crazy himself to want to be saddled with a raving loony, but in his opinion marrying him would be the best thing I could do. "You've got to *live*, Annie," he said, sounding like George. "You've got to get out of your rut. How long can you go on like this? Lusting after somebody else's husband just because he nailed you one night on a back lawn when you were eighteen years old."

He made me cry. We left the balcony and went inside, and he propped up pillows on the bed. We sat there together while he talked to me. He dried my eyes and brought me tissues and stroked my hair. I don't remember most of what he said—just that he was persuasive, tender, insistent. We drank a lot of vodka. When the bottle was nearly gone, we were tentatively engaged.

I agreed to it because I was tired of being lectured, tired of crying and arguing, and just plain tired, but also because what he said touched me—not his opinions about Will but his own feelings for me. *I'm suffering*, he said.

"I don't want to set a date or anything," I told him. "I don't want to get married next week, Hal."

But he seemed satisfied. "Don't worry," he said. "We're only tentatively engaged. You decide what to call it. Moderately engaged? A little bit engaged? Engaged up to a point? All I care about is that I can count on you and you love me." He'd give me a rhinestone instead of a diamond to show what a sleazy, semisort of engagement it was. In the end, we were laughing together against our pillows, and we tried to make love again, but we were too drunk.

I woke toward morning with a massive headache. Hal was asleep on the bed beside me, still in his clothes. I got up and took an aspirin, and when I came back to bed I looked at his face in the dawn light: thin cheeks, pointed chin, bushy eyebrows. All right: yes, it was a dear face. He woke suddenly and smiled at me. I put my arms around him and kissed him, and he went back to sleep instantly. I lay there for a long time before I fell asleep, listening to the familiar sound of his breathing and wondering what was wrong with me that I could care for nothing, no one, but Will Westenberg and music.

5

IBM sent Hal to New Jersey for a two-week seminar called "Possibilities in Management Theory and the Decision-Making Process."

Hal said he probably could work it out so that I could accompany him this time—as a semimoderately engaged fiancée. "I know New Jersey isn't Bermuda, but on the other hand it is New Jersey."

But I stayed home. I had thought I wanted to be without Hal for a while, but I missed him fiercely when he was gone. Everyone I knew seemed to be out of town at the end of that hot summer. Business at the bookstore was desultory at best, and Lydia was away, so I didn't have a voice lesson. My top-floor room was warm and airless. I tried out for the Boston Light Opera Company's fall production and only made the chorus. I was gaining weight. I caught a summer cold. I lost my favorite pair of earrings. When my father offered me the money for a train ticket, I went home for a long weekend.

Jean was expecting again, in November, and she was swollen and crabby. It always surprised me how quickly Jean had gone from glamorous divorcée career woman—the bleached blonde my grandmother had disapproved of—to harassed mother. She still dyed her hair, but she had cut it short because she had no time to tease it into an upsweep, and it waved limply and unfashionably around her face. Patty, nearly three, was full of beans. I did my best to keep her busy and out of Jean's way, but she wouldn't leave Jean alone. "She wasn't like this last spring," I said, and Jean just sighed wearily and said, "The pediatrician calls it mother-hunger. He says she'll get over it, and while it lasts I should feel flattered."

We were sitting on the porch, drinking lemonade, and Patty

was on Jean's lap. It was very hot. The plastic straps of the aluminum folding chairs cut into the backs of my bare legs. "And do you?" I asked. "Feel flattered?"

Jean smiled at me over Patty's head. "I'll tell you the truth, Annie," she said. "I feel like shit."

It shocked me that she would make such a confession, use such a word. I felt immediately closer to her. She was forty-two, my father's pregnant wife, all the mother left to me. It occurred to me that I should talk to her about things—about Hal, and George, and Will, and my singing, and the vague feeling of loss that accompanied me always, wherever I was, whatever I did. But before I could speak, Jean said, "Someone's been calling you here, Annie. Some man who won't give his name."

Can I say that my heart leapt? It did, and I could hear it beat, I could feel the pulse thudding in my temples, as if it had been stopped for a long time and had just revved up again. I thought: *Will.*

"He calls every couple of weeks and asks for you," Jean went on. She put Patty on the floor, and Patty, miraculously, got involved with a box of plastic farm animals. "I always just say you're not home. He asked me the first time if there was a number where you could be reached, and I said no. I didn't know if he was someone you'd want me to give your phone number to."

"Does he say anything else?"

"No. He's rather pleasant, but all he says is that he'll keep hoping to catch you when you're home. He obviously knows you live out of town."

Will. I remembered the last time I saw him—all the things that had returned to me with a jolt that night on Hal's balcony: our hands joined, his leather jacket, the voice from inside the house, his ironic little salute.

"He called two nights ago," Jean said. "I told him you'd be home this weekend. Do you think I should have? He seems harmless enough, and he's certainly interested in getting hold of you. I hope he isn't some creep you're trying to avoid."

Patty looked up at me with curiosity. "Tweep," she said. "Some tweep," and lifted her arms to Jean to be picked up.

When Jean went inside to get dinner, my father came out to the porch. He wanted to talk to me about my career, as he called it. "You're a singer, Anna," he said. "You're trained to be a singer, not a clerk in a bookstore."

"I'm still a singer, Daddy. I'm still going to be at the Cantabile. I open October eighth."

He shook his head, looking impatient. "That's not the kind of career I mean."

"You said you were proud of me." He and Jean had come to Boston twice to hear us. Jean liked the Beatles—she thought they were cute—and I had sung "Yesterday" for her and "Danny Boy" for my father. "I love doing it, Daddy," I said. "I'd sing at the Cantabile for the rest of my life."

"You were wonderful," he said. "I wish your grandmother could have heard you. God, she would have enjoyed it—all those old songs."

"I can't wait to get back to work. I miss singing them." I was trying to put an act together in little chunks: the old sentimental songs, then Gershwin, then some Brecht-Weill, then a miscellany of more current pop tunes, then "Marble Halls" for the closer— my signature tune, Eric called it.

"I miss hearing them," my father said. "Maybe you'd sing for us a little before you leave."

I said of course I would, and he sighed. He seemed melancholy. I was always afraid he was ill and not telling me— he was so thin and pale. He wouldn't be fathering all these children, I told myself, if he weren't well. But I watched him carefully as he stared out past the bushes that lined the porch, trying to read the lines in his face, too many for a man just fifty. It scared me, suddenly, how much I loved my father and how old he was. When had the years begun to overtake him? When did he get so thin? When did his hair go so gray? There was a brown bottle of pills in the medicine cabinet with his name on it. He would die—not soon, but some day. Twenty years? I would not be ready.

Inside, we could hear the radio, and Patty singing along to "Eleanor Rigby."

"Listen to her," I said, to cheer him up. "She's right on key."

"She likes the part about picking up the rice."

I leaned over and patted his hand. "Maybe she's the one who'll finally take the family talent to the Met, Daddy. It isn't going to be me."

"You still don't want to go to graduate school?" he asked. "Go to New York and study? Europe?"

"Me?" I leaned back in my chair and put my feet up on the

railing to show how lazy I was, how ambitionless, how content with my modest lot. "God, no."

"I hope you're not hesitating because of the money. Jean and I have some saved, quite a bit really, and your uncle Phil would help us out. I ran into Sister Cecilia the other day and she said you should be studying in Europe. She even gave me the name of someone in Paris."

"Daddy, please—no. I don't want to do that, you know I don't."

"I don't understand you. A gift like that."

"It's a small gift," I said gently. "Really. It's very small. It's not enough, Daddy."

"There are plenty of people who don't agree with you."

We had been through all this before. "I'm the one who's got to do it, though, and I know I can't. And if I did do it—I mean, if I did actually manage to have a big career, I'd feel like a sham. Like I was putting one over on everyone. At least at the Cantabile I never feel that. I know I'm giving them their money's worth."

"You're a little too subtle for me," he said. "All I know is you're capable of better."

We sat in silence. I felt resentment building up: it was no one's business but mine if I wanted to sing in cabarets and work in bookstores. I'd sing on a corner by the Common and collect money in a cup if I wanted to. I imagined doing that, wearing the Edwardian dress and the plumed hat that still hung in my closet, singing "Danny Boy" and "Summertime" a cappella. There wouldn't be a dry eye on Tremont Street. My cup would be full.

My father said, "So what are you going to do with your life? Sing in a bar forever?"

I knew I should tell him about Hal, about being a semifiancée, but I didn't. Even now, missing Hal as I did, the engagement seemed unreal. I said, "Oh, I don't know, Daddy. Don't worry. I'll be all right." He looked over at me with a smile, hopeful again after his brief melancholy. Years ago I had promised him that I would be happy, and it occurred to me that he trusted me to do this. I thought for the thousandth time how fortunate—how improbably fortunate—it was that his own life had turned out so well. I took heart from that fact—from Patty's voice in the kitchen, from the morning glories climbing the corner pillars of the porch, from the smell of chicken frying. "You and Jean are such a good example—maybe I'll get married. I'll marry this guy who keeps calling me on the phone, and I'll come back to Syracuse and settle down and have babies and sing in the choir at St. Joseph's."

His smile widened. "That'll be the day," he said.

"Don't be too sure," I said. "I can imagine a worse life."

At dinner, Jean said, "I wonder what happened to the mystery man. He hasn't called back."

"Maybe I'll get in touch with him," I said.

Jean looked at me in surprise. "You know who it is?"

I shrugged. "I have a pretty good idea."

Patty banged her spoon on the table. "Some tweep," she said.

"Oh, I don't think so, Patty," I said, and felt myself blushing. "I really don't think so."

After dinner, I got out of my cutoffs and T-shirt, showered, made up my eyes with liner, mascara, and two shades of shadow, and put on a white gauzy dress embroidered in blue, which Hal claimed made me look like a wholesome tart. I borrowed Jean's car and drove over to Danforth Street. I pulled into the Westenbergs' driveway and sat there a minute, watching the pink sunset sky over the trees behind the house. This is a mistake, I thought. I should have called first, at least. And it probably wasn't Will.

But it was, I knew it was, and I didn't hesitate long. I looked in the rearview mirror—face, hair, lipstick—and got out and went up the path. I didn't even notice the house; I assume it was still shabby and neglected. The front door was open. Through the screen I could hear a television, and dishes clanking. I rang the bell, and Will's mother came to the door, wiping her hands on a dish towel.

"Yes?"

"I came to see Will."

She looked puzzled. "Will?"

"I'm Anna, Mrs. Westenberg. Will and I went to school together."

"But he doesn't live here anymore."

"No—I know that. But I thought he might be in town for a visit."

I couldn't see her well through the dirty screen, and the light was wrong, but I remembered that her face was shaped like Will's, she had the same pointed chin. She shook her head. "No," she said. "I'm sorry. Will hasn't been home for a long time. He lives in the Midwest now."

At first I didn't understand. She still had the slight German accent that turned *w*'s into something more like a *v*. Vill. Vest.

"He's out in Indiana now. He works for his wife's father."

"Ah. Of course." Vife. I laughed. "Oh, dear. Somewhere I got the impression he and his wife had split up or something. I'm sorry. I guess I was misinformed."

I could see her smile through the screen. "No," she said.

I waited for more, but that was all. *No what?* I laughed again. "God, what a dumb mistake. I'm really sorry. I'm sorry I bothered you."

"That's all right."

"Well." I watched her wipe her hands over and over with the dish towel, looking at me disapprovingly: the dress, the eyeshadow, the dangling earrings. I didn't care. I went on, "If you see Will, will you say hello for me? I live in Boston now. Tell him to look me up if he's ever in the area." She said nothing. I imagined her thinking: *hussy, homewrecker, loose woman.* I said, "My name is Anna Nolan."

She said, "Yes, I remember you." Then she surprised me. She opened the screen and held out her hand. I took it, and she gave it a firm squeeze. "I'll tell him you were asking for him," she said, and—oh, God, was it my imagination?—her face wasn't disapproving at all, and it seemed to me that there was some deeper meaning to her words and her handshake, some message she was trying to communicate about Will.

But she said nothing else. I gripped her hand, and thanked her and left.

It was getting dark, a warm fall night. Will was in Indiana with his wife. I was in Syracuse with no one, driving down Court Street looking at black trees against red sky. There would be the same sky, similar trees, out in Indiana. The Westenbergs might be sitting down to dinner—Mom, Dad, and the kids. Or would Will be alone somewhere, looking at the approaching sunset with his soul reaching east to me?

When I got home Jean said, "He called again, not ten minutes ago. He's going to call back."

"Oh, Lord—Jean, it's not who I thought it was," I said. "Unless—I don't know, did it sound like long distance?"

She said no. She said, "In fact, he said something about coming over and taking you out for a drink." She looked at me curiously. "May I ask who you thought it was?"

I leaned my elbows on the kitchen counter and put my head in my hands. Will had been so real to me while I was at his old house talking to his mother. Now he was fading again, dissolving like the opposite of a Polaroid photograph. He was somewhere in Indiana, maybe unhappy, maybe in trouble, but he was a shadow, far from me, unreachable. "I thought it was an old friend, someone I used to love," I said, and while Jean was patting my shoulder and saying "Oh, dear, Annie, I'm sorry," the phone rang.

I said, "I'll get it. Whoever it is, I'll get rid of him." I picked up the phone and said hello.

"Anna? I can't believe I got you at last. It's Trevor."

"Who?"

"Trevor Finch. How are you? Long time no see and all that. I can't believe you're really in town. Listen—do you want to get together for a couple of beers? Have a chat about the good old days, so called?"

I'm not sure why I agreed. I was taken by surprise, I didn't even think. I said, "Sure, why not?" When I hung up I wished I hadn't: Trevor, for God's sake. I remembered his weaselly face, his greasy black hair and sharp little teeth, his rotten drunken temper. I remembered the main fact about him, which I had somehow forgotten over the years: that he was the one person on this earth that I despised. And yet he was, in spite of everything, undeniably a link with Will, part of my history with him.

I met him at the Green Horseshoe, a bar I used to go to with George that summer before we left for college. It was a bad choice—too familiar and full of memories. Unlike so much of my life, it hadn't changed a bit. The shuffleboard game was still there, the neon Black Label sign, the ancient piano with its yellow keys, the dusty plants on the windowsills. Even the bartender looked familiar.

And Trevor, sitting in a booth near the back waving at me as I walked in—Trevor hadn't changed either. The details were different—his black hair was tamed down and longer, he'd put on some weight, his light-blue summer suit looked expensive—but it was the old Trevor. His eyes were the same, narrow and watchful, and so was his mean, mocking mouth.

He stood up when I came in, hugged me and kissed me on the cheek. He smelled sharply of some astringent aftershave, and he had bad breath.

"Hey, that's some dress," he said in a way that made me wish

I'd changed into jeans and a sweat shirt. He indicated that I should sit beside him on the bench, but I sat down across from him. He was halfway through a beer, and he ordered another for himself and one for me. Then we sat there facing each other. "Well," he said. "Good old Anna. Tell me what you've been doing with yourself."

I gave him a condensed version, slightly glamorized, of the five years since high school, and he told me at length what he'd been doing since he got out of college three years before—mostly working in a bank and spending his vacations on various Caribbean islands looking for women.

"Miss Right hasn't come along, though," he said with his snarling smile. "How about you? Engaged? Going with anyone?"

"Sort of," I said. "He's away at the moment."

"Not in Vietnam, I hope."

"New Jersey," I said.

Trevor said, "Beats Vietnam, I guess. My back's keeping me out." He laughed. "I told that to a guy at work the other day, and he said, 'Oh, yeah, Trevor, you mean that big yellow streak down it,' and I said, 'Fortunately I've got a slipped disk to go with it, sucker.' I mean, let's face it. Who isn't afraid to go over there and get shot at? You've read *Catch-22*? Jesus, who wants to go to war?" He laughed again, then sobered. "You heard about George Sullivan? There a couple of weeks and bam! And for what? He was evacuating some guys into a helicopter—wasn't even fighting. That's what gets me. He didn't even get to kill a gook. God, what a shame. He was a good Joe."

"You used to call him a jerk, if I recall."

"Ancient history," Trevor said. "Water over the dam." He looked down at his fingernails. They were perfectly manicured, oddly tiny. I remembered Martha's little hands. Trevor stared mournfully at his nails as if the story of George's death were written there. But when he looked up at me he said, "There's a lot of ancient history I'd like to forget, Anna. I was a shit after Martha drowned, I know I was. I was in bad shape. You have to understand that. I mean—that night."

"It doesn't matter, Trevor. We don't need to talk about it."

"That was the last time I saw you, that graduation night. I can't stand to think you've been left with that impression of me all this time."

"Don't worry about it," I said. I wanted to tell him to shut up, that there was nothing he could say that wouldn't disgust me, nothing he could do that would make me dislike him less. And at the same time it was weirdly thrilling to hear the words *graduation night* on Trevor's lips, the same way it used to be thrilling to talk in church, in the presence of the Blessed Sacrament. "As you say, it's ancient history."

He looked into my eyes. Martha's eyes had been dark brown—large and earnest; Trevor's were lighter, golden with specks in them, like an animal's. He had the most untrustworthy face I have ever seen. But I believed what he said next; it fell between us with the sharp click of truth, a key fitting into a lock, a door opening. He said, "I was always in love with you."

I didn't say anything. I was remembering how filthy I felt, for days afterward, the time he pulled down the top of my bathing suit. I was remembering Will's blood on my white graduation dress.

Trevor said, "But you probably knew that. I didn't really make much of a secret of it. I was crazy about you for years."

I said, "I'm sorry to hear that, Trevor."

Under the table, his knee touched mine. "I'm not exactly over it, either, Anna." I waited a second, then moved my knee away. He looked at me, but not with love. What was in his animal eyes was more like hate, and I had the impression that it wasn't only me he hated but the world, and that any love Trevor ever said he felt for anything would be sick and cruel. Trevor chuckled, as he probably would have chuckled if I had said my thoughts aloud. "Who would believe it," he said. "Trevor the lady-killer. Love 'em and leave 'em. Who would believe I could be such an old faithful."

He ordered me another beer, and one for himself with a shot of Wild Turkey on the side. I looked clandestinely at his left wrist; his gold watchband was surrounded by thick black hair, like a fence among brambles. We had been there only an hour. I wondered how soon I could decently leave.

"Well," Trevor said, "water over the dam, damn it," and he laughed at his joke. "So what else is new?"

I got him talking about people we had known. Did I know Ed Kuminsky was an actor in New York? He'd been on TV, in a commercial for Allstate Insurance. Joey McCoy was teaching history at a high school in Albany; his twin sister, Kathy, had left the convent and married a man twice her age. I told him what I knew about Johnny Tenaro, who was now a high school chemistry teacher, and Marie Barshak—now Marie Reissdorf, married to a veterinarian and expecting her first child.

"Very interesting," Trevor said. "Isn't it great how everyone has made good? All those assholes." He drank his bourbon in one gulp and ordered another one. I poured the last of my beer into my glass; when I finished it I would leave. "Most of them, anyway. Not everyone." He looked at me expectantly. I took a sip of beer and said nothing. The Beatles came on the jukebox singing "Help." Trevor said, "You heard about Will Westenberg?"

I thought: This is why I'm here, this is why I came. On the off chance. It was like another key turning, another door opening. I hadn't known it before, not really—not *thoroughly,* as sitting in that dim bar I suddenly knew it. It astonished me, because now it was so clear: that Will wasn't a weird adolescent hang-up, as Hal claimed, and he wasn't someone I used to love, as I'd told Jean. Will was someone I still loved, and would always love. I felt breathless for a moment, sick and dizzy, as if I'd had much more to drink than two beers. "Help!" the Beatles sang. "I need somebody. Help! Not just anybody . . ."

"No," I said. "What about him, Trevor?"

"He's in a nut house in the Midwest. Alcoholism. You didn't know that? About his little problem?"

"No."

He grinned. "See? Aren't you glad I called you? Hey, I could tell you a lot about little Willie."

The Beatles sang "Won't you please, please help me?" Trevor went up to the bar to get me another beer. When he returned, I said, "Like what?"

"What what?" He poured for me.

"You could tell me what about him?"

"Who? Will?" He sat back, studying me. Then he smiled. "Kiss me and I'll tell you."

"Go to hell, Trevor," I said.

"Will you listen to this?" he asked, looking around, talking to no one. "She sits there drinking my beer and she tells me to go to hell. I like that."

I said, "I'm sorry."

His knee pressed mine. I drew away again, and he captured my knee between both of his. He said, "That's better," and drank off another shot of bourbon. "Now. Willie. Well. I ran into him a couple of years ago, down at Tino's. I was there with a date, getting pizza, but he was in the bar drinking. I've never seen anyone so drunk, not even me." Trevor laughed, showing his little teeth, the canines so sharp they looked filed. "I talked to him for a couple of minutes. We let bygones be bygones. I mean, he was too drunk to hold much of a grudge, and let's face it, I don't give a fuck about anything anymore. He told me he was married, he knocked up some girl. I said, 'That's not the first one, is it, buddy?' Shit, he was too far gone to know what I was talking about. He couldn't even hold his head up."

"So what happened?" How did he get home? I meant. Who took care of him? Where did he go?

"What happened? I don't know, I left with my date. Then, last summer—"

"Wait a minute," I said. "That night, when you ran into him." My throat was so tight I could hardly talk. I imagined him in that dingy bar at Tino's, his finely cut mouth slack with drink, his eyes sad, his thin fingers around the glass. I didn't look at Trevor. "Did he mention me, I wonder?"

"He said he saw you at your grandmother's funeral. He said you looked fat and ugly."

"He didn't!"

Trevor cracked up. "I'm glad to see I can still get a rise out of you. Jesus, Annie, you kill me."

"You're a real scream, Trevor. You're just hilarious." He sat there giggling. I said, "Tell me what he really said," and that made him laugh harder. I sipped my beer, waiting.

"Oh, God," he said, pretending to wipe tears from his eyes. "You're too much. Still carrying the torch after all this time. Holy Christ, I thought I was bad." He laughed again—fake guffaws calculated to annoy me. I waited patiently. Finally he said, "Well. What I really heard from old Willie was what I just told you, that he ran into you at your grandmother's funeral."

"That was all?"

"That's it, baby. Sorry." I knew he was lying, but I also knew I wouldn't get anything else out of him. "So anyway," he went on. "Then a couple of months ago I got talking to his sister Ruth. She came into the bank for a car loan, as a matter of fact, and she told me he's living in the Midwest someplace, some two-bit town out there where his wife came from. He's drying out in a hospital or something for alkies."

"What else?"

He shrugged. "That's it. End of story. That's when I got the idea to call you. I got thinking. I wanted to apologize for all that crap, back when I was in such rough shape after Martha died. You know." He licked his skinny red lips. "I wanted to see you. I never forgot you. I remember how you used to stand up on that stage and sing at those stupid glee-club concerts. It was worth it, just to hear you. God, you were a sexy broad." He reached across the table and took my hands; his were damp with sweat. I remembered his B.O. problem, the special deodorant in the Finches' bathroom, and I would have laughed if my mind wasn't full of Will, Will. God: *Will*. He would be staring out a window: would there be bars on it? By now, the sun would be nearly gone out there. He'd be staring into darkness, seeing things. Seeing what?

Trevor said, "You still are, Anna. One goddamn sexy broad. You wouldn't believe how you turn me on."

He held my hands and gazed at me. I looked away, up at the wall as if there were a clock there. "Oh, Lord," I said. "I've got to get home."

I started to stand up. He kept my leg tightly between his. "So soon?"

"I've really got to. I have to catch an early train tomorrow."

He let me go, and I got up with relief and slid out of the booth. There was something so menacing about Trevor that I wouldn't have been surprised if he had pulled a knife on me to keep me there—if he had dragged me under the table and raped me with a gun to my head. "Trevor the lady-killer," he had said.

We walked together to the parking lot. "This has really been great, Anna," he kept saying. "It's been great to see you."

He wasn't entirely sober. I wondered suddenly if it had all been lies about Will, if it was Trevor himself who had the problem and had been to a hospital to dry out. At my father's car I turned to him and said, "Trevor, tell me the truth. About Will Westenberg. Was that true, what you said? Do you know it for a fact? That he's in a hospital? That he's sick? An alcoholic?"

He stood close to me. I could smell his bad breath and the faint chemical scent of his aftershave. "Kiss me and I'll tell you the truth."

"Leave me alone, Trevor," I said, and I turned to get into the car. I was shaking. He grabbed my arm and pulled me to him and pressed his mouth against mine, jabbed in his tongue. I pushed him away, but he held me tight and stuck his hand between my legs.

"Get away from me." I pushed him with all my strength, clawed at his face, pushed him again. He fell back, and I got into the car and locked the door. Trevor banged on the windshield. His face was the face of a fiend.

"Bitch," he kept saying. "Bitch, bitch, you bitch, come on out here, you bitch."

I started the car and reversed out of the parking space, Trevor hanging on and beating his fist on the front window, then the side, his face contorted next to mine through the glass. "Bitch!" he screamed one last time before I peeled out of the lot. In the rearview mirror I saw him standing in the light from the Green Horseshoe, watching me as I drove away, one hand raised to give me the finger.

My father and Jean were on the porch. Patty had been put to bed. "Thank God you're home early," Jean said. "I'll bet you forgot you promised to sing for us."

Sing: oh, God, yes, I had. "Of course I didn't forget."

"Was it fun?"

I blinked in the porch light. "Fun?"

"Tonight. With Trevor."

"Oh." I laughed. "Tonight. No, actually, I'd have to say it was the opposite of fun, whatever that is."

"Oh, dear," said Jean.

"I never liked that kid," my father said. "Kid—he must be twenty-five, twenty-six. But I remember him when he was little. His mother was a friend of Elinor's." He was talking to Jean. "She was a wonderful woman—salt of the earth. But that Trevor was a sneaky little cuss."

"He's worse than that now, Daddy."

My father stood up and put an arm around my shoulders, and we all went inside. I washed my face and hands and brushed my teeth and drank a tall glass of cold water, but it would take a long hot shower to get rid of the stink of Trevor, his sweaty hands and sour mouth. I remembered the night I lost my virginity, when Mamie sang and played the piano while I soaked my underpants in the sink and sat in the tub to wash away the blood.

I went downstairs to her old Emerson upright. Fred the cat was perched on top next to the metronome, looking down at me. "What'll it be, Fred?" I asked. "Any requests?"

"Anything," my father said. "Fred likes 'em all."

He and Jean settled together on the sofa, he with his arm stretched out behind her, she with both hands clasped on her big stomach. Because my father loved it, I sang the Yeats song cycle I had learned the year before, and then I sang Mamie's songs, to cheer myself up: "Danny Boy" and "All Through the Night" and "Long Long Ago." Jean smiled into space. My father wore his melancholy look—thinking of my wasted gift, no doubt. I ended, as I always did, with "Marble Halls," and as I sang I thought of the James Joyce story "Clay," in which the spinster Maria sings that song and it's so obvious that any dreams she might have will not come true. I sang the second verse, the one Maria got wrong in the story:

> *And I dreamt that one of that noble host*
> *Came forth my hand to claim,*
> *But I also dreamt which charmed me most,*
> *That you loved me still the same . . .*

And I thought of Will, whom I wouldn't ever again forbid myself to think about—Will out in Indiana in the dark, looking east.

The next morning, before I left for the train, I telephoned his mother. Was it true, I asked her, that he was in a hospital, that he was ill. I didn't say alcoholism. "I heard a rumor that he hasn't been well," I said. "I wondered if I could do anything for him."

"It's good of you," she said.

"I can't help being concerned."

"Well," she said, and stopped.

"Is there anything I can do?" I asked again. "I hate to be a pest, but would it help if I got in touch with him? Can you give me his address?"

She took an uneven breath, and I realized she had been choked up. She said no, paused again, and said, "I'd better not do that."

I closed my eyes. I concentrated. I would drill my resolution into her mind, I would overcome her reserve, her scruples, her family pride. I would be a demon, a terror, not myself. I said, "I want to help, Mrs. Westenberg. Please let me help."

"No," she said, and her voice was under control and distant. "Really. There's nothing you can do." Her face was like Will's, but old, with circles under the eyes and deep lines framing the mouth. Her face would be closed up, lips set, eyes wary. She said, "It's very kind of you, but he's all right, he's better."

"He's better?"

"He's getting better."

I clutched the phone with both hands, I prayed into it: *Give me his address, tell me where he is.* But I knew I was beaten. Her face would be like Will's the night he fought with Trevor, when he kept telling us all to leave him alone, he was fine.

"I'd love to give him a call," I said desperately. "Or write him a letter." My father was in the room behind me, waiting to drive me to the station. He was still, and I knew he was listening. "Could you give me his address? I could send him a get-well card. Cheer him up, maybe."

I thought that if she said *no* again I would scream, but she said it, and I didn't. She said, "No, I really can't. But I'll tell him you called. I'll give him your message. Anna Nolan. You live in Boston, and he should look you up sometime."

I said, "Yes. Anytime. Be sure to tell him. I'm in the book. Or he could always get in touch with me here, at my father's."

"Yes. I'll tell him."

I could tell she was getting ready to hang up, and I said quickly, "Mrs. Westenberg? Please, just tell me one thing. Just tell me—is he happy, do you think? Is he happy out there in Indiana?"

I didn't expect anything. It was like graduation night, when I walked out on the porch and found Will. But I heard her sigh, and then she said, "Just one moment. I'll get his number for you."

I was afraid to breathe. She came back and recited the number. I wrote it down on the pad that hung near the phone, but I didn't need to. It was tattooed on my soul.

I could hardly speak, but I thanked her and we hung up. My father said, "Anna?" I leaned against him and wept. I could have cried for a long time on his shoulder, against his old white sweat shirt—out of relief and·fear and the plain childish comfort of it.

When I stopped I said, "I'm all right, Daddy. Really I am. Everything's all right." And that was true. Even as I cried and was comforted, I was aware that hope sustained me. It was like a birthmark, or a sixth toe: it would be with me forever, and I would be forever all right because of it. I had a sense of myself teetering at the edge of something, some pit I'd always be conscious of but into which I would never leap.

I blew my nose and washed my face, and then my father drove me to the train station. I waved good-bye to him, the train started, and I took out my book, but I couldn't concentrate on *The Mill on the Floss*. All I could concentrate on was what Trevor had said, what Will's mother had said, the picture I had in my mind of Will looking east. The tight bloom of hope that I had recognized back at my father's house flowered into a plant, a bush, a tree of optimism. I said the phone number over and over to myself like a spell or a mantra. I could reach him if I dared, just by picking up a telephone and dialing ten numbers. I would hear his voice in my ear, he would speak my name. Thinking of it, I had to squeeze my eyes shut so I wouldn't weep at the prospect.

Somewhere around Springfield I made a decision: when Hal got back I would tell him I couldn't marry him. And I would get in touch with Will.

A feeling of perfect peace took me over. The crowded train, the woman beside me with her gray dress and bag of knitting, the sunny afternoon, the diet Pepsi I got from the diner, the tuna sandwich Jean had made me—all of it seemed right and inevitable and complete: perfect. I turned back to my book and began to read about Maggie Tulliver and her doomed love. I read, looked out the window, read some more, looked up again, and day-dreamed. The light began to fade, and I could see my reflection in the window: a face preposterously calm, under the circum-stances—my hair pulled back with barrettes, my brow smooth, my eyes showing nothing. Looking at me, no one would guess that I harbored a secret healing spell, that this quiet dull person was as powerful as a dope dealer, or a saint who could work fabulous cures: what happiness lay within my reach. I smiled at myself. I didn't have to call—not yet. There was no hurry. The number in my head was enough. It was more than enough. It was everything.

6

When Hal returned from New Jersey, he got a notice from his draft board saying he'd been reclassified at last. He was 1-A, and he was so upset about it that I hadn't the heart to break up with him.

I would wait and see what happened. I didn't want to think about any of the things that might happen: that Hal would be sent to Vietnam and get killed there, or that he'd go to Vietnam and return safely and I'd marry him out of gratitude. I tried not to think about it at all, but I had nightmares about George, and once I dreamed about Trevor in the parking lot, only he was Hal, in uniform.

I inscribed Will's phone number on several pieces of paper and folded them into hard little squares; I·kept one with me at all times, tucked into a pocket or at the bottom of my purse. As if they really were magic talismans—good-luck charms—my life suddenly improved dramatically. I got a call from the musical director of the Boston Light Opera Company telling me I'd been promoted from the chorus to a major role—Lady Angela—in *Patience.* I applied for and got a full-time job at a bookstore in Kenmore Square. A woman who had heard me sing offered me the soprano-soloist gig at St. Elizabeth's Church on Beacon Hill—hymns every Sunday and a Bach cantata once a month.

And every fourth Saturday I appeared at the Cantabile—black dress, cigarette, piano, sad love songs, wry little jokes in between; Eric called me "a large economy-size Blossom Dearie," so I went on a diet and lost ten pounds. Hal used to come in on Saturday nights for the last set. He sat in back at the tiny corner table, drinking the English ale he was fond of. He was sometimes with friends, but often alone, and when he came alone he talked to no one, especially Eric. Looking down at him from the stage, I couldn't see his eyes, just the reflection in his glasses of the candle in a wine bottle on the table. His unhappiness was something almost tangible, like the smoke from his cigarette. I imagined him, as he sat there, thinking black thoughts about Eric, thinking about Vietnam, thinking about me, and I sang directly to him. "You Made Me Love You," I sang. "I've Got a Crush On You," "Poor Wand'ring One," "I Loves You, Porgy." I was always trying to cheer him up, but his exuberant, foul-mouthed humor had become bitter, and his only jokes were cynical wisecracks.

That winter, I acquired a bass player named Duncan and a drummer named Mart. Mart's girlfriend was a violinist named Alice Weeks. She moved in across the hall from me, and we became friends. The BLOC *Patience* was a smash, and I got the part of Josephine in *H.M.S. Pinafore*.

I was busier than I'd ever been in my life—BLOC rehearsals, rehearsals at St. Elizabeth's, rehearsals with Mart and Duncan, a full-time job, Hal, Lydia. I was always consulting my watch, waiting for the MTA, hurrying somewhere, getting home late. The importance of keeping busy became overwhelming. If I had a few minutes to spare, I panicked. I didn't know what to do with them. I stopped reading—couldn't concentrate. My life was packed with motion, but it felt like an airplane flight: time passed, things happened, but each individual minute, each day, seemed stagnant, going nowhere.

Hal's reclassification radicalized him. He began going with me to the Back Bay Peace Council on Tuesday nights and Saturday mornings. Our job was to operate the ditto machine, running off letters that we later folded and stuffed into envelopes, and flyers that the more adventurous council members distributed at subway stations and on the Common. The flyers, badly typed and inked in pale purple, told the history of American involvement in the war, made impassioned pleas for grass-roots action, announced rallies and speeches. The letters were mostly to influential people—senators, civic leaders, university officials—asking for money.

Hal sent them routinely to his parents; all I knew about them was that they lived in Detroit, played a lot of bridge, and supported the war. The mere thought of them infuriated Hal in those days—but then, everything infuriated him. The madder he got, the faster the letters poured out of the ditto machine. "None of it does any good," Hal used to say, turning the crank in a doleful rhythm: *crunch-a, crunch-a.* "Noth-ing, noth-ing, noth-ing, does any frigging good." He talked almost entirely about IBM and his 1-A classification. He said the 1-A was a gigantic Steinway concert grand hanging over his head by a piece of catgut.

On weekends we went to parties. There were always parties, and always rallies: the two went together. There would be a peace rally at Harvard Square or on the Common, and afterward the same people who'd carried signs and chanted "Ho-Ho-Ho Chi Minh" would be dancing and drinking beer at somebody's apartment. Hal used to get drunk and make pronouncements: "There's nothing positive about America anymore, all we are is anti-Communist," and then, his voice raised, "You know, when you come right down to it, this fucking war has very little to do with Vietnam."

What the war was all about, he'd go on if he drank enough, was getting him, Harold Aaron Jacobs, personally killed, maimed, mutilated. There was talk in the air of a march on Washington. If anyone asked Hal whether he was going, he always said, glumly, "I'll probably be marching, but I doubt that it'll be on Washington."

He went to a series of draft-counseling seminars, and he began spending his Tuesday evenings advising other men in his position about support groups in Toronto, and ways to get into graduate school without any money, and how to register successfully as a conscientious objector.

"Physician, heal thyself," I used to say, and begged him to apply to graduate schools. Capitalize on your formidable managerial talents, I told him, and get an MBA. Or go back to music, get a degree in music ed., get an MFA. Surely *some* combination of initials appealed to him. We had the same discussion over and over. He was always very patient with me, very depressed. "I'm not interested in going to graduate school, Annie," he would say. "If I did go, it would only be to play their game, like Nicky's doing."

Nicky was a friend of ours from the conservatory, a pianist who was in a master's program somewhere in Nebraska learning to teach second-graders to play the recorder.

"What's wrong with that, Hal? It *is* a game."

He shook his head. "There's not anything wrong with it. I counsel guys to do it all the time. I just have trouble with it."

We talked about going to Canada. He had trouble with Canada, too. "I don't want to leave the country," he said. "Rats leaving the sinking ship. And I sure don't want to swim out of here alone."

He didn't look at me as he said this. My reply was always the same and always unhesitating: "You know I'd go with you in a minute." But he'd just wave his hand and say, "Well—" and look off into space. Then he'd start talking about his job at IBM. "You can laugh at it," he said, though I wasn't laughing. "But I like it. I don't want to just walk out on it." His boss at work told him that if he kept on the way he was going, he'd be head of the Card Order Department at the Boston branch by the time he was thirty. "Hey, man—heavy," he said to me with his twisted grin, but I knew he was pleased.

I tried to stay optimistic. "Maybe you'll never be drafted," I said. "Maybe the war will end. Maybe they'll announce tomorrow morning that negotiations are beginning."

Hal always laughed—his laugh that was not a laugh. "Maybe an angel will carry me off on a pink cloud. Maybe I'll chop my dick off and be 4-F. Maybe LBJ and Ho Chi Minh will fall in love. Maybe we'll be invaded by Martians."

This went on until April. It was a messy, cold, late-arriving spring. Hal grew thinner, gloomier, angrier, more absorbed in his job. We weren't able to spend as much time together as we used to. My *Pinafore* rehearsals became intense—the performance was scheduled for the end of May—and the Cantabile act, with Duncan and Mart, got better and better. *Boston After Dark* reviewed us and said, "Though her traditional material and refined manner evoke an Eisenhower-era ideal of suburban gentility that's slightly at odds with the seedy ambience of the Café Cantabile, Anna Nolan's operatic-caliber voice and simple, direct way with a song are a welcome addition to Boston nightlife—and bassist Duncan Maguire and drummer Mart Appel provide the perfect backup for her unique talents." Duncan and Mart and I pored over that for a long time and finally decided it was a rave. The *Globe* dropped in one night and mentioned us the next day in passing as "the always pleasant, often exhilarating, and occasionally electrifying trio at the Café Cantabile." There was a poster outside the café with my picture on it every week before my Saturday appearances. Eric appended to it, " 'Exhilarating! Electrifying'—Boston *Globe*. 'Unique! Perfect!'—*Boston After Dark*."

My purses and pockets still carried their grimy little squares of paper, and there were still images in my head that troubled me and that I assumed would haunt me always: of Will Westenberg sitting at a barred window somewhere in Indiana, waiting in some ultimate, mystical, eternal sense for my phone call. But I tried, for the moment, to forget Will. He had become unreal to me again. It was Hal who was real and who needed me. In bed, I held him tight until he fell asleep. I was always expecting him to cry in my arms, but he never did; he was just silent and glum, and so thin that I wondered why the army would want him.

Then one Friday night in April he came over to my place for dinner. He was later than usual but I didn't ask him where he'd been. I knew he sometimes took a walk after work. I met him at the door, and kissed him—I hated to think of him gloomily trudging the streets, alone, hands in pockets, seeing nothing—but he pushed me down on the bed without a word and started pulling off my clothes. I had a casserole in the oven—a macaroni, ground beef, and tomato thing Jean had sent me the recipe for—and I said, "Hal, wait, let me turn the oven off, for heaven's sake," but he held me there, and we made love, and it was so fast and furious the casserole wasn't even done yet by the time we were.

He lay beside me, on his back, with his eyes shut. I put my head on his chest, over his heart, and heard its rapid beat, like footsteps. "Hal?" I said. "Are you all right. Is anything wrong?"

He didn't open his eyes. He told me he'd gone down to the Common after work, to the army-recruitment tent they had set up there, and he'd enlisted.

I stared at him and said, "You what?" I assumed it was a joke, and I got ready to play straight man to his sour humor.

"I enlisted," he said, and I knew he wasn't joking because he kept his eyes squeezed shut. After a while he got out of bed and walked restlessly around the room, picking up a book, a record, my knitting. He snapped on the radio. We listened to Frank Sinatra wobbling out "Strangers in the Night," then a Pepsi commercial and a disk jockey giving the weather—warm and dry at last, a glorious weekend ahead.

I said, "Hal."

"I couldn't take it anymore, Anna," he said. He stood by the window, naked. He was so thin and slight he broke my heart. He weighed less than I did. I felt like his mother.

I got out of bed and went over to him, and we stood there together with our arms around each other's waists, looking out at the Boston rooftops against the dark-blue sky, the Prudential tower in the distance, the building across the alleyway where someone grew a windowful of plants and someone else kept a Siamese cat that yowled.

I waited for him to say more. After a while he said, "I wanted to get it over with, Anna. So I just went down there and talked to them. Some sergeant. He seemed like a good guy. He reminded me of my uncle Charlie."

"You're not kidding me, Hal, are you?" I knew he wasn't, but I wanted to hear him say it. I wanted him to look at me.

He said, "No, I'm not kidding. He really did look like my uncle Charlie."

"Ha ha."

He looked at me then, his goggly, nearsighted stare. "No, I'm not kidding."

"I didn't think you were."

He said, "It's the suspense that's driving me crazy, Annie, even more than the prospect of being sent to Vietnam. I've thought about it a lot. I can handle that. What I can't handle is not knowing."

All I could think of was George. I tried to imagine being blown to bits: What was it like? At what point did you die? Where did it hurt? I remembered George—dear old Wilbur—the one night we had made love, back in high school; he had been eager and clumsy, inexperienced, slightly ridiculous as always. I had endured it, pretending it was Will on top of me. I thought of George and said, "Hal, I can't let you do this."

"Well, I've done it."

I said, "I don't understand, I don't get it. Why just cave in? Why can't you go back to school like everyone else? Or keep trying for the C.O. classification? Or go to Canada. We could leave now and be there by midnight. You're the one who always says this country has nothing positive to offer anymore. It's not only rats who leave sinking ships, you know."

He just looked at me and said, "Annie," shaking his head.

We stood there in silence listening to the radio. The Tijuana Brass finished up "What Now, My Love?" and the Supremes came on.

I said, "So you're going to get yourself killed because you can't stand the suspense."

"I'm being as practical about this as I know how, and I'm not planning to get myself killed." There was controlled exasperation in his voice, an edge to it. I thought of George when I yelled at him, defending himself. For what? So he could die.

I said, "It's nice to know you're in such complete control. I had no idea you had this power over life and death."

His fingers at my waist squeezed, pinched flab. I felt his nails in my skin. "Goddamn it, I could use a little support," he said. "A little affection." I pulled away from him and headed for the bath- room. "Annie, for Christ's sake." I slammed the bathroom door. I heard him shout, "You tell me—what's my goddamn fucking alternative?"

I went to the sink and looked into the mirror. I looked—God, I didn't look the way I felt, I looked rather beautiful, my hair in a tangle, my shoulders bare, my skin flushed from anger and from sex. I began to cry. I watched myself cry in the mirror, then I watched myself, deliberately, stop. Hal called, "Annie?"

"Just a minute."

I lingered in the bathroom, looking around as if I'd never seen it before—the salmon-pink walls, the psychedelic shade over the ceiling light, Hal's ancient, heavy safety razor on a shelf next to my makeup case, a framed portrait of Lotte Lenya over the toilet, yellowed *New Yorker* cartoons taped up around the mirror. I studied one for a long time—a picture of a thuggish little kid carrying a sign that read, THE WORLD IS ROOLED BY DOPS.

I peed, washed my face, brushed out my hair. When I opened the door, the Supremes were still telling me you can't hurry love. I turned off the radio and stood there looking at Hal. He sat on the edge of the bed in his underwear—a white T-shirt and his black IBM socks and faded red boxer shorts with a pattern of little white hearts that I'd given him one Valentine's Day.

"I'm sorry I yelled at you," he said. "This whole thing is such a mess."

I said, "I just can't take it, Hal. I've told you about George. He was a medic, and he was loading wounded men into a heli- copter, and he was blown to bits. Just gone. He wasn't even there a month. They couldn't send anything home. There was nothing left to send. Not an eyelash. Not a fingernail."

I could see that in the midst of our misery Hal was jealous of my feeling for George. This irrelevancy was momentarily com- forting, and I let him draw me down to the bed again and cover me with the sheet. But when he touched my shoulder I turned away from him. I said, "I don't want to be your semifiancée if you're going over there. I don't want it to happen again."

It was all so predictable it nearly made me laugh: I would cry when he left, he would be brave and manly, he would write me letters full of cynical army jokes in those thin little envelopes like the ones George had sent, my life would dwindle to mere expectancy, waiting for letters, for news, for an end to the war. It was all such nonsense, the whole ritualized load of crap, like some tearjerker movie—when you knew the hero would be killed before the final reel and the soggy violins would soar over the credits.

I said, "I'm sorry to be so selfish, but that's the way it is, I can't do it, I won't." I would have been glad, at that point, to cry: every tear would be a weapon against his decision, a grenade thrown in this stupid war. But I had no tears. He stroked my hair, my neck, my cheek, but I had no desire for him. It was shockingly clear to me that the fact of our love for each other, our long association, our music, our semiengagement, made no difference at all in the great crooked scheme of things. I imagined us as two tiny dots on the vast globe, lying on a bed arguing while the dark-blue sky turned black, and somewhere a million miles away another dot was living a life, learning to set a land mine, to drop a bomb from a plane, to fire a machine gun, to kill Hal.

We talked again about going to Sweden or Canada, but Hal kept saying he couldn't just walk out on it. I accused him of joining the army to force his parents to oppose the war, or to piss them off. I tried to persuade him that going to Canada would accomplish the same thing. I called him a stupid bastard and said he was cruel and told him he had delusions of heroism.

He kept saying, "Annie, stop it, don't worry, calm down, it's not going to happen, no one says I'll be sent to Vietnam, I'm going to be all right." He spoke decisively, firmly, in that irritating masculine way, as if all he needed to keep himself safe were that patronizing tone of voice, that mindless conviction. But I knew he would go to Vietnam and be killed. I hadn't known it with George, but I knew it with Hal, and the knowledge made me hate him.

The casserole dried out in the oven while we argued. I wouldn't let him stay overnight. I fell asleep as soon as he was gone, slept hard and dreamlessly, and woke up at noon the next day. All that afternoon I played the piano and practiced. I sang until I was exhausted: scales and exercises, my Josephine songs, every Gershwin and Kern tune I knew, the Puccini aria I was singing with Lydia. When I couldn't sing anymore, I played records, filling the peace of Saturday afternoon with Violetta and Mimì and Butterfly. I invited Alice over for supper. We ate grilled-cheese-and-bacon sandwiches, and I told her the whole story. She said I was right to uninvolve myself, that Hal had an advanced case of masochistic egotism and I was well rid of him. Mart had a gig somewhere, so she stayed and watched *Gunsmoke* with me and we killed a bottle of cheap Chablis, and when the phone rang I didn't answer it.

But Hal wore me down. He could always wear me down. He was waiting for me after work on Monday. He took me out for dinner and drove me to my *Pinafore* rehearsal, and he picked me up afterward. He was there again the next day; it was our Peace Council evening but we went to a bar in the North End and drank beer instead. He told me he had seen Sergeant Hawley again, he'd taken the ASA test, had a physical. It wasn't so bad, he said. The people he'd met were really great. The whole experience was interesting— another world. He would be inducted on the thirtieth of April, and get on a bus for Fort Dix. I asked: And then Vietnam? He hedged, finally said probably—but not in a combat position, he'd be doing something safe. The sergeant had talked about his becoming a chaplain's assistant. He asked me to marry him. I said no.

The next day he was there again at the bookstore, wearing a new suit he had bought at Brooks Brothers. I cut rehearsal. He took me to dinner at the Ritz-Carlton, and afterward we stayed to dance. We were the youngest people there by many years. The orchestra was tame and tasteful. The lights were dim. We were surrounded by elderly people fox-trotting in each other's arms. One old couple danced like teenagers, close together, nearly unmoving, his cheek against her white hair. Watching them, I began to cry, and Hal and I sat down. I sipped ice water and he talked, whispering to me his unconvincing litany of love and comfort. I kept crying, hating every tear, hating the mechanical music, the old people shuffling by us, the whole stinking world. Finally Hal pulled a velvet box from the pocket of his suit jacket and put a little diamond on my finger. I groaned loudly and blotted my eyes with a napkin. The dancing couples looked in our direction, then away. Hal held my hand tightly, as if I might fly out one of the long silk-draped windows if he relaxed his grip.

We went back to his place and I clutched him to me tight, pulled him into me and set my teeth against his bare shoulder, tasting salt on my tongue, his slick and sweaty back hot against my hands, and gave in to the pleasure he gave me, the hard little ring on my finger like a dead weight.

We spent his last eleven days together. The big cheese at IBM promised him he'd have his job back when he got out of the army. It took him a couple of days to clear up his work there. Al, his boss, gave him some sort of parchment citation; his fellow management trainees took him out to lunch. The rest of the time we were together.

I moved into his apartment and skipped as many rehearsals as I dared, to be with him. Twice I called in sick to the bookstore. When I did go to a rehearsal, Hal accompanied me and sat stolidly in the front row watching with folded arms while I rehearsed dance steps with the fat tenor. When I went to work, we ate lunch together, and then he walked me back to the store and hung around all afternoon, looking at books, browsing through them and chatting with Reed Bell, my boss, until it was time to walk home.

We stayed for long hours in bed, but we did other things, too—went out for food, listened to records, took long slow walks around the city. Sometimes in the evening he played the piano and I sang—our old numbers and a couple of new ones. "You never know," Hal said. Sergeant Hawley and the U.S. Army—the certainty he had craved—had given him back his old cheerfulness, though a slightly manic form of it. He played wildly, long improvisations on the old familiar tunes, then he'd suddenly break into a bit of Schubert, part of one of the impromptus, and then break off entirely and stare into space. I thought of George Gershwin playing the piano at a party and hearing all the notes go awry and realizing he had something wrong with him. I sat beside Hal on the piano bench. I looked at his bony fingers on the keys, his hairy knuckles, and I thought, irrationally, How can a man who plays the piano like this go voluntarily to kill other men? To be killed. I wanted to knock him out, tie him up, stuff him in the trunk of his little MG and carry him away to somewhere safe. I imagined hiding him up in my attic room at my father's house. I wanted to put my hand on his arm and say, "Please, Hal—" but I wouldn't have known how to end the sentence.

At first I kept crying at odd moments; the visions of death

and blood and doom wouldn't leave me. I'd look at Hal's hands on the keys or his glasses on the table and the tears would come. I tried not to let him see this lest his precarious good mood slip away. I took to running suddenly to the bathroom and turning on the water, hard, while I cried and banged my fist against the wall.

But as the days went by I quit crying. I forced myself to look at the situation in a new, fatalistic way that seemed to me hateful but was the best I could do. I thought of those eleven days as an interlude in my life that would have no sequel, as a time whose future was composed of nothing but memory. It was something perfect I would look back on, my own personal war experience, a time of tragic beauty: eleven days with my doomed lover. It was like a half dozen operas I could sing the heartrending concluding arias of, where the heroine weeps over the dead body of her lover. I remembered George—George, in fact, haunted me those eleven days—and I looked on Hal as a condemned man, as someone already dead.

And all this was made worse by the knowledge that though I loved him more than I'd thought I did, I still didn't love him enough.

Two nights before Hal was due to leave, Duncan Maguire turned up at the door while we were cooking dinner. Hal hadn't told anyone but me and his parents and the IBM crowd that he had enlisted. He said his friends wouldn't understand; he'd see them when he was home on leave. I figured he was embarrassed. But when Duncan came over and Hal told him what he'd done, Duncan said, "Oh, Christ, Hal, goddamn it to hell," and crossed the kitchen to enfold him in a bear hug.

He understood immediately why Hal had made his decision. This amazed me. Duncan had been arrested twice for disorderly conduct during peace marches. He'd been in a fight with a policeman and been carried away in a paddy wagon. I would have expected him to slam out of the apartment, calling Hal a traitor or at least a tool of the establishment. But the two of them went into the living room to have a beer together, leaving me with the cooking and a confused, resentful feeling that I was sheltered, out of it, not very bright. Where did one get such detachment? the ability to blank things out and move on, always *on*? to say as I heard Hal say to Duncan, "What the hell, it's an experience, man"?

Later that night Duncan returned with Alice and Mart, and some Peace Council people came over. There were about ten of

us, and we all got drunk on gin and orange juice. We played
Beatles and Stones records and we danced. Someone asked me to
sing, and I'd had a lot of gin by then, so Hal sat down at the piano
and I leaned against it à la chanteuse and sang a little Gershwin
and did my Joan Baez and Barbra Streisand imitations. Somebody
asked for Gilbert and Sullivan, so I did a couple of numbers from
my usual routine. Then somebody else wanted the sentimental
Irish stuff, so I started in on that with everyone singing along. I
ended with "Danny Boy"—I must have been very drunk—and I
made my way through it the way I got through "You'll Never
Walk Alone" when Martha Finch died. I hated myself for doing it,
but once I got going I couldn't stop. Everyone else shut up and I
went through it alone. My voice didn't even wobble. I sang glori-
ously—all the beautiful sad bits about leaving, returning, waiting—a hell of a song to sing to a departing soldier. When I was
done, Alice blew her nose, Mart sat with his head in his hands, a
girl named Susan sniffled loudly. Hal sat staring down at the keys,
and I went over to him and put my arm around his shoulders. No
one knew what to say. Then Duncan cleared his throat and said,
"As a special favor to me, could you do the Immolation Scene
from *Götterdämmerung* for your first encore?"—making everyone
laugh. We poured more drinks, and someone put on a record and
we danced. We became rather hilarious, and the people downstairs complained. Sometime around two in the morning the party
petered out to a tired silence, and finally everyone left. They
shook Hal's hand, embraced him, embraced me, and went down
the stairs quietly. When I turned off the hall light, and the blackness of the long stairwell rose up to meet me, I felt suddenly sick
with horror. Everything—not just that dark hall—seemed blank
and empty.

I turned back to the apartment where there was light and
where Hal stood in the terrace doorway looking down at
Huntington Avenue. I came up behind him and heard him say
softly, over and over, "Fuck it, Annie. Fuck everything, fuck 'em
all."

We woke up with hangovers and had to spend our precious
last day in bed. We dozed and woke, took aspirin, dozed again,
woke up in the early evening feeling better, and went around the
corner for Mexican food.

I asked him if he was glad, after all, that he'd been able to say
good-bye to everyone. He said yeah, he was, they were a good

bunch—speaking absently, looking down at his plate where he was digging a road through his chili—and then he said "Annie" in such an unfamiliar voice that I looked at him with concern. His face was the same as ever, but the determined cheerfulness was gone, and had, I realized, been missing for a while. When had it disappeared? When I sang? Before that?

"What is it, Hal?"

He put down his fork and said, "I don't know why I'm doing this, I must be crazy." There were tears in his eyes. He reached for my hand. "You're right, I should have done the things I'm always advising all those other guys to do. It's perverse, it's stupid and destructive, I don't know what's wrong with me. Jesus, I think I'm going crazy."

I didn't say "It's not too late, let's get going, let's leave right now, we can be over the border by midnight." It was his turn; I was sick of being the weepy woman begging her man not to leave her. But neither of us said anything—we just sat and stared at each other, holding hands. The song from the night before was still going through my head:

> It's you, it's you must go,
> And I must bide.

I watched the tears slide from his eyes and down to his chin. He wiped them away with his napkin, and then he picked up his fork, again and began to eat his chili.

We were tired; we fell asleep early that night. Toward morning, I dreamed I was buying something in a shop—something formless and elusive that I coudn't quite catch hold of. The dream woke me. There was an odd silence, and I knew right away that Hal was gone—not just from the bed beside me but from the apartment. His duffel bag was no longer in the middle of the floor, his car keys weren't in the ashtray on the desk. By the time I found his note, which was taped to the bust of Schubert on the piano, he was probably no longer in Massachusetts. The note said, "Dearest Annie, it's 4 A.M. and I'm going to Canada. Don't worry about me. I'll write."

I found the note at 4:45. All I could think at first was: He hasn't been gone that long, I could call Mart or somebody and we could head north, we could catch up with him, spot that little MG anywhere, I'd jump in and go with him.

I got back into the cold bed with the note in my hand, thinking that I should call Mart, call Alice, but not doing it, and trying to figure out why I was doing nothing but sitting there shivering and staring at Hal's jagged handwriting. It took me a long time to remember that I didn't love him enough, and to recognize the emotion I was feeling as relief. When I did, I buried my face in his pillow and cried.

I went to rehearsal that afternoon and walked home to my own apartment. It was a perfect April evening. Petals from spring-flowering trees lay on the sidewalks like confetti from a dozen weddings. "Hey—cheer up," a man said to me on the B.U. bridge, but I didn't have the heart even to smile at him. Marlborough Street was a long way from the church basement in Cambridge where we rehearsed; when I got home I had a huge blister on my left heel, and I was so tired I wasn't even angry anymore. I tried to sleep and couldn't. I broke the blister and soaked my feet, and then I baked a batch of chocolate-chip cookies and ate half of it. It wasn't, thank the Lord, a Cantabile night. Alice wasn't home. That was all right with me; food and advice were not what I needed. What did I need? I had no idea. Guiltily, furtively, as if I were being watched, I dug down into an old purse and found the little paper nugget that was Will's phone number, my drug, my comfort. Was that what I needed? To call Will Westenberg and take a bus out to Indiana to find him?

I did nothing. It was Saturday night. Marilyn Monroe had committed suicide on a Saturday night. Saturday night is the loneliest night of the week, everyone knew that. I half-expected someone to telephone—the army, Sergeant Hawley, Hal's hawkish parents—and try to pry his whereabouts from me. The bus had gone to Fort Dix without him: they'd called his name and no one answered. What would they do? Send out the dogs? Maybe at that moment his apartment was being sealed off, his belongings sifted through by FBI men, the IBM citation and the mountains of piano music and the letters from old girlfriends being photocopied and analyzed. But Hal would be safely in Toronto, taken in by some earnest group of draft dodgers who would shelter and succor him. I composed a careful prayer: *Take care of him, O Lord, let him be happy, let him prosper, and let him not mind that I didn't love him.*

I missed him—everyone missed him, even Eric, who said, "The guy was a bastard, but underneath it all I've got to admit he was a decent son of a bitch." There were songs in the Cantabile act that I could no longer sing without getting depressed, especially the Gershwin numbers we'd done together so many times. And I missed hearing him play the piano—his light, almost conversational touch, as if he were speaking to a group of friends he was especially close to. I'd had no idea I would miss that, I'd taken it for granted for so long.

But my life, the life of the city, closed around his absence as if he had never been. *Pinafore* was opening at the end of May. I was grateful for those last hectic weeks of rehearsals, then the disastrous dress rehearsal and the four blissful nights of performance. Music was something I could count on, always—my little niche in its great edifice, the quiet corners where Gilbert and Sullivan and Gershwin lived, and the grander ones that housed the Sunday morning Bach cantatas and the Puccini I was singing with Lydia. *Pinafore* was a success. The *Globe* review said, "Anna Nolan, known to Boston audiences as a popular Café Cantabile chanteuse, acquitted herself admirably as Josephine, with a sweet, accurate soprano and an acting ability several notches above the standard usually adhered to by the Boston Light Opera Company." On the strength of it I was offered the part of Mabel in a production of *The Pirates of Penzance* at a summer theater, and my salary at St. Elizabeth's was raised from eight dollars a Sunday to ten.

Eventually, Hal and I wrote each other letters. His were from his old cheerful self, upbeat and friendly—not the letters of a lover, or of anyone with a claim. I could see that they were designed to let me off the hook, and to reassure me. I was grateful to him for that, but there was no way I could tell him so, and so I wrote back in the same vein, feeling heartless and guilty, knowing with every word that I'd failed him. Don José, Pagliaccio, Jack Point—he was right.

Only once, after I had sent him the *Globe* clipping, did he indulge in anything like a reproach. He sent a postcard of the university, where he was, after all, enrolled in a couple of graduate courses. The card said, "Check out these marble halls. Nothing the same without you. Congrats for Josephine. I always believed in you, baby. Love always, Magic Fingers." I didn't know what to do with the diamond he gave me. Eventually, I sent it back to him via a friend of mine who was going to Toronto. Hal never mentioned it. By late summer, we weren't writing to each other anymore.

I began dating Duncan, my bass player. Duncan was in law school at B.U., a tall, lanky guy with wire glasses and a bald spot.

139

When he wasn't working down at the Legal Aid Clinic, he smoked too much dope, and he was always looking for a new way to get high. One night I found Duncan and Wally, our new pianist, drinking tea in which they had soaked the insides of Vicks Inhalers—laughing like idiots until they began throwing up. Once, he got hold of LSD. I wouldn't take it with him, though he begged me to, and I have to admit I was tempted. But when he was tripping his eyes were like hot coals, and he didn't speak, and he scared me to death.

But I liked him. We spent pleasant summer evenings in his apartment, drinking wine and listening to old Bill Evans records. One September night, he and I were walking down Huntington Avenue to a concert at Jordan Hall. We went by Hal's old apartment building and Duncan told me Hal's parents had disowned him. His father had come to Boston and cleaned out the place, taken everything away to be stored in the Detroit attic. The piano had been sold to a conservatory student.

I had always imagined Hal, when I thought of him in Toronto, sitting at his ancient Steinway, still playing Gershwin and Schubert. I said, "Oh, God, Duncan, he must be so lonely up there, he doesn't even have his piano."

Duncan laughed. "Hal?" he said. "I hear he's living with some woman, somebody with big bucks."

My heart dove down, then lifted, settled. I smiled at Duncan. "Then I guess he's got himself a piano."

"Count on it," Duncan said.

We stood there looking up. From the street, the second-floor windows looked cleaner. There was a tub of bright flowers on the little terrace. Young marrieds, I thought, and remembered the night Hal and I had stayed up half the night while he browbeat me into agreeing to be semiengaged to him. Looking up at Hal's windows, I had trouble for a moment remembering what he looked like: I could see his Groucho Marx eyebrows, his glasses, his wild hair, but I couldn't put it all together to get a fix on his face.

Duncan took my hand. "What is it, Annie? You miss him a lot?"

I said no, I didn't miss him anymore.

On another Saturday night, when Duncan had a gig somewhere, I was home alone, listening to my recording of Victoria de los Angeles singing *Butterfly*. At the end of "Un bel dì," I turned it off and rummaged through my purse for Will's phone number.

What the hell, I thought. What the hell, I'll call Will. I said it aloud, and hearing his name my heart began to pound. Will, my God, *Will*.

I dug out one of my grimy little wads of paper. It reminded me of a relic—the scraps of paper and cloth and hair we used to believe came from saints and were holy. I held it between my fingers and thought: it *is* holy. If I concentrated, I was fourteen years old, and I was in Latin class looking at the back of Will's head—his light hair and beige neck and green sweater. I used to write his name in the back of my Latin grammar: "WILL," and then make it into two triangles and three squares, the secret geometry of my devotion. Remembering, I had to catch my breath: it was like yesterday.

I still knew part of the number, but not all of it. It will have faded away, I thought, crumbled to nothing after all this time, but there it was in bold-blue pen, as neat inside its folds as the heart of a rose. I sat looking at it, and then I went to the phone and dialed.

A woman's voice answered and said something I didn't catch: Summer? Sumner? I thought, O God, she gave me the wrong number, she just wanted to get rid of me. I felt disappointment gather in me like the start of an illness, but I said, "Hello? I wonder if Will Westenberg is there? Have I dialed the wrong number?"

"One moment, please."

Even then I didn't think I could reach him. I thought she'd gone to check and she'd come back and say sorry, there's no one here by that name. But a voice said, "Yes? Who is it?" and it was Will's voice.

I said, "Will? It's Anna Nolan. I'm calling from Boston. How are you? I just wanted to know how things are going." I gave a small, hysterical gasp that I meant for a laugh; I heard it and rushed on. "I haven't seen you in so long, and I got thinking about you and wondered." He didn't speak. "How you are," I said. "How everything is. I thought maybe we could get together next time we're both back home for a weekend, or something." *Un bel dì.* I closed my eyes and leaned against the wall. "It's been a long time."

He said, "Anna," and his voice sounded strange—flat and muffled. I had never heard it long-distance before. Was that it? Or had life done something to it? I wondered how my own voice sounded. Crazed, probably. Pathetic.

I took a deep breath. "I heard you got married. Congratulations. And I guess you heard about George Sullivan."

He said, "Yes."

"God, that was so horrible, this damned war. And then—do you hear from anyone else? I get Christmas cards from a few people, the old gang." I gave the laugh again. "That's one good thing you can say for holidays, they keep people in touch. I heard from Johnny last summer—a real letter. He sounds pretty good. I think he'd probably like to hear from you."

I stopped. The silence from the other end was so profound I thought he'd quietly hung up. "Will?"

There was a pause, and then he said, "Anna, will you do me a favor?"

"Yes. Of course. Anything." I pressed my mouth to the phone. I could feel all the little holes against my lip.

"Leave me alone. Please, Anna. Stay out of my life."

Neither of us said anything. The long-distance silence stretched out. In the hall mirror I could see my face, red and stricken, the face of a hag. I sat down on the edge of a chair and said, "Will—I'm sorry if I've bothered you, I didn't mean to." By an immense effort, I kept my voice under control. It was like singing: no matter how sad the song, you couldn't cry. "I just wondered how things are going. I'm sorry. I certainly didn't mean to intrude."

The flat voice was raised. It said, "Just forget it. Please. Forget me. Leave me the fuck alone." There was a click and it was gone.

LONELY BOY

1

I walked out of the Sumner Clinic one October morning, just walked out the front door and down the path to the gate, and hitchhiked to my mother's house back in Syracuse.

The actual leaving was simple. Everything at Sumner was voluntary. There were no bars, no locks, no guards. Nothing expected of the inmates (clients, customers, patients) but good intentions, personal cleanliness, and attendance at the compulsory daily therapy session. And payment of the bills, but that wasn't my concern. Cindy's father paid the bills.

When I left, I didn't know if I was paid up or not, and I didn't know if I ever would be. Sam financed my stay at Sumner because I was married to his daughter. I assumed that was also why I was sent to such a posh joint to dry out, so that in case the subject came up Sam could say, "My son-in-law is out at Sumner for a while," as if Sumner were a luxurious resort up on Lake Michigan. If you had to have an alcoholic nut case in the family, better to hide him away in style than to send him to the state hospital.

When Sam's daughter decided to divorce me, I didn't know if he was going to disown me immediately or continue to stake me as a kind of severance pay. For all I knew, Mona or Ralph would present me with a whopping bill for my three months at Sumner. But I didn't hang around to find out.

I left on a Tuesday morning. Cindy came to see me the Sunday before, bringing Freddie and a picnic lunch. We sat on a blanket out by the pond and ate ham and cheese, Italian bread, pickles, potato salad—the usual food supplied by the family business, the C & R Quik-Stop Market. For years we had lived on this stuff. Deli food, cold meats and cold salads, cheese slices, packaged desserts. When I wasn't craving booze, I used to crave my mother's good German cooking. I'd dream about sauerbraten and spaetzle and rye bread and apple kuchen and real potato salad, not the mushy, sweetened glop the Quik-Stop dished out. And then I'd wake up and eat Pop-Tarts for breakfast and salami on Italian for lunch and shrimp salad and macaroni salad for dinner.

Cindy rolled slices of ham into tight little tubes for Freddie. "He won't eat ham any other way," she said. "It's his new thing." He also had to have his Swiss cheese rolled up, and his bread smeared with mayonnaise and cut into chunks. Cindy kept up a conversation, mostly about Freddie's latest oddball habits. What else did we have to talk about? And Freddie sure was an unusual kid.

"Everything he does is weird," Cindy used to say. I could never tell if she was impatient with him or proud. There was that period (age twenty-one months) when he would do nothing all day but lie on his back under the dining-room table, with the thumb of one hand stuck in his mouth and the other resting on the flank of Laramie the collie dog, his favorite record playing over and over on the hi-fi (Patti Page singing "How Much Is That Doggie in the Window?"). If anyone tried to change the record, or if Laramie got up and left, or if we had to take Freddie out somewhere or even remove him to change his diaper, he screamed. This went on for weeks, the record driving us bananas, until Freddie got sick of it. Cindy used to bitch about the situation to me and brag about it to everyone else. "Everything he does is weird"—as if weird were a synonym for brilliant. Maybe it was, I don't know. All I knew was I loved the kid, weird or not, Patti Page or no Patti Page.

You'd look at us having our little picnic in the sunshine, chatting, laughing at Freddie, and you'd think we were a nice ordinary family. Mom, Dad, cute toddler. Forget that the picnic is on the grounds of a hospital for alcoholics. Forget that Mom has been threatening to walk out for the last two years. Forget that Dad's been keeping busy screwing one of his fellow patients (in-mates, customers, clients) whenever he gets the chance. Forget that Mom and Dad have been subsidized since the day they got married by Mom's pop, the filthy-rich C & R Quik-Stop chain magnate. Forget that the cute product of these two mixed-up kids has a screaming, breath-holding temper tantrum whenever his bizarre whims are not meticulously catered to.

Forget all that, and we probably looked just great, a healthy blond family with tans, not bad-looking, Cindy and me putting on the act while Freddie sat between us in his Oshkosh overalls, eating ham tubes and looking at the pictures in a book about a collie pup who gets lost and then gets found and ends up with a big red ribbon tied around his neck and a dog biscuit. That was me, I sometimes thought when I read that book to Freddie (it was one of his "things" for a long time, and we all knew it by heart), a lost puppy taken in and given a home by kindly folks—a nice home and all the C & R Quik-Stop dog biscuits he can eat, the red ribbon around his neck attached to a short leash.

As always, we went into the common room for coffee before Cindy left. Gwen was there with her husband. They were sitting by themselves in the window seat holding hands. Her husband, Forrest, was talking nonstop. She told me that was one reason she drank, because Forrest wouldn't shut up. Consequently, Gwen and I didn't spend much time talking, though there were other reasons for that. When I walked by them, she threw me a slitty-eyed look, and her tongue snaked out between her teeth.

I didn't introduce Gwen and Cindy. There was no point, except for the cheap morsel of private amusement I might get out of it. Cindy headed straight for Mona. She liked to talk to Mona because Freddie was one of her favorites. Mona didn't think he was weird—either that or she was so used to weirdos he didn't faze her. Also, she and Ralph never had any kids—too busy drying out drunks. Anyway, she liked telling Freddie stories, so after Cindy and Mona finished hashing over his amazing progress at nursery school, Mona took Freddie on her lap and told him about a dog she used to have when she was a kid (Freddie was obsessed with dogs—among other things, like light switches and tree bark and his old tin A & P bank full of pennies). Cindy and I stood there in silence, drinking coffee and eating the homemade cookies Mona always provided on Sunday afternoons, laughing when Freddie did. On our own, we had nothing to say.

At least, I didn't think we did, but as it turned out we would have had a lot to talk about if I'd known what was going on in Cindy's mind. The next evening, when she got home from work, she called up to tell me she was divorcing me.

"But we had such a good time yesterday," was the first thing I said. A dumb remark—good times had been beside the point for two years.

"Not that good," Cindy said. Her voice was brisk. "Ted's drawing up the papers. You'll be getting a bunch of stuff in the mail. Or Ted'll stop by with it next Sunday. I'm not sure."

I wondered if Sam knew. He must, I thought, if Ted Lombardi was handling it. Ted was my father-in-law's Indiana lawyer and investment counselor. I wouldn't trust him with a can of dog food, much less my millions. I said, "Well, well."

"Well, well, what, may I ask?"

"It's all so neat," I said. "You got me into this, and I see you're getting me out with your usual efficiency and your old man's usual money."

"It's me I'm getting out of this, Will," she said. I pictured her mouth forming these words, that hard red line. "Did you honestly think I'd be able to go on like this?"

"No," I said. "I honestly didn't think you could go on like this. Human nature can only bear so much."

"Don't joke about it, you son of a bitch," she said, and I rushed in, quickly, because she sounded as if she might hang up, with, "Okay, okay, but what about Freddie?"

"What about him?"

I could see her, still in her red Quik-Stop shirt, one hand holding the phone, the other on her hip, one foot tapping. I said, "What are we going to arrange about him? How are we—"

She interrupted me, using her Sam voice—loud and sarcastic, with laughter in it. "Arrange? Are you crazy? There's no *arranging* here, Will." Indignant, as if I'd suggested some perversion, some crime. "Do you honestly think there's a judge on this earth who would award you any kind of custody?"

"Yes," I said.

"Think again."

I thought again and saw Ted Lombardi, and Sam, and Cindy's foot tapping. "Wait a minute here, Cindy," I said. I was suddenly so hot I thought I was going to faint, I was on fire, the sweat was dripping off my face, tears gathered in my eyes. I had to sit down. "Wait just a minute. Are you saying you're taking Freddie away from me?"

"I don't know if I'd put it like that. You made your choice a long time ago. The booze or the kid."

I tried to keep my voice calm. I said, "Cindy, I'm in this fucking hospital to dry out. When I get out I'm going to live a normal life. We've talked about all this a hundred times. What in hell do you think I'm in here for, if after all I've gone through I'm just going to lose Freddie?" I felt as if I were hanging on to something deep in myself by a thread, and it was going to snap loose any minute. My voice rose and became furious, out of control. I hated for Cindy to hear how frantic I was, how desperate, and I stopped talking so that I wouldn't scream at her, or howl, or burst into tears.

She said, "Will—Will—I don't have time for this. Sunday's picnic was bye-bye. I'm not saying it's forever. I'm not a monster, no matter what you think. But for now this is best. I'm getting out of this marriage, and I'm keeping him with me, and I want you to stay away."

I was sitting on the edge of my bed, doubled over with my head on my knees—sick, sicker than I'd ever been from booze or flu or anything. "I'll fight this," I said to Cindy. I wanted to call her names, every filthy name I knew, but I refrained: the first bit of strategy in my battle. "I'll fight this, Cindy."

There was a short silence. For a minute I thought I'd persuaded her of something, but then she said, "I know about that woman," and after another pause she said, "You just try fighting it, Will, and see how far you get." Then she hung up.

I tried to call her back on and off until midnight and got nothing but the answering machine. I didn't leave a message. What could I say: "Which woman do you mean?"

The next morning I hit the road, right after breakfast. I ate a huge meal, not just my usual Wheatena and coffee. I had orange juice and melon and bacon and eggs and two English muffins. I didn't know when I'd eat again. Gwen walked by me on her way out and leaned down to murmur, "Catch you later, lover." I smiled and nodded, and half an hour later I was gone.

I had zero money, and I didn't take luggage—obviously. I left wearing corduroys and a plaid shirt, with the Shetland sweater Cindy gave me for my birthday slung over one shoulder. The day was hot, but I figured I'd need a sweater if the weather turned cool. And I wore my comfortable old sneakers, in case I had to do a lot of walking.

I didn't know how long it would take me to get from Richmond, Indiana, to Syracuse, New York. It had taken Cindy and me twelve hours to drive it the other way two years before in Sam's Buick. We took three days to get there, stopping at Holiday Inns and eating fabulous meals courtesy of the company credit card. Freddie was a baby, too young to be eccentric (although even at four months, I swear, he had that smart, figuring frown), and Cindy and I were still speaking. We were even hopeful, off to Indiana to make a new start. I'd sworn never to touch another drop, and I didn't have one drink all the way out there. I didn't miss it, either, while we were on the road. Those were the days. But no they weren't, and I knew it. I was better off walking through the gates of the Sumner Clinic with nothing in my pockets, my divorce papers in the mail, my nose pointed east. If it weren't for leaving Freddie behind I might even have been happy.

I got a ride right away, at the corner of the main drag, from a Coca-Cola truck. The driver stank of sweat, and the radio blasted out what was passing for rock 'n' roll in the late sixties, but he supplied me with free Cokes, he didn't talk much, and he drove me all the way to Ashtabula, Ohio.

Once I got the hang of mentally tuning out the Monkees and the Turtles, I was free to think. It took me nearly the whole ride to get things sorted out—past, present, and future. The present wasn't a problem, except for what to do when my Coke-swilling friend dropped me off in Middle-of-Nowhere, Ohio. Something would work out. I had a superstition that the more I thought about it, the more of a problem it would be, so I didn't bother thinking about it at all.

As for the future that would begin when I got to Syracuse—that was pretty easy, too. I'd hole up at my mother's house, get myself a job, settle down, prove myself a straight-arrow guy, and find a lawyer to help me get at least part custody of Freddie. I'd move back to Richmond if I had to. What did I care where I lived? But I had to wait until I was fit to be a father. I had to be further away than a couple of months from the drunken excesses of the summer that had landed me in the Sumner Clinic. A year of sobriety, I figured. A year of solid citizenship, a good year at some responsible job, and then I'd be ready to tackle Cindy and Sam.

All right. That part was easy. At least, I had to believe it was. What was hard was the past, the stuff I'd been dragging out every day since August for Dr. Cross. I told Cross everything, beginning with Cindy's tricking me into marriage and ending (we were just getting on this when I left) with the horrors of the summer.

Cross was a cool guy. He said, "When you found out she'd lied about being pregnant, why didn't you walk out then?" He was a big, handsome, confident shrink with a beard, and I could imagine him doing just that. He'd say, "You blew it, baby," and go out the door, too cool even to slam it. He asked me, "What made you stay with her after a stunt like that?"

"By the time she told me she really wasn't pregnant, she really *was* pregnant," I said, and then I gave him the story of Martha Finch.

Cross said, "You're a fertile son of a bitch."

"Just stupid," I said, and he didn't disagree.

"How can you be sure she drove off the bridge deliberately?"

"I can't be sure. I'll never know. I just believe she did."

"And you're going to pay for that the rest of your life?" I shrugged. Cross said, "Let's drop that for the moment. Tell me about Cindy's father."

That took a while. I had to go all the way back to my fight with Trevor Finch on graduation night to explain why I left town. And Anna Nolan, I even had to drag her in (though I didn't tell Cross about her calling me at Sumner and what a shit I was to her). And my job at St. Luke's Cemetery in Albany, where I was probably happier than I've ever been in my life, mowing the grass between the graves, trimming the bushes, walking slowly between the rows reading the names. It was a big cemetery, and the rows of stones seemed endless. I took it on myself as a duty to read every single name, but they went on forever, and I never could be sure I got them all. I used to walk along reading names and dates, beloved wife and devoted husband and all those little kids, thinking about how many dead people there are, how everyone who isn't living is dead, how the earth is full of them. It sounds like a simple idea, and I suppose it is, but it had never hit me before and it was important to me—to Cross, too, because I saw him write it down. I told him that job made me realize that not only wasn't death so bad, it was natural and right.

"Except in the case of Martha Finch," he said, scribbling away.

"Nobody's supposed to die at eighteen," I said.

"All right. So you went from the cemetery to Sam."

That made it sound like I died and went to heaven, and in a sense I did. The cemetery job was for the summer only, and when it was over Sam hired me at the C & R Quik-Stop in Schenectady. I was living with my sister in Albany, and I had to take two long bus rides to get there and back, but it was worth it. It was a good job, better than I deserved.

Sam was a big bald Polack, a good-natured, trusting guy with biceps like thighs and enormous thighs like ham hocks. He could have killed me with one swat, and he probably would have if he'd known what the Petraskis were in for from me, but instead he liked me, and he gave me the job in spite of the fact that my only experience, not counting bagging at the supermarket in high school, was busboy at Deluxe Pizza and groundskeeper at St. Luke's.

I started at the Quik-Stop as a cashier, but within a couple of months I became something called assistant manager, which meant that I got to wear a Quik-Stop shirt and take the cash deposit to the bank every morning. And my pay was raised from minimum wage to fifteen cents above it. But I was still basically a cashier. Cindy Petraski was the *C* in C & R (her sister Renee was the *R*). She was also the manager—my boss—and right after I was promoted we started sleeping together.

"Why?" Cross wanted to know (he never shrank from a personal question), and all I could reply was, "Why not?" She was female, she was there, she wasn't bad to look at. And she was willing, to put it mildly. At least, she was the one who began it. She grabbed me in the stockroom one slow day, kissed me and pressed her pelvis against me and dug her nails into my back. She had her own apartment, and we went there every day after work. She dished up the ham and potato salad and then we went to bed, like the old married couple we were soon to become.

She was twenty-nine, eight years older than I, though she didn't look it. She was short, very blond, and skinny, with little pointy breasts. She said she hadn't had a man in two years. I believed her at the time, but as I got to know her I realized Cindy could never have gone two years without sex, and eventually she told me about the guy who delivered milk to the C & R, the guy from the real-estate office down the street, and the guy she met in her night class in accounting at the community college—others, too. I don't know why she was so reluctant to tell me about them. I didn't care how many men she'd slept with. I didn't care a lot about Cindy. I liked her, and I liked her family, and I liked working at the C & R Quik-Stop. If she'd ditched me I wouldn't have minded, except that I probably would have lost my job.

We went together for a year and half, and eventually we were one of those couples who are always considered as a team. Cindy and Will (never Will and Cindy). We used to alternate Sunday

dinners at the Petraskis' house and at my sister's in Albany. I liked
eating at Sam's. He wouldn't eat C & R deli crap if you held a gun
to his head. His wife, Rose, was Italian, and she lived for food. She
cooked all day Saturday for a dinner that took us most of Sunday
to eat: antipasto and braciole and meatballs and sausage, big plat-
ters of spaghetti, bowls of tomato sauce heavy on the garlic. That
was the standard stuff, same thing every Sunday. Then, in addition, she'd make stuffed-veal things, and homemade ravioli, and
pork roasts, and rum-soaked cakes. My mouth still watered remembering my mother's German dishes, and I loved my sister
Ruth's meat loaf and macaroni and cheese, but I've never eaten
anything, anywhere, before or since, like Sunday dinner at the
Petraskis' house.

Sam always said he ate like a horse, and he expected to see
everyone else eat at least like ponies. In this respect, Cindy was a
constant disappointment to him. He and Rose were both tall and
beefy, and Cindy's sister, Renee, was definitely in the pony cate-
gory, but Cindy apparently took after someone named Margy,
Sam's cousin, who didn't eat enough to keep a bird alive, was just
skin and bones—"She didn't dare go outside in the wind," Rose
always said—and wasted away to nothing at the age of thirty-five.
They were afraid this would happen to Cindy, and they were
constantly urging her to eat, eat, eat, look at Will, look at Renee,
look how they enjoy their food, remember Cousin Margy, eat, eat.
Not that it did any good. Cindy ate plenty of cold cuts and ice
cream bars on those nights after work when I went home with
her—to keep up her strength for what came after, she said. But at
Sam's table, faced with Rose's cooking, she had no appetite. I
think it was her one tiny rebellion against them. In every other
respect, she was Mom and Daddy's little dumpling.

If Sam was disappointed when he and Rose produced girl babies instead of sons—and he seemed like the type—he had gotten
over it by the time I knew the family. He'd groomed them both for
success, and Cindy and Renee were ideal daughters as far as Sam
was concerned. Renee was two years older than Cindy, and married
to a guy named Ace Lesser. Ace managed a movie house called the
Schenectady Fourplex—four theaters in one, a new idea in those
days. He was also a slumlord, and he gambled heavily on the horses.
Renee was his right-hand man, as it were. She had a degree in business from the State University of New York at Albany. When I met
Ace and Renee, they had three kids and were working on the

153

fourth, and they were filthy rich—like everyone the Petraskis associated with, except me and Alberta, the cleaning lady.

Cindy was a different kind of success story. While Renee had gone out on her own—graduated from college, married young, gotten involved in her husband's business ventures—Cindy had stuck close to home. She'd been in on the C & R Quik-Stops from the start. They'd opened the first one in Chicago, where Sam and Rose were from, when the girls were little. Even then, Sam bragged, Cindy liked to work the cash register and inventory the soda pop. Sam brought the stores gradually east as the girls were growing up, to Indiana, Ohio, western Pennsylvania, now New York State. The family moved with the Quik-Stops, and the ones they left behind were managed by relatives—Sam's three brothers and their spin-offs, plus the endless ramifications of Rose's enormous family. And every one of them was loaded. The public's desire to make a quick stop at a cute little fake-wood–shingled Quik-Stop for cold cuts and deli salads and packaged desserts and soda was apparently overwhelming and insatiable and unstoppable.

Cindy and Sam were expanding all the time. Cindy used to say, "After Schenectady, Springfield. After Springfield, Hartford. After Hartford, Boston."

"After Boston, what?" I asked her. "London? Paris? The Fiji Islands? Moscow?"

"Providence," she said. "New York. Philly." She saw it, literally, as a chain, snaking east to the sea and then back west. She was full of ideas. It was she who'd thought of including a few "nonfood items" at the Quik-Stops (panty hose, Dinky toys, cigarette lighters), and they'd paid off so handsomely, Sam bought her a Corvette. "Phoenix," she said. "L.A." She'd get a dreamy look in her eyes, the same look she had that first day when she pushed me up against the storeroom wall and started kissing me.

So when Daddy's dumpling told me she was pregnant, it was serious. The news almost killed me. I thought we'd been careful. Except on Cindy's safe days, we used rubbers, but either one of the safe days wasn't safe, or one of the rubbers. I knew about the unfathomable complexity of the female reproductive system, and I'd heard stories of Catholic employees in condom factories sticking a pin in every tenth one, as a protest. I'd also heard of women who tricked their lovers into marriage by pretending they were pregnant. But I never suspected Cindy of it.

We got married immediately. We drove to Binghamton, where Sam didn't know anyone, and found a justice of the peace. There was no question of abortion, adoption, toughing it out. It was less than four years since Martha Finch drove off that bridge because I gave her money instead of an engagement ring. All those years I dreamed of her—I still do—usually a dream where I can see her off in the distance, and I call her name, but she doesn't hear me. Sometimes I dreamed she wasn't really dead, and she'd rise from the water like a mermaid, smiling at me and saying "It was all a joke," her black hair dripping in her face.

I never told anyone the truth about Martha, except Anna Nolan and my sister Ruth, and that haunted me, too—the desire to confess. I actually toyed with the idea of writing a letter of confession and sending it around to everyone Martha and I used to know. Or taking out an ad in the paper, even putting it in the personals column of the Syracuse *Herald-Journal.* "I killed Martha Finch, she committed suicide because of me, she was pregnant and I refused to marry her. Forgive me. Signed, William J. Westenberg."

When Cindy told me she was pregnant, I told Ruth and said we were getting married right away. We planned to tell everyone we'd been secretly married since April. "I don't think Mom and Daddy would want to know this baby was conceived out of wedlock," Cindy said, and I agreed with her. Sam wasn't someone I wanted to alienate.

Ruth said, "I think you ought to think about this carefully. Do you really want to get that involved with Cindy?"

I said, "That involved? Ruthie, she's pregnant, how much more involved can I get?"

"You sure it's yours?" I couldn't believe she doubted it. Cindy and I spent nearly every second of our lives together. If she was seeing someone else, it would have to have been while I was in the shower. "And you're sure she's pregnant?" She had terrible morning sickness, I told Ruth. Sometimes she didn't get to the store until ten o'clock. She could hardly eat at all. Ruth asked me, "Does she show?"

I said, "Ruth, she's only two months."

"Has she been to a doctor?"

We sat looking at each other. I said, "Yes, she's been to a doctor. Ruth, why don't you like her?"

Ruth said, "I do like her. Do you? Would you marry her if she wasn't pregnant?"

At that point, I didn't know. The fact of the pregnancy, the rushing around making plans, the endless discussions with Cindy, the memories of Martha—all of it had confused me. The only thing that would have prevented me from marrying Cindy was that I didn't love her. But I was fond of her, she was easy to be with, we had great sex. I said, "We would probably have gotten around to it eventually."

"This is so romantic I can't stand it," Ruth said.

The next Sunday we were due at her house for dinner. There were Ruth and her husband, Vic, and their twin babies, Jimmy and Joey, and Cindy and me and my mother, who'd taken the train from Syracuse. Ever since my father died the year before, Ruth had been trying to get Mom to move in with her and Vic in Albany, but Mom resisted. She said she wanted to keep the old house forever. And my sister Jane wasn't settled yet—settled meant married. And my mother still had a little dressmaking business, and she still did custom tailoring for the dry cleaner on the corner. She liked being independent—especially of Ruth, who could be bossy. But she took the train to Ruth's once a month or so and stayed the weekend, so she knew Cindy pretty well. She viewed the Petraski empire with awe and considered me lucky to be in on it.

At dinner, Cindy and I announced our marriage. She stood up at the table and hit her wineglass with the side of a spoon for silence. "We have an announcement," she said. Everyone looked up immediately, all sappy little smiles. Engaged at last, they were all thinking. Then, when Cindy went on, "Remember that gorgeous weekend in April?" everyone looked puzzled. "The weekend of the eighteenth?" She was really throwing herself into it. She'd looked up a date and chosen April 18—not too close to Christmas or to either of our birthdays. "The weather was so incredible," Cindy said. "Just like summer." She reached down for my hand, and I stood up beside her like a good boy. "Will and I got a license, and then we drove up to Lake George on a whim and got married by a nice old justice of the peace named Mr. Skelly. Remember, Will? That long white beard? Wasn't he great?" Cindy's upstairs neighbor was an old man with a long white beard named Mr. Skelly. He was always complaining that Cindy played the television too loud. I remembered the unsmiling justice of the peace in Binghamton, his falsely sweet wife, the brisk ceremony. His name, R. L. Cloke, was carved into a little wooden plate on his desk—as if the room were full of desks. After he married us, he said, "Well, I guess that just about does it, folks." I avoided Ruth's eye and agreed that Skelly was great. Cindy shrugged adorably and smiled around the table at all the stunned, happy faces. "You can now pronounce us man and wife."

My mother hugged us and kissed us and cried, said, "Oh, why didn't you have a real wedding?" and Cindy kept saying impulse—spring—a mood—Nature. She promised we'd have a big party to, as she put it, solemnize the marriage. I kept waiting for her to say she was pregnant, but she didn't, and I didn't know how to bring it up. I figured Cindy had a scenario all worked out.

We repeated the act the next Sunday at Sam's. "I don't want to hit them with the baby until they've digested the wedding," Cindy explained. "Just stay cool, and remember—it was a wild whim, it was spring, we got carried away. And don't forget Mr. Skelly."

"But your father knows Mr. Skelly," I reminded her. "Ace knows him. Ace owns this building."

"Oh, God, that's right. Will, you're so smart." She looked around the kitchen, and her glance stopped at a jar of mustard. "Mr. Gulden, then. And scratch the long white beard."

Except for the fact that they missed out on a wedding, the family was overjoyed. Sam clasped me to his huge chest and called me son. Rose couldn't stop crying. "Tears of joy," she said, and hung on my arm. She said, "Oh, Cindy, you picked a good boy," and went on and on until I felt like shit. I'd knocked up their daughter, I didn't even love her, and they were treating me like a messiah.

The celebration party Sam threw is probably still being talked about in certain Schenectady circles. Rose cooked for two weeks beforehand, Sam ordered enough champagne to keep a poor, starving family in India drunk for ten years, and they invited friends and relatives and business associates I didn't know existed. On my side, there were Ruth and Vic, Jane and my mother, and my aunt Claire. We had the marriage blessed at St. Stephen's, and then everybody went back to the Petraskis'. Sam gave us a lengthy toast, not omitting a clause expressing his hope that we'd be blessed with little ones like Renee and Ace, and going on about how beautiful young love was, what wonderful kids we were, what a great life we were going to have. His big bald head gleamed with sweat, tears stood in his eyes. Cindy, beside me, laid her head on my shoulder. She had washed her hair that morning, and it hung around her shoulders, fluffy and pale, the way I liked it. She wore a white silk dress and a little circlet of white roses. My mother and Rose stood together, big Rose towering over my little mother, both of them dabbing at their tears with handkerchiefs. Even Ruthie and Vic looked pleased. I thought, This should be the happiest day of my life. Nice wife, good business, a baby on the way, all these people raising their glasses to celebrate with us. I looked down at Cindy and felt infinitely sorry for her because I didn't love her. It was a while before it occurred to me that she didn't love me, either.

They clanked their glasses and drank, and by the time everyone left I was blind drunk on champagne and had to be put to bed in the guest room.

When I described all this to Cross, he asked me, "But you'd been drinking steadily right along, hadn't you?"

"Of course. I mean—who doesn't drink?"

"I don't," Cross said. "And neither do you, anymore."

"Well, in those days the world was full of drunks," I said. It seemed like a lost paradise, the days when I simply used to drink and not worry about whether I was drinking too much, whether it was too early to drink, whether I could get away without Cindy noticing I'd been drinking, whether I was going to do something stupid. I said, "When I had that cemetery job, I used to let myself into the cemetery at night when it got dark. I'd unlock the gate and take a bottle to my favorite spot, this little grove of trees where some guy named William West was buried. Born 1822, died 1898. Big marble stone. He had two wives, Harriet and Elizabeth, and he outlived them both. I liked him because our names were so similar. I used to sit there and drink my vodka until I could hardly make it back to my car, and then I'd drive home and sleep for twelve, fourteen hours, and never dream once."

Cross said, "And you were drunk the night Martha Finch died."

"Plastered. And plenty of nights after that. And that graduation night I ended up in somebody's bushes with Anna Nolan and had a fight with Trevor Finch. And when I moved to Albany I used to go out barhopping with this guy Ed Santoli. We used to try to pick up girls, but we'd get so drunk we'd end up passed out somewhere, puking on some back road."

"Sounds like a lot of fun," said Cross, writing furiously. "Okay. So what happened after the wedding party?"

I told him how I was sent away in disgrace after my bad behavior. It wasn't just that I got drunk. I got stupid. I danced with Renee and tried to wrestle her to the kitchen floor. I threw meatballs for the dog to catch. I sang old rock 'n' roll songs. I wore Cindy's crown of roses on my head. I tried to take off my clothes.

There was more, but that's all Cindy would tell me. We had a fight the next morning in the Petraski guest room. She called me a drunk. I defended myself and called her a nagging bitch. The Petraski guest room had two beds, two bedside tables, two glass lamps with pink shades. I picked one up and waved it at Cindy. She screamed. Sam burst in and said, "Get out of here, damn you. Get out of my house before I throw you out," and so I left.

That was the first time I walked out on Cindy—walked out, was thrown out, what does it matter? It was the first time I went home to Mother. Where else was I going to go? The apartment? I didn't want to face that cramped domestic atmosphere, the sharp familiar smell of Cindy's Jean Naté, the mumble of the refrigerator, the bowl of fake fruit on the TV. And I didn't want to face Cindy. Let her stew, I kept saying to myself. Let her sweat.

I left the house with a ten and three ones in my pocket. No credit cards. No car. No friends who weren't Petraski friends. I couldn't go to Ruth and Vic. My mother hadn't made it to the party—sometimes I think the prospect of the Petraskis was too much for her—but Ruth and Vic had been there, and Ruth had made it clear before they left that she was mad as hell. I vaguely remembered her cornering me in the kitchen or somewhere and gripping my arm tight while she told me to get myself under control. I remembered her hard blue eyes, and the disgust in her voice, and I was sure that if I inspected my left arm above the elbow there would be a bruise.

So I took a bus to the station and waited for a train to Syracuse. I had a killer hangover. It seemed to me in my weakened condition that I was doing something judicious and wise. I'd take a week off from work, get a lot of sleep, eat Mom's home cooking, make Cindy worry a little bit, make Sam appreciate me. By the time I got on the train, I was thinking they could all damn well apologize.

I was in Syracuse for ten days before I heard from Cindy. I told my mother Cindy and I were having trouble. I told her about

Cindy's pregnancy, and she crossed herself and said, "Dear Lord." She asked me how I could desert her, in her condition, and I said, "I'm not deserting her, I'm taking a vacation from her." My mother just looked at me, didn't say a word, and I realized how that sounded. Married six months and I needed a vacation. I tried to imagine my parents, for all their bickering, needing a vacation from each other. Except for when we three babies were born, I doubt if they'd ever spent a night apart.

She didn't say anything else about Cindy, and I didn't either. I was afraid that if I spoke her name she'd be on the doorstep, or the phone would ring and I'd hear her voice. I wondered if she'd told Sam and Rose she was pregnant. I wouldn't have put it past her to juice up their anger a little with that fact. On the other hand, I'd expect Sam, if he knew, to show up on my mother's porch with a shotgun.

I went to St. Joseph's Church with my mother on All Saints' Day. I don't think I'd been to mass since high school, and it really got to me—the mass in English, no bells, and Father McNulty facing the congregation like an emcee counting heads. I hated it. All I could think of was getting back to Mom's and having a beer.

At the sermon we were asked to pray for the soul of Mamie Nolan, and I realized that was Anna's grandmother. "Old Mrs. Nolan died," I said to my mother afterward.

"The grandmother of one of your classmates."

"Anna."

My mother remembered her, and she remembered old Mamie, the lady with the loud voice and the funny hats. I asked her if she ever saw Anna around town, and she said she thought Anna was in school in Boston. Then I remembered that she'd gone to the music conservatory there, and I remembered in detail (after a couple of beers) that night on someone's lawn, and what it had been like making love to her. If Trevor hadn't started making trouble, we probably would have been seeing each other all that summer. How would my life have been different, I wondered, if I'd stuck with Anna Nolan?

I went to her grandmother's funeral. My father was a Lutheran. His last rites, short and brisk, had been held at the German Lutheran church on James Street. I'd forgotten how moving Catholic funerals can be, and Mamie Nolan's was in Latin, which surprised me. The ancient words stirred me unexpectedly. I sat in the back row at St. Joseph's, in my old black suit from high school, and when I heard *"Requiem aeternam dona eis, Domine,"* I remembered what a joy it had been to sing it—the Gregorian chant that could put you to sleep unless you really listened and heard how beautiful it was.

Anna was sitting in the front row with her father and his second wife and a baby. For a disoriented moment, I thought it must be her child, and I wondered if she was married, but after a while I realized that the baby was her father's. I sat looking at the back of Anna's head, the Gregorian chant running through my brain. Her voice had really been something. I choked up when she sang "You'll Never Walk Alone" at that glee-club concert after Martha died, and was embarrassed at the tears in my eyes until I saw that everyone around me was crying, too. The whole school had been sure she'd go on to be an opera singer, rich and famous, and we'd all be able to brag about how we knew her in high school. I wondered if she would really do that. I wondered what had happened to her since I saw her last, and if she'd still speak to me if she saw me.

I had my mother's car, and I followed them to the cemetery. It was a grim, dark day, snowing a little, and I was freezing in my old suit coat, but I watched as the coffin was lowered into the grave. I saw Anna crying, blowing her nose, leaning on her father's arm. I wanted to go up to her and say I was sorry about her grandmother, and I almost did it, thinking that I'd ask her how long she was in town and if she wanted to go out and have a couple of beers. Then I remembered that I was married to Cindy, and I turned and walked back to my car.

I got drunk at Tino's that night. I half hoped that someone I knew would come in, some of the old crowd, but there was no one out boozing on a cold Monday night except, late in the evening, Trevor Finch of all people. He had a girl with him, and he looked more than ever like a weasel, but he was civil to me, even friendly. We talked for a minute, and if I hadn't been so drunk I probably would have confessed to him what was on my mind so much— "Yeah, Trevor, I killed her, you were absolutely right to hate me"—but I was pretty much out of it by then. I don't even remember how I got home, just that I woke up the next morning on my mother's living-room floor to the sound of her sewing machine coming from upstairs, and that the sick, crazy dream I'd been having wasn't of Martha Finch but of Anna Nolan.

My mother begged me not to drink so much, and I laid off

the beer for the rest of that week. I sat watching television with Mom after dinner, and went to the store for her, and took long dull walks around the old neighborhood, and read a couple of James Bonds. I was bored and happy, like someone in the hospital recovering from an illness. With just a little effort, I could have forgotten my other life completely.

But when Cindy showed up, finally, to claim me, I was almost glad to see her. I could have used another few days, even another week, with my mind blank and nothing happening except my mother sewing and James Bond saving the world, but I was coming to the end of my period of cold storage, and I knew it. If nothing else, I was beginning to miss Cindy's skinny little body in bed, the warm core of her that had become my refuge, my consolation for a lot of things. But it wasn't only that. I missed the whole Petraski thing—the joking around, the family feeling, the little kids yelling, the big table filled with food and surrounded by people. If I remembered Sam at the party toasting me with champagne and saying "To the son I never had," I even missed Sam.

Cindy showed up on a Saturday morning, unannounced. We kissed primly in front of my mother, and then she left us alone together. We sat down on the sofa with our hands joined. When I asked her how she knew where to find me and she said, "Where else would you be?" I took it as an insult and had no desire to kiss her again, but I did, and she kissed me back, passionately, and pressed her body to mine. She said, "I want you to come home, Will, I want you back. I'm going crazy without you."

Cross once said, "Excuse me for asking, I don't mean this the way it probably sounds, but what made Cindy decide to marry you and what made her stick with you as long as she did? I'm not even talking about the alcohol problem or the in-law problem or any of that. But you told me you two didn't love each other, and you explained why you married her in spite of that, and stuck with her—but what did she see in you?"

I didn't have much of an answer. I was there. Propinquity, as Dobie Gillis used to say. And, of course—I didn't like to talk about this with Cross, I didn't really know how to say it—sex had a lot to do with it. We were crazy for each other. I'd never really gone with anyone before long enough to learn about what sex was. Except for Martha—and that was all quick backseat stuff, those awful nights with Art and Arlene at the drive-in and at Burnet Park, that one time in Martha's bed when no one was home and the guilt and fear were so thick on us we could barely get our clothes off, barely kiss each other—except for Martha, I'd never really had a girlfriend when I met Cindy, no more than a couple of one-night stands, two nights now and then. And I never knew exactly what it was women *do* in bed, aside from lying there while you put it to them. Cindy showed me that. Cindy was—God, she was a maniac.

"Well—sex," I said to Cross, reluctantly. "We had a lot in common. You know."

He dismissed that with a grimace, a hand held up. "Please. You've got to forgive me again, but somebody like your Cindy wouldn't get married for sex. Come on. Think harder."

I shrugged. "What am I supposed to say? That she married me because she knew she could dominate me?"

Cross snapped his notebook open and began to write. "Yes," he said. "That's what you're supposed to say."

Sitting with her in my mother's living room, I said, "I don't know, Cindy. I don't see how we can keep going with this." I didn't really know what I was saying or why I was saying it. I felt that I had, for the moment, the advantage with her. Her leg wedged between mine, her hands on my chest under my shirt— she wanted me a lot more than I wanted her. I said, "If your father's going to curse me and kick me out of his house every time I have one drink too many—"

She said Sam was under control, not to worry, all was forgiven. All Sam had to do was see how much she loved me, how solid our relationship was, how a few drinks, a little shouting, were nothing compared to the importance of our marriage. She was kissing me while she talked, her mouth on my neck, my collarbone, she was unbuttoning my shirt. Her voice came in gasps. I put my hand between her legs and she let out a cry and lolled her head back, with her eyes closed. I couldn't stay distant from her. I was rock-hard, and I unzipped my pants and made love to her on the floor of my mother's living room, on the old gray carpet.

"Dad's going to be glad to see you," she said later. "In spite of everything. You know he's fond of you, Will."

I asked her, "So what am I now—on parole? Do I have to report to Sam every week?"

We were driving down the Thruway in the Corvette. Cindy always drove like a crazy person, and she never once got stopped for speeding in all the time I knew her. She was an incredibly lucky driver. We must have been doing eighty when she pulled off the road suddenly, skidding onto the shoulder with dust and stones flying up around the car and the brakes squealing. I was sure we were going to turn over, and I braced myself, but her luck held and we came to a stop right side up. I turned to her, shaking, and said, "What the hell are you trying to do?"

She was perfectly calm. She cut the motor and said, "You listen to me, Will. You keep drinking like you did at that party and I'll murder you. I'll do something. I'm not going to stand it, and I'm not going to listen to you make your dumb jokes about it, either. You're my husband now, damn it, and I'm not going to put up with a husband who can't hold his booze and who makes an ass of himself in front of my friends and my family."

She stopped. Neither of us said anything; we just sat there while the traffic on the Thruway whizzed by and the cold gray sky got colder and grayer as night fell. It was freezing in the Corvette without the heat on. Finally I said, "I'm sorry, Cindy. I'm really sorry about that night. I don't know what got into me. I guess this whole thing scares me—marriage and a baby on the way. But I'm all right now. I've done a lot of thinking. It won't happen again."

This speech seemed endless while I was making it, and false, but Cindy put her arms around me and we sat huddled together in the cold. Then she said, "Oh, Will, I do love you, I really do," and I realized that she didn't and never had.

Sometime that same month, she told me she was pregnant. I said, Ha ha, I know you're pregnant. She said, No, you don't understand, I wasn't pregnant before, I made a mistake, but now I am—isn't that great, the baby was conceived in wedlock after all? I said, What do I care if the baby was conceived in wedlock or not, what the fuck did we get married for if you weren't pregnant? She said, We got married because we loved each other. Then she began to cry. And I went out and got drunk.

We spent Thanksgiving at my mother's that year. Cindy and me. Ruth and Vic and the twins. Sam and Rose, who drove in just for the day. Jane and her boyfriend and my mother's old friend Mrs. Gleason. Ten of us around the table, plus the twins in their playpen. I drank a glass of the wine Sam brought to go with the turkey, and I would have drunk a lot more, but Cindy saw to it that my glass didn't get refilled when the bottle went around—a skill she was to perfect in the months to come. I would have given anything for a drink. I'd looked out the window that morning and seen Anna Nolan pull up in a car. I met her on the path. She wanted to get together and talk sometime, maybe go out for a drink. She wore a coat with a fur collar, and she looked very pretty. I thought about sitting with her in a booth somewhere and talking about Martha, about Cindy, about old times. I thought about kissing her, burying myself in her, getting some comfort from her soft white body. I looked at her mouth and remembered how we used to sing together. I wanted to throw myself at her feet and beg her to save me. But all I could do was mumble, and then Cindy called me from the house and I fled.

I sat in the Coca-Cola truck listening to bubble-gum music and drinking sodas until I thought my teeth would fall out. By the time we hit Ashtabula, I had resolved to get in touch with Anna when I got to Syracuse. It seemed important that I see her. I felt I couldn't retrieve whatever it was I was trying to get at with Cross unless I could talk to Anna Nolan.

My Coca-Cola friend dropped me at the entrance ramp to the interstate going east. I stood there for two hours before anybody picked me up, and then it was a kid in a souped-up Ford who drove me as far as Erie, Pennsylvania. He smoked pot all the way, rolling joints while he steered with his elbows, the Ford zigzagging all over the road. At least ten times I thought: This is it, good-bye Freddie, don't forget your dad who loves you.

I arrived in Erie after dark, freezing and starving. Breakfast had worn off, and the sweater wasn't enough. I thought with lust of my plaid wool jacket, hanging on a hook in the back hall next to Cindy's blue raincoat. I'd been dropped at a small shopping area. Winkler's Pharmacy, Janine's House of Beauty, Chan Village Take-out, Erie Home Bakery—I was in Quik-Stop territory. I looked around for one. Would it be funny to present myself to whatever Petraski connection was running it and demand some food? Or would the family network have an APB out on me by now? Would my picture be taped up by the cash register? WANTED. Wanted for what? I doubted if any of the Petraskis wanted me for much of anything. They wanted me out of the picture, was all.

I walked around, looking in the stores, thinking about stealing food, rehearsing it in my mind until I got up enough nerve to take a couple of candy bars from the drugstore. I walked half a mile down the road before I dared to take them out of my pocket and eat them. I immediately felt better, but I didn't know what I was going to do next.

I was on a suburban road lined with tidy bungalows, lawns browned in the Indian summer heat, yards littered with tricycles and hot wheels. It reminded me of Arbor Street in Richmond, where Cindy and I lived. I imagined the insides of the houses—dinner just over, the dishes washed, baby being put to bed, toys all over the floor, the evening news on TV. Just like home, except for the guy slumped in his chair swilling vodka.

I considered knocking on a door and asking if I could sleep in a garage or on a back porch. What would I do if someone knocked on my door with that request? Slam it in his face. I decided to find myself a bed I wouldn't need to ask for, and I walked those cozy dark streets for an hour or more, partly to tire myself out and partly to case the neighborhood.

It's amazing what freedom you have in the dark. I strolled through people's shadowy backyards and, when the house wasn't lit up, I checked out screened porches and every garage whose door was open enough for me to slide under. It was in one of these that I found a place to sleep. The house seemed deserted. There were two newspapers on the front walk and mail in the box, and the garage door was up a foot or so—permanently, I suspected, something probably wrong with the track. I rolled under it into a smell of oil and dead leaves. Inside was a VW van up on blocks, its sliding side door conveniently missing. There was a blanket inside on the seat. I peed in the backyard and climbed in. I was tired, and I planned to sleep fast and hard and wake up early and get the hell out of there, but I had trouble drifting off. The blanket smelled strongly of dog, for one thing, and I had visions of a great big Weimaraner or Great Dane whose nightly sleeping place I'd taken over. Any minute the garage door would open, somebody would say, "Attaboy, Tiger, see you in the morning," and I'd be dog meat. But the time went by, and it was ten, then eleven, and I quit worrying about Tiger and began worrying that I'd never get to sleep. And I worried about Freddie.

Oh, God—Freddie. I remembered the day he was born. He was small, only six pounds, but Cindy had a hard labor. Twelve hours and a lot of stitches. I spent the time in the hospital waiting room, leafing through *Newsweek*s, dozing off, and going over all of Cindy's good points in my mind. Her pretty blond hair, her patience with me, her intelligence, her efficiency. I remembered a picnic we went on once when I got stung by a bee and Cindy put meat tenderizer on it. She'd packed meat tenderizer in the picnic basket for just that purpose. That amazed me. She was always amazing me. She'd carried Freddie for nine months as if she were carrying a lunch bag. Her real pregnancy included no morning sickness—and no backaches, no fatigue, no weepiness, no weird cravings. She worked at the Quik-Stop right up to the first labor pain, which came when she was unpacking a carton of potato chips. She finished unpacking, and then she sat down with her watch and started timing the pains. I said to myself, She's what I need. All this, and she's good in bed, too.

When I saw her and Freddie afterward, I was ready to fall in love with Cindy the mommy and make up for all my sins against Cindy the wife. I was half-laughing and half-crying when I picked up Freddie—red, sleeping, wrinkled thing, looking barely human, more like some animal that's born helpless and without fur. Kangaroo? Wombat? He was soft and floppy and warm against my shoulder. He made a small snuffling noise, and I felt drool on my neck. My heart flipped over.

"Isn't he fantastic," I said to Cindy. "Look at this kid." I sat down on the edge of the bed and laid him on my lap to check him out: hairless red skull, fat face, no chin, navel stump wrapped in gauze, minipenis under the diaper. I took his two feet in my hand and admired their skinny redness, their fat toes. Freddie, who until an hour ago had been "the baby" or (Cindy's joke) "the little monster." And here it was, Frederick William, those toes, those noises, this warm sack of baby wrapped up in a blue blanket. "Look," I said. "Toenails, honey. Look at these little feet."

I was going on and on, and then I realized she wasn't saying anything, just lying there with her eyes shut. For one mad moment I thought she had died, and—God forgive me—I was filled with joy. Just me and Freddie, I remember thinking.

This moment was so brief it almost didn't exist. Then I heard her sigh, and she said, "I don't think I'm ready for this, Will. The motherhood bit." Tears slid down her cheeks from her closed eyes, and the corners of her mouth turned down. "Shit," she said. "Shit, shit, shit."

A classic case of postpartum depression, said her doctor. Lying there under Tiger's smelly blanket, I wondered if I could use it against her. She called it "the motherhood bit," Your Honor. She kept saying "shit." She wept when the baby was put in her

167

arms. She refused to breast-feed him. Contrast that attitude with mine, ladies and gentlemen of the jury. I worshiped that baby from the day he was born. I'm the one who did the two A.M. feedings and the four A.M. feedings. I'm the one who stayed home with him all day changing his diapers and singing "Pop Goes the Weasel" (that particular song was another one of Freddie's "things" for a couple of weeks) and spooning in the baby food while his mother chased the almighty dollar at the C & R Quik-Stop, first in Schenectady, New York, then in Richmond, Indiana. All right, so I drank beer while Freddie drank formula—a couple of beers and a little vodka. At least I loved him.

Be fair, Willie, I said to myself. She loved him, too. She got over the postpartum depression even before Sam sent us to Indiana. No one can say she didn't turn into a fond mother, a model mother. It's just that I did all the work, I spent all the time with him, and—here's the important point, Your Honor—I loved it. Faced with a choice between selling cold cuts at the Quik-Stop and singing "Pop Goes the Weasel" to my son—well, there's no contest, as far as I'm concerned, even if I did have to sing "Pop Goes the Weasel" ten thousand times wearing a cowboy hat.

Sam sent us to Indiana when Freddie was four months old because his brother Stanley's son Stanley junior, who ran the Richmond Quik-Stop, was deserted by his wife. She robbed the till and took off with her lover, and Stan had a breakdown. Cindy asked Sam if we could go out there and replace him. For fun, she said. Will's never seen the Midwest. And Sam could put Ace's smart little brother Artie in charge of the Schenectady store. Artie needed a break. He was destined for better things than selling tires at Sears. And in Cindy's opinion—she and Sam went over the books every month—the Richmond store could use a shot in the arm.

Sam agreed, and Cindy was overjoyed, because the real reason she wanted to get out of Schenectady was that she was having trouble keeping my drinking from Sam and Rose. I used to stay pretty sober all day while I was home with Freddie (I would never have endangered my boy, Your Honor). I had a few beers and limited myself to one shot of vodka. I used to pour it around noon and sip at it all day, about a sip an hour. I had it timed so that I drank the last bit just before Cindy walked in, and when I heard her on the stairs I'd have another shot, fast, and then I'd pour myself a beer. When she opened the door—she'd be in her red

Quik-Stop shirt, carrying a bag with our nightly potato salad and slaw in it—I'd say, "Hi, honey. Boy, I sure am beat. I think I'll just have a beer and relax a little before dinner."

By nine or ten I'd be drunk. Usually I drank at home, but sometimes I didn't, and Cindy lived in perpetual fear that one of her innumerable relatives would see me being drunk and disorderly in some bar. Or that, if I were home, Sam or Rose or Ace or Renee or some damned Petraski clan member would stop in and I'd keel over before their eyes or, worse yet, say something like "Hey, motherfucker!" as I did once to Ace.

So we drove out to Indiana in Sam's Buick, leaving the Corvette for Artie. Cindy said she prayed night and day that I'd stay sober out there. "Away from the stress and pressure," she said, though I didn't know what she meant exactly. She took care of all the Quik-Stop stress and pressure while I stayed home and drank with Freddie in possibly the world's most nonstressful, unpressured situation. Except for the booze, even Sam approved of it. He said he liked to see Cindy in the store instead of cooped up at home wasting her talents. The assumption was that I had no talents, therefore there was no waste. Sam clapped me on the back and said, "Don't sweat it, Willie. When Freddie's older you'll be able to take a more active part."

"I feel like a kept man," I said.

"Don't feel that way," Sam said. "There's nothing to be ashamed of."

"I'm not ashamed of it," I told him. "I like it." He didn't think that was funny, I could tell, but he laughed anyway. Sam was essentially a nice, easygoing guy. I really had to persevere to turn him against me.

I suggested to Cindy that we have another kid. "Let's have five, six more. Let's outbreed Ace and Renee. This is a good life."

"If you're so happy," Cindy asked me, "why are you drunk every night?"

"I'm not drunk every night," I said. "I have a couple of beers and fall asleep in my chair. So would you if you were up all night with the baby. I wouldn't exactly call it *drunk*."

"Whatever you call it, you're in no condition to make babies."

That sobered me up, in a manner of speaking. We tried to get our sex life going again, but it was never the same. In bed, I could sense in Cindy the desire to get it over with. I sensed it in her because I felt the same. We became adept at quickies, but everything we did together was distasteful to us both, like some gross bodily function we were forced to perform together instead of in private. Most of the time we could cover up the fact, even to ourselves, that there was no love between us, but in bed the real truth became apparent, and to avoid it we avoided each other.

Business at the Quik-Stop in Richmond picked up when Cindy took over. She could manage a cardboard box and make it turn a profit. She took Freddie to day-care every day, which meant I could start earlier on the vodka. It also meant I was lonely. Sometimes I'd wander over to the store and help out, but mostly I used to put Laramie on his leash and walk around the town— nice town, with a pretty river and lots of good bars. My favorite was called the Oasis. I liked it because it was within walking distance of Arbor Street and they let Laramie in and it had a lot of old songs from the fifties and early sixties on the jukebox. I'd get there around eight in the evening, get myself a dollar's worth of dimes, and play them over and over. "The Great Pretender" and "Only the Lonely" and "Tears on My Pillow" and Dion and the Belmonts singing "Where or When." The one I probably played the most was "Lonely Boy" by Paul Anka. It was a song I hated back in 1959 when it was a hit (all the girls were crazy about it), but now that I was lonely and blue, all alone with nothing to do, it really spoke to me. I wondered what had happened to Paul Anka. When he was seventeen he was a millionaire teen idol. Now he was probably a junkie, or dead, or drunk in some sleazy bar in a town like Richmond.

I stayed too long at the Oasis one night, and when I got home Cindy was waiting up and she called me a filthy son of a bitch no-good bum—something like that. It didn't bother me, but when she went on to tell me I didn't deserve to be Freddie's father and if she decided to leave me no court in the world would give me a second's visiting rights not to mention custody in any form, I hit her. And two days later Sam was in Indiana holding Cindy's face out to me so I could get a good look at the big purple bruise on her cheekbone, and I was packed off to the Sumner Clinic for the first time.

I didn't see Dr. Cross on that first visit. I was there two months, and every day at ten A.M. I trotted down to see Dr. Sack. I grew to hate Dr. Sack, who was as sarcastic and insulting as Cross was (that was part of the Sumner philosophy—brutal honesty was supposed to help you understand yourself and shock you out of your old behavior patterns) but lacked Cross's brains and charm. With Cross, I felt I was being understood—even liked. I had the feeling Cross might be an ex-drunk. Sack, I suspected, had never touched a drop—had grown up in a family where alcohol was equated with cod-liver oil and where anyone who even contemplated taking so much as a teaspoonful of Manischewitz for a sore throat was locked in a dungeon with the rats.

To get away from Sack, I became a model patient (client, whatever). I should have been out of there sooner, but two months was the minimum. And after I was sprung, I became a model husband, father, son-in-law, and citizen. I went to work in earnest at the Quik-Stop and became an energetic shelf stocker and floor cleaner. I even received the Samuel Seal of Approval for an idea I had to stock individual cans of soda in the cooler so the local lunchtime crowd could buy a Coke to go with their shrimp salad and Fritos. I got a bonus of one hundred dollars for that one (fifty dollars was the standard bonus for bright ideas, and I pulled an extra fifty for being a Petraski clan member).

Cindy and I were getting along a little better. She was impressed by my post-Sumner resolutions and behavior, and Sam— I knew because he told me—had recommended that she give me another chance. But she had the day shift at the Quik-Stop and I had the night shift, so we were still having trouble getting together for baby-making. My heart wasn't in it anyway, and not only because of the trouble between me and Cindy. I was seeing someone else, a woman named Claudia Freedman whom I'd met at the Oasis when I used to hang out there. (She was also partial to "Lonely Boy." She said it heated her up.)

She came into the store for some salami one day after my reformation. She said I was missed at the Oasis, that "Lonely Boy" wasn't the same without me, why didn't I come down some night and she'd buy me a welcome-back drink. I told her I wasn't drinking. She invited me over to her apartment for coffee. I went, next day on my lunch hour, and we went straight to bed. No surprise there. We both had known, as I passed her the salami and took her dollar and thirty-eight cents, that we weren't going to be drinking any coffee.

We did, though, eventually drink a lot of coffee together. Claudia became my best friend—aside from the fact that we were lovers. She was somewhere in her late thirties, passably pretty, a little overweight, a drinker. Maybe she was a type—I've seen them in movies—the type that has a heart of gold. I used to tell her my troubles, all about Cindy and Sam and Freddie and booze. I told her how I walked the streets of Richmond lonely and blue, and she said all I needed was a friend, and that turned out to be the truth. Once I met Claudia I was happy.

So why did I start drinking again? Because Claudia was a drunk, I suppose. I started going to the Oasis with her some nights when I got off work. I found that if I talked a lot, ate plenty of beer nuts, and drank Cokes in between, I could hold it down to a couple of beers. I successfully kept my Oasis visits secret from Cindy by telling her incredible whoppers. I told her I walked at night to tire myself out. I told her I played checkers with a guy named Gary Llewellyn, a character Claudia and I invented complete with personality quirks like extreme shyness, a passion for Ovaltine, and a talent for checkers that bordered on genius. I told her I decided to stay a little later at the store because I'd seen suspicious characters around the place. She either fell for all of this or didn't really care what I was doing until one in the morning, as long as I didn't come home drunk.

And I didn't, not once, until that second summer. Cindy found out about Claudia. I don't know how, maybe I'd been seen by one of her relatives at the Oasis or coming out of Claudia's apartment house. Maybe Stanley junior, always on the lookout for marital infidelity, had me followed just for the hell of it. Maybe Cindy herself followed me. She never told me how she knew, just told me that she did, and that if I didn't dump Claudia ("that old whore"), she'd take Freddie away from me; she'd take him so far I'd never find him, not if I looked for ten years, and I could hit her all I wanted but that wouldn't make her any less determined.

I went out and got drunk at the Oasis with Claudia. I started closing the store at ten, then at nine, and I'd go out drinking. I came home later and later. Some nights I stayed at Claudia's because she wouldn't let me go home in the condition I was in. A couple of times Cindy bolted the door on me and I slept in the car. I don't remember, during that time, ever asking myself what I thought I was doing. If I had one rational thought, I don't remember what it was. I just drank.

Finally Sam showed up again and told me to shape up or ship out. I remembered what Cindy had said about taking Freddie so far away I'd never find him. Freddie was two and a half. He'd just finished his "Doggie in the Window" mania and was absorbed in light switches. I'd fixed him a dummy switch on a piece of plywood, and he'd switch it on and off, on and off, for fifteen, twenty minutes at a time, looking thoughtful. And he and I used to play a game where we'd stack up the pennies from his bank in rows of six and then knock them over with a toy dump truck. Six was his favorite number, and also (after his second birthday) two. We used to bake cakes together, putting in six spoonfuls of this, two cups of that—cakes that no one but Laramie would eat, but we sure had fun baking them.

I said I'd shape up. I went back to Sumner. I told my troubles to Cross. I was prepared to reform again, once and for all. And then Cindy called up out of the blue to say she was divorcing me, she knew about that woman, and I could forget about Freddie.

And I finally fell asleep under a dog blanket on the backseat of a van in Erie, Pennsylvania.

I was awakened by voices. I opened my eyes. Sunlight pushed through the dust on the garage windows. Someone outside said, "Okay, then, see you later." I looked at my watch. Eight-twenty A.M. Jesus! I'd meant to wake early and slip out of there before anyone was stirring. How could I have slept so long? It was a bad sign, my first stupid move—to let myself sink in so heavily. And I had to take a leak. More than anything in the world, I wished I'd awakened in the night and sneaked out to piss in the bushes again.

"Hey, Carl," someone called. Adolescent-male voices. Worse than a dog, I thought. A bunch of Teddy boys looking for a fight. I crept from my backseat bed to the van door and lowered myself lightly to the floor. I heard a motorcycle begin to rev up. Whoom, vroom, vroom, real tough. More voices.

I looked around. In daylight I could see that it was a tiny garage, more like a shed, and crammed with junk—a couple of old lawnmowers, part of a kiddie swing set, bushel baskets full of nothing, a stack of hubcaps in one corner, rakes and hoes and God-knows-what standing up against the walls. It was pure luck that I hadn't knocked something over when I came in and had the Teddy boys down on my neck in the dark.

I looked for a place to hide. At the far end was an old kitchen table covered with tools, rusty junk no one would be caught dead using. I could crouch under the table if someone came in. I tried to put myself in the position of a hulking, leather-strapped teenager walking in to add a stolen hubcap to the pile or pick up a wrench to bash some old lady's head in with. Would he see me? In an instant.

My only other choice was the back door. It was next to the table, and it didn't appear to have been opened since the last time the tools were used. What was this place? A memorial to the boys' pop who'd died working on his van? Nothing touched since the old man passed on . . .

The vrooming stopped and someone said, "Fuck it."

"What's the matter?" asked the "Hey, Carl" voice.

"It don't look like I'm going anywhere today."

"Oh, God, then what about Elaine? You can't let that chimney go."

"Fuck, Elaine. Just tell me what you're doing with *that* thing."

The "Fuck Elaine" voice was coming closer. I quit trying to figure out what they were talking about—was *"that"* thing" a gun? a sledge hammer? a killer cockroach? Who was Elaine, and what about the chimney?—and moved toward the back door. Spider city. The door had a Yale lock, which meant it would open from the inside, but it also had a latch bolt. The latch bolt looked rusted for the ages. I tried to wiggle it free. Nothing. Gingerly, like playing pick-up-sticks, I took a hammer from the table for leverage and leaned into the bolt with all my strength. It moved, but the hammer slipped from my grasp with the surprise of the release and fell to the cement floor.

I froze. Nothing. Safe, still safe, I said to myself, but the thought had barely registered when I heard "Fuck Elaine" say, "Well, I'm getting out of here before noon, I'll tell you that," and then the front garage door began rolling up and I was out the back.

I was in a skinny strip of yard bordered by a chain link fence. I got a toehold and went over the fence, and when I dropped down my bladder gave and I peed my pants. I didn't stop, though, I kept running, through two more backyards to a street. I had heard a yell when I first shot through the door, but no one was following me. My relief was enormous, but with it came my first real moment of panic. I realized with the force of a punch that I had no money, not a dime. I had the clothes on my back, including a pair of pants that were wet in front and going to make me stink like a derelict. I was miles from my destination. And my destination was my mother's house, in the town where I was born and grew up. I said to myself, I'm twenty-four years old and I might as well be twelve. Except that what I wanted more than anything on earth was a shot of vodka and a cold-beer chaser.

I was on the corner of a main drag. At that hour, work traffic snarled the intersection—all those normal people leading their normal lives. For a minute I longed to be one of those guys in suits on their way to the insurance office or the Erie branch of G.E. or whatever. Maybe it was dull, but at least you knew who you were and what you were supposed to be doing. At least your pants were dry.

Across the street was a gas station. I crossed over. A pretty young woman at a bus stop glanced at me—wet pants, no shave—then away. She was holding the hand of a little boy who had a curious, open-mouthed stare like Freddie's, the same blond hair, same skinny sturdiness. I looked back after I passed them. The kid was turned around watching me. His mother jerked his hand. I checked my watch. Cindy would just be dropping Freddie off at the day-care center. He would run straight for the big blocks and start building a house. Architect, we always said, but all of a sudden I thought: *father*. It's what fathers do—make a place to keep their families safe. I had to blink back tears.

In the gas station men's room, I blew my nose on rough toilet paper and took a look at myself in the tin mirror over the sink. I looked dirty and insubstantial. I peeled off my corduroys and rinsed the front in the trickle of water that came out of the rusty faucet. They'd be wet, but maybe less smelly, and they'd dry soon enough in the warm morning. In spite of the heat, I kept my sweater on to hide my rumpled shirt. I combed my hair with my fingers, not improving it much, and washed my face and rinsed my mouth with the foul tap water. The mirror was cloudy and wouldn't give back details—my eyes were two smudges, like a snowman's eyes—but I knew I looked like hell, and my stomach was so empty it hurt.

After that I was lucky, if you can call it lucky to be on the road, starving and penniless, and hounded by the knowledge that your soon-to-be ex-wife is plotting to take your kid away from you. But I tried to keep all that in the back of my mind while I filled the front with practical details, and with the continued sense that the farther I traveled from Freddie, the closer I was coming to him.

I rode as far as Rochester in a tractor-trailer with a guy who was so lonely he hardly stopped talking all the way, and who

175

bought me coffee and a greasy double cheeseburger at a Savarin on the New York State Thruway. Just before we got back into the cab, he popped a pill into his mouth, washed it down with the dregs of his coffee, and winked at me across the table. "I'd offer you one, but that was my last," he said. "I gotta see my man in Rochester." He went the last ten miles at eighty-five and kept his right hand on my knee all the way.

I got a ride into Syracuse with a college boy on his way to S.U. to see his girlfriend. Her name was Lorraine Giraldo, and before we'd gone five miles he'd told me what a hot ticket she was. "She'll do anything," he said, looking at me sideways with his eyelids half shut. "Know what I mean?" He smacked his lips and licked them. He said, "What about you? You getting much?" And when I mumbled something about being too busy, about having other problems at the moment, he said, "Man, how do you stand it? I go without pussy for a couple of days I begin climbing the walls, I get zits all over my face, I feel like shit." I smiled weakly, nodded, shrugged. He said, "I mean it, it's a physical thing, I just gotta have it." He told me he was majoring in psychology at the University of Rochester. He wanted to be a shrink and make a bundle. I tried to imagine this twerp doing what Cross did, and the idea was so ludicrous it put me in a better mood. When he asked me where I was going, I told him I'd graduated last June from UCLA law school and I was hitching around the country for a year before I entered my father's law firm in Milwaukee. I told him my knapsack was stolen in Buffalo. I told him my girlfriend was in Paris working as a model. I told him my name was Desmond Petraski. His was Kurt Bundy. I smoked his disgusting menthol cigarettes. He said, "What are you doing about the draft, Desmond?" I told him I was 4-F. He said, "Jesus, you don't look 4-F." I said, "I'm an insomniac, Kurt. I'm on medication."

We were great pals by the time he dropped me off. He gave me his address in Rochester. I made up an address in Milwaukee. He left me at the corner of Erie Boulevard and Teall Avenue, and I walked the rest of the way. It was getting dark, and it was chilly in Syracuse, even with my sweater, but I warmed up as I walked, and I was glad to get a little time to myself before I showed up on my mother's doorstep.

The streets were as familiar to me as my own hands. It wasn't such a great city, it was probably a dump, and I sure didn't have many happy memories of it, but I always had a funny feeling coming back to Syracuse, as if I were in the right place, like a ballplayer who's reached home plate. The feeling made me uncomfortable, and so did the anxiety that I might run into someone I knew—one of the priests from St. Joseph's at Carbone's Cleaners, Trevor Finch coming out of the Clover Club on Grant Boulevard. I walked fast.

I was starving again, though, and I stole two more Milky Ways from a drugstore on Teall that was just about to close. There is nothing easier than stealing candy from drugstores; you could live forever on them. I kept passing the North Side dives of my youth. The Clover Club, Del's, the Track, the Green Horseshoe. Yellow windows and neon beer signs, the throb of the jukebox, people laughing. I tried to think of how I could get someone to buy me a drink, but I couldn't come up with a thing. I was getting to the point where I wouldn't have minded running into Trevor when I came to Danforth Street if he'd buy me a beer.

I stood there on the corner—the corner I'd turned how many times in my life? how many thousand times? I stood there looking down into the dark of that familiar street, unchanged since I was a little kid riding a tricycle on the sidewalk, and I was unable, all of a sudden, to move. There I was, forty-eight hours away from Cindy's voice on the phone, thirty-six hours of traveling behind me, and it came to me like the voice of God that I'd done something stupid. I should have gone straight to Sam, I thought. I should have gone to Arbor Street and had it out with Cindy. I should have waited for Ted Lombardi to get in touch with me. I should have stayed in Richmond, got a job, proved myself right there where I could see Freddie and influence Cynthia and impress the Petraskis instead of fleeing back to what I always persisted in calling home. Like some mamma's boy. Like someone unfit to be anybody's father. Like a loser. It came into my mind that I should retrace my steps, back down Grant Boulevard to Teall to Erie Boulevard to Rochester to Buffalo to Erie to Ashtabula to Richmond. I should go back and scoop up my life.

But here I was, at the corner of First North Street and Danforth. I tried to remember why. To get my head straight. To prove I could survive without the Petraskis. To talk to Anna Nolan about Martha Finch. To wolf down some food at my mother's kitchen table.

I went down the hill and rang the bell. Through the window I could see the blue glow of the television. The screen door was full of bulges and rips. The house needed painting badly. My mother came to the door, peered out through the screen, looked at me as if I were something from outer space, and pressed one hand to each side of her head. She said, "Oh, my God, Will, what have they done to you now?"

2

My parents bought that house before I was born, when Jane was a baby and Ruth was in kindergarten. My first memory is of the big rhododendron in our backyard—a small rhododendron then, full of huge rosy blooms. I remember pulling on one, hard, and when it detached itself from the stem I fell backward and cried, and Ruth came running.

The house is full of photographs of the three of us. My two sisters propping me up (a drooling, smiling baby) between them. Me on my tricycle, the sun in my eyes. My parents and my two sisters lined up on the porch—a picture taken by me. Ruth and Vic's wedding picture. Various high school graduations. Jane at the piano. Me in short pants and blond bangs, looking just like Freddie.

I woke up the next morning, late, and found a note from my mother saying she'd gone to the store. With me in the house, she suddenly needed food—my mother, who survived on coffee and doughnuts and the big German stews she'd make on Saturday and eat for dinner all week. And now she was out spending money she didn't have on hamburger and chops and bags of frozen vegetables and butter and beer and big containers of milk. I sat down with the morning paper and read the funnies and "Dear Abby" and "Ask the Doctor" and the bad news from Vietnam and an editorial on Bobby Kennedy's plans to run for president. I was just getting to the Help Wanted page when my mother came in with my sister Jane and the groceries.

"Look at you," Jane said as soon as she set down her grocery bag. She stood there doing just that, hands on hips, mouth tight, but the expression in her eyes said she was glad to see me in spite of my crimes.

179

"Leave him alone," Mom said. I got up and took her bag and set it on the counter. I felt the six-pack heavy on the bottom. She reached up to pat my cheek. "He's got problems."

"So what else is new?" Jane said, but she smiled then, and I went over to hug her.

My sisters resemble each other, both tall and toothy, with my father's long face and wiry dark-blond hair. But Ruth is angular and Jane is ample. *Built,* we might have said in high school. She finally got married—*settled*—not long after I married Cindy, to a widowed plumbing contractor named Richard Flanagan. She inherited his two kids, Tanya and Wendy, and she and Richard had one of their own, little Gilbert, age ten months.

"What are you doing here? And where's the baby?" I asked her. I had a hunger to see her kids, any kids. I remembered the little boy at the bus stop, thought of Freddie and his blocks. "Do you realize I haven't even *seen* this one yet?"

"He'll keep," Jane said. "He's at day-care."

"And why aren't you at work?" Jane worked in a hardware store out in Fairmount as bookkeeper, sales clerk, stock girl—a little bit of everything.

"I wanted to see my baby brother. God, Will," she said, raking her fingers back through her hair. "What in hell is this? What are you doing with your life?"

I shrugged, widened my eyes, and said, "Eekie tookie boogoo"—the Martian language we made up when we were little.

Jane laughed and took me by the shoulders and shook me. "You really are from Mars, you jerk," she said. Jane never changed. She was two inches taller than I, and sarcastic. Whenever I was with her I was her little brother, an eight-year-old in a cowboy suit.

The three of us sat down for coffee. I think of my mother's house, and it's the kitchen table that comes to mind first. There were always people sitting around it drinking coffee. My father could spend the whole day there, especially after he got sick and couldn't work. I remember him, morose and irritable, drinking cup after cup. There was always a pot on the stove ready to be warmed up, the ancient Drip-o-lator with its container of grounds in a saucer on the sink.

The last time I saw him he was sitting at the table. I was working in Albany, but I was home for Christmas. When I left the morning after, I stood next to him and said, "I'm going, Pop." He didn't look good. In his last year he had become frailer, and gaunt, and he was always in a bad mood, my mother said. I wanted to lean over and kiss him, but I didn't, of course. I just put my hand on his shoulder and said, "Happy New Year."

He said, "Bah!" Then he laid his hand over mine where it rested on his shoulder. "You be good, Will," he said in his gruff German accent. *Vill,* he called me. *Villi.* When he told me to be good, it was on the tip of my tongue to say, "It's too late for that." I've always been glad I didn't say it. I said, "Don't worry about me, Pop." He died on New Year's Day, in front of the Rose Bowl game.

Jane went through the want ads, looking for a job for me. "Something respectable," she said, running her finger down the page. "Something that doesn't require much in the way of brains—"

"Hey, watch it." I reached over and punched her on the arm.

"Or charm," she said, and then looked up at me, frowning. "Or references, I presume? I don't suppose Cindy's old man's going to give you a recommendation."

"Ha ha," I said. "If I know Sam, he's only got one thing to recommend where I'm concerned." I made a throat-slitting gesture.

Jane put down the paper. "Will, what happened? I mean, all of a sudden total alienation. I don't understand it. You went willingly to Sumner, you were being a good boy."

I looked from Jane to my mother. Mom was sitting there shaking her head, her coffee cup poised by her chin. Those Petraskis, I imagined her thinking. My poor boy. The unfairness of it all. She took a sip and put down her cup. "I got involved with this woman at the clinic," I said to Jane. "Cindy seems to have found out."

My mother said, "Oh, my God," and struck the table with the flat of her hand. "Will, Will, my God, what's the matter with you?" She stood up and went over to the sink, rinsed her cup and set it down, came back to glare at me. "You say you want to be a father to your son, and what do you do? You get drunk, you fool around with these women. The Lord only knows what else."

"What's that supposed to mean?" I said. "And I don't *get drunk,* I don't *fool around with these women.* Once or twice I drink a little too much, once or twice I run into someone who's a little less of a bitch than my wife. I try to stay sane, Mom. I try to keep myself going."

"You're going to keep yourself going right into the gutter," she said.

I said, "Christ!" I stood up, then sat down again. Where was I going to go? "I don't believe this," I said; "I don't believe I'm still getting nagged at like this." My mother's voice brought it all back—those hopeless high school years, this kitchen with its faded wallpaper printed with pots and pans, this shabby old house, this broken-down neighborhood, the nuns bugging me at school, my mother nagging, my father badgering me to do my homework, do this, do that—all of it had seemed like a prison and the only thought in my mind half the time was escape. I said, "What the hell am I doing here, anyway? Maybe I should have let Sam slit my throat instead of coming back here."

My mother said, "Don't you talk like that, William. Don't you sit there feeling sorry for yourself when you've brought all these troubles on your own head."

Jane put her hand on my mother's arm. "All right, everybody," she said. "All right. This doesn't accomplish anything. Mom?" My mother sat down again, her hands folded in front of her on the table, her thumbs rubbing together in agitation. "Okay," Jane said. "Let's stay calm. Let's be practical." She looked at us both, bright-eyed and wary, as if expecting one or the other to leap up in a fit. Then she picked up the paper again and began to read. "Accountant—nope. Accountant, accountant, blah blah blah. Administrative assistant, health center, experience preferred—nope. Assistant manager—here you go, Will. College bookstore, assist in all phases of bookstore operation, bookstore experience necessary—forget it. Auto-body repair person, reliable, experienced—nope."

I grabbed the paper from her. "I don't want to hear it, don't read them out loud. I'll go through it later."

"Will—"

"Later," I said. I threw the newspaper on the floor and slumped over my coffee. I had honestly never considered the problem of references. If Sam would recommend me I could get any of a dozen jobs. But the chances of Sam giving me a reference were about the same as Cindy giving me Freddie without a fight. The chances of my calling Sam and asking him for help were even smaller.

I sensed my mother and Jane looking at each other across the table. I imagined Jane's exasperation, my mother's angry despair. I put my head in my hands. Jane said, "Will?"

"Leave me alone," I said. I sat there looking into my cup until the milk began to congeal and break up into clumps like continents. My mother finished putting the groceries away. Jane left, calling, "I'll see you later, Will." I didn't answer. I sat there thinking about Freddie. I felt as if I were drowning, being washed out to sea, while Freddie played with his blocks on the shore, getting more and more distant until eventually I wouldn't be able to see him at all. I remembered how I'd taught him to wave bye-bye during those long good days when Cindy was at the store. He used to wave bye-bye to Laramie. When Cindy came home one day he waved at her and said, "Bye-bye, doggie," and we both cracked up.

My mother went upstairs, and before long I heard her sewing machine begin to hum. I heated up the coffee and took a cup out to the porch steps. Danforth Street was quiet. When I was two, three, four years old, on a sunny fall day like this, at this time of the morning, nearly lunchtime, the sidewalks would be full of little kids with their tricycles and doll carriages and scooters. You'd hear kids shouting, crying, calling to each other, making shrill woo-woo Indian noises, fighting. Then, a couple at a time, their mothers would call them in for lunch. All morning I used to look forward to lunchtime, the bologna and *Sülze* and spicy gray liverwurst we got from Keller & Weber up the street, and rye bread, and coarse mustard, and a big glass of milk, and if my mother had baked there was *Apfelkuchen* or *Lebkuchen* with what my mother called *falscher Schlag*, cheap fake whipped cream made out of milk and cornstarch. If I ever went to another kid's house for lunch, the food seemed boring and bland, even though there was more of it. My mother told me years later how she and my father had suffered during those war years and just after. There were certain kids who weren't allowed to play with Ruth and Jane and me. There were people who called us Krauts and Nazis. My father got into fights at Bendix, lost his job there, and was unemployed for several hard months. By the time I started school, this had all passed, but I have hazy memories of those preschool days playing out on the sidewalk and sometimes being tormented, called names for no reason, turned away from somebody's door by a tight-lipped mother.

Now there were no kids on the street. "Everybody works," my mother said. "All the little ones are farmed out." My mother had been approached by a contingent of parents and asked to serve as a Helping Hand—someone who was always around when the older kids came home from school in case one of them needed an adult. There was an orange pair of hands on blue construction paper in the front window of the house, and my mother was conscientious about it. No matter what she was doing, she was always home by three, and there was often a child there who had forgotten a key or developed a nosebleed or needed to call a parent at work and didn't know the number. "They ought to pay you," I told her. "It's free baby-sitting." But she said she liked it, and she always added, "Those poor kids."

I planned to sit on the steps until three o'clock. I'd watch the kids come down the street from the schools—good old St. Joseph's, three blocks away, and Lincoln Elementary, down Spring Street past the funeral parlor, and Northside High in the other direction. I'd watch the high school girls stroll past, arms full of books, their skirts above their knees. Then I'd eat some lunch. Then I'd look at the want ads. Then it'd be dinnertime, watch a little television, go to bed early. But the longer I sat there scanning the empty street, watching the leaves drift down red and yellow and get blown into piles by the wind, seeing the shadows change position as the sun moved overhead—the more I wanted a beer.

I had made several resolutions that morning before I got out of bed. One was not to just sit around doing nothing. Another was not to feel sorry for myself. Another was to lay off the booze entirely, beer included.

But it was hot out on the steps. The sun came around and got me. I'd already broken the first two resolutions. I kept thinking about the six-pack in the refrigerator. Genesee. I'd seen it when I got milk for my coffee, the six little brown bottles nestled on the shelf between a gallon of apple cider and some Swiss cheese. One. I could have one bottle. One now and one after dinner. Two lousy bottles of beer don't make an alcoholic. Limit myself to one every afternoon and one every evening. When I found a job I'd have to cut out the afternoon beer. Hell, one beer a day! What harm?

Certain things from my childhood stick in my mind no matter what I do. The Baltimore Catechism was the gas that powered St. Joseph's Catholic Academy. Math and English and geography were the chrome and the windshield wipers and the whitewalls, but the Baltimore Catechism kept it moving. Everyone memorized it, and we were supposed to live by it. The nuns were always quoting it. The thing is burned into my brain. In the chapter about angels there's a picture of a wimpy kid in baggy pants standing at a crossroads. He resembles Hanky Wheeler, class nerd. His eyebrows are slanted down in a worried frown, and who can blame him? On either side there's an angel tugging at his arm, one with black wings and black halo, a cruel face, and slicked-back hair, the other gentle and white-winged, looking like Bing Crosby. I remember the picture because it always annoyed me. Where was the contest? Who wouldn't go with the nice guy in the white wings? Who'd let himself be led away by Mr. Sourpuss who, if he was the personification of evil, made evil look pretty unappetizing. Even at a tender age I knew real-life choices were never so simple.

My mother came downstairs and made herself some lunch. She didn't offer me any. I could hear her through the open screen, opening cupboards, running water, rattling silverware. Then I knew she'd sat down with a sandwich and a magazine because I could hear pages turn, and because my mother always ate lunch over *Family Circle* or *Good Housekeeping*. When she was done, she came to the door with an armful of dresses on hangers.

"I have to deliver some work," she said. "You going to sit out there all afternoon?"

I shrugged, still sulking. When she pulled past me in her old Plymouth, I gave her a little wave, and she waved grimly back. The Plymouth disappeared down the street, and I went inside and got myself a beer and went back to the porch. Not that I thought I could fool her, even if I'd wanted to. I just wanted to postpone the nagging. I knew my mother didn't object to my drinking. She came from a beer-drinking culture and a family of beer swillers, and my father had drunk himself to sleep after dinner every day of his life, no matter how hard up we were. My mother's only quarrel with my boozing was that it made me idle. I was supposed to be pounding the pavement looking for a job. I was supposed to be consulting a lawyer. I was supposed to be— who knows? Making phone calls, making lists, striding around looking purposeful. If nothing else, I could fix the porch steps or put new screening in the door.

I went back to the porch and drank the beer slowly, sipping, making it last the way I used to do with my shot of vodka. The bottle was cold and wet against my hand. My first beer since August. Hell, it was only my first day home. Why shouldn't I spend it loafing? I'd get to the want ads. I'd get to the screen door, too. But for the moment, I'd let those black wings lead me away.

I put in a week of depressing battles with the Help Wanted pages. Accountant to zookeeper's assistant, there wasn't a damn thing I was qualified for without references. Even if I'd had a fistful of glowing Petraski letters, the only things I could go for were busboy jobs. Pizza-slinger. Counterman. I called about a dishwasher job, but it was already filled. I saw myself sliding into middle age washing dishes, ringing up groceries in some market—or living on welfare in one of those hotels down on Clinton Street. Whenever I thought about it, my limit of two beers a day seemed like a sadistic joke.

My mother said, "You should have gone to college. You should have got those Petraskis to send you." My mother still saw the Petraskis as the chance of a lifetime that I'd let slip through my fingers, an Irish Sweepstakes ticket tossed out with the trash. "Even now," she said. "You should call Sam. He's a nice man. He'd listen to reason. The worst he could do is hang up on you."

"He's not a nice man," I told her, but I wasn't sure I believed it. Maybe he was a nice man. Maybe I was the one who wasn't nice. "He's a businessman who's crazy about his family. I done his daughter wrong, Ma. He hates me. And he could do a lot worse than hang up on me. He could screw me in this custody thing."

I saw Sam as my enemy—Sam even more than Cindy. I thought I could probably still sweet-talk Cindy if I saw her. I knew Cindy, all her soft spots. Sam had no soft spots that I'd ever seen or heard of.

"You've already screwed yourself," was my mother's helpful comment.

The job I finally got was thanks to my sister Jane. Wendy's nursery school—Grace Hill, out in Lyncourt—needed a teacher, preferably young, male, good with kids. I was all that. The only reference they required was that I was Jane's brother, Wendy's uncle.

"It's not what you know, it's who you know," Jane said. "Lucky for you."

I was interviewed by Dorcas Kyle, who ran Grace Hill. The school was in a building that used to be a real-estate office, squeezed in between two wood frame houses. Out back, swings and seesaws under the trees. Inside, three rooms, a block corner, a row of

cubbies labeled GINGER, WENDY, MICKEY, LISA, JOSH . . . no Freddie.
It was a Saturday morning, no kids around, and the silence of the
place made me feel irrationally mournful, as if all the Gingers and
Mickeys had been annihilated by a bomb, and these cubbies, these
papier-mâché dinosaurs, these abandoned block houses were their
remains. Looking around, I missed Freddie with a pang that was
as real as a stomachache.

Dorcas and I sat at a kiddie table on kiddie chairs. She was
double-chinned, pretty, with dark hair and dark eyelashes and big
blue eyes—a plump, motherly, warm-hearted spinster, past thirty,
who obviously liked kids better than any adult she'd ever met. I
felt immediate kinship with her.

"We just adore little Wendy," she said. "And your sister has
been such a help to us here, as a volunteer for field trips. I'm very
happy to meet you, Will." She said it sincerely, emphasis on the
very. I wanted to put my hand on her heavy thigh and suggest that
we make babies together, now, before it was too late—fat little
dark-haired Freddies.

She described the job to me: eight to three, five days a week,
minimum wage, minimal benefits. She talked about Morning
Songtime, Snack Break, Quiet Corner, Story Hour. She told me a
little about the kids—this one was a bully on the swing set, that one
wasn't toilet trained yet, somebody else could already read whole
books at the age of four . . .

I could scarcely pay attention, I wanted the job so badly.
Even aside from Dorcas, even if she had been ugly and witchy and
beat the children with a strap, I wanted the job. It seemed to me
that it was what I was born to do—play with little kids all day and
get paid for it. I wanted the job so much I set out to charm her,
something I hadn't done since—when? Had I ever tried to charm
anyone? Cross, maybe. Cindy, once or twice, a long time ago.
Claudia? I talked about how much I liked kids, chuckled sadly
while I told her about Freddie, even described the Petraski brats
as if they were angels. The amazing thing was that it worked; after
we'd talked for a while she offered me the job. I don't know if it
was the charm or not. Maybe it was because of good old Jane,
maybe because Dorcas knew I was sincere—Christ, talking about
Freddie I had to fight back tears. Or maybe I was the only young,
good-with-kids male she'd interviewed who was willing to work
for minimum wage.

"I admit the pay stinks, but it's the best we can do," she said.

She frowned apologetically, wrinkling her dark, winged eyebrows. "We work on a very tight budget. Our families pay on a sliding scale according to income. Some pay nothing."

I said I wasn't complaining, I didn't need much. "Minimum wage is better than no wage at all."

The frown smoothed out. "There are other satisfactions, of course."

I smiled at her. "The kids." She smiled back. I said, "I miss my son like crazy. He's all the way out in Indiana."

"Jane told me." She made a gesture, and for a second I thought she was going to touch my hand. "I'm sorry." The gesture petered out. Her hand turned palm up and became part of a shrug. "So many of our children come from broken homes."

We were silent a moment, pondering this, pursing up our lips and shaking our heads. I looked past her to the cork-covered wall where a dozen finger paintings were hung with pushpins. They were all of animals, more or less: something striped, something spotted, something long-tailed. Field trip to the zoo, I decided, and remembered the day I'd taken Freddie to a little petting zoo that was part of a carnival run by the fire department near our house. Goats, sheep, a family of piggies, a couple of shy calves, and a machine that dispensed some dog-foodlike fodder at a nickel a fistful. Freddie loved the sheep. Their silly baa's made him laugh, and the way they nuzzled his hand for the food, tickling. He stuck his fat little fingers into their thick wool. When we ran out of change, the sheep deserted him for another, better-stocked toddler, and Freddie ran after them, crying, "More sheep! More sheep!" The sheep clustered together at one side of the pen, looking back at him in terror, bleating wildly. Freddie sobbed, holding out his empty hands. On the way home, he said "Sheep" from time to time, sitting up straight in his car seat, looking thoughtfully out the window. I sang "We are poor little lambs who have gone astray" for him, and he cheered up a little, sang along: "Pore yitto yams . . ." But for days afterward he talked about the sheep—mournfully and wistfully. I figured it was an important experience for him. Loss. Maybe it would be his first memory, something he'd tell his wife about, his children.

Dorcas handed me a form to fill out. I could sense her watching me while I worked on it. I filled in my name, address, phone number, Social Security number, work experience. It seemed strangely unreal to write "Assistant Manager, C & R Quik-Stop,

Schenectady, N.Y. and Richmond, Ind."—as if it were all lies, or a previous incarnation. I fudged the dates, merging my drunken excesses and my months at Sumner into one vast Quik-Stop experience. I handed it back to her and she read through it and asked me, "What about skills?"

I had left that blank. "Skills," I said. "What am I supposed to say? I can play the farmer in the dell? I can color inside the lines?"

She smiled. "Can you sing? Can you build things? Could you make costumes for a play out of newspaper and old socks? That's the sort of thing we mean."

"God, I don't know," I said. Eekie tookie boogoo. I could feel the job slipping away from me. "I used to play with Freddie. My son. I mean—I was his what-do-you-call-it. Primary caretaker. For a while. Sure, we did all those things. Cut out snowflakes and everything. I can read music. I can pick out tunes on the piano." I stopped. She seemed to expect more. I said, "I'm not a bad carpenter. I can fix things."

"You don't play guitar, do you?" I shook my head. She stood up and went over to a closet, opened it, took out a guitar with a red-and-white woven strap attached to it. She handed it to me. "You can learn," she said.

"I can?" I hung on to the thing, ran my fingers over the strings. *Twanggg!* "I don't know the first thing about it."

"Get a book." She sat down again and pulled her little chair closer to mine. Her thighs spilled over the sides, straining against her denim skirt. "Listen, Will," she said. "I think you'd be wonderful for this job." I felt a rush of excitement that I thought at first was sexual, part of Dorcas's kind and earthy presence, until I realized it was the thrill of being taken seriously. Me, Will Westenberg, champion loser, being pronounced right for something. She went on, "We'd really like to have you with us. It's so good for the kids to have a man around. We had this guy Gary, but he turned out to be—" She waved her hand, making a face. "How shall I say it? I don't want to be judgmental. I mean, he had problems—"

I watched her hand turning on her wrist. Her hands fascinated me. They were dead-white, plump, solid. Long fingers with tiny pink nails filed short and perfect. Silver ring like a snake coiled around her wedding-ring finger. Big turquoise on the other hand. Looking at her hands made me horny. I imagined pressing my lips to the palm of one, biting into the firm flesh.

189

I asked her, "What was his problem, exactly?" She still hesitated, and I wrenched my gaze away from her hands and said, "I think I ought to know." God, I thought, was he a child abuser? Did he come to work in drag? Force the kids to march like Nazis? Or was he simply a loser like me, a jerk who couldn't even play guitar?

"Well—" She put her hands back together, folded them firmly on the table like we had to do in third grade, and looked me in the eye. "He used to smoke pot on his lunch hour," she said.

I almost laughed, she was so solemn about it. A couple of joints out under the trees didn't seem like a big enough sin to thin Dorcas's lips into a line and make her eyes so hard. I said, "You don't have to worry about me. I've never smoked pot in my life."

That wasn't quite true. I tried it three or four times with Claudia, and once with some of the guys at the pizza place where I worked. I never liked it. I hate smoking, anyway, that hot rush into your lungs, but most of all I hated the way I felt when I was high. I disliked everyone. I noticed all the dumb things they said and all their flab and pimples and big noses and ugly feet—things I never thought about normally. I remember looking at Claudia once when we were high and being repelled by her enormous sloppy breasts. I didn't tell her that, but one time when we were smoking I told her marijuana made me feel mean and I didn't like the feeling.

"That's the real you," Claudia said. "That's all your repressed hostility coming out."

"Bullshit," I said, and Claudia said, "See what I mean? You don't normally talk that way to me." Maybe she was right—who knows? But I think pot simply didn't agree with me.

I said, "I can't imagine doing something like that in front of the kids." I wondered what she'd do if I said I'm a drunk, gimme a pint of vodka and who needs marijuana?

Dorcas unpressed her lips. "I don't want to sound prudish or anything," she said, and she glanced at me quickly and then away, at the zoo paintings on the wall. "But we do need to be careful around the children. I mean, we're responsible for them. And we're their role models, like it or not. Of course, what the staff does on their own time is their business," she added, and her eyes slid from the zoo back to me.

"Sure," I said, trying to interpret her words, her look. Was she inviting me to an after-school pot orgy? Or was she pretending to invite me to an after-school pot orgy, as a test? Or was I just going crazy from imagining the things her hands might do? I began to wonder what Jane had told her about me. *He's a decent guy but keep an eye on him, he really needs this job but don't let him get away with anything . . .*

She sighed. "Unfortunately, Gary was a fantastic guitar player. The kids were fascinated by him. He played like a professional, and he knew every song on earth, and he was really good at getting them to respond and sing along." She looked sadly at the guitar. "We were sorry to let him go." I wondered if she'd been sleeping with Gary. "Really sorry," she said.

I slung the guitar into playing position and tried to look musical and smart. "I can probably pick it up."

"We're not asking that you play as well as Gary. Even some simple chords. Maybe you could get a book at the library."

I nodded, twanged it again, pressed down a string and plucked it. *Twong.* "Sure," I said. "No problem."

"Take it along," Dorcas said, and stood up. "See what you can do. And the sooner you can start work, the better. A week from Monday?"

"Why wait?" I said. "What about this coming Monday?"

"Well." She smiled. "Make it Tuesday, so we can prepare the children." She gave me her hand. It was warm and muscular, and it seemed to me that she held the handshake just a split second longer than necessary.

My sister Jane said, "What a perfect job for someone who's basically an overgrown kid." She said it in a friendly way, but it was meant to be a home truth. All my life my sisters had insulted me for the purpose of improving me, disguising the insults as jokes.

I said, "I really don't think you have to be an overgrown kid to work in a nursery school." We were sitting at the kitchen table later that afternoon, drinking iced tea. I hadn't had a beer yet that day, and I told myself I'd have only one, with dinner. I was still drunk on the prospect of the job. "You think Dorcas is an overgrown kid?" I asked her.

"No. She's a frustrated mommy."

"Why can't I be a frustrated daddy? It's a lot more dignified."

That shut her up for a minute. In the ten days since I'd been back in town, she'd gotten used to prying into my life and twisting it the way she thought it should go—just like the old days. It was as if the last six years plus didn't exist, and she'd forgotten I'd left home, married, had a kid, and was being sued for divorce. She looked at me sadly and said, "Oh, darn it, Will, I wish you'd been able to bring Freddie with you. He could be playing with Wendy and Tanya, they'd love him, and he'd be like a big brother to little Gil." She stopped. "I'm sorry. All you need is my going on and on about it."

"It doesn't matter, Jane," I said. "I'll get him back, eventually."

"You really think so?"

"Obviously. I mean, I doubt if I can get full custody, but it's obvious that I love the kid. They're not going to keep him from me. I'll get him weekends, vacations, whatever. And maybe when he's old enough to decide these things for himself he'd want to come and live with me permanently."

That was my new vision: Freddie at eleven, twelve, thirteen, showing up on my doorstep saying "I want to live with you, Dad. I miss you so much, and Mom is a complete bitch."

"You should get a lawyer," Jane said.

"It's not going to come to that. I can handle this myself. It's simple. She tells her story, I tell mine. All right, there are points on both sides, but no one can say I wasn't a good father. Even Cindy couldn't say I wasn't devoted to that kid. And look at me now." I laughed. I'd thought about this a lot. "Working in a nursery school! I couldn't have a better job, under the circumstances. I play daddy to a bunch of kids all day—who's going to say I'm not fit to be Freddy's father?"

Jane looked dubious, and when she got up to go she hugged me hard, and I hugged her back. "I'm sorry if what I said sounded like a put-down," she said.

"You mean I'm not just an overgrown kid?"

"Oh, no—you *are*," she said. "I'm just sorry I said it." It was one of her jokes. I had to pretend to punch her, pretend to be kicking her out the door, to make her laugh, and make my mother put her hands on her hips and say "You two," shaking her head like she did when we were little.

But it bothered me, what Jane had said. I wondered how I'd appear to some judge in court. I went upstairs and looked in the mirror. To myself, I looked old, responsible, somebody who'd led a dog's life and survived it by strength of character and force of will. I wondered if a moustache and beard would make me look fatherly or too much like a hippie. Keep my hair short, keep the beard trimmed neatly. It would go with the guitar. Would the kids like it? Gary the pothead probably had a beard. Would it scare Freddie when I saw him again?

Jane had brought me a book called *300 Guitar Chords and How to Play Them.* I went up to my old room and worked at it while my mother got dinner. First I tuned the guitar, from a section called "How to Tune Without Piano." Easy enough. I learned which string was which, what a fret was, how to read chord diagrams. I cut my nails as short as they would go. Then I taught myself the C major and A minor chords, and I was working on G major when my mother called me for dinner.

"It sounds good from down here," she said.

"The chords are easy," I told her. "I know there's a lot more to it than just strumming chords, but so far it's okay. My fingers are a little sore. I guess I'll have to develop callouses." I began to fill my plate. She went all out on weekends: sauerbraten, applesauce, potatoes, hot rolls.

"You were always good at music. I was sorry we couldn't afford piano lessons for you from the nuns, like Jane."

I used to envy Jane, the way she could dash off all those minuets and sonatinas—showing off—while all I could do was play things like "Silent Night" and "My Country 'Tis of Thee" by ear. The old piano, junked long ago, used to take up a large corner of the dining room. I remember sitting there trying to figure out how to play, trying to match the music in my sister's books with the long, confusing row of keys—and getting mad at the whole process, banging the keys with my fists until my father bellowed at me to cut it out or he'd take his belt off.

I said, "I wouldn't have practiced anyway, Ma."

She put her hand on my head and ran it through my hair. "I think you've changed, Will," she said, and looked down at me, nodding. My faded little mother, all the color and stuffing gone out of her in her old age—just like the house. It had always been shabby, but she used to keep it so clean you could lick the floors. Now there were dust kittens under the beds, an ocean of thread bits all over her sewing-room floor, crud in the corners, stains in the sink. I'd been helping her some since I got home—not enough.

I cleaned out the garage, raked some leaves, helped with the dishes. I was too edgy and low-spirited to do much. It didn't matter, though. I was her favorite, in spite of my sins. She said, ever-hopeful, "*Ja,* Will, I think you're changing all the time."

She didn't eat much. Mostly she watched me eat, looking pleased. I felt guilty, eating such huge amounts of food. And not just the food. In general, I felt like a sponger. I was always borrowing her car, and I knew I was screwing up her whole routine, all the rituals she'd set up to organize her life and fill her days. "My son, Will, is home for a while," I'd hear her say on the phone—meaning she couldn't go play bingo or meet Mrs. Gleason for lunch or whatever because she had to slave over my dinner or my laundry or because I was using the car. I even disrupted her sleep. I wasn't sleeping well myself, and I'd developed a collection of compulsive nighttime habits—checking over and over to see if the doors were locked and the oven was off, getting up every ten minutes to take a leak, turning on my light over and over to check the clock, and toward morning going downstairs ten times to see if the *Post-Standard* had been delivered yet. My mother was a light sleeper, and I knew she suffered.

"Now that I've got a job, I can get a room somewhere," I told her. "Get a hot plate and do my own cooking."

"I don't mind your staying here," she said. "I like having someone to cook for. You could stay right here and pay me a little room and board. It'd be cheaper for you, Will."

I knew that was what she wanted. I would have liked it myself, but I thought it would be better for my Freddie campaign to have my own place, to show I was a responsible citizen who pays rent and cooks and gets along with his landlord. Not just an overgrown kid living at home. I told her I'd think about it, see what my finances were like once I started working; I wasn't sure what I'd do. But I already had in mind a one-room apartment, neat and bare and functional. I imagined taking women there—fantasy only. I was determined to stay uninvolved. No booze, no women, just single-minded work on my son's behalf. But I could think. I thought about Dorcas, her plump capable hands. I thought about taking Anna Nolan in my arms and finding some sort of comfort. I thought about all the nameless lonely women eating dinner somewhere at that moment, home alone on a Saturday night like I was.

My mother looked at me with her little bright eyes. "Just don't forget you're still a married man," she said.

*   *   *

I surprised myself with the guitar. I mastered it in record time—at least, I learned enough basic chords to accompany some basic songs. I sat in my room all that weekend singing and strumming. My first real victory was "Pop Goes the Weasel," in honor of Freddie—mostly G and D chords, with a short trip into C and a quick A minor that I was proud of. I tried a combination of picking out the tune on the strings and filling in the rhythm with chords, and it worked pretty well on "Pop Goes the Weasel," but I got into trouble with "The Yellow Rose of Texas," my second attempt. The chords were simple, but the song—another Freddie favorite—had too many notes, and I got confused trying to combine them with chords. I kept thinking, If I could just have one lesson with somebody like the lost Gary (who was probably standing downtown in an unemployment line smoking his furtive joint), if somebody could just show me a couple of basic techniques, I could be pretty good by Tuesday morning, in a primitive kind of way.

But I kept at it on my own, all that weekend and into Monday. I remembered a lot of the good old songs my sisters and I used to sing when we were kids. On car trips the three of us would belt out "Red River Valley" and "I Didn't Know the Gun Was Loaded" until my father would yell *"Hört doch endlich auf!"* Then, when Freddie was born, it gave me an excuse to sing them all again. He loved to be sung to, loved to sing along. All that long guitar-playing weekend, I thought about Freddie. What was he doing? Was he playing with Laramie, was he playing outside, was he rolling cheese slices into tubes, was he still crazy about light switches? I sat in my old bedroom surrounded by the junk of ages—St. Joseph's Academy banner on the wall, schoolbooks and baseball cards and a pile of faded game boxes on the closet shelf, my ancient record player (broken) and a stack of old 45's. Elvis, the Shirelles, the Everly Brothers, Duane Eddy and his twangy guitar. I thought once how funny it was that so many elements from so many parts of my life were there together in that shabby bedroom: Chutes and Ladders, Willie Mays, Freddie, "Pop Goes the Weasel," "Bye Bye Love," *Amsco Review Book for Latin II*, my sisters singing in the car, and me picking out chords on the Grace Hill Nursery guitar—all of it mixed up together, all of it present in the old songs I tried to play.

I had a whack at almost everything I knew, and when I forgot the words, I hummed or played the guitar louder. I was probably driving my mother crazy, although she was full of encouragement and compliments. Finally, on Monday morning, I took my sore fingers outside to rake leaves, but I kept thinking about the guitar, the songs kept going through my head, and I never did finish the backyard. I went back up to my bedroom and tried out a new bunch of chords for "Lonesome Road," a song I particularly liked:

> *Look down, look down that lonesome road,*
> *Hang down your head and cry . . .*

It was complicated, but my inspiration was to play it with D chords, and then it fell into place and sounded good. I thought the kids would like it.

> *The best of friends must part someday,*
> *So why not you and I?*

I knew from singing for Freddie that it wasn't only cheerful, funny songs that turned kids on. They liked the sad ones, too. Who can relate to poor little lambs, and hanging down your head and crying, better than a bunch of four-year-olds? Except maybe overgrown kids and frustrated daddies.

By Tuesday morning I had a batch of songs I could play pretty well, and some more that I could fake or play haltingly. I took the bus to Lyncourt and walked into Grace Hill at five after eight. The kids—twenty-four three- and four-year-olds in overalls and pinafores—were assembling in a circle on the floor. Morning Songtime. Dorcas stood in their midst holding a rabbit handpuppet. Maria, the other teacher (a skinny, stringy-haired girl who looked about eighteen), introduced herself and led me by the hand over to the group. Dorcas made the puppet say, "Children, this is Will, our new teacher. Let's say good morning to him," and the kids yelled out, "Good morning, Will!"

I hung the guitar around my neck and took a seat on a stool Maria placed for me just outside the circle. I said, "Hi, kids," feeling like Buffalo Bob. I didn't know what else to say, I was so nervous. Then I strummed a few chords and lit into "On Top of Old Smoky." Dorcas smiled approvingly, Maria started singing, the kids joined in, the place filled with music, my nervousness fled, and the unfamiliar certainty came to me that there, sitting on that little red stool, surrounded by singing children, my arms around a guitar, for the first time in my life I was in the right place.

ALL YOU NEED

1

I wrote to Cindy asking for pictures of Freddie—I had gone away with nothing. Or some drawings, stuff he did at day-care. Or news. Anything. I sent him a Halloween card: a ghost saying "Whoooo's wishing you a Happy Halloween?" and inside the ghost throws off his sheet and it's a puppy saying "Me, that's whoooo!" No reply to any of this. I tried to call a couple of times and got the answering machine. I couldn't think of any message to leave that wouldn't sound pathetic or seem like harassment. "Cindy, *please*" or a string of obscenities, there seemed to be nothing in between.

Fortunately, I had Grace Hill to keep my mind off my troubles. I loved it there. The kids would hang on me, grab my shirt or my arm or my pants pocket and beg me to sing for them or push them on the swings or help build a castle. I was *popular*. I couldn't get over that. They kept me busy, and they wore me out. I'd get off the bus on the corner after work and trudge up the hill like an old man. I'd think how glad I was to be home, to be free of their demands—and then I'd talk about them for an hour to my mother, or call up Jane to discuss each of them in depth. Josh, who pushed the other kids around. Sandy, who wouldn't talk except through a puppet. Maureen, who could read. Mickey, who was always happy no matter what happened. My niece Wendy, who cried a lot.

I was glad of my days off because I needed, physically, a rest, but I never got tired of the children. It was as if I were in love with them, the whole crew. That was the only thing I could compare it to—the fascination I felt for them, and the endless appetite for their company.

Dorcas wasn't much of a complimenter, but at the first staff

197

meeting (we held one every Friday) she said, "You're going to work out great," and a week later she came up to me after a hard morning and said, "You're really amazing—you know that? Your instincts with these kids are perfect."

Maria and I became friends. She was a skinny, outgoing kid, just out of high school, and she treated me like a classmate. She liked to call me WW, and she teased me so much about the beard I'd begun growing—as if I were a teenager who'd just begun to shave—that I got rid of it. Then she got mad and said I was too sensitive, so I started growing it again. Sometimes I went to the movies with her and her boyfriend, Dave, who was quiet and good-natured. We'd go out for a pizza afterward, and Maria would sit there talking, on and on, forgetting to eat, while Dave and I smiled and listened and devoured the pizza.

Dorcas puzzled me. I never felt comfortable with her. There was something about her that made me want to look down at my shoes and say, "Aw shucks, Ma'am" when she spoke to me, like a hick in a cowboy movie when the schoolmarm comes to town. And there was something else that made me want to throw her down on the floor and rip her clothes off. The same confusion seemed part of her feelings toward me. There would be these awkward silences. Once, she drove me home because she was going that way for a dentist appointment, and neither of us could think of much to say. We didn't seem to get to know each other any better, no matter how many weeks we worked together. But sometimes I'd catch her looking at me. When she dropped me off that time, she leaned toward me as if she wanted to touch me, or as if she expected to be kissed.

But I was never sure, and so I was afraid to do anything about it, even if I hadn't sworn off women.

There were times, though, when I thought I'd crack up if I didn't have a woman. It wasn't sex I craved so much as just sitting close to someone, talking, holding her hand. You ought to be able to hire someone, I thought. Not a whore, but some nice, gentle, cozy woman who would curl up on a couch with you and listen. Maybe put on a record and dance. Rent-a-Sweetie. Listeners Anonymous. If the Quik-Stops added it as a sideline they'd make a fortune.

I guess I was lonely. I had my job, the kids, Dorcas and Maria and Dave, my mother and my sisters and my brothers-in-law, the poker games I went to from time to time next door at Walter

Kennedy's. It wasn't that I lacked people in my life. I wasn't even alone all that much. But I had no friends. I was close to no one. In bad moments I almost missed Cindy.

My sleeping problems were getting worse—the old vicious circle. I slept badly, and as a result I was always so tired that I'd have trouble not falling into a nap when I got home from work, and then I'd be too wide awake to sleep at night. Sometimes I'd keep myself awake in the evenings by talking to Mom, or calling Jane after her kids were in bed, or taking long walks in the cold autumn air, but there were other nights when I was too tired to make the effort and I'd sit down in front of the television and give in to my fatigue, resigned to the knowledge that I'd wake up at three or four A.M. in a panic and prowl around the house until the morning paper landed on the porch with a thump.

The funny thing was, I wasn't drinking, not even my one beer a night. From my first day at Grace Hill, I gave it up, and it wasn't a problem. I'm not saying I didn't miss it. I even used to dream about it. Ace once told me that for years after he gave up smoking he'd dream that he was lighting up after dinner, and in the dream he'd feel guilty as hell. My dream was that I confronted Cindy. There were no words, just unfocused anger and hate, and then I'd go to the refrigerator—the one in our apartment, with Freddie's magnetic letters and numbers stuck all over it—and get myself a beer. I never felt any guilt in this dream. I felt great, and I'd wake up with such a thirst that no matter what time it was, four in the morning, I'd be tempted to go downstairs and get a beer and take it up to my room to drink while I waited for the paper. But I never did, and as the days went by and I still didn't have a drink, and *still* didn't, I began to be proud of myself, and to resent the fact that for so long everyone—Sam and Cindy and Cross, even Gwen, Claudia, Jane, Ruth—had called me an alcoholic. I was no alcoholic if I could go on the wagon with such ease. It became one of my compulsive middle-of-the-night habits to open the refrigerator and check to see that the three bottles of Genesee were still lined up on the door—as if I feared I'd gone berserk and guzzled them, or finished them off in my sleep. Seeing them there gave me, in a diluted kind of way, the same reassuring lift I used to get when I'd look in on Freddie in his crib to see if he was okay.

I told Jane about my sleeping problems, the weird behavior that I couldn't control, the endless checking and pacing and worrying I went through in the night. I expected her to laugh at me, make it into one of her jokes, but she surprised me. She said, "Believe me, Will, that's *nothing*. After the hell you've gone through I'm surprised you haven't had some kind of breakdown." Her sympathy stunned me. I felt I had indeed been through hell, was still going through hell, but I'd assumed everyone else on earth thought of me as a spoiled brat who'd screwed up his life and deserved what he got. Jane said I should go to a doctor and get a prescription for sleeping pills, but I didn't want to spend the money. And it seemed to me that it would be cheating. I had the idea that the sleeplessness and the rest of it was something I had to go through and find my own cure for. I told Jane that and she said I was hopeless.

I sent Freddie a Thanksgiving card ("Know what I'm thankful for?" Open it up. "YOU!"), and finally left a message on Cindy's goddamn machine. I wrote it out on paper and read it into the phone, trying to keep my voice cool and neutral but not unfriendly: "Hello. This is Will. If it's not too much trouble could you please communicate with me in some form? I'd like to know how Freddie is and what's happening. And tell him his daddy misses him. And give him a kiss for me. Thanks." I screwed it up. "If it's not too much trouble" came out sarcastic, and my voice broke at the end. I called home from work at mail time for days afterward, and I tried to keep the phone free in the evenings, but there was no reply. Nothing.

My sisters and their families came to my mother's for Thanksgiving dinner. Ruth and Vic sat me down right away and started giving me advice. They'd been thinking about my situation, they said. They'd been talking it over. They thought I should go to college, maybe get a degree in elementary education since I liked little kids so much. They'd be willing to pay for me to take courses at night for a year, starting in January, and if I liked it they'd help me go full time next fall. I could live with them and go to the state college in Albany.

"You're such a bright boy, Will," Ruthie said, looking at me wistfully, as if she really wished it were true.

"I'm not a boy," I said. "I'm almost twenty-five years old."

"It's never too late," Vic said, and began to tell me how he wished he'd gone to college, and then, without noticing he was contradicting himself, how he'd made good in spite of it.

I hadn't seen Ruth in a while. She looked older—she said the twins were wearing her down—and with her hair cut short she looked so much like my father it was as if his ghost had taken her over. She told me she ran into Renee in a shoestore and Renee had been friendly enough, but when Ruth asked about Cindy and Freddie, Renee said, "I'm afraid I'm not at liberty to discuss that." Ruth pushed it and Renee put her shoes back on and left the store.

I told Ruth to keep out of it, mind her own business. It made me sweat, thinking of goddamn Renee and Ace and Sam setting family policy. *If you run into him or his family, keep your mouth shut, don't tell him anything, say you can't discuss it.*

"Just do me a favor and don't try and help me out," I said to Ruth.

She shrugged and said, "You need a lawyer, kiddo."

There was the usual mountainous dinner. I'd kicked in a good chunk of my week's pay for turkey and trimmings and a couple of bottles of Rhine wine. But I couldn't eat. It seemed to me that my family couldn't open their mouths without giving me a piece of advice I didn't want. Go to college, get a lawyer, tell Dorcas you need a raise (that was Richard's brilliant contribution), call Sam, don't you dare call Sam, get yourself a decent sweater for heaven's sake (Ruth), take your elbows off the table (Jane).

I got—as Claudia would say—hostile, and the meal ended with me barely speaking to anyone except my mother, who bustled around nervously, bringing out the pies and getting coffee. I sat there scowling, glad I took after my mother, who was quiet, who kept to herself and didn't yell and rant and ram things down your throat. Not that my mother didn't indulge in some subtle nagging of her own. She was the master of the hint, the meaningful silence, the gentle little suggestion repeated a dozen times. But my sisters were loud and bossy like my father. I remembered how mad he used to get because my mother wouldn't yell back. I never saw him hit her, but he would look at her when she disagreed with him, especially if she was right, and the corners of his mouth would draw down and his lips would purse as if something were making him sick, and he'd say, "You idiot." My mother would turn her back on him and walk away—to cry, to curse at him in peace, I never knew. But there was no question in my mind as to who had won the battle, whose way was best.

The women washed the dinner dishes and sat around the kitchen table talking and nibbling at the mince pie that was left. Rich and Vic turned on the television and watched college football, Gilbert sleeping between them on the couch. The older kids ran around outside until it got dark, and then they came in and whined and fought and the baby woke up and started screaming. I sat in my room with the door shut, playing the guitar and trying to make my mind go blank, and when everyone was gone (Ruth yelled upstairs, sarcastic, "Good-bye, Will, it's really been fun!"), I came downstairs and sat with my mother and watched *Perry Mason* and *Hazel*.

The day after Thanksgiving was sunny and almost warm, with a bright blue sky. I had the day off with pay and no claims on my time. I woke up in such a good mood that I called Jane at the hardware store and apologized for being nasty and antisocial, and then I telephoned Ruth in Albany and apologized again, and thanked her for the offer of help with college and said I'd think about it (a lie).

Then I went outside and spent the morning pulling the rotting porch steps apart. My mother's friend Mrs. Gleason had picked her up for a trip out to the shopping center in Mattydale. The house still smelled of turkey, and I was glad to be outside. I wished I had someone with me so I could say, "God, what a perfect day." I wished I had Freddie, so I could show him how to use tools as my father had shown me. The summer I was seven, Pop and I made a knickknack holder for my mother. If I concentrated, I could bring back every detail: how we cut the fancy scalloped sides with a jigsaw, and made slots for the shelves to fit into, and whittled out, by hand, a heart at the top and a hole for the nail to go through. Last of all, my father had let me stroke varnish onto the wood and then clean the brush by scrunching it up and down in a soup can full of turpentine. And when it dried, we gave it to my mother for her birthday. It was a day late— varnish dries slowly in July, my father said—and so I had to make her a card that said, at Ruth's dictation, "Surprise! Happy Belated Birthday! Your present will arrive in a couple of days, depending on weather. From your two carpenter boys." My mother hugged me and cried. She said to my father, "You spend your time on this nonsense when the roof is full of holes and the porch is falling apart," and then they had a big fight in German. But she kept the thing forever. I could walk into the living room and see it still hanging by the stairs, its three dusty shelves crowded with miniature teacups and a family of figurine cats and a tiny picture of baby Gilbert in an oval frame and two brass candelabra into which were fitted pink birthday candles.

When I finished knocking the steps apart I drove over to Jane's to get some scrap lumber Rich said I could have, and on the way back, driving down Court Street, I saw Anna Nolan.

I slowed up. She was walking with her back to me, but I knew her right away, even before she turned her head and I saw her profile. She wore a fake-fur jacket, short skirt, black tights, and a red wool hat that, as I watched, she took off and stuffed in her pocket. She shook out her hair. It was long, and the sun turned it a nice shiny brown, like a piece of furniture. She crossed the street near the dry cleaner my mother worked for. I stopped the car by the side of the street and watched her, and when she'd gotten half a block ahead of me I drove along a little farther and stopped again.

It's not difficult to follow someone. Drive a little, pull over, watch, drive on. She never looked back. She walked with her hands in her pockets, quickly, as if the route were laid out for her. Maybe it was—all the landmarks of her childhood, like a guided tour. I thought, If she became a big-time opera singer this route would become famous. She walked by Smitty's. Here she hung around after school, here's the jukebox she put dimes in. Here's where she went to school. Here's where she went to mass on Sundays. She passed St. Joseph's and turned up Park Street. Here's where a drunk punk screwed her the night she graduated. . . .

I wanted to get out of the car and talk to her, but I couldn't, after what I'd said to her on the phone. I regretted it the minute I hung up. I'd just arrived at Sumner. I was at the low point of my life. I needed a drink so badly I thought I was going to die. I'd had my first two sessions with Cross and they'd left me shaking. I don't remember what I said to Anna—this voice from my dismal past intruding on the hellish present. I do remember that I said something insulting, that at that moment I needed to be cruel to someone. Watching her walk up Park Street hill, I wanted to confront her and explain. I wanted to talk about Martha's death, about my life since, about Freddie. I wanted to revive the strange, backhanded sort of friendship that had been between us all those years.

I wanted—let me be honest—I wanted to stop the car, have her get in, drive to some quiet spot, and screw her again in the backseat of my mother's Plymouth. I wanted to bury myself in her and weep.

She turned north down Kirkpatrick Street and circled around

back down Carbon to Danforth. I kept following her, right to my mother's house, the orange helping hands in the window, the stepless porch. She didn't stop or slow down. What if I'd been out there fixing the steps when she passed? What if I'd called out, "God, what a perfect day?" Would she have crossed the street to avoid me? refused to answer? I thought: I know what I would have done if I'd seen her coming—I would have sneaked inside and hidden behind the door, holding my breath. My mother said she had stopped by once, thinking I was home. And she'd called up to get my phone number.

I parked in the driveway, got out of the car, and watched her walk away from me down the street. Her hair blew in the breeze. Her legs looked long and thin in the black tights. She used to be a little pudgy—always dieting, I remembered. She and Martha. Always laughing, the two of them. I used to call Martha on the phone and the line would be busy and when I finally got through I'd say, "Anna, I presume?" and Martha would giggle and say, "Of course."

I watched her out of sight, and it occurred to me as I stood there in the sun that she had wanted to get in touch with me for a *reason*. She'd called, stopped by that Thanksgiving morning after her grandmother died, traced me out to Sumner. Why? Could she perhaps want to talk to me as badly as I did to her? Maybe she had her own past to sort out and get rid of. In my mind, I was getting back in the car and following her, running up to her, saying "Anna, forgive me, let's talk." What I did, though, was to haul the lumber out of the car and go back to work on the porch steps.

As if Fate wanted to keep hitting me in the face with my adolescence, I ran into Johnny Tenaro a couple of weeks later. I was coming out of the pharmacy on the corner one night after dinner. I had walked down there for Christmas wrapping paper. I'd bought Freddie some stuff—mainly a big, plush puppy, plus a couple of books, a few odds and ends. I couldn't afford much. The thought of Freddie in Indiana with Cindy for Christmas, or, worse yet, in Schenectady with the whole goddamn Petraski bunch, drove me crazy. I almost did call Sam—or Rose, actually. If Sam had answered I was planning to hang up. But something told me not to, to send a gift instead. *Keep a low profile,* I said to myself. *Don't make waves.* And so I bought this huge floppy puppy and a card that said "Merry Christmas to a Big Boy" and went down to the drugstore for wrapping paper.

DUET

This guy came up to me as I walked out and said, "For Christ's sake, I don't believe it." It was dark except for the store light and the streetlamps, but under the hair and beard and moustache I could see it was Johnny Tenaro. "Willie boy," he said, and held out his hand. I shook it and we said all the usual things: good to see you, what a coincidence, you haven't changed a bit. He asked me, "What are you doing back in town?"

"I'm not here for long," I said. "Six months, maybe a year, I don't know. My wife and I are separated and I'm just trying to get a little money together and—" I shrugged, not knowing what else to say. It wasn't a story that could be told in a few words out in front of the Court Street Pharmacy.

Johnny hit me lightly on the shoulder. "So you're a single dude again."

"Yeah, I guess so. Sort of."

"Sort of single. Ha! I like that." He did a little dance step, snickering. When he moved into the light I got a good look at him. He was a short guy, handsome in a Latin-lover kind of way. His wavy hair, down to his shoulders, was black and wet-looking, and so was his beard. He wore gold-wire glasses like my father used to, and a khaki jacket designed to look like army issue. I wondered if he was high, then I thought how unfair it was to assume that every long-haired bearded guy was a junkie. The feeling crept up on me as we stood there and talked that it was truly weird that here in my old neighborhood, which I always imagined as stuck somewhere around 1954, this new Johnny could be walking around, that even the possibility of his being high could exist.

"What about you?" I asked. "What are you up to?"

"I teach at Pendleton. That private high school out in Dewitt?" I vaguely remembered crazy rumors of stuck-up, hot-to-trot girls who'd pay you to do it to them in the backseats of their fathers' Cadillacs. "I teach chemistry," Johnny said. "And I coach the soccer team." He laughed again, did his dance. "We're one and six this season. I don't know why they don't fire me. I'm a good chem teacher, but I'm a lousy coach, and let's face it—what's more important?" He slammed his fist into his palm. "Soccer! Yeah, man!"

I said, "I'm surprised they let you get away with—" I gestured. "You know. The beard and all that."

He stroked his beard, smiling, as if it were a pet. "That's why they keep me, I think. The resident hippie-peacenik type. Having me on the faculty proves they're liberals. The good guys. Not that

205

I do much, believe me. If I started organizing the kids and spreading sedition I'd be out on my ear, and my draft board would ditch my teaching deferment and ship me over before you could say Ho Chi Minh. Hey—" He quit smiling and said, "You heard about George?"

"Yeah. I was out in Indiana when it happened but my mother sent me the clipping. Poor bastard."

"I really miss old George," Johnny said. "We were best friends from the time we were little. First grade. When he went off to Yale we weren't so friendly—I mean, Christ! The stuff he was involved in. Goldwater, for Pete's sake. But we still hung around together on vacations. Then when he went to France—"

He stood in silence for a minute, looking down at his shoes, mourning George. I was never crazy about George Sullivan, personally. He was a loudmouth who liked to throw his money around. I didn't know he'd gone to France, forgotten he'd gone to Yale. I hadn't thought about him once, probably, after we graduated. But I was sorry when I heard he got killed in Vietnam. In fact, that clipping hit me hard. The only other person I'd known who died young was Martha Finch. I was sitting with Freddie on my lap when I read it, and I had to set him down and go in the bathroom and press a cold washcloth to my face. That night I went out and got drunk.

Johnny said, "It's hard to keep up these old friendships, but I've always been sorry I didn't try a little harder with George."

It had begun to snow lightly, and it was getting cold standing on the sidewalk. Johnny asked me if I wanted to go up to the Green Horseshoe for a beer. I said I wasn't drinking. He gave me an odd look, as if I'd said something clever that he didn't quite understand, and suggested a cup of coffee somewhere. In the end we walked up to my mother's.

"You're living home?" he asked, meaning *why* are you living home.

"Just until I find a place. I'm looking for a room—some kind of studio apartment, I guess." Actually, I hadn't started looking yet. I'd had to buy some clothes—God forbid Cindy should send mine. I had written and asked her to but she didn't answer. I was also helping Mom with the groceries, paying her a little rent, and then, before I knew it, it was almost Christmas. "After the first of the year," I said.

It was snowing harder, and when we walked in we scattered

wet drops in the front hall. Johnny took off his boots—heavy brown clodhoppers that had seen better days. There were holes in the toes of his socks. My mother was watching Huntley and Brinkley in the living room. Johnny said, "Hi, Mrs. Westenberg, remember me?"

I could tell she was shocked by his appearance, but she only said, "I was sorry to hear about your mother."

Johnny said, "Oh—yeah—thanks. Goddamn cancer—excuse my language, I just—"

She raised her hand. "That's all right, I understand. It's hard."

Johnny stood there, arms folded, his eyes on the television screen. A map of Vietnam appeared, and Brinkley's voice said, "Allied intelligence reports that there are signs of a move to liberate the capital city in Quang Tin province ..." Arrows zigzagged across the map.

"And how's your father?" my mother asked.

"He was all broken up," Johnny said. "He's down in Philly now, with my sister. I've been trying to get the house in shape so we can sell it. He says he never wants to go back there."

A chill went through me. When I followed Anna up Park Street past Johnny's I had been shocked by the awful familiarity of that house. The last time I saw Martha was at Johnny's New Year's Eve party, and six months later the graduation-night party was there. Johnny said, "A lot of memories in that old place," and then he looked at me, embarrassed, as if he'd made a major goof, and said, "Well. Where's this coffee I was promised?"

My mother started to get up, but we made her stay there and finish the news. I made a fresh pot, and Johnny and I sat in the kitchen waiting for it to drip through. Johnny talked about George some more—his political activities in college, his year in France, his decision to enlist. I tried to act interested. I could see Johnny was full of guilt about his old friend. Couldn't anybody die without leaving behind a crowd of guilty people? I sympathized, but I didn't want to hear about George Sullivan. What I wanted was to ask Johnny if he ever saw Anna. But I listened patiently, poured coffee and set out milk and sugar, and finally, just like the nuns used to say, my patience was rewarded. "He was a funny guy," Johnny said after a long monologue about the 1964 election. "Never got over his big crush on Anna Nolan."

"No kidding. I didn't know he—I mean, I knew they used to date, but—"

"George was crazy about her, right up to the end. He wanted to marry her when he got out of the army." Johnny sighed and finished his coffee. "Poor old George," he said, and clattered his cup into his saucer, smacked himself on the stomach and gave a little burp.

"You want another cup? I think we've got some doughnuts. Or a beer?" I didn't want him to leave until I could get him firmly onto the subject of Anna. He said, "Sure. Give me another cup. And a doughnut. Sounds good."

I poured, put the box of doughnuts on the table, got out the milk again. I tried to think of a casual way to ask my question. *Do you hear anything from Anna?* I kept remembering graduation night, how Anna had laughed about George, and then we went back to the party and Johnny made some smart remark and George Sullivan had looked at us through the screen door with the same sad look as Jesus on the cross. Not mad, even, just sad as hell. And then when Trevor broke my nose George offered to take me to the emergency room. And when I left he was crouched on the floor beside Anna. And then when Anna came over the Thanksgiving after Cindy and I were married and said, "It's been three years and five months, to the day." Something like that. Reproachfully, as if I owed her something. And I did owe her something. I'd fucked her and walked out, and she still didn't hate me. She'd called my mother to get my phone number, and she'd called me at Sumner that horrible October night . . .

Well, she hated me now. She must hate me the way I hated Cindy—worse, the way Cindy hated me, probably. But I still needed to see her. It seemed to me—this had occurred to me often since I'd come back to town—that it was on that lousy graduation night, the night I got drunk and screwed Anna and fought with Trevor and decided to leave town, that my whole life had been set into motion, and that seeing Anna would complete some kind of circle. I'd see her, talk to her, and my life would be lifted out of its rut and stretch out straight again.

"Do you ever see Anna?"

Johnny gave me that funny look, as he had when I'd said I'd stopped drinking. "Yeah. I do. In fact, I saw her a couple of months ago, in Boston. I went up and caught her act."

"What act?"

"You don't know? Hey, Willie—" He leaned across the table and punched me on the shoulder again. "I thought you kept up with things, at least a little. I didn't think you were *completely* out of it."

"You know me," I said, and we both laughed a little, but in that second it was just like high school all over again. I felt myself getting irritable. There was that same sense of being forever on the edge, forever a misfit, and in the end—what I admitted in my honest moods—not even minding it that much. But being touchy about it anyway, partly for the hell of it, partly from habit, partly because it was easier. Except for that strange period when I was going with Martha, and those few times with Anna. Standing around the jukebox at Smitty's, singing. Going to dances. Johnny's parties. "You know me, old buddy," I said. "Out of it is my middle name."

He reached out again to punch my shoulder, but this time he just gripped my upper arm and gave it a little shake. I didn't like it, that he kept doing that—the phony jock buddy-boy stuff that ex-athletes like so much. Johnny had been a basketball player in school—good, in spite of his size. He was fast, and he could jump. He was nicknamed "Mex" for a while, the Mexican jumping bean, and it evolved into "Sexy Mexy" and then was dropped. I'd been on the team my freshman year, and what I'd hated most, except for the fact that I was a lousy player who was on the bench most of the season and scored a total of six points, was all that shoulder-whacking and ass-patting and fake punching. Everybody did it to everybody, whether you hated each other or not. All the guys disliked me, and yet the few times I was sent into the game they'd whack me and pat me and say, "Atta boy, Willie," as if I were not only their best pal but the hope of the team. Crap.

"Hey," Johnny said. "I apologize. Hell, let's not start reliving high school. All the old grudges and shit. That's all we need. I didn't mean anything, Will."

I said, "Okay." From the living room came the voice of Huntley, then the voice of Brinkley, then a commercial for Alka-Seltzer, the funny one with the bride who couldn't cook. We heard my mother's little chuckle. Johnny and I looked at each other for a minute, and then I had to smile. *Ease up, Will.* I was so used to not trusting people. I said, "So tell me about her act. What is she, an opera singer?"

"No, she sings in this club. The Café Cantabile in Kenmore Square. You ever been to Boston?"

"No."

"You should go and hear her one of these weekends. Saturday nights. She's on at nine and again at eleven. Oh, man, she's terrific. You'd love it. She stands up there in this red dress and belts 'em out for all she's worth. Plus drums, bass, piano—three guys backing her up. They're really good—I mean, it's not just because she's an old friend. This is professional stuff. In fact—hey, you want to drive up this weekend? No—shit, I better not, I've got these real-estate people. Maybe next weekend we could—or hell, don't wait for me, you could go on up there yourself. It's not a big deal—five hours, straight down the Thruway to the Mass. Pike. Catch the show, have a couple of drinks—or coffee, whatever. Have a chat about old times, and drive back." He grinned. "Nothing to it. You're home in time for early mass, ha ha."

"You think she'd want to see me?"

He gave me that look again. "Are you kidding? Is the Pope Catholic? Was Attila a Hun?"

"She called me, not long before I left my wife. She caught me at a bad time. I treated her like shit on the phone."

Wasn't the first time, I expected him to say, but he spread out his hands in a who-cares gesture and said, "So catch the show, and then go backstage and apologize. Perfect opportunity."

"Maybe I will," I said, and as I spoke I knew I would, and the idea excited me so much I wanted, suddenly, for Johnny to go so I could go up in my room and play my guitar and think about it

But we ate another round of doughnuts and talked some more. Johnny told me he'd gone in with his brother to buy a cabin in the Adirondacks. He asked me if I wanted to go up there for a weekend sometime. "It's a shit hole, but it functions. Stove. Toilet, more or less. Beds." He stroked his beard. "We could take a couple of girls with us, take some grass. I could fix you up. Maybe in the spring."

I said sure, why not. What else was I going to say? *I've given up booze, and I've given up women, and I don't smoke pot either.* I said sure, sounds like a gas, and all I could think of was Anna Nolan in a red dress under a spotlight, singing to me.

2

I didn't hear from Cindy at Christmas. No card, no phone call, no response to my presents for Freddie, no communication from Sam's lawyer. It occurred to me that the Petraskis were trying to drive me crazy by ignoring me. Last I heard, in October, Ted Lombardi was going to be serving me with papers. Since then, silence. If Ruth hadn't run into Renee, if Cindy's answering machine wasn't still in operation, I would have assumed some hereditary disease had wiped out the entire clan.

Of course, I could have called Lombardi myself, or hitched back out to Richmond, or waylaid Rose when Sam wasn't around and forced information out of her. A dozen times I almost called Sam's house, assuming Cindy and Freddie were in Schenectady for the holidays, but I knew it wouldn't do any good. None of them would talk to me. On Christmas Eve I hit on the idea of driving up there and casing the place, but my mother refused to give up the car, and the more I considered it the more I decided it was a lousy plan, anyway, that would net me nothing but irritation and would possibly jeopardize my position.

So I spent my Christmas vacation without my son or any news of him. I kept thinking how, with a whole two weeks off, I could have had Freddie with me for a long visit. He could have slept in Jane's old room next door to mine, and if he was scared in a strange house I'd have taken him in with me. I'd zip him into his snowsuit, put on his boots, and take him for walks around the neighborhood. I'd show him my old school, my old hangouts. Sing about the doggie in the window and the pore yittoo yams. I'd make a snowman with him, make a fort. He could play with the Kennedy kids next door, and Jane's little girls. He could help his grandma make the Christmas pies, he'd come downstairs on

211

KITTY BURNS FLOREY

Christmas morning and see his presents under the tree, he'd sit at the table with his cousins and I'd roll up his turkey into little tubes for him . . .

Sometimes when I thought of Freddie, and Cindy, and Sam and his lawyer, and what Renee said to Ruth in the shoestore, I wanted to drive up to their house with a sawed-off shotgun and take Freddie by force—just grab him and bundle him into the car and beat it out of there, go to—shit, I don't know. Anywhere. Drive out to Richmond and pick up Claudia and head for Mexico. Or stop at Sumner and spring Gwen—Gwen had money—and take off for Canada or get on a plane for Europe or some South Sea island. I had fantasies that Cindy died, that Sam died, that some priest or social worker would talk to them and persuade them to give me back my son, that Freddie would cry and cry and nothing would make him stop but Daddy and so they'd frantically call me up and—

That was all I was good for, those idiot fantasies, those desperate plans I was never going to put into effect. Sometimes, lying awake in the middle of the night, or walking alone through the streets to make myself sleepy, I'd admit to myself that the real problem was that the Petraskis scared me. I was afraid to get Sam on the phone yelling at me, or Cindy threatening me with the loss of Freddie, or Ted Lombardi laying out a lot of legal jargon. In the end, not knowing what to do, I did what I'm best at: nothing. Eekie tookie boogoo.

I spent the vacation in a daze, working around the house and shoveling snow and taking long daytime naps. A day would go by and at the end of it I couldn't remember one thing about it. I considered giving Johnny Tenaro a call but couldn't get up the energy. He called me one night, though, and we went up to Danzer's for hot-pastrami sandwiches—his treat, when I told him frankly that I couldn't afford it. Johnny ordered a Budweiser with his. I had a ginger ale. I watched him drink the beer. I followed every drop, painfully. After a week of being a zombie on vacation, all I could think was that a beer would get my brain going and bring me back to life. Johnny saw me watching, and after he'd drunk half of it he asked me, "What's this ginger-ale shit, Will? Why no booze?"

I decided to be honest. "It was getting to be a problem."

"What kind of problem?"

"Certain people thought I was getting too dependent on it."

212

He gave me a knowing smile. There was a shard of pastrami between his front teeth. "Like your ex-wife?"

"Her especially."

He nodded, as if he had a dozen ex-wives and had been through it himself. "But she's not actually your ex yet."

"Not yet. This whole thing is pretty slow."

He was looking at me with an expression that took me a while to interpret, I was so unused to it from guys like Johnny Tenaro. It was interest, I realized finally. He wanted me to tell him about Cindy and the booze and the divorce. He wanted me to tell him my troubles! But by the time I grasped that fact, the moment had passed and Johnny had changed the subject to complain about what a dump Syracuse was. I knew it was what you were supposed to say about your hometown, but I liked the place. I had nothing against it except my bad memories.

"It's all right," I said. "It depends what you want." I thought: What do I want? My son, love, understanding, justice. Those things are as attainable here as anywhere. As unattainable. "One place is like any other," I said, looking at the inch of beer left in his glass.

Johnny laughed and drained it and said, "Oh, yeah, right. Listen, Willie. You want to see some real action, go up to Boston or down to New York one of these weekends. You'll see whether one place is like another or not."

He laughed again, as if I were an outer-space alien who had to be shown how humans have fun, and all of a sudden everything was a drag and a pain and a headache. The long, idle remainder of my vacation stretching ahead. The warm, good-smelling restaurant full of people who looked like they enjoyed living their lives. Johnny Tenaro sitting there full of beer—him and his beard and his McCarthy button and his fat paycheck from a snob school.

I tried not to give in to it. Lately, these bad moods were always on the edge of my consciousness, surprising me when they took me over, making me despair of everything—except when I was at Grace Hill. At work, there was a certain kind of peace, satisfaction, I don't know what to call it. It had something to do with the kids being so natural, so lacking in bullshit. But the rest of the time I was plagued by these black clouds, and one came to surround me at Danzer's, fogging up the evening, making me want to be out of there, away from it all, away from Johnny. What the hell was I doing, hanging around with Johnny Tenaro, letting him buy me supper, letting him pry into my life? I remembered when we were kids, eleven or twelve, Johnny Tenaro and George Sullivan used to come charging down the sidewalk on their bicycles, clanging their bells and yelling "Coming through!" Big deal—as if they were an army, or royalty, and the rest of us were peasants. Johnny hadn't changed. I didn't need his stupid advice.

I thanked him for the sandwich and said I had to get going. I didn't have time for coffee, I had to get back, I was expecting an important call. I didn't want a ride, thanks. I left him sitting there, knowing he'd pissed me off but not knowing why. In ten minutes he wouldn't care, he would have forgotten the whole thing; he'd go to the bar and pick up some girl and drink beer with her all night. I walked the six blocks home down the dark snowy streets. Even the sky looked ugly and cold, like an old piece of metal suspended over my head.

Right after Christmas, I got the papers in the mail. The divorce hearing was scheduled for the end of April. I filled out the financial statement and the rest of the crap they wanted and sent them back, and then I spent a couple of days trying to empty myself of the hopeless, scummy feeling that filling out the papers had given me. And on Saturday night, the eve of New Year's Eve, I drove up to Boston to hear Anna sing.

I went on an impulse—just begged the car from my mother, told her I'd be home late, and took off. It was another gloomy, overcast day, threatening more snow. The drive to Boston was the most boring five hours of my life. I spent it mostly twiddling the radio dial, trying to get something decent and generally failing. I spent my first hour in Boston completely lost. By the time I finally got some rational directions to Kenmore Square, it was late afternoon. I found a parking lot on Commonwealth Avenue and paid the guy the three dollars I couldn't afford to leave the car there all night. I thought I might as well be prepared. Then I set out on foot to explore the area and find out where the Café Cantabile was.

There was a booth set up by the subway entrance, with a bearded guy in a ponytail passing out antiwar information. It was bitter cold out if you were just sitting there, and I felt sorry for the guy, freezing his balls off for what he believed in. He was obviously what Johnny Tenaro was pretending to be. I went up to him and asked for directions. He pointed across the square, across a sea of traffic and people, and there it was, a wooden door and a dingy sign reading CAFÉ CANTABILE, not what I expected. He asked me where I was from, and when I told him Syracuse he started reeling off names of people at the university, antiwar honchos, asking me if I knew them.

"I'm not at the university," I told him.

"So what's keeping you out of the war, man?"

"Why?"

He handed a leaflet to a passing hippie and said to me, shrugging, "I'm a draft counselor. I'm just curious. Don't mean to pry."

I shrugged back and said, "I've got a drinking problem. I've been hospitalized for it. My draft board out in Indiana classified me 1-Y. Last resort." I remembered that I was supposed to notify them if I left town. I'd never given it a thought. I imagined Cindy calling them, telling them—what? Could Cindy be vindictive enough, or Sam powerful enough, to get me drafted?

The peace guy looked at me, impressed. "No shit," he said.

"What's the matter? You've never seen a drunk before?"

"No—hey—I mean—listen, good luck to you, buddy." He put down his stack of leaflets and held out his hand and I shook it, who knows why? We were comrades, sharers of my terrible secret.

I said, "I'm on the wagon, as a matter of fact. But don't tell my draft board."

He laughed, too heartily, and I walked away accompanied by his chuckles. I walked around the square, dodging traffic, looking in windows. Looking at women coming out of the subway station, walking fast in the cold, carrying packages. Dresses for New Year's Eve. Black satin, and sequins, and shoes with high heels. The New Year's Eve before, Cindy and I went to a party. I wasn't supposed to drink but I sneaked a couple of shots in the kitchen. At midnight I was talking to a woman named Carolyn. She was leaning against the wall in the hallway and I stood in front of her, my arm stretched out, palm against the wall behind her, our faces close. She had long, straight black hair and wore a necklace of red stones. We were talking about cars—she had just bought a Corvette, or a T-bird, I forget which. Cindy came to get me and dragged me away for the ritual midnight kiss, after which she squinted at me with that look that was supposed to be sad and disappointed but was really pure contempt, and said, "You've been drinking."

"My God," I said. "You're a genius. You should get a job as a hot-shot detective. Joe fucking Friday. Or a smell analyzer. One of those dogs that can trace people by their scent. You missed your calling, Cin."

She slapped me, not very hard or very noticeably—only a few people saw, and they pretended they didn't—and I went back to the hall and found Carolyn and hustled her upstairs to one of the bedrooms. We necked on a bed full of coats for half an hour until her date came looking for her and she had to leave. When Cindy and I got home we had one of our fast, angry sessions in bed—you couldn't call it lovemaking—and after she fell asleep I got up and sat in a chair in the living room, waiting for morning and thinking, thinking, until the sky got light and I heard Freddie stir and went to lift him down from his crib, and Cindy got up and wouldn't speak to me. And so began that wonderful year, 1967.

By the time I made my way around to the Café Cantabile it was nearly dark, but as I stood there somebody inside must have thrown a switch because, like magic, lights came on, the sign above my head was illuminated by a hundred tiny bulbs, and the glass case outside the entrance revealed a poster:

SATURDAY NIGHT
NOW APPEARING
ANNA NOLAN
&
THE DUNCAN MAGUIRE TRIO

There was a picture of Anna. She had on a low-cut dress. She was smiling, just a little. Her hair was pulled into curls on top of her head, and she wore dangling earrings. She was heavily made up. She looked beautiful and sexy. She looked like the Anna I knew and also like someone else I didn't know at all. The picture awed me, and the café, lit up, looked more impressive than it had from across the street in the dusk. My first thought was, She won't want to see me. My second was, What the hell, I'm here, what have I got to lose? I felt like I had the first time I called up Martha Finch and asked her for a date. If she had said no, things couldn't possibly get worse than they already had been.

I walked around until eight o'clock or so. I looked up Anna Nolan in a phone book in a booth, thinking I'd find out where she lived and stroll by, check it out, but there were three Anna Nolans and seven A. Nolans, and I had no idea where any of the streets were, so I gave up. I got a hamburger at a cafeteria—the Hayes-Bickford, full of hippies—and counted my money. I had left the house with thirty dollars. Dorcas gave me and Maria a Christmas bonus of ten dollars cash, something I hadn't expected. She also gave me a little box of Christmas cookies she'd made herself, and Maria gave me a coffee mug with my name on it. I was embarrassed because I hadn't thought to give either of them anything. I kissed them both on the cheek, and when I kissed Dorcas she held me by the shoulders and then kissed me, very lightly, on the lips. I kept thinking I should do something about Dorcas, but I wasn't sure what it should be, or if doing it would be wise or insane.

Anyway, I had her ten, plus the five bucks my Aunt Claire gave me for Christmas, plus money of my own I should have socked away in the bank. I'd dropped almost nine already on gas and tolls and parking. Another three for a hamburger and fries and a root beer. A quarter in the peacenik's cigar box. And two quarters for a violinist who was fiddling up a storm on a corner by the Café Cantabile, a pretty girl who must have been a student—maybe at the conservatory where Anna went. Her nose was red with the cold. She was playing some classical thing. When I tossed fifty cents into her violin case she smiled at me, and I thought: That's what I'll remember about this trip to Boston. If I don't get anywhere with Anna Nolan, I'll remember this shivering blond girl and her violin.

I got bored and tired walking around Kenmore Square. It was beginning to be as familiar as my old neighborhood at home. The First National Bank, the National Shawmut Bank (with an exhibit in the window of a tepee and tomahawks and fringed moccasins, et cetera, that I studied for a long while), a dozen restaurants and cafés and pizza joints, a movie theater showing *Belle de Jour*, crowds and cars, and, every hour, a chime somewhere bonging out the time. I went up Commonwealth Avenue past my car and came to some B.U. buildings and watched the trolleys going down the middle of the street on tracks, and when I walked down a short street I was surprised to see a river, wide and black and not frozen like the river in Richmond but choppy-looking, with an icy wind blowing off it. I walked back to the square.

The violinist was gone. There was a line at the movie theater. It had begun, very gently, to snow. People rushed by me, paying me no attention, and I didn't have a friend in town but Anna Nolan and a bearded peacenik whose hand I'd shaken. But for some reason—it was as unexpected as the onset of one of my black moods—I felt a kind of elation. I was here, in a town where no one knew me. I had moved, I had acted. I felt reckless, almost joyful. I had less than twenty dollars in my pocket. But I was here, and anything could happen.

I went back to the Café Cantabile. A young couple was going in—Harvard-looking kid, a girl in a fur coat—and I looked past them through the door. There was a guy in a tux standing by one of those pulpit things with a reservation book on it. I thought, Oh, Christ, and there I was in corduroys and desert boots, the brown crew-neck sweater Jane gave me for Christmas, my old blue duffel coat, and the start of the beard I kept growing and shaving off and growing again.

I went in and the guy gave me a look. I said, "I don't have a reservation, but—"

He interrupted me. "One?" I said yeah, and he said he had a table, and then I saw the sign saying there was a five-dollar admission fee, so I gave him five and he showed me to a corner in the back of the room with a table the size of a basketball hoop.

I ordered a rye and ginger, with the rye on the side. I'd hit on that as my solution to the oddness of going to a nightclub and ordering a soft drink. I nursed the ginger ale until the show started. The place was filling up quickly. It was a stuffy room, not very big, with dark-red walls. The tables were crowded together, each one with a lit candle. There was a stage at one end of the room and on it a drum set and a piano and a microphone on a stand. A seedy little guy played jazz on the piano, but no one seemed to be listening.

A couple of miniskirted waitresses bustled around with trays. The Café Cantabile served food, it turned out, as well as music and booze, but most people seemed to be there only to drink. The Harvardy guy and his date were at the table next to me. They started necking, and I could see their mouths open to each other and, under the table, his hand under her skirt. When the waitress leaned over and set down my drink on a little red napkin, her breasts were two inches from my nose. I felt my good mood receding a little. I was horny, and lonely, and wishing I knew someone there I could sit with. I imagined how weird I looked, alone in the corner in my sweater with my ginger ale. I would have given almost anything for a couple of sips of the whiskey, but I pushed it to the far side of the table and pretended it wasn't there.

Finally, the lights dimmed, the stage lights came up, and a fat man in a suit made of what looked like red velvet stood in the spotlight. He said, "Good evening, ladies and gentlemen. I'm Eric Silver, and I'd like to welcome you to another of our terrific Saturday nights at the Café Cantabile." There was some scattered applause which he stopped for briefly, smirking, holding up his hand. A pinky ring gleamed. He went on, "Tonight is love-song night—an album of love songs to usher in 1968. It's not quite New Year's Eve, so we don't have champagne and noisemakers and party hats for you. You'll have to come back tomorrow night for that." He paused again, and the piano player played a few bars of "Auld Lang Syne." There were a couple of cheers and whistles from the audience. Red Velvet held up his hand. "But we've got something even better for tonight, something you can really celebrate. And so without further ado let me introduce our own Anna Nolan and the Duncan Maguire Trio!"

His voice rose on the last words, which were drowned by a burst of applause. The guy at the piano began to play, and the rest of the trio came out, one with a bass fiddle and one who sat down at the drums. They chimed in, though you couldn't hear much because the applause kept going on. Then the spotlight brightened and Anna swept out onto the stage. The applause became a roar. She hugged Mr. Red Velvet, who ducked off the stage, and then she smiled and bowed at the crowd for what seemed like ten minutes before she held up her hand to stop the applause. It faded away gradually, reluctantly, and the music became audible. The band was leading into "The Man I Love," and when it was quiet, Anna began to sing—very softly but you could hear every word:

> *Someday he'll come along,*
> *The man I love . . .*

She was—I don't know what to say. She was wonderful, perfect. She was so good tears came to my eyes. I don't know what I expected. A girl in a white dress singing "O Holy Night" at the Christmas assembly. A girl smiling at me across Johnny Tenaro's rec room while we harmonized to "Moonlight Bay," or singing along with Elvis on the jukebox at Smitty's. Not this assured, dazzling woman in slinky black with a voice that began almost in a whisper, then rose and rose until it filled the room, then quieted again before it died away to wild applause. Not tears in my eyes, and not a sick ache of longing that began in my stomach, or my crotch, and rose to my throat. I tried to calm down. I said to myself that it was only a song, it was only a woman—it was only *Anna Nolan,* for Christ's sake, I'd known her since kindergarten. But I couldn't even clap. I was overwhelmed.

She said thank you, thank you, and introduced the musicians. Duncan Maguire was on bass—tall, skinny guy with glasses like Johnny Tenaro's. The others' names I didn't catch. Anna joked with them a little. They each seemed to have some characteristic the audience was familiar with. Duncan was a law student, the little guy at the piano was a vegetarian, I don't remember what-all. She began to talk about what a good year 1967 had been for her, and then she said, "As usual, on the nights we do our love-song album, we organize the music around the progress of a love affair. You're lonely, and then you meet someone, you fall in love, you're happy, and then—" She shrugged, and her smile became sad. "Something happens. Who knows? It doesn't work out. You break up. But if you're lucky you've got your memories. And so—" The music started up. She did a dance step and her black dress swirled out around her ankles. Then she threw her head back and said, "Let's move on here, from wishing he'd come along to—"

She paused, and began to sway to the music, and then she began to sing again. "Where or When." "This Can't Be Love." "Tonight." Old songs, show tunes, a couple of hits from our shared past. Her voice was stronger than I remembered it, more emotional, and everything she sang sounded absolutely true, every word seemed an expression of her own deep personal feelings. The waitress brought me another rye and ginger. Anna sang "Let It Be Me," the old Everly Brothers song, and "Love Me Tender," with a funny little Elvis imitation thrown in at one point. And then she began to sing,

> *Tonight you're mine completely,*
> *You gave your love so sweetly,*
> *Tonight the light of love is in your eyes—*
> *But will you love me tomorrow?*

It got to me, that song, and the more I thought about it the more I became sure that it had been playing the night Anna and I made love on the grass and my life began its complicated path toward Cindy and Sam and Freddie and Sumner and the place I was in at that moment—a table at the Café Cantabile in Boston where I sat alone with tears in my eyes and two shots of whiskey untouched in front of me, listening to Anna Nolan sing.

But will my heart be broken
When the night meets the morning sun?

She sang it slowly and quietly—it was different from the old Shirelles hit, more affecting, more of a blues. As she sang, I could swear she was looking straight at me, though I knew she probably couldn't see me. I was too far back, and the stage lights were too bright. But it seemed to me that she knew I was there, and that she'd dragged out those songs of our youth as a way of erasing the guilt and sadness and failures of the hard years that had passed. I was certain that, as Anna sang and I listened, she and I were both thinking the same things: what if Trevor hadn't shown up that night, what if I hadn't sneaked out of town in embarrassment and anger and disgust? Where would Anna and I be now?

So tell me now, and I won't ask again,
Will you still love me tomorrow?

This time I applauded. I got up out of my seat and clapped until my palms hurt and the necking couple turned around to look at me. I wanted Anna to see me. She looked out over the crowd with her serene, happy gaze, bowing and smiling, smoothing her hair, stretching out a hand to the three musicians. I couldn't tell if she saw me or not. I imagined going backstage between sets. She'd have a dressing room or something. I'd knock on the door, she'd say "Come in, who is it?" and I'd go in, she'd turn to me, we'd say each other's names, and those six terrible years would be gone for good. I imagined her in my arms. I imagined our lives, somehow, after all this time, intertwining.

I ordered another drink, and there were three shots of whiskey lined up on the table. I sat there in a dream, drinking my ginger ale, watching Anna and listening to her sing. I didn't know when I'd been so perfectly content—not since the pre-Sumner days, those long afternoons at home with Freddie while Cindy worked. Maybe this was even better. I knew that I'd never drink again, never desire a drink, if Anna Nolan and I could get together, if she would sing to me periodically for the rest of my life. I'd never want anything else.

She sang for forty-five minutes without an intermission. She sang "Let's Call the Whole Thing Off" and "They Can't Take That Away from Me," and talked a little about George Gershwin, whom she said she revered, and she ended with a medley of sad songs—"break-up songs," she called them. She said, "The waitresses are prepared with boxes of Kleenex for anyone who needs them," and everyone laughed. She sang, "Wish You Were Here" and "Smoke Gets in Your Eyes" and "The Party's Over" and "Yesterday" and a bunch of other songs, some of which I didn't know. But it didn't matter. She made everything sound good, everything special.

After more applause, she said, "I'd like to close with what Eric insists on calling my theme song." Everyone in the place seemed to know what it was, because they began clapping again, and whistling. Anna smiled, waiting for silence. I looked at her face, trying to connect it with the girl I had known. That crazy night in the church after Martha died when she had offered to let me make love to her. Once when she got me out of a jam with her Latin homework. Her solos at the glee-club concerts. The time Martha and I doubled with her and George Sullivan. The more I looked at her, the less she seemed like the same person. I thought of all that had happened to me in those years, and I wondered what had happened to her. I wanted to know. I wanted to know why she had kept trying to contact me. I wanted to know everything, I wanted to touch her, I wanted to sit with her for long hours and talk and talk.

This was going to be her last song. I signaled to the waitress and she started toward me across the room. Anna said, "This is a song my grandmother used to sing, an old-fashioned song that was popular around the turn of the century, from a now-forgotten opera called *The Bohemian Girl*. And you literary giants in the audience will recognize it as the song Maria sings in James Joyce's story 'Clay.'" There was more applause. The Harvard type at the next table clapped and grinned knowingly at his date. The waitress gave me the check: a dollar a drink. Anna said, "It's a song that's been special to me all my life. It means a lot to me. Maybe Eric is right, and it *is* my theme song. Then she pulled a white handkerchief from the front of her dress, waved it, and said, "But I warn you, it's very sad—a two-Kleenex number." There was laughter, and the piano started, and she began to sing:

DUET

I dreamt that I dwelt in marble halls
With vassals and serfs at my side . . .

I had a flash of memory that came to nothing. It wouldn't
connect. I had heard Anna's grandmother sing that song. I didn't
remember when, or where, but I recalled old Mrs. Nolan's loud,
incredible voice. She was like one of those big opera singers in a
comic TV skit who bursts onstage in armor, waving a sword and
singing at the top of her lungs. Mrs. Nolan was the soloist for a
while in the church choir; I remembered her voice leading "Holy
God, We Praise Thy Name" on Sundays after mass and belting
out carols at Christmas. And I remembered something else I hadn't
thought of in years—when Anna's mother died and our whole
class was at the wake, Anna was led in weeping to see her mother,
and she took one look at the coffin and turned to her grandmother crying "Mamie!" and sobbing and screaming. They had to
take her out.

I tried to think what the circumstances were when I had
heard this song, this operatic-sounding number that I associated
with that huge, booming voice. I could remember nothing except
a vague, useless suggestion of snow and cold, so I gave up and quit
thinking and just listened to Anna.

But I also dreamt which pleased me most,
That you loved me still the same,
That you loved me,
You loved me still the same . . .

It was unforgettable—even if I hadn't known Anna, even if
all the nagging memories weren't there, our shared childhood,
graduation night, Martha Finch—even without all that, her voice,
that song, in that dark and smoky little room, would have affected
me strongly. It struck me again that she must know I was in the
audience, that she had chosen those particular songs for my benefit, and that the bond between us was something real, something
almost visible in the room.

She got a standing ovation. Even the neckers at the next table
were on their feet cheering. Anna smiled and bowed and blew
kisses and mouthed thank-yous. She had a funny way of bowing:
she'd clasp her hands in front of her and swoop down, then stand
straight and spread her arms wide. Every time she did it the
cheers intensified. Eventually, she held up her hand for silence

223

and said, "I want to thank my wonderful band." She introduced the piano player and the drummer, and then she said, "And of course my partner, the incredible Duncan Maguire," and she went over to the bass player and kissed him on the lips and stood there with her arm around him while the audience clapped some more, and then the four of them disappeared offstage. The clapping stopped, chairs scraped, a couple of people left, the waitresses began to circulate.

I needed to get out of there, but I couldn't move. Duncan fucking Maguire. It was obvious that they were lovers. *Partners.* It was obvious that I wasn't going to go backstage, there wasn't going to be any happy reunion, and she sure hadn't been singing to me. Why hadn't I assumed that her life had gone on like every normal person's did? That she'd grown skin around her old wounds and the wounds were healed? What had made me think she was an alien like me, a Martian, a misfit?

The black cloud descended on the Café Cantabile, the black wings fluttered nearby. I drank off each of the three whiskies in my little row, and then I put on my duffel coat and left. Anna's last song followed me out the door and into the cold, and it was like a thin echo of what I had felt when I heard about Martha's drowning—that something precious was lost to me, and I could have prevented it if I weren't such a jerk.

3

Early in Spring, Johnny Tenaro called me up and asked if I wanted to go up to his cabin in the Adirondacks for a weekend. "Bring a girl," he said. If I couldn't get a date he'd fix me up.

I didn't want Johnny to fix me up. It would be just one more thing for him to lord it over me about. We had become friends, I suppose, though we weren't particularly close and I was hardly ever honest with him. My rudeness at Danzer's and my general lack of cordiality didn't faze Johnny. I think he barely noticed—he had so much self-confidence it never occurred to him that he could offend anyone, or that people wouldn't like him. So we'd been going out for a beer every couple of weeks. He didn't comment on the fact that I'd started drinking again. I suppose he was waiting for me to tell him voluntarily, but I never did. I didn't even know, myself, why I was back on the booze. I wasn't drinking a lot—beer in the evenings, once in a while a shot of something. If Johnny had asked me, I'd have said it helped me to sleep, and that was as much the truth as anything else.

I didn't tell him I'd made the trip to Boston, either, so he was still nagging me to go. But mostly we talked about college basketball (which he was crazy about, though I wasn't) and his new girlfriend, a senior at S.U. named Ingrid. I had met Ingrid, and she was another reason I didn't want Johnny to fix me up with a date. The date would be bound to be a friend of Ingrid's and I didn't like Ingrid much. She was good-looking, a skinny blonde, taller than Johnny, supposed to be a hot ticket, but she talked a blue streak and never let you forget she was an English major.

Dorcas and I had been carrying on our small flirtation, or whatever you want to call it, all that winter and spring. I knew she liked me, and there was a kind of comfort in knowing that, but I didn't have the heart to pursue it very far. She made me a cake on my birthday, and I took her out for a fish fry on hers (she was thirty-three). When I dropped her off at her apartment afterward, she didn't ask me in or even let me walk her to the door, but she gave me a fast kiss (not as fast as her Christmas kiss) when she got out of the car. At school, I pondered that kiss while I watched her white hands buttoning the kids into their snowsuits or turning the pages of *The Cat in the Hat*. I knew I should do something more, but every time I thought of the implications of it, of getting involved in the whole scene of sex and commitment and guilt and the awful intimacy it carried, I backed away. I went home and drank a couple of beers and masturbated and daydreamed. My latest fantasy was of being reclassified 1-A and drafted (due to some Petraski plot), and of heading for Canada with Dorcas and Freddie and the Grace Hill guitar. I looked at a map and found a town called Lynn Lake way up in the north of Manitoba. It sounded pretty, and it looked isolated. Dorcas and I would open a nursery school for the little Manitobans. Freddie would grow up in the cold and wholesome air, playing ice hockey on the lake eight months of the year and hunting moose.

I used to spend my free time lying in bed, or sitting on it strumming my guitar, making up these fantasies. I had a million of them. They were like an addiction. I'd run them through my head, elaborating on them, getting the details down, and all the time I'd be disgusted with myself, that I could do nothing *real* to ease my loneliness, that I was letting my life idle in neutral—the only life I was going to get.

When Johnny proposed going to the mountains, I surprised myself with a desire to go—somewhere, anywhere, anything to get away from my stupid daydreams and that dusty old house. My sisters' constant suggestions for improving my life. My mother's *Family Circles*—"Feed Your Family for $1 a Day!" Mrs. Gleason, who came over and talked to me about her dog peeing on the rugs. And the war news my mother was so fascinated by. She watched Huntley and Brinkley every night—soldiers slogging through rice paddies, women and children screaming, fat generals mouthing off. My mother would sit there saying how terrible it was and how she didn't know what to think, you couldn't trust anyone, was this a good war or a bad war. She wanted my opinion. I told her I didn't have one. LBJ said he wouldn't run, Bobby

Kennedy said he would, a zillion people marched in New York City, ten zillion Vietcong were killed. All it meant to me was a kind of sick, oppressed feeling. I didn't want to hear it, and I usually ended up escaping to my room with the guitar.

I had reached a point, over that long snowy Syracuse winter, where I didn't care what happened—to the country, to me, to anyone. I still wanted Freddie, but aside from that I felt, most of the time, the way I did the few times I smoked marijuana—alienated and abusive. I told Johnny I'd go to the mountains with him, and I'd get my own date.

I asked Dorcas because I had no one else to ask, and because I knew she would say yes. I thought, If I screw up with Dorcas and lost my job or whatever, the hell with it. And after months of celibacy, I'd stopped fearing that an affair with a woman would jeopardize my chances with Freddie, as long as I was discreet. What could be more discreet than a primitive cabin in the Adirondack wilderness? It wasn't exactly Quik-Stop territory. If Sam was having me watched (in my lowest anti-Petraski moments I suspected him of it), he wouldn't have me pursued all the way to the mountains.

The four of us drove north on a sunny Saturday in Johnny's little Volkswagen. It was close quarters in the backseat, and I put my arm around Dorcas. She shrank away when I did it, and she seemed nervous in general, but as we got away from the city she relaxed, and we sat there leaning against each other in a friendly silence. Ingrid and Johnny did most of the talking. They talked movies, which they called films, all the way to Utica, and then Ingrid began to talk about an idea she'd come across somewhere that if people just touched each other more the world would be a better place.

"My physics professor, for example," she said, and turned to Dorcas and me in the backseat. "You know? If I could just go up to him and put my arms around him—nothing sexual, just pure friendliness and goodwill—I think I could relax and do a lot better in that course."

Johnny said, "Yeah, Ing, and he's a dried-up old toad—right?"

"Well, actually, he's kind of cute," Ingrid said, and we all laughed. Ingrid got fake-mad, and Johnny had to pull her over to him and give her a kiss. "I'm serious, Johnny," she said. "This isn't just my idea, you know. It's a legitimate psychological theory."

"Our friends in the backseat are doing okay in the touching department, I see," Johnny said, and Dorcas blushed and moved a little away from me.

They began to talk about Columbia—the student riots, blah blah blah, what was going to happen at Syracuse, who was truly radical and who was a phony, who was passing out antiwar pencils for the Syracuse Peace Council. I didn't give a damn about a bunch of rich-kid hippie draft dodgers. I leaned back into my side of the seat and looked at Dorcas. We twisted our hands together, smiling at each other. She wore some kind of Indian shirt over a turtleneck, and long silver-and-turquoise earrings. Her lips were pink and unlipsticked, her eyelashes looked false but weren't. She smelled of something it took me a while to recognize, something that made me think of Freddie. Baby powder! I imagined her sprinkling it over herself after her bath that morning, rubbing it into her pink skin. I liked her plumpness, her double chin, the way her thighs strained against her jeans. I realized that I liked big women, and thought of Cindy's slippery skinniness with distaste.

"What's keeping you out, Will?" Ingrid asked me. They'd been talking about the draft, some friend of theirs who swallowed a wad of bubble gum before his preinduction physical hoping it would show up as an ulcer.

"I've got medical problems," I said, "I'm 1-Y."

"What's that? National emergency only?" She swiveled around to look at me. "Jesus, you look healthy."

"I am healthy," I said. I felt Dorcas's eyes on me.

"Then what—"

"Old Will is a sharp character," Johnny put in quickly. I saw him wink at me in the rearview mirror. "He pulled a Felix Krull on them at the induction center."

"My God, that's fantastic." Ingrid looked at me with admiration.

"A what?" I said.

"Felix Krull did it too, Willie," Johnny said. "In the book. *The Confessions of?* Faked an epileptic seizure to stay out of the army."

"You did that?" Dorcas said to me. I couldn't tell if she shared Ingrid's admiration or was disgusted. I appreciated Johnny's rescue, but now I had to live up to his lie.

"More or less," I said.

"And you actually got away with it?"

DUET

"It beats swallowing gum," I said.

Ingrid laughed, turned back to the front, then turned to look at me again. "I'll be damned," she said. She looked something like the Kenmore Square violinist—thin lips, thin nose, thin cheeks. She made a face, a contortion of her features that seemed to mean she found me interesting. "That's really something." I knew she'd tell people about me, draft dodgers back at S.U. *This guy looked so harmless, so sort of dull, but let me tell you what he did at his physical . . .*

When we hit the mountains, Ingrid and Dorcas kept exclaiming about how beautiful everything was, but it seemed bleak and desolate to me. The trees were still bare. In fact, this far north there was still plenty of snow on the ground, and the mountains, up close, looked forbidding, studded with black trees. We got to a town called Witherbee around three o'clock and stopped at a store to buy beer. Then we went down a couple of two-bit roads to a dirt track rutted with snow, and at the end of it, backed by woods and lonely-looking mountains, was a shack. Johnny's cabin.

We unloaded and dumped everything on the floor of the kitchen. Beyond it was a living room and stairs going up. There was some grungy-looking furniture, no rugs, no curtains. Bathroom with an ancient sink, rusty toilet with a pull chain, no tub. The place was colder inside than out, a damp, bitter cold that seemed eternal. There was a filthy fireplace with a stack of firewood next to it, and Johnny built a fire right away, but it was a long time before it made any difference.

"I was going to suggest we take a little hike up Cascade Mountain," he said. Ingrid groaned. She huddled in front of the fire in her white sweater and long wool skirt. Johnny grinned and winked at me again. "But maybe it's a little too chilly out there."

"Damn straight," Ingrid said.

Johnny passed out beers all around and dragged a portable stereo out of a locked cupboard. "This place may look like hell, but it does have a couple of modern conveniences." He put on a record and Bob Dylan's whiny tenor came wobbling into the room telling us we had to get stoned.

There was an old couch in front of the fire, and a big armchair. Johnny and Ingrid sprawled on the couch. Dorcas took the chair and I sat on the arm of it, one hand on her shoulder— awkward as hell but Dorcas filled the seat. We couldn't have fit into it together. I wasn't even sure I could survive if she sat on my lap for very long. What I imagined was being on top of her big

229

sweet body upstairs in some cold bed, the two of us warming ourselves on our own heat, on raw sex, on endless lovemaking. I kneaded her shoulder with my fingers.

Johnny reached under his sweater and pulled a plastic bag out of his shirt pocket. "Fantastic stuff," he said. "Friend of mine brought it back from Mexico, from outside Tijuana somewhere."

"How come everybody always feels they have to give you a pedigree when they drag out the grass?" I said. "Who cares where it comes from?"

Ingrid laughed and looked over at me with her how-interesting grimace, but Johnny frowned. "This happens to be, quite simply, the best there is, buddy," he said. He took out a pack of papers and began rolling. "I guarantee it's unlike anything you've ever had before. And it cost me a small fortune."

"You want us to pitch in?" I asked him, hoping he'd say no. After buying my share of the beer I was down to three dollars and change.

"Not necessary," he said, and lit up. "My treat." He took a drag and said through his teeth, "I suppose I should ask. This okay with you, Dorcas? You turn on?"

She said sure, and took it from him. When she inhaled it she threw her head back and looked into my eyes. I said, "But not in front of the kiddies—right?" and she smiled up at me. I took a drag, figuring that although I might very well develop what Claudia called hostility toward Johnny and Ingrid, I could never be hostile to Dorcas. I imagined, later, after dark, upstairs in bed, telling her I loved her.

We listened to Dylan and stoked up the fire and smoked for a while, and then Johnny decided we had to go outside and watch the sun set, so the girls bundled blankets around themselves and we went outside and down the road to a little hill where there was a better view of the range of mountains behind the cabin. We climbed it, slipping in the hard snow, Ingrid complaining all the way that she was ruining her shoes. Dorcas, I was glad to see, had sensible little boots on with her jeans. When we got to the top, Johnny rolled a couple of more joints, and we sat on the cold rocks, smoking and shivering and watching the pink sky turn red and gold and purple.

Dorcas said, "God, it's beautiful."

Johnny grinned in the fading light. "Worth freezing our asses off—right?"

DUET

It was a strange moment. I was sitting there, wrapped in a blanket with Dorcas, cold but getting warmer, and—I don't know what it was—maybe the prospect of having Dorcas in bed, or the magnificence of the sky with the black trees outlined against it. Maybe nothing more than Johnny's hot-shot Mexican grass turning everything to Technicolor, multiplying the significance of every little thing. But whatever it was, it came over me almost like a physical sensation, or a religious one, and it made me believe that there was hope. I didn't even know what I meant by that—by *hope*. I didn't mean just Freddie, that I'd be able to retrieve him—I'd never really doubted that. I meant something more general. Hope for the human race? For my own life? I can't explain it, but it was a powerful, peaceful certainty that I had been wrong all that winter not to care what happened to me, to resign myself to the awful loneliness of my bed and my guitar and my daydreaming. I watched the sun disappear behind the triangular mountains, and then I turned urgently to Dorcas. I wanted to kiss her but her eyes looked unfocused, and there were tears in them. I figured the moment, the sunset, the pot, whatever, had gotten to her too. I tightened my arm around her and whispered, "Are you glad you came?" and she nodded, smiled through her tears, and wiped her eyes on her sleeve.

Johnny and Ingrid went back down the hill. "You guys coming?" Dorcas started to get up, but I said, "We'll be right along," and they went on. "Let's sit here a minute," I said to Dorcas.

We moved from the rock to the ground in front of it and sat with our backs against the cold stone. There was snow beneath us, but the blanket gave us some protection. We sat in silence for a while, holding hands, and then I turned her face toward me and kissed her. She hesitated before she responded, but then some restraint seemed to slip from her, and she kissed me urgently, open-mouthed, and when we drew back and looked at each other she gave a little moan and put her mouth back on mine. I pressed her backward on the ground. The snow crunched beneath us. I put my hand between her soft thighs. She gave a sort of shuddering gasp and took my hand away, but she continued to kiss me, and we lay there kissing until the snow began to melt through the blanket. We sat up. The sun was gone, the sky a dark gray-blue. It was almost completely dark, but I could see her face. I whispered, "Dorcas, I want to make love to you."

She lowered her head away from me and murmured something I didn't hea·

231

I put my hand on her shoulder and said, "Is anything wrong?" She turned back to me, and in the dimness her face looked fierce and remote, even sad. I remembered the tears in her eyes when the sun set. "Dorcas? What is it?"

She shook her head. "Nothing." She stood up, shivering, and gathered up the wet blanket. "Let's get back."

"Wait." I stood beside her, put my arms around her, and forced her head down to my shoulder. I stroked her thick, tangled hair. I meant to say something about my moment of truth in the sunset, but the words that came to mind sounded false and sentimental, like part of some corny seduction scene in one of those movies where the lovers sprint in slow motion through meadows. I ended up saying nothing, just holding her tight, thinking of all the times I had almost despaired and been saved. Then I let her go, and we went back to the cabin together, holding hands.

Inside, Johnny and Ingrid were making dinner. We had brought hamburger and rolls and frozen potatoes. The burgers were sputtering in a pan and the oven was on. Johnny and Ingrid were high as kites. Bob Dylan was still whining and snarling from the other room. We ate burgers and drank beer. Johnny passed around a couple of joints after dinner, but Dorcas and I declined, and when he and Ingrid settled down on the couch in front of the fire, I led Dorcas by the hand up the stairs and into one of the bedrooms.

I drew her down to a mattress on the floor. The cabin had become warmer—not much, but warm enough so that I could take off my heavy sweater and we could huddle together under another blanket. Dorcas was reluctant. She stayed stiff and shivering, and her face was troubled. I wondered if she was a virgin—at thirty-three. I said, "We don't have to do anything. I promise we won't do anything you don't want to do," and I remembered saying those same words, years and years ago, to Martha Finch in the backseat of Art Brewer's car. We were at a drive-in—some Elvis movie. Martha had whispered back, "I want to do whatever you want to do."

I said to Dorcas, "Just lie here with me. Relax, Dorcas. Please." She curled up beside me on the mattress, and I drew her close and kissed her neck, her hair, her lips. She kissed me once, then pulled away again, and I lay back and said, "Okay. What is it? What's wrong? Please tell me."

She didn't say anything for a while, but I waited. I imagined mice in the far corners of the room, birds nesting in the dark, under the eaves outside our windows. The blanket over us smelled of long, closed-in winters. There was a transom above the door, and the hall light coming in was golden and faint. From downstairs, Dylan had given way to the *Magical Mystery Tour*. There was no more noise from Johnny and Ingrid. I pictured them screwing, quietly and efficiently, on the couch. I lay there waiting, feeling Dorcas's heat beside me, through "Strawberry Fields Forever" and "Penny Lane," and then the album started again, automatically, and still Dorcas didn't speak. Finally I said, "Dorcas?"

She stirred slightly and took a deep breath, and I realized she was crying. She said, "I went with a guy for a while, a couple of years ago. He was married. He was always going to get a divorce, but he never did. It went on and on, and nothing happened."

I pulled her close and stroked her hair, looking into the dark beyond the windows. A great calm settled over the room, a spreading satisfaction. The Beatles said that all you need is love, love is all you need. "Is that what's the matter?" I said. "I thought it was something serious."

She said, "It *is* serious," and she buried her face in my shoulder. I started to speak, but she said, "Will, I'm thirty-three years old. I like you a lot, you know I do. But I can't make love with you, I can't let myself get involved like that again with someone who's married."

She was crying. My shirt was wet. I said, "Shh, Dorcas. Don't cry. Listen. I'm not *married,* for Christ's sake. I'm separated from my wife, we're in the process of getting divorced. A couple of weeks ago I couldn't have said that, but there's a date for the hearing now, later this month. This is not bullshit, Dorcas."

She sat up and looked at me. Her face was wet with tears, her nose was red. She said, "He broke my heart."

I said, "So he was a bastard. I'm not him."

Her face crumpled up and she started to cry again. "I'm sorry," she said. "I just can't do it."

I couldn't talk her out of it. Nothing worked—persuasion, promises, explanations. Hell, I knew how determined she could be. She'd fired Gary the pothead, just like that. I'd seen her be firm with bratty little Josh when he started pushing the other kids around. I remembered her handing me the guitar, saying "Get a book." No arguments, please. She'd either turn her face to stone or smile pleasantly, it didn't matter which. She'd hold out until the bitter end, and she always won.

So finally I shut up. I was afraid that if I said anything to her it would be sarcastic. My disappointment was absolute—so intense, in fact, that I examined my motives. Was it only sex that I wanted from Dorcas? Was there any love in what I felt for her, or was it something I manufactured because I hadn't made love to a woman in six months?

"Will?" She was beautiful in the dusty light, with her hair loose around her face. "Are you mad at me?"

I said no, and took her in my arms again, stroked her hair. The Beatles went on and on. Strawberry fields, Penny Lane, and love, love, love is all you need. Then the record stopped, suddenly, as if it had been kicked. In the sudden quiet, I imagined Dorcas with her clothes off. I imagined her smooth white skin, and the way she would smell—baby powder and sweat and the sweet smell of sex. I had never wanted anything so badly. Her big soft breasts pressed against my chest, her belly against my cock. I wondered if we would lie there all night, her head on my shoulder, her breathing slow and easy, while the light behind the windows got darker and darker and I became so swollen with lust I would die of it. I leaned down and kissed her, insistently, and then I fumbled with the zipper of her jeans, murmuring her name, murmuring that I loved her, I wanted her. She moaned, and kissed me, but she fought me off, and when I managed to get my own pants unzipped and halfway down she struggled free and turned her back to me and said, "No! I won't! I can't!"

From the stairway we heard the sound of Johnny and Ingrid coming up—whispers, a scuffle, a laugh. Their shadows passed our door and went into the room across the hall. Then there was silence. Dorcas and I lay there in it, she on her side of the mattress, I on mine. No one moved. I had never heard such silence, inside and out. No wind, no night birds, no planes flying overhead, no creaks in the old house. Even Dorcas's breathing was soundless. Listening to the quiet, I was seized with the old familiar loneliness. Nothing, nothing mattered except that I get rid of it. Irrationally, I thought of those dinners at the Petraskis', the table loaded with food and the room full of noise and bickering and laughter. I leaned over and touched Dorcas on the arm. "Dorcas?"

"No!"

"Shh," I said. "All right. I'm sorry. Forget it. Just don't go to sleep. Stay up and talk to me. Come on. We'll keep our clothes on. Let's just sit here and talk. Sometimes I think if I don't have someone to talk to I'm going to go crazy. Please? Dorcas? Talk to me?"

She forgave me. I calmed down. We put on the light in our room, talking in whispers. She went downstairs to the bathroom and got into her nightgown—a long, loose granny thing that I teased her about—and she put her hair into two short pigtails. She brought two bottles of beer with her, and some Fritos, and we sat there together with the blanket tucked around us and talked. I told her all about Cindy and Freddie and Sam, about Sumner and the truth of my 1-Y, about my fantasies of our kidnapping Freddie and opening a nursery school in Lynn Lake, Manitoba. She told me about the married guy, some creep named Brian, who turned out to be a rabid Catholic who thought divorce was a sin. And she told me about somebody else she was engaged to who died in a car crash a week before the wedding. And about a Greek guy she had an affair with on her trip to Europe in 1965. And she told me about her parents in Rhode Island and her twin sister in Oregon and how she wanted to have children before it was too late and lose twenty pounds and travel to Europe again. I told her I thought I loved her but I wasn't sure. She said she felt the same way. We kissed until I couldn't stand it, and then she fell asleep with her back to me, her lovely rump curved against my hip.

I couldn't sleep. I hadn't expected to sleep. If I couldn't sleep at home, how was I going to sleep on this moldy, lumpy, bare mattress in Johnny's freezing cabin? But I didn't care. I felt eased, lightened in a way that was almost sexual. I thought about Martha Finch, and Anna Nolan, and Cindy. I thought of the ways I'd screwed up my life, and wondered if I'd come to the end of them. I kept thinking about a news clip I'd seen on Huntley and Brinkley—some Vietcong guy in a plaid shirt like the one I walked out of Sumner in, executed by having his head blown off at close range by a South Vietnamese general. My mother had turned the television off, said they shouldn't show things like that, but the image had stayed with me for months. I knew I was lucky compared to those poor slobs in Vietnam, compared to a lot of people—the blacks rioting after King was killed, the welfare families living in hotels, people like old Mr. Tenaro who was sick and widowed and kept telling Johnny he wanted to die. But sometimes I felt like that guy in the plaid shirt, as if there were a gun at my temple that might go off any minute. I wondered if Dorcas, this beautiful sleeping creature, would be my reprieve.

I lay there a long time waiting to fall asleep, but nothing happened. My eyes were wide open, my feet were ice cold, I had an erection that wouldn't go away. I needed a beer to make myself sleepy. I inched myself silently out of bed, put on my socks, and tiptoed down the stairs and into the bathroom to pee in the dark. When I came out, there was Ingrid with a flashlight.

She whispered, "Hi, Felix," and came over to me. She pointed the flashlight straight up. It turned her face into an eerie mask, the bad angel in the Baltimore Catechism. She set it down on a table and put her arms around me. She was as tall as I was. I felt her breath on my lips, and then she was kissing me, pushing me backward to the bathroom door and inside. She closed the door behind us. It was pitch dark in there, no window, no light. "What is this?" I whispered.

"You don't know?" she answered. She giggled, then knelt on the floor and lay down, holding my hand, pulling me down with her. The floor was old linoleum. "Come on," she said, and pulled at the belt of my jeans. "Hey—don't tell me you don't want this."

I said, "What about Johnny?"

"Asleep," she said. "I wore him out." She seemed to be wearing a sweat shirt and nothing else. She directed my hand between her legs. She was wet, her pubic hair was stiff with Johnny's semen, and when I touched her she closed her legs tight around my fingers. I could sense her smiling in the dark. "Count your blessings," she said. "I'm a nymphomaniac."

It took us about thirty seconds after I got inside her, and then she went down on me and sucked my cock back into action and we did it again, though this time I was nervous, afraid Johnny would get suspicious or Dorcas would wake up and come looking for me. Ingrid whispered, "Relax, baby, relax," and she kept saying, "Fuck me, fuck me, oh, Christ, fuck me hard," and when she came she cried out, a long series of sobbing gasps that, it seemed to me, were loud enough to wake that silent house. But no one stirred, and we lay there panting for a minute. Then she pushed me off her and said, "Well. Not bad for an epileptic."

We stood up. She opened the door. The flashlight on the table lit the room with a pinkish glow. Ingrid smoothed back her hair and grinned at me. Her sweat shirt had Greek letters on it. Her legs stuck out under it, white and skinny. Her eyes were gleaming in the strange light. She was still high. "People should touch more," she said. "Nothing sexual, of course."

I took her arm and said, "Ingrid, you're crazy."

"Maybe. Who cares?" She pried my fingers away. "Anyway, that was fun. Just do me a favor and don't call me or anything. Okay? I like to do it with almost complete strangers, preferably."

She picked up the flashlight, and, still breathing hard, I watched her little white ass go up the stairs. When she was gone I got myself a beer from the old Frigidaire and sat down with it on the couch. The fire had dwindled to a few red coals. I stoked them up and put on some kindling and a small log. Flames flared up. I wanted to laugh. I wanted to tell someone about it. Who was I going to tell? Johnny? Dorcas? I wished Claudia were there. Claudia would appreciate it.

I put on the Beatles again, with the volume turned way down, and listened to side two, straight through, while I drank my beer. I was warm, I was getting sleepy. I felt good. Penny Lane, strawberry fields, and all you need is love. I said to myself, "You got what you wanted, Willie," and I sat there chuckling like a maniac.

But I had enough sense to know that Ingrid's hard-used cunt in the dark on the bathroom floor wasn't what I wanted. If people got what they wanted as easily as that, the world would either be a better place or a worse one—I couldn't decide which.

I took a bus out to Richmond for the hearing. It was brief. I knew the minute I walked in the door of Room 4 at the Wayne County Courthouse that something was wrong. On one side there was Cindy (in a new short hairdo and a mannish-looking suit, refusing to look me in the eye), and with her was her team— Lombardi and a pediatrician and a child psychiatrist, all of them armed with notebooks and folders and piles of papers.

On the other side was me, teamless, paperless, all alone at my big table.

The judge was in the middle. Lombardi dragged his paunch out from behind the table and started telling the judge about some sleaze who deserted his family, who walked out on his treatment for chronic alcoholism. Who during the time he stayed home like a bum caring for his son (and boozing heavily), while his wife busted her ass bringing home the bacon, turned the kid into a virtual nut case who had trouble with reality perception, peer integration, and small motor coordination at nursery school. Who hadn't visited his son once in the six months since he'd deserted him. Who had never maintained steady employment or an independent residence and was certainly in no position to contribute to the child's support.

"Wait a minute," I said to the judge. "This is all wrong. I love my son. I'd do anything—"

Lombardi said, "Objection, Your Honor," and the judge said, "You'll have your turn, Mr. Westenberg." He put his glasses on and looked at my financial affidavit, took them off again and listened to Cindy talk about the time I hit her, the nights she had to lock me out, my affairs with Claudia and Gwen. The judge didn't like any of it. He didn't like my salary, he didn't like what Lombardi called the aimlessness of my life, he didn't like my leaving Indiana without a word to anyone. He listened patiently to what I had to say, but he didn't like me, either.

It took him hardly any time to decide that in the face of my insolvency and general irresponsibility, the sensible and just thing to do in the best interests of the child was to deny me all visitation rights for eighteen months, at the end of which time there would be another hearing, and if I could then prove myself a fit father the law would reconsider the case. And then we all stood up and the judge left, and Cindy and her team marched out stone-faced.

I sat in Room 4 through two more hearings, watching complete strangers fight over support money and mortgage payments until some lawyer asked me who I was waiting for, and I said nothing, nobody, and I left.

ANNA

REPRIEVES

1

After Duncan moved in with me, I began to find my apart-ment oppressive. Even when he wasn't there, which was often, the walls and windows and the jumble of old furniture, Duncan's books and papers, my music stacked on the piano, the tiny closet jammed with Duncan's clothes—all of it would weigh on me until my mind got as cluttered as the rooms and I had to burst out of there so I could breathe.

I walked a lot that late winter and early spring. I started walking home from work, even when it was still nearly dark at closing time. Reed, my boss, didn't like it. He'd look up from winding his plaid muffler around his neck, peer at me as if I were a misshelved book, and say, "You're not going to walk home again, are you?" When I told him yes, he always said, "It's not safe out there for a woman alone," and I always pronounced some impa-tient variation on "Oh, Reed, don't worry, the streets are full of people at five-thirty, the bad guys don't come out until later," and he would smooth down his scarf with a fatherly frown.

But I walked later, too, in the cold dark. Duncan would be at the library or the *Law Review* or the Legal Aid office, or he'd be hunched over the card table he used as a desk, his books spread out all over the place, and I'd be out in jeans and boots and the wool pea jacket I bought at Goodwill, walking the streets of Back Bay: Marlborough to Arlington to Beacon and up Beacon Hill, past the bars and antique shops on Charles Street, up the shadowy side streets, then back down past the Public Garden to Copley Square and up Exeter and home.

I was never threatened; no one noticed me at all, good guys or bad. Maybe it was the pea jacket. It was big and broad-shouldered, made of heavy wool that even the spring damps of

241

Boston couldn't penetrate. Wearing it, I felt like a longshoreman or a sailor, someone tough and masculine and invulnerable. "A woman alone," Reed called me, and it seemed, each time he said it, that a woman alone was exactly what I was, in spite of the fact that the paper slot on my mailbox now had D. MAGUIRE squeezed in beneath A. NOLAN.

As I walked, I tried to figure out why I didn't want to be home. I loved Duncan, I kept telling myself. It was logical for us to be together. I'd been feeling lonely and old and unloved, and I hadn't thought twice when, just before Christmas, he suggested moving in. "Wouldn't it be more sensible if I just lived here?" he asked one morning when we woke up together and had to make love in haste so Duncan could dash out the door to an appointment he was late for. "Everything would be so much less frantic."

"Yes!" I called to him as he ran down the stairs. "It would! Let's!"

"Right! Okay! Dig you later!" he yelled, and he showed up at nine that evening with his briefcase, two suitcases, a trunk, an armful of dry cleaning, four cartons of junk, and a duffel bag— his worldly goods, his dowry. And his living there did make everything less frantic. Was that the problem? Was it the old helpless urgency I longed for, when we had to squeeze in our sex life between my voice lessons and his work at Legal Aid? When he would race up the stairs and start undoing my buttons before he even had his coat off and tell me how he missed me, was obsessed with me all day, couldn't concentrate, thought only of this moment?

Sometimes on my walks I'd stop at my friend Alice's place on Berkeley Street if her lights were on. On cold nights, she made cocoa with a shot of whiskey in it, and we'd sit in her underheated living room wrapped in blankets, talking. She was forever having problems with Mart, and I had this nagging dissatisfaction with Duncan, so we usually ended up talking about our men. It was her opinion that Duncan was so wonderful that I didn't know what had hit me, that after some of the wackos I'd been involved with Duncan's wonderfulness was something I didn't know how to deal with, that I should be down on my knees thanking Jesus or Eros or Apollo or whatever god I happened to favor for introducing this marvel into my life.

"I don't see what your problem is, Anna," Alice said. "Of course you love him. How could anybody not love Duncan?"

"Yes, Alice," I said. "But *love* him? Commit myself to him? I'm not saying he's not a lovable guy and a terrific human being. I'm just asking myself if I want to live with him, much less settle down with him. Especially since something about his presence drives me out of the apartment. My claustrophobia is trying to tell me something."

"You need to move to a bigger place," Alice said. "Or see a shrink."

"Why is it the apartment that's the problem? Or me? Why doesn't anybody ever consider that it might be Duncan? I mean, if he's so great why aren't you in love with him? Why do you stick with Mart who just plays drums all day and smokes too much grass and won't get a regular job and never washes his hair and all the rest of the stuff you complain about?"

Alice smiled. "You know I don't mean half of it. Mart's okay. I love the little turd."

"That's what I mean, Alice. Why don't I love Duncan like that? And why should I?"

"Because he's so good for you, obviously." She was always saying that—as if Duncan were a B vitamin and I was dangerously anemic. Not that it wasn't true, in some abstract sense in which love is seen as a system of checks and balances, that he was good for me. He was energetic, I was lazy; he was ambitious, I was content to stick in ruts; he was involved with the Great World, I was inclined to withdraw from it; he was idealistic, I tended toward cynical despair. But I was always waiting for someone to say *I* was good for *him:* I was a musician, he was an appreciator; I was versatile, he was a specialist; I liked to spend the evening sitting around with people drinking beer and laughing, he was a loner who liked to work, work, work . . .

"Besides, you're nuts about each other," Alice said. "Anybody can look at the two of you onstage together Saturday nights and see that."

It was true that I loved Duncan most on those Cantabile nights. He was not a great musician; he was a hack. I knew that Mart and Wally sometimes wished we had a better bassist, but the wish remained unspoken. Duncan brought other virtues to the group; the Duncan Maguire Trio was named after him because of his dedication and his energy and his organizational skills. And there was something else about him, an intensity, some force he transmitted that inspired us and made us into a unit onstage.

Maybe it was just the look on his face when he played—confident, in love with the music, turned on by us and our abilities. Or maybe it was the knowledge that we could depend on him absolutely, that he could do with life itself what we could do only with music: take it in his hands and mold it to shape and make it do what he wanted.

Duncan was competent: that fact informed every aspect of his existence. It was the main fact about him. Everything he did was absolutely right. I don't know how to explain this. He was tall and lanky and wore clothes beautifully, and in those days, when it was the custom to look more or less scruffy, Duncan, who had been raised on extravagance, wore plaid vests and cashmere socks and pigskin driving gloves. Even during his druggy activist phase, he was always beautifully dressed; he got carried off in paddy wagons wearing not army surplus jackets and fatigue pants but pin-striped trousers with suspenders. It wasn't vanity; it was only a habit of taking certain things for granted. He wore a gold watch that had belonged to his grandfather, who had also been a lawyer for the underdog; on the back it read, in elaborate old-fashioned script, "To William Duncan Maguire from his friends, 1938." The old man's grandson, Duncan William, was born in London; he had vague memories of a nanny named Hackett and the crowds in the streets at Queen Elizabeth's coronation and his grandfather's estate south of London where the low green hills were dotted with sheep. He had come to America at the age of nine, and had had the kind of privileged childhood you'd expect for the son of a Manhattan psychiatrist (his father) and a professor of classics at Barnard (his mother). He was born with the knowledge of what fork to pick up, what shoes to wear, what word to use. He had, just possibly, never experienced an awkward or uncertain moment in his life.

Sometimes I thought of my childhood in comparison with Duncan's (St. Joseph's Catholic Academy versus Choate, Mamie versus William Duncan Maguire, Esq., summers lying on a towel in Martha Finch's backyard or hanging out at Smitty's versus summers climbing in the Rockies or bicycling through France) and marveled that we had inhabited the same planet. And maybe it's true that Rumpelmayer's and F.A.O. Schwarz and Young People's Concerts and soccer and cashmere and trips to Europe on the *QE2* build character, because when Duncan's parents and brother were wiped out in a car crash during his senior year at Harvard, he paid the unexpected but enormous family debts, got a job, and put himself through law school.

When I met him, he was a reckless participant in the wilder side of the antiwar movement, and he was involved with drugs to a degree that made me nervous—not just marijuana but mescaline and bennies and LSD and the bizarre homemade medicine-chest hallucinogens that were doing God knows what, I told him, to his brain. Shortly after we met, he gave everything up, even quit smoking pot. He got his head straight—not that he'd put it in those words; it was Mart who called it that. "You find the love of a good woman, and you get all your shit worked out," Mart said, with a mixture of admiration and disappointment, and perhaps a little resentment against me, whom he saw as the agent of change who had robbed him of his old dope-smoking buddy.

That was probably the only time anyone saw me as being good for Duncan. But in truth, Duncan's transformation from dopehead to idealist-on-the-make had nothing to do with me. In his thorough, capable way he began seeing a therapist who helped him realize that drugs were a reaction to his failure to confront the tragedy of his family's death; faced with their loss, he had degenerated into infantile behavior. Duncan appreciated the neatness of this interpretation, and he could process information and act on it quicker than anyone on earth. He saw the therapist for six weeks; that was all it took.

Part of his new personality involved working within the system. He began volunteering his time down at Legal Aid and became one of the legal advisers to a straight-arrow Harvard liberal named Jack Sparks who was running for state representative. He got a job as research assistant to a senior professor at the law school who was working on a book about the lower courts. He was on the *Law Review,* of course, and began working like a demon there. It seemed obvious to me that work was his new drug, more dangerous than any of the others because it was socially acceptable: he was admired for it, and praised as a saint.

"Marry him," Alice said. "That boy's going to be attorney general of the United States some day."

"I don't want to be married to the attorney general of the United States," I said. "I want to be married to a man who has time to sit down and talk to me, or go out for a beer, or play Scrabble."

"Honey, he can't help it that he's busy," Alice said. She got the same slightly loony look on her face that she wore when she played the violin—a spaced-out, rapturous half-smile. She took a generous pride in Duncan and me as a couple: her friend the well-known chanteuse, her friend the hot-shot lawyer who was heading straight for the attorney general's office. What a pair! "It doesn't mean he doesn't love you," she said hopefully.

But that wasn't the problem. I did believe that Duncan loved me, as an individual, slightly more than he loved humanity in the mass. And I knew his work was important. My pianist, Wally, once complained to me that his girlfriend had said, "If you really loved me you wouldn't go off and leave me to do a gig every weekend." I didn't want to be like that. Duncan had his life, I had mine. We even had a life together: the Cantabile, an occasional evening out, friends in common, chats over breakfast, sex when there was time. And the day Bobby Kennedy was shot, that June, he cried in my arms: I found myself being grateful even for that, for those few minutes when he clung to me as if I were important to him.

But there was so *little* for me. I didn't want everything. I didn't even want much. I only wanted him, just once, to ask my advice. I wanted him to move heaven and earth to spend an unscheduled evening with me. I wanted him either to help me find a bigger apartment or at least get his stuff organized so we could live less squalidly. I wanted him not to look up from his books when I spoke to him as if, for a small second, he couldn't quite recall who I was.

The worst thing was the pettiness I saw in myself. I'd walk the streets of Boston, unable to keep out of my head a dialogue with some imaginary antagonist, someone who was trying, quite reasonably, to talk me into a greater appreciation of Duncan— some Duncanesque lawyer, someone who was always right, and to whom I was forever defending myself. And my defense was so lame: he left without saying good-bye this morning, he didn't notice my new sweater, he was on the phone for two hours with Jack Sparks Tuesday night discussing school integration but he didn't say one word all through dinner.

"Doesn't it matter to you that he devotes himself to the needy and wretched?" my mental prosecutor asked. "Doesn't it matter that he's helping build a better world?"

Alice used to ask pretty much the same questions. Once I answered her, "But *I'm* needy, Alice—*I'm* wretched. And what about him? Why isn't he ever needy and wretched so I can be a

DUET

comfort to him and help him out?" She looked at me with such
exasperation that I gulped down my cocoa and left before she
could answer. I went home to Duncan, massaged the tense muscles of his shoulders, and got into bed with him to perform the
efficient erotic rituals that he had devised to bring us both the
maximum pleasure and release. And then I lay awake and thought
of Hal, who had said "I'm suffering, Anna" because he had loved
and needed me.

On my walks, I allowed myself fantasies of going to Toronto
and begging Hal to let me live and die with him an expatriate, an
outcast, a criminal. As the nights got warmer and lighter, and
tulips and daffodils came up in the Public Garden, I began to see
that these fantasies meant not that I should go to Hal but that I
should give up my commitment to Duncan. The tulips gave way
to beds of annuals—pansies and marigolds and geraniums—and I
walked and walked, and the fantasies died a natural death, and
I resolved over and over to do something about Duncan, but I
couldn't think what. I couldn't even think of a way to discuss with
him something so personal, so trivial, so irrelevant to the world's
greater miseries. And so for a long time I did nothing.

247

2

In mid-June, I was offered a singing job on a cruise ship. Mr. Galliard, who was a booking agent for Worldwide Talent in New York, caught the Cantabile act when he was passing through Boston, and called me from the Sheraton. The ship was the *Festa*, bound for the North Atlantic and the Mediterranean on a six-month hitch: from England along the west coast of France to Portugal, through the Strait of Gibraltar to Morocco and Spain, then the south of France, Greece, up the Italian coast to Venice—and back again if I wanted to sign on for another six months.

Mr. Galliard told me I'd be perfect for it. "You can sing, but you've got personality, too," he said when I went to see him. He had a suite at the Sheraton, a room with a desk and beyond it another room in which I glimpsed an enormous bed. I didn't entirely trust Mr. Galliard. He was silver-haired and dignified and quite elderly, but he kept reaching across his desk to touch my arm. Every time he did, I felt a little thrill of horror, as if this job on the *Festa* were the first step on the road to perdition that Mr. Galliard seemed to represent. Without Duncan to anchor me, would I become the kind of woman who took up with men like this? Would I reach the point where I'd loll back on the pillows of that huge bed while he wrote a check or reached into his pocket for a wad of bills? Was that what people really meant when they said Duncan was good for me?

"Well, thank you," I said.

"And looks." Mr. Galliard touched my arm. He wore a diamond pinky ring, and a diamond stickpin in his silk tie, and I had the impression of corsets beneath his blue suit, polish on his neat, ridged nails. "Those are the important things," he said. "Looks and personality. Not that I'm trying to downplay your singing

You have a very nice way with a song. Those old tunes get me here." He thumped his silk tie, below the diamond. When he smiled, a gold tooth flashed. I decided that he was just a nice, sentimental old man. As if to reinforce that, he began telling me long, meandering, old-codger stories about his travels in Europe and South America—he had grandchildren in Peru—and about the chef on the *Festa*, who had trained at the Four Seasons and who had devised a dish involving pheasant, champagne, and heavy cream that was served on the first night of every cruise. "It gives the passengers a taste of what shipboard life will be like," said Mr. Galliard. "Right at the start they see it." He leaned forward and smiled, all his gold gleaming. "Unparalleled luxury." I told him I would consider the offer seriously.

He gave me a week to decide, and on my walks I pushed Duncan to the back of my mind and began thinking about traveling. The job paid badly, but I would see the world. The world! I barely knew it was there. Duncan, in his privileged past, had traveled all over; Alice had studied in Germany for a year and then backpacked through Europe; my old roommate Laurie was married and living in Italy. Even George Sullivan had spent a year in France and came home with a terrific accent and a taste for good wines. Except for parts of New York State and Massachusetts, and, once, New Haven, where I went with Duncan when he had an interview with a law firm there, I had never traveled anywhere. The only ship I'd ever been on was the *H.M.S. Pinafore*. God! Greece and France and Portugal after three years in a shabby little Boston walk-up with a view of the Pru. The fact that six months' absence on a cruise ship might untangle my life was almost secondary.

I was about to call Mr. Galliard in New York and accept when my father was hospitalized. He hadn't been well all that spring. He'd become weaker, had lost weight, was running a fever, and the blood tests that had looked harmless back in March now indicated pancytopenia.

Jean tossed the word at me over the phone. "What in hell is that?" I asked, hating the word, resenting her expertise, her familiarity with the esoteric terminology of my father's illness.

"Both the red-blood-cell count and the white-cell count are down," she said. "They've done a bone-marrow biopsy. Dr. Malone has a specialist in, this guy Greifinger. He says we should have the results, I don't know, Monday morning, Tuesday at the latest. I can't see why it takes so long with these damn tests. They've done them a million times, you'd think they could move a little faster."

I interrupted her rambling. I could recognize panic in her voice. "Jean, just tell me what this is all about. What do they think it is?"

"Leukemia," she said.

I forgot about the cruise ship, got time off from the Cantabile, took my vacation from the bookstore earlier than I'd planned, and got on the first train home.

He was in Memorial Hospital, where I was born and had my tonsils out. My mother had died in that hospital ten years before. I hadn't been there since then, but it seemed to me that my father's room was in the same wing, on the same corridor—it could have been the same room. The walls were beige, not the sick green I recalled, but it had the right layout—windows to the left of the bed, bathroom in the far corner—and the same view of the parking lot that I had looked out on so often during that long afternoon I spent with my mother before her operation. It was winter then, and instead of a belt of green around the back edge of the lot and a blur of pink flowers in tubs, there had been dark, stark trees reaching into a white sky, a landscape of death. Now the sunny weather, the flowers and leaves, the soft air of June, made death seem absurd and impossible.

And yet there he was—my father—in the same hospital, same room, same condition: dying.

I wondered if he would notice and be oppressed by the room's similarities, but when I saw him I realized that he was too ill to notice or be oppressed by anything but his own condition.

I hadn't seen him since Christmas, when Duncan and I went to Syracuse for three days. I considered it a triumphant achievement to pry Duncan away from his work, though in order to do so I'd had to nag and threaten and throw his briefcase and his *Trusts & Estates* hornbook across the room—nothing breakable, because it had to be half a joke. I had to jolly him into it. I had to become an exaggerated parody of the shrewish mate—Lucy Ricardo, Alice Kramden, Maggie brandishing a rolling pin over the head of Jiggs. I had to tell Duncan I'd kill him, I'd murder him in his sleep, I'd bury him alive beneath a pile of law books, if he didn't take two days off and go home with me. By the time the scene was over, Duncan was chuckling, saying all right, all right already, he'd go, and I was exhausted and resentful.

But we had a wonderful Christmas. Duncan and my father got along like old pals. They even looked alike—tall, balding, and nearsighted. Jean said to me that if I married Duncan, he'd be taken for my father's son and me for the daughter-in-law. It was obvious that he charmed Jean, as he charmed all women, and that she was hoping for the marriage. When we all sang carols around the piano, the way we used to when Mamie was alive, I saw Jean and my aunts and my cousin Roseanne looking approvingly at Duncan, as if I'd brought home Santa Claus himself. Patty, too: she was hooked when, no more than ten minutes after we arrived, Duncan offered to pull her down to the drugstore on her sled to buy candy canes to hang on the tree. And when he got back he carried baby Jonathan around the house, singing "Good King Wenceslas" in his off-key baritone until Jonathan fell asleep.

My father had seemed fine at Christmas—thin, of course, and older, and tired in a way that had nothing to do with sleep. I assumed it was the children; both my father and Jean were always a little haggard. Jonathan was barely a year old and beginning to walk, and Patty, at four, was almost superhumanly energetic. But my father was his usual quiet, cheerful, serious self—a man who said everything, even "Gee, it's good to see you two," as if he'd given it a lot of careful thought. He ate more Christmas turkey than anyone; his appetite for turkey was an annual family joke. One night he even stayed up with Duncan and me drinking the Courvoisier Duncan had brought and talking about McCarthy's chances in the New Hampshire primary—my straight-living Daddy, who for years had gone to bed punctually at eleven.

Dr. Malone, our family physician who had seen my mother through her illnesses—who had, in fact, held her hand as she died—had told Jean frankly that the prognosis was lousy. "Leukemia in adults is nearly always fatal," she told me on the phone. Her voice was steady but pitched high and strained, as if she'd gotten all her crying, hours of it, out of the way before she called me.

I took a cab straight to the hospital from the train station, and went up to my father's room. They had done the biopsy the day before. He was alone, asleep. There was an oxygen hookup in one corner, a yellowish tube in the back of each hand. I sat beside the bed on the green metal chair that I would have sworn was at my mother's bedside. I looked down at my father. In the hospital gloom, he was all gray: hair, face, lips, hands. He was barely fifty,

but he looked elderly. If I hadn't recognized his reading matter
on the stand beside the bed (*Time* magazine and a worn Modern
Library edition of Chekhov's stories) I might have thought I'd
come to the wrong place.

He opened his eyes and said my name, and I took his hand.
It was hot, burning. He said, "They think I've got leukemia, Anna."
I was unable to speak, so I nodded, and concentrated as hard as
I could on not crying. He said, "If I die, will you help Jean with
the kids?"

"You know I will, I'll do anything, everything." I gave up.
Tears ran down my face. I said, "But you won't die, Daddy."

"I might." He gripped my hand tighter. I tried to take comfort from that, that he still had some strength. He said, "All I
worry about is the children. What will happen to them if I die."

"You won't die. You can fight it."

"Malone says there's not much hope. He told me that, Anna.
And Greifinger, the specialist, says the same thing. Not much
hope."

"That's not the same as no hope."

"Well." He smiled at me. It reminded me of when I was little,
when I'd beg for something and he'd give in. "He's a good man,
Greifinger. There's always hope." He let go my hand. "I'm so hot,
Anna. My head hurts. I get so short of breath." He smiled again
with his eyes shut. "I felt a lot better before they put me in here
and stuck in all these tubes."

"Go to sleep," I whispered, and sat there crying. I tried to cry
softly, but he opened his eyes again and saw me. "You're my girl,
Annie," he said. "You know that, don't you? You'll always be my
number-one girl." He winked at me and closed his eyes again, and
I left his side to go down the hall and cry in the women's room.

Jean came in a little later, and we sat with my father until
visiting hours were over. He slept most of the time while Jean and
I sat there whispering about him—going over and over what
Greifinger said, what the blood tests showed, what the biopsy
would prove, what the chances were, what Jean had read in some
magazine. In the pauses between our whispers, she closed her
eyes, and I had the feeling she was praying, though I'd never
known her to be religious. I wished I could pray, but I'd lost the
knack years ago if I'd ever had it. I ran the words through my
head: *Give us this day our daily bread, blessed art thou among women,
pray for us sinners, I believe in the Holy Ghost, the holy Catholic Church,*

the communion of saints . . . I couldn't see what any of them had to do with my father, or with Jean sitting by the bed holding his hand, or with this grim beige hospital room that smelled like pills and antiseptic. When I kissed my father's cheek before I left, my face came away wet. He lay in a pool of perspiration, the pillow was sopping with it. His fever was steady at 103 and wouldn't come down.

Jean and I drove back to the house. The children were sleeping at my aunt Gert's for the duration, and the place was strange without them or my father there—oddly smaller and shabbier, the furniture ugly, the rooms dark and uninviting. There was new wallpaper in the hall, a pattern of antique cars on red, and I wondered what on earth had prompted them to choose it. In the living room, the lid was down over the piano keys, all the music stored away in the bench.

The night was hot. We opened windows, turned on the fan. I took a shower and got into my nightgown while Jean cooked hamburgers, and we sat at the kitchen table eating. She made us each a gin and tonic, a drink I hated, but I drank it anyway. When I held the glass to my forehead to cool it, the house was so quiet I could hear the ice cubes sizzle and pop.

Jean was abstracted, frowning. She dipped her forefinger in her glass, picked up crumbs from her plate on the tip of it, put them in her mouth, wiped her fingers on a napkin.

"Jean?" I said. "This guy Greifinger is good, isn't he? He knows what he's doing?"

She shrugged. "He was recommended to us by Dr. Malone. I have no idea." Tears appeared in her eyes and ran down her face, suddenly, as if she'd pressed a switch. "It doesn't matter, anyway," she said. "It's almost hopeless, Anna. They told us that. If the biopsy is positive, everything they do for him is just a formality. Chemotherapy, drugs, whatever. They'll be able to give him, I don't know, a few more months." Tears dripped from her cheeks to the front of her blouse, dark stains on the blue material. "Maybe the summer," she said. "And then that's it."

"You can't believe that, Jean," I said. I didn't believe it, not for a second, that my father would be dead in the fall. Everything was too fast for me to make sense of it. It was like a condensed book with all the vital parts missing, the connections that explained events. How could I drink Courvoisier with my father at Christmas, joke with him on the phone two weeks ago, and today be listening to his death sentence? I could barely believe in the gray, feverish man on the bed. I didn't want to think about him.

"If Michael dies," Jean said, "I will lose my mind."

"No, you won't," I said. "And he won't die, anyway."

I spoke briskly, sensibly, reassuringly I hoped, but I didn't take in her actual words so much as the fact that she'd called my father by his name. Since their marriage, I couldn't recall her ever referring to him as anything but "your father." I didn't like this new intimacy, what looked like loss of control. Life was rolling over us, ironing out every subtlety, every nuance of my pleasant, auntish relationship with my father's family, making everything flat and ugly. In the space of a day, we had become a family in crisis. Jean and I had become partners in tragedy, gropers after the bewildering vocabulary of death. My father had become a wasted gray man in a hospital bed who had lost eighteen pounds, whose fever was a relentless 103, whose cell count was dangerously, grotesquely low. "He won't die," I said stubbornly, and wished, all of a sudden, that Duncan were there.

"I envy you your optimism," Jean said, as if in her real opinion optimism were a fault.

I wanted to tell her that I wasn't optimistic, I was just plain stunned, but I said, "I have to keep hoping, Jean. It's like those fairy tales where as long as you believe in magic the hero will be saved. If you stop for even a minute it's all over."

Tears ran down her shiny red face. I was afraid she would become hysterical and I wouldn't know what to do. Should I slap her in the face, like they did in movies? And why wasn't *I* getting hysterical? Why was I so calm? What was wrong with me? I imagined that a good case of hysterics would be like singing, a soaring release into another dimension, a heightening of reality.

Jean said, "I wish life was a fairy tale, Anna, but I'm afraid it isn't." Her voice rose to a sob, then subsided into sniffles and little moans.

I said, "Well," in my wildest tone. I tried to think what Duncan would have done. He would forgive Jean for condescending to him, he would eat his hamburger, he would read the evening paper, and then he'd go to bed and sleep eight solid hours. It occurred to me that for all his rushing around and working late and fast-talking on the phone, for all the cramped and stifling mess of our tiny apartment, Duncan's life was fanatically orderly at its core: he, Duncan, remained pretty much untouched, like the

254

silver spoon that stirs the big, aromatic simmering stew. The silver spoon could sleep at night, and take his cashmere to the cleaners, and arrive punctually for every appointment because his grand-father's watch kept perfect time.

I drank my gin and watched Jean cry, reaching over once to touch her limp hand. That reminded me of Mr. Galliard. What-ever the biopsy results showed, I could still sail in July on the *Festa*. I hardened my heart: why should I sit around there all summer watching my father waste away, watching his hair fall out from the chemotherapy, watching my stepmother lose her mind?

The kitchen, usually kept so neat by the house-proud Jean, was a shambles. The sink was full of dirty dishes, there were pans all over the stove, the floor was littered with the children's toys—plastic blocks, a carriage with a bare-bottomed doll dumped into it head first, coloring books opened to scribbles, a box of broken crayons, a box of animal crackers, two cups and a saucer from the tea set I gave Patty for Christmas.

It would have seemed tactless just to get up and start clean-ing, but I found the mess profoundly, personally depressing: looking at it, I knew I would never pack up my looks and per-sonality and my nice way with a song and sail around Europe eating pheasant cooked in champagne. In the dirty dishes and the chaos on the floor and the dying sizzle of the ice cubes in my glass, I could see my fatal inability to harness life to my needs the way Duncan did. The clincher was the promise to my father to help Jean with the children. I knew exactly what I would be doing after the ghastly biopsy results came in. I'd move in with Jean and the kids, a graying Cinderella with two hyperactive step-siblings and a stepmother who did nothing but cry. There I'd be forever, mop in hand, shrewish and pathetic, always hoping for a prince. And what prince was I going to find back home in Syracuse? Trevor Finch. Yes, perfect: I'd marry Trevor the repulsive, adopt Patty and Jonathan, and let Jean be the mad woman in my attic.

As if she saw the joyless scenario going through my head, Jean sat up straight suddenly and smoothed back her hair. She said, "Anna, my dear, forgive me. I don't mean to sit here crying all night." She pulled a pink Kleenex from the box on the table and blew her nose. "It's just going to make us both feel worse. Talk to me, Anna. Tell me about what you've been doing. Tell me about Duncan. Was he pretty broken up about Bobby Kennedy? And how's that guy Sparks doing? Is he going to get anywhere?"

I talked, and Jean hung on my words, smiling, her eyes bright: the mad woman feigning wellness. But gradually her interest became real, and we talked about Jack Sparks for a while, and about what Duncan was going to do now that he had his law degree. "I wish we could have come up for his graduation," Jean said.

"Duncan didn't go," I told her. "He said he doesn't have time for empty ceremonies. And he didn't approve of the speaker. They had Scranton. He wanted them to get McCarthy or Cesar Chavez or at least somebody like Ed Muskie."

She studied me across the table, her red-rimmed eyes narrowed. She was calmer. The small change of my life and Duncan's soothed her. But she looked terrible. Her hair needed washing, and the roots were showing. Without makeup she looked her age and more. She had put on an old bathrobe, a short faded muumuu type with big plastic buttons, the kind of thing my father hated. I knew she had a pretty one, a dainty lace-trimmed seersucker. I wondered if it seemed inappropriate at such a time, or if she was practicing for a dowdy widowhood.

She wiped at her nose again, then smiled crookedly, genuinely, and became young again. She said, "Anna, this may sound strange, but sometimes I think you aren't as fond of Duncan as the rest of us are." She poured a little more gin into each of our glasses with the air—a little studied—of settling down to a long girlish gossip. "I don't mean to pry but I can't help wondering if you two are getting along all right."

"No—I mean you're not—and we're not." My own eyes filled up. What a horrible spring this had been, what a horrible day, what a horrible life. Jean pushed the tissue box toward me. I said, "No, we're not getting along okay. He's driving me crazy."

Saying the words, I felt something flutter away from me, some pressure lift—like the way you're supposed to feel in confession, telling your sins. Was that a sin? That Duncan drove me crazy?

Jean said, "What's the trouble? Don't tell me. He's too perfect. Too dedicated to his work. Too superhuman." I stared at her. She stood up to get some more ice cubes. "He's a great guy," she said, "but I can see where he'd be hard to live with. He's so wrapped up in everything, and he does tend to go on and on, doesn't he? I mean, about this guy Sparks and McCarthy and that book he's working on with what's-his-name—the famous professor. I can see where it could be tiresome. And I don't suppose he has much time left over for personal relationships."

She was struggling with the ice-cube tray, banging it on the sink, running water on it. Had I heard her right? Was she saying these things? It was as if I'd just been declared sane. At the same time, I had a brief, contrary, dutiful impulse to defend Duncan, to floor Jean with the arguments of my mental prosecutor—my better self.

Jean dropped an ice cube into my glass, and then she began picking up the blocks on the floor. She dumped them into the carriage and wheeled it into a corner, out of the way. I looked again around the kitchen, at the mess of daily life that was scattered there, and my vision of myself as Cinderella with a mop was transfigured. There was a halo around it, like the holy glow on the pictures of saints that the nuns used to give us for good conduct. Yes, surely that was as useful a path: to sacrifice your life, if necessary, for the people you love instead of for faceless humanity.

The urge to defend Duncan passed. I took a drink of my fresh gin and tonic; it was evil-tasting, bitter, with a medicinal stink, but it was cold and strong. Jean gave up on the kitchen and sat down again across from me. "Tell me," she said. "Is he as tough to live with as I think he is?"

When I said yes, he was, he was impossible, my voice came out so fiercely it surprised me, but Jean nodded sympathetically. "God—*men,*" she said. "You know?"

I saw this enigmatic remark for what it was, not a cheap and undeserved reproach to my wasted, feverish father but a comment designed to encourage me, to show sympathy for my uncommitted generation and our troubled relationships, to demonstrate the solidarity of all women, whether they be hooked up with bad men or good. I appreciated this.

"Sometimes I hate him," I said. I noticed that I was getting drunk, and I didn't care. I drank more gin. "Every time he ignores me I hate him. Every time he doesn't answer me because he doesn't hear what I said because he's thinking about something more important. I hate him, and then I feel like such a shit because he's so good. He's a saint, Jean. That's a true fact, and everyone knows it. I don't deserve him."

"If that's the way he treats you, you deserve better," Jean said.

"I don't know about that, but—oh, God, Jean, you know, there was no question of his coming down here with me. He didn't even try to get away. I know he's busy, the bar exam is next month, but he didn't even ask me to call him when I got here to tell him what was going on. He just kissed me good-bye and said he hoped Daddy would be okay, he said treatment for cancer has made tremendous strides, he—oh, I don't know. It was all so inadequate, I thought. And then I wouldn't let myself think it. You know?"

My voice slid into a drunken whine. I didn't tell Jean that when I was going out the door he had embraced me, kissed my neck, slid his hand up under my T-shirt, told me he'd miss me, and I had said, "For Christ's *sake*, Duncan," and run out the door. "I should probably call him," I said. "But he wouldn't be home."

Jean sat there frowning, arms folded across her chest. The tear stains on her blouse were drying. I saw that this was good for her, my little complaints a happy distraction from her own larger ones, my trivial tears balm for her anguish. We'd crucify one man to divert us from the fate of another.

Jean said, "It sounds pretty bad, Anna."

"I can't stay in the apartment, I get so restless," I said. "I walk. All the time, all hours, I'm out walking the streets, thinking until my head aches, trying to talk myself into this relationship." As I spoke I wondered why I let it go on if it was as bad as I described it. Was I exaggerating? I felt fuddled, and for a minute I could only recall Duncan as he was on the stage of the Cantabile, draped over his bass, lovable, smiling at me. I pushed on, into Jean's flattering sympathy. I said, "Maybe it's just that I didn't know it would be such a big deal to live with someone—such a commitment. I didn't know I'd have such a hard time handling it."

"It's obviously not commitment that's bothering you. It's commitment to Duncan."

"I'm not so sure," I told her, and that made me start to cry again. "I'm not really good at committing myself to anyone, I don't think. Sometimes I see myself alone forever, Jean. I see Duncan as some kind of test. If I can't make this work I'm not going to want to chance it another time."

"Oh, nonsense," Jean said. "At your age."

I blew my nose again, trying to feel young and carefree, with my whole life ahead of me, but the tears wouldn't stop, and I cried and pulled tissues while Jean took her turn at patting my hand. After a minute, she said, "Hush, Anna, stop that for a minute, listen to me."

DUET

I quit crying, feeling foolish and self-centered. "Oh, I'm sorry, I'm sorry, I hate weepy women," I said. "I hate women who snivel and cry because their men make them miserable. All this boo-hoo, oh-poor-me stuff." That was what Mamie used to say. "Boo-hoo, oh, poor me, oh, dear, oh, dear"—in her sarcastic voice when she knew I'd been crying in my room. And then she'd say, "Come here to your old grandma now, and give me a hug. It can't be that bad."

Jean said, "Nonsense. People need to cry. If men did it more they'd be easier to get along with."

I wiped my eyes. "I don't think it's that simple." The day after Duncan had wept in my arms over Bobby Kennedy he barely spoke to me, he was so embarrassed.

Jean said, "Well, anyway, I'm having a major insight." She smiled. "Really. Listen to me. I know you think of yourself as a drifter, a sort of semihippie, a Bohemian. But I don't see you living that way for long. You're going to find some nice man and settle down and have a wonderful family, a wonderful life. It doesn't look like it will be Duncan. It'll probably be some terrific guy you don't even know exists yet. But I see it happening, honey."

I smiled at her from behind my tissue. I didn't know how to answer. I didn't even know if I wanted what we both foresaw for me: each our own version of mop, prince, halo. But it comforted her to say it, and it cheered me up to hear it said with such conviction.

"Meanwhile, keep walking," Jean said, getting up to add our dishes to the precarious pile in the sink. "Until you decide what you want to do. At least you're probably losing weight."

"But I'm not," I told her. "I'm always stopping for ice cream at Brigham's or a bagel someplace or a drink at Alice's. I'm always hungry lately, always eating."

"He's starving you," Jean said. "Emotionally. If you'll pardon the *Ladies' Home Journal* psychotherapy."

We went through the silent house to the stairs. Jean turned out lights, I picked up a magazine to read in bed. "I'm not tired," I said. "I'm so hopped up by our talk. I can't tell you how grateful I am to you for not yelling at me and telling me to count my blessings."

"That's good, Anna," she said.

I turned to look at her because her answer was so slow in coming, her voice so odd, and saw that her face was stricken. She was staring at the little three-legged table next to the wing chair in

259

the living room. On the table were a library book—I couldn't see the title—and a pair of glasses folded up: my father's spare reading glasses. I imagined her thinking, He'll never sit there again, never put those glasses on, never again read the Russian novels that he loved. I remembered why I was there with her, in that house. I remembered my gray father lying in a pool of sweat.

"Jean?"

She sat down, heavily, in the wing chair and stretched her arms out along its arms. She looked up at me and smiled wanly. "You go up, Anna. I'll stay down here awhile."

"I don't like to leave you alone."

"I'm all right. I'm just not ready to sleep yet."

I stood before her clutching my magazine. I said, "You know it's not going to happen, Jean. Don't you? He's going to be all right. This whole thing is unreal. He's going to come through it."

She closed her eyes. "We'll see, Annie. You go on up to bed now." I felt about thirteen, naïve and silly, but I was sure that what I said was true, and I wanted to convince her. My vision of Cinderella the martyr, Jean the madwoman, the ennobling sacrifice I would make—it was all crap. People must have a sense of these things, I thought—an intuition for disaster. Somewhere inside you *know* when it's going to strike, and I knew it wouldn't. I couldn't see why Jean didn't know it, too.

"You have to have faith, Jean," I said. She didn't answer. I stood there a while longer, looking at her, but her eyes stayed shut, and I couldn't think of anything else to say except good-night.

"Good-night," she said. "Sleep well."

I went upstairs reluctantly to my old attic room. One end of it was used for storage now, neatly stacked with cartons labeled in Jean's neat printing—BABY CLOTHES, BOOKS, ODD DISHES, KNITTING PATTERNS—but my bed was there with its blue spread, and a bookcase full of my books, and all my old junk in the closet under the eaves. I got into bed and lay awake with my magazine, listening for Jean to come up, but there wasn't a sound in the house. She was sitting down there in silence, either with tears rolling down her cheeks or dry-eyed in anguish, thinking of my father's reading glasses and Dr. Greifinger saying "not much hope" and her two fatherless children. And this was what she foretold for me, this connection and dependence and wifely love, this kind of desperate falling apart when it was threatened. And eventually I fell into a drunken sleep, wishing, yes, for just that.

3

The biopsy confirmed the low cell count, but Dr. Greifinger also found granulomas in the marrow: cells being produced to combat not leukemia but tuberculosis—miliary tuberculosis, a rare form that affects the bone marrow rather than going directly to the lungs. That was what was wrong with my father. It wasn't leukemia. It wasn't even very serious.

He told us all this on a sunny Tuesday morning, in his office at the hospital. They had already started my father on antibiotics. He'd have to take them for a year or more, but he would be out of the hospital in ten days and back at school in September. Jean and the children might be carrying a low-grade form of TB and would have to be skin-tested. Dr. Greifinger explained to Jean the three antibiotics he'd prescribed: pills for isoniazid and ethambutol, and streptomycin to be given by injection every day. The nurse would show her how to do it.

Jean cried all through this, and when he was done she got up to hug him. Dr. Greifinger patted her back, looking pleased, winking at me over her shoulder. "There, there," he said. "You've been through the wringer, haven't you?"

"I knew it all along," I said.

His eyes twinkled at me. "You knew it would turn out to be miliary tuberculosis? I'll have to get you on my staff, young lady. That's a pretty sophisticated guess."

"I knew he'd be okay. Didn't I tell you, Jean?"

She came over to hug me, still crying, and then we went up to the sixth floor to see my father, who already looked better. The fever wasn't gone but it was down, and he was drinking orange juice through a bendable straw.

"Anna knew all along," Jean said to him. She told the nurses

261

that when they came in, and my various aunts and uncles and her brother Don and his wife when they arrived to rejoice with us. I was hugged and kissed by relatives who, I knew for a fact, disapproved of what they considered my sinful Boston life, and I saw myself being transmuted from renegade to heroine, a legend in the family: Anna, who could foretell the future, whose faith could move mountains, whose mere presence was a lucky charm against illness and death.

I talked to Duncan a couple of times on the phone. When I told him I'd known all along, he said, "Hey, if you can foretell the future, what do you think Jack's chances are?" He phoned my father at the hospital to congratulate him on his reprieve, and they talked about Bobby Kennedy's assassination, the riots, the escalation of the war—a depressing conversation that perked my father up noticeably.

When he hung up, he said to me, "I like that young man more and more, Anna," and I said, "I admit it was nice of him to call." My father gave me a look but didn't say anything except would I fluff up his pillows.

In the hospital, my father became uncharacteristically sociable, perhaps as a reaction to his miraculous return to life. Sometimes he was another personality entirely, a funnyman, a card, a master of the comic insult, the off-color innuendo, the well-placed bit of foul language. When he introduced me to people as "my little girl—isn't she something?" he sounded exactly like Eric Silver.

He had an ongoing routine of ribald jokes with the nurses, and he got into long debates about Nixon with his roommate, Ed Kreiger, who was recovering from surgery on his foot. Sometimes I could hear them from down the hall as I approached the room, my father shouting, "He's a nothing, a nobody! Just a little jerk who wants power!" Ed's voice would break in. "He's what this country needs right now, Mike," and my father would say, "Bull*shit*! When it comes to politics, you don't know your ass from a hole in the ground."

In the evenings Jean sat with him drinking gin and tonic, watching *The Prisoner* and *Gunsmoke* on television, and joining in the arguments and the jokes. The nurses would peek into the room and giggle, as if Mike and Ed were naughty, high-spirited little boys let loose after a bout with measles. Dr. Malone said it was good for my father, even the shouting, even the foul language.

My father said to Ed, "You and that goddamn Nixon brought my fever down."

I was in no hurry to get back to Boston. More and more, as my father's health improved—so rapidly and steadily that the gray, wasted man who asked me to look after his children seemed like a figure in a nightmare—his reprieve seemed a mysterious example of divine intervention, a genuine miracle, as if God really had reached out from his celestial aloofness and gently, enigmatically, purposefully touched—not my father but myself. It seemed to me that I had been drawn away from Boston and Duncan and Mr. Galliard for a purpose. It was like a mystery novel, in which every element of the plot, no matter how trivial—every spilled martini, every misplaced cushion, every case of the flu—exists for the purpose of leading to Lord Castlethwaite's discovering his wife in bed with the chauffeur and pounding them both to death with a tire iron. I kept thinking that if there was no larger purpose in my father's escape, then the whole episode was nothing but an absurdity, a joke, a divine comedy.

I found it hard to believe that God had that kind of a sense of humor, and so I hung around with a half-hopeful, half-abashed feeling that something was going to happen. Jean was finishing up the school year, and I took care of the children after dinner while she did end-of-the-year paperwork and then went up to see my father. I liked the nighttime routine, bathing Patty and Jonathan and tucking them into bed. They were tired then, and less boisterous, their clean little bodies relaxed and smelling sweetly of soap. Jonathan always went instantly to sleep, but I used to read fairy tales to Patty until her head drooped and her eyes closed, and I would ease her down onto the pillow, pull up the sheet, and kiss her cheek. At times like that I felt such tenderness for those children, such painful love, that I'd think maybe I should marry Duncan after all, have some children, and settle into Jean's vision of my future. Then I'd go sit in front of the television and hope that when the phone rang it would be not Duncan calling but Fate.

I realized on Saturday that I missed my walks, and after lunch I dumped the kids next door at Mrs. Neal's and set out for my old neighborhood on the north side—a longish haul that I felt vaguely possessive and superstitious about. I walked it every time I was home. At Christmas I had talked Duncan out of coming with me and walked there alone in a small blizzard, arriving home freezing and exhausted but pleased, as if I'd fulfilled some ancient promise to myself.

That June day, though, was sunny, perfect, not too hot. I walked slowly, enjoying my freedom and the feeling of rightness I always had in my hometown—that things here were as they should be, that here I was safe and protected, that this was the real world and everything else was through the looking glass.

I walked down Court Street to Smitty's, past my old house, past the pizza places and the Oz Boutique and the drugstore with its black marble front that had been there since before I was born. I intended to avoid the block of Danforth Street where the Westenbergs lived. In a note Johnny Tenaro had sent me that spring, he mentioned that Will was staying at his mother's house. He didn't mention Will's wife, or say why Will was in town. "You might be interested to hear that good old Will W. is living here at his mother's place temporarily." I read that sentence over and over, and in the months since, it had drifted in and out of my head like a song. He was there. Why? How long? Was he there at Thanksgiving when I walked by? At Christmas when I struggled down the street in the snow? Was he looking out a window at me as I passed, hiding so he wouldn't have to speak to me? Afraid I'd come looking for him, to force my way into his life?

At the thought of never seeing him again, I felt a sick emptiness, a sort of horror—something, I realized, like what I felt when Jean first called to tell me my father was sick, a feeling of loss as dire as death. And yet I sincerely hoped, with all my soul, that I would never see him again.

Why I walked by his house, then, I couldn't say. I did it automatically, because I always did it when I was in town on my ritual walks around the old neighborhood. I did it without thinking, without analyzing. If I had been honest, I would have admitted to myself the degrading truth, which was that I did it because no matter how sincerely I never wanted to see him again, I wanted to see him, wanted him, more than anything. I walked by his house because no humiliation or hopelessness could have prevented me if there was the chance of a glimpse of him, a word.

His mother was on the porch, washing windows. If I had seen her from up the street, I would have turned back. Would I have? I can't say. But I didn't see her until I was almost opposite, and then I stopped because she saw me and called out, "Well, hello there," and put down her bottle of Windex and waved.

I hesitated. "Anna Nolan," she said, smiling, and came toward me down the walk. She wore a flowered housedress with an apron over it. "Excuse my appearance," she said, and we shook hands. "We're finally getting a little work done here, now that we're going to sell it."

We. Who is we? She had Will's face, older and softer and more—what? More contented. *Where is he?* "You're moving?" I asked.

"I'm going down to Albany with my daughter. Ruth. I hate to sell it. I've lived here since I was married. Thirty-four years. But—" She shrugged, and looked back at the porch. "I think it looks pretty good. I think it will sell fast."

The place did look better with a new coat of paint—green, with white trim. The porch steps had been fixed. Yellow marigolds scraggled along the walk. "It looks great," I said. "Good luck with it."

She asked after the family, and I told her about my father's illness. "It was a miracle," I said. "They were so sure it was cancer, and it was nothing. It was this piddling little thing you can take pills for." It still made me supremely happy to tell people this, and I could see it made them happy to hear it, as if my father's reprieve somehow contained their own.

Will's mother crossed herself and said, "Thank God." Then there was a pause that seemed to last an hour but was probably three seconds, during which I tried out a dozen ways to ask, *What about Will? Is Will here? Didn't I hear Will was home?* But I just stood there, smiling vaguely at the fresh paint, the flowers, until divine intervention prompted his mother and she said, "Go say hello to Will, why don't you? He's out back painting the garage."

How could I have gone? But I did go. How could I not? I went around the side of the house to the back, and there he was, in jeans and a ripped undershirt. He had a beard, longer hair. He was on a short stepladder. Paintbrush, green paint, smell of latex, bright sun on his hair. He turned and saw me and looked confused, then pleased, then embarrassed.

Mrs. Westenberg was right behind me, like an honor guard. She said, "Will, here's Anna Nolan, come to say hello."

"I was just passing," I said quickly. "I'm in kind of a rush, I'm on my way home, actually, but—" I gave up, I went toward him over the grass. I said, "Hello, Will."

He descended the ladder, put down his paintbrush, wiped

his hands along the sides of his jeans. He gave my hand half a shake—a European gesture, like his mother's—and dropped it quickly. We stood looking at each other. He was smiling. I had forgotten his shy smile, remembered his small white crooked teeth and his full underlip, forgotten what his speaking voice sounded like. "It's good to see you, Anna," he said. "You look great."

My hair was all over the place, I was sweating, I had on a miniskirt that showed off my fat legs. I doubted I looked great. I said, "Thanks. So do you. You haven't changed a bit."

"Ach! That beard!" his mother said.

"I like it," I said shyly, and Will's smile widened. He touched his beard.

"It feels good," he said. "Feels right, for some reason."

"The spirit of the times," I said.

"Yeah—something like that."

"Hippie," his mother said.

Will and I snickered, and then a silence fell during which I tried madly to think of something to say, half-expecting him to mutter, "Well, it was nice seeing you, Anna," and return to his paintbrush and ladder. All I could think of saying to him was, *I've waited years for this moment.* All I could think of doing was flinging myself into his arms.

"How about a glass of iced tea?" his mother asked, looking from me to Will and back, her hands clasped at her bosom, as if to get me a glass of iced tea was her dearest wish. "Or a beer? Such a hot day."

Will said, "I could use a beer. Can you stay for a while, Anna?"

My knees were shaking. I said I could. Mrs. Westenberg went inside and Will and I sat down on lawn chairs under a tree. I looked at his tanned arms, the golden hair that grew on them, his slender fingers. No wedding ring. Not that that meant anything. Holes in his T-shirt. His smooth chest, white, untanned. His short, neat beard. His small ears. On my own hand, in the web between thumb and forefinger, he had left a crescent of green paint, like a new leaf.

"So," he said. "Anna." I looked at his face, and he blushed—the rose-pink bloom, high on his cheeks, that I remembered. He said, "I just want to say—that time you called me—" He shook his head, frowning, and stopped. I was probably supposed to say something, but I couldn't speak. *Stay out of my life. Fuck off.* I had cried all night, drunk half a bottle of whiskey, considered walking over the B.U. bridge and leaping into the cold black river. "I want you to know I'm sorry," Will said. "You got me at a bad time. My life was falling apart. I was in terrible shape. I can't believe I was such a shit. I felt so bad afterward. I really wanted to talk to you."

I inhaled, unsteadily, and tried out a careless laugh. "It's okay. I've had days like that."

He said, as if I hadn't spoken, "After you called I really began to miss you. I began to want to see you more than anything. I thought I'd go crazy if I didn't see you and apologize. Talk to you."

I stared at the pink flush on his cheeks, his brown eyes that darted toward me then away. I wondered if what he said was true, or if it was merely exaggerated courtesy, part of the apology.

I said, "Where's your wife?"

"We're divorced."

"I'm sorry."

We were silent again. Our words lingered rhythmically in the warm air, like a bit of opera. I said, "After that phone call, I wanted to die."

"Oh, God, Anna." He put his head in his hands and rubbed his forehead as if it ached. "You know I'd never do anything to hurt you."

The sun was shining all around us, breaking here and there through the leaves in spots of brilliance. There was the smell of paint, a cat asleep in the driveway next door, red roses on a trellis. Under the tree Will was bright, golden, an angel of light in the cool green shade, more beautiful even than my memory of him. He said he'd missed me, he wanted to see me. He was divorced. How wonderful the world was, how full of good things.

"No," I said. "I didn't know that."

"Well, it's true."

"Why didn't you call back?" I asked him, hating the way it sounded: the aggrieved woman. You done me wrong. "Why didn't you write? In all this time, Will?"

He raised his head. "My life," he said. "My life has been hell."

My eyes filled with tears. "I'm so sorry," I said, and then, I couldn't help it, I said, "Oh, Will, I'm so happy to see you, you can't imagine."

"No," he said. I saw him look quickly at my legs and at my breasts, then at my face. "You're right. I can't imagine. I can't believe you'd ever want to see me again."

"I've wanted that for years," I said. "Just to see you."

A loaded silence settled between us. A power mower started up somewhere, a bird said *Scree!* Will lifted his hand from the arm of his chair and held it toward me. I clasped it. His hand was warm, a little sweaty, and his fingers tightened urgently around mine. Desire for him overwhelmed me, and I remembered one of the cool, sophisticated, devastating remarks I used to say over and over to myself and write in my diary and practice saying to Will: *I get more of a thrill out of holding hands with you for one minute than from screwing all night with somebody else.*

He turned his hand in mine, and his fingers caressed the inside of my wrist. He whispered, "Anna."

We sat there like that, holding hands, looking at each other, until Mrs. Westenberg came out with a tray: brown bottles, glasses, a box of potato chips. "Well!" she said, and beamed at us. "Isn't it nice when old friends get together again?"

He picked me up at six-thirty. We were going to drive up to the Adirondacks, to a cabin that belonged to Johnny Tenaro. Jean was at the hospital with my father, the kids were at my aunt's. I stuck a toothbrush and a change of underwear in my purse, and I put on white slacks and borrowed a red sweater from Jean; it would be cool in the mountains.

He was driving an old Plymouth, his mother's car. All the way up Route 8 he talked about the car's quirks, and I talked about my father's illness, and we discussed people we used to know and what they were doing now. He told me about his sisters, who they married, their kids. I tried to think of funny stories about Patty and Jonathan. We talked about everything but the oddity of our being there in that car together after all those years. I didn't tell him my theory of the divine hand that had contrived the infinite number of events that had to occur to make it possible: My father had to get sick, then get well; it had to be Jean's afternoon at the hospital; Will had to be home painting the garage, not out getting the car greased or shopping for groceries; his mother had to be in the front yard, she had to recognize me, I had to be passing the house at exactly that moment . . .

Around Pottersville we ran out of small talk. Out the window, the sky was darkening ahead; inside the car, the light was rosy-gold from the sunset sky behind us. I kept wondering what he thought of me—did he think I was a whore, a slut, to agree without thinking twice to spend the weekend with him? But he had said he missed me, he wanted to talk to me. He had held my hand.

It was strange to be there with him, and yet familiar, like a movie seen a million times coming suddenly to life. I sneaked a look at him from the corner of my eye—as if years were erased and I was in Latin class again, lusting after Will across the aisle, watching his hands fiddle with his pen, the dog-eared corner of *Third Year Latin,* the wire spiral of his notebook. Wishing they would fiddle with me.

Now I watched his hands on the wheel. They hadn't changed. The thin, sensitive fingers. His skinny wrist with its prominent bone. He had green paint under one thumbnail. Between my own fingers I still wore the green streak of paint he'd left there. In the shower I had shielded it, amused at myself, remembering my uncle Phil's handshake with JFK—this sacred hand.

The light in the car became less rosy, more brown, dimmed. Will asked me to get him a beer. There was a grocery bag in the backseat, with eggs and bread and coffee and potato chips and six-packs in it. There was a church key in the glove compartment. When I handed the can to Will, his face in the sepia gloom was indistinct, and for a moment he seemed a stranger, a phantom, the invisible man I'd been pursuing all these years, and that image seemed more fitting than this mad reality: me at his side in a speeding car, driving through the mountains toward our destinies.

Then he glanced at me and I saw his crooked teeth, his small smile, and he became Will, the solid blond Will I had held in my arms that long-ago June night—seven years ago almost to the day—and I became weak with desire again, and with the need to hide it, not to scare him away, not to make a lovesick idiot of myself. I smiled stiffly back at him. He drank from the beer and tucked the can between his thighs. "Hey," he said. "How about a little music?" He turned on the radio and I fiddled with the knob, finding mostly static until the sudden bray of a disk jockey burst through loud and clear, telling all of us cats and chicks about a record hop at a high school in Glens Falls that night, admission free for every gal in a miniskirt. Then, cutting into his words, music: "Mrs. Robinson."

"Ah," Will said, and he began to hum, then to sing. I joined in and we sang it through, drowning out Simon and Garfunkel,

269

looking at each other in embarrassed delight, Will beating time on
his knee. His voice sounded exactly as it had years ago at parties
in Johnny Tenaro's basement—strong and steady and unfailingly
on pitch. We ended up in harmony and broke into laughter.

"You're so *good*," I said.

He laughed. "Well, hey. So are you." Something by Step-
penwolf came on, and Will made a face and turned the radio
down. "I don't like much of this new stuff. There's a place I used
to go in Richmond where they had all the oldies on the jukebox.
God. The Drifters. Dion and the Belmonts. The Shirelles."

"They don't write 'em like that anymore. Right?"

He grinned over at me. "Damn right. Hey, Anna. Remember
how we used to sing?"

"Every note," I told him. And then I said, "I remember everything, Will. Every word you ever spoke to me. I've thought
about you all the time, all these years. I never stopped missing
you." He reached for my hand, and I pressed my lips to his palm,
then held it to my cheek. I said, "Tell me what you've been doing.
Why your life has been hell."

He said, "Well," and paused. He took his hand back, raised
the beer can to his lips and drank from it once, twice, put it back
between his legs and wiped his mouth on the back of his hand.
"Please," I said. "Tell me, Will." And then he took a breath and
started in, fast, as if he were afraid he'd lose his nerve.

He told me about his wife, whom he had gotten involved with
out of loneliness and who tricked him into marriage, and about
his remarkable little boy who was taken from him. He told me
about his drinking problem, the hospital they'd put him in, his
crazy escape from it, his job at the nursery school. Every once
in a while he'd turn to me and say, "Is this boring you?" or "I'm
sorry to keep yakking like this," and I would say, "Please, go on,
tell me."

He talked compulsively, as if he hadn't spoken a word in
seven years, and I listened in amazement. This was his life, years
and years of it, a life of which I had known only a few bare facts.
I had pictured him, all that time, doing essentially nothing while
life somehow happened around him. I had seen him sitting somewhere looking out a window, and instead he'd been working in a
grocery store and taking care of his son and learning the guitar
and arguing with his sister Jane. As we drove north and the sky
blackened, an idea came to me that filled me with shame: I un-

derstood that Will was not merely the chief inhabitant of my day-dreams, the person around whom my childhood memories organized themselves, a dream to comfort me when life turned rotten. He was a real person. He was Will, he had nothing to do with me, he had a life as rich and complicated and full of struggle and indecision and promise as my own.

This idea stunned me. It filled the car like light, as if God himself had just appeared there with a terrifying message that could change the world. I hardly heard what Will was saying—something about his lawyer, his wife's father. I wanted to inter-rupt him to ask his forgiveness. I wanted to tell him I'd turned him into a toy, a cartoon, a piece of myself. I wanted him to know that all those years I'd been false to him.

He stopped talking and silence fell between us again. The air was cool this far north, and we rolled up the windows. The radio station was long gone. I wanted to move closer to him, to curl against him with his arm around me, but I was afraid to make a false move. I had a sense that my entire life was pointed toward this day, and I thought of those posters every shop in Boston was selling: "Today is the first day of the rest of your life," with pic-tures of sunlit meadows, or kittens, or women photographed through gauze—the sappy paraphernalia of pseudoprofundity. And yet—there were times when your life did turn a corner, you could almost feel the force of its acceleration. And if such dra-matic events did happen, if a life could really be changed in the space of a day, if epiphanies did occur outside the pages of liter-ature—then this ride to the mountains with Will would change my life. Will would be my Mediterranean cruise, my trip to Greece, my liberation from my narrow existence. He would be the equiv-alent of my father's miraculous reprieve.

In the quiet, after a while, he said, "So. Tell me. What about you?"

"Me? Oh—there's not a lot to tell. Compared to yours, my life has been pretty quiet."

"What about Duncan?" he asked.

"Duncan?" It was another disorienting moment. On gradu-ation night he had said, "What about George?" and I said, "George who?" and we cracked up.

"Did you say what about *Duncan*?"

"Duncan Maguire." He looked over at me with a sly smile. "You're wondering how I know about him."

Duncan. I had talked to Duncan on the phone the night before. I asked him if he missed me. He said, "Believe me, I miss you in bed. That's the only place I have *time* to miss you." He didn't ask me if I missed him. If he had, I would have said yes. I wasn't ready yet for a confrontation.

"I went to see you," Will said. "In Boston, the Saturday after Christmas. I caught your show. It was great. You were fantastic."

"Will! Why didn't you tell me you were there? Why didn't you at least come backstage afterward?"

"I don't know. I went to see you, and I felt sort of—I mean, it was obvious that you and this guy were pretty heavily involved."

The Saturday after Christmas. He was there. He had come to see me. If I had known, this whole winter and spring could have been different. I closed my eyes. Duncan, that persistent presence at the bottom of my mind. When I thought of him I saw his head bent over a book, his abstracted smile. I heard his key in the lock late at night. I said, "I live with him."

"Oh."

"But—" Did I need to explain? Did he care? "I won't say he means nothing to me, but—" Will glanced at me, waiting. "Almost nothing," I said.

"You live with the guy and he means nothing to you?"

"He did once, or I thought he did. But he doesn't anymore." The words sounded like a betrayal. They were hard for me to say. This surprised me, because the words were true.

He didn't speak for a while. He finished his beer and tossed the can into the backseat. The car wheezed along, going seventy. I wondered what he was thinking, if his thoughts bore any similarity to mine—if this whole evening seemed to him, as it did to me, like a scene in a science-fiction story in which the ailing old Plymouth speeding north through New York State was a fabulous machine that made time pointless and unreal, as insubstantial as clouds. This was the reality—this car, this twilit road, Will beside me in his plaid shirt and khakis. Those seven years that lay between us were the dream.

He said, "I needed this, Anna. To be with you like this, to talk to you."

He took one hand off the wheel and put his arm around me. I moved over and leaned my head against his shoulder, smiling. Yes: things can come true. He smelled faintly of paint. I could feel his sharp collarbone under his shirt. I pressed my lips to it.

"Why did you come to Boston?" I asked him.

"I wanted to see you."

"But why?"

"I don't know. You were the person I kept thinking I had to talk to. I screwed up my life so badly, and for some reason I thought talking to you would bring things together again."

"Maybe it will."

"It feels better already." He pulled me closer. "Maybe you're going to be my salvation."

I turned on the seat and put my arms around him, my cheek against his shoulder. We sat like that all the way to the town of Witherbee, where Johnny's cabin was. Will turned, one-handed, at a little closed-up general store and then down a dirt road. The cabin was at the end of it, isolated and dark, barely visible in the scant light. Behind it I could see the double hump of mountains rimmed thinly in red. We trained the car headlights on the little porch while Will located the key on a ledge, and then we went inside and closed the door and fell into each other's arms.

4

There are no words—or, rather, there are hundreds of
words (romantic, poetic, biological, pornographic) that
could be drawn upon to describe sex with someone beloved, but
the words fail, none of them is enough, no combination of them
describes it accurately. Music, maybe, comes closer—but to say
that making love with Will was like "Rhapsody in Blue" or a
Beethoven string quartet is to say nothing—to be ridiculous.

And so I won't attempt it. I will say that we were awake all
night in Johnny's filthy and decrepit cabin, talking and making
love, and that Will finally fell asleep in a hazy wash of morning
sunlight that gradually covered his face, his neck, and his shoulders with radiance as the morning sun rose higher, and that when
we woke and he kissed me his mouth was hot and musky from
sleep and we made love again instantly, without having to speak,
like lovers who have spent a lifetime together, and who know each
other so well they can communicate with a touch, a nod, a quick
breath. It seemed to me that we compressed our seven lost years
into that night and day we spent at Johnny's, and that as a result
those were the richest hours of my life.

I will also say that making love with him again was everything
I knew it would be, he was everything I wanted, I needed nothing
more than what he gave me.

Even the talking we did was like some very concentrated
intoxicating drink. We had known each other since we were five,
but we said more words to each other during our one night together than we had in all the twenty years before it. It had never
occurred to me until, thirsty and hoarse from talking, Will left my
side to get some more beer from the refrigerator, that all those
years I had loved someone I never knew at all. I lay there in the

274

dimness, waiting for him to reappear in the light from the stairs, and I saw how badly I had been cheated, having to rely on my dream-created Will when the real Will was there all along, just out of my grasp. When he came up the stairs and through the bedroom door, arms at his sides, a beer can in each hand, his pale, skinny, compact body caught the light and seemed to glow like the body of an angel. What the body of an angel would be like if angels had bodies. I smiled at the thought: *willful nonsense, Anna.* The pun delighted me. *Willful:* that was me.

"What's so funny?" he asked me.

"That you've always reminded me of an angel," I said to him.

He laughed and held up his can of beer. "Angels don't drink." He lay beside me again. "Angels don't do any of this stuff, the poor bastards."

Eventually, we talked about Martha—her death was still on his mind. "I dream about her," he said. "It wasn't that I loved her, Anna—hell, we were only seventeen years old." My heart lifted disloyally: he never loved her. "But I could have saved her," he went on. "I dream about trying to save her. Lately I've dreamt that she's drowning and I try to throw her a rope or hold something out for her to catch, but she can't, she's just out of reach, and I see her face going under."

We were huddled together on a filthy mattress, drinking beer out of the cans. He drank three for every one I got down, and watching him finish one and open another, guzzling beer as compulsively as he talked, I saw how obvious it was that his drinking problem (in which I didn't really believe—God, everyone *drank*) was caused by that seven-years-long nightmare, that white face under the water. I took the can out of his hand and set it down and touched his cheek so that he would face me. I said, "Will, listen to me. I've thought about this for a long time. She was my best friend, and when she died it was the worst thing that ever happened to me—worse than when my mother died, don't ask me why. But listen, Will. Martha didn't do it on purpose."

He shook his head impatiently. I put my hand over his lips and went on. "Listen to me. I knew Martha better than you ever did, and I know she didn't kill herself. At the time I wasn't sure, but now I am, after years of trying to see it clearly. She wasn't the type, Will. Martha—I don't know how to say this—she liked herself too much to destroy herself."

This was all improvised. The years hadn't given me any certainties; I hadn't even really thought about Martha much since I left Syracuse. And the odd thing was that as I spoke I felt an opposite conclusion growing in my mind: Martha *had* driven off the bridge deliberately; the truth was that she liked herself too much to be able to endure rejection and notoriety and suffering. And it was New Year's Eve, and she'd been drinking. And she was impulsive. It was as if the years that had passed were a kind of telescope, and I could look through it and see Martha, desperate and angry and betrayed and drunk on an icy road, deliberately give up control of Trevor's car at the bridge and go through the ice. I *knew*.

But I said to Will, "Martha couldn't have killed herself," and I saw in his face a profound willingness to believe what I said. It was terrible to see—how much it meant to him. "And she was the worst coward I've ever met," I said. "A physical coward. God, I remember how Trevor used to tease her about it. She was afraid of bugs, she was afraid of thunder, afraid of the dark, afraid to ride her bike down steep hills—she was afraid of seaweed, for heaven's sake." None of it was true except the seaweed. I remembered Martha at Skaneateles Lake screaming when she got tangled in a long dripping piece of it. But she would ride down John Street hill on her bike, no hands, her eyes shining, and once she told me that thunder made her feel sexy. "Don't you remember what a chicken she was?" I asked him.

I watched Will's face smooth out and lose its desperate look. "If that was true," he said, clutching my hand. "'If I could believe that."

I said, "I'm sure you hurt her that night, Will. And she was angry and upset. But she had good friends, she had an understanding family—she had plenty of other choices besides suicide."

He was sitting propped up on the ratty, stinking pillows. I knelt in front of him, holding his hands. I looked into his face. *Believe me,* I instructed him silently. *Believe me.*

He said, finally, "Maybe you're right."

"I'm right." *Forgive me, Martha.* But Martha was unreal, a ghost, unimportant. "I'm right, Will, I know I am." He dropped his head and covered his face, and I put my arms around him and pulled him down on the mattress beside me. He said, "Maybe I won't have the dreams anymore."

"You won't." His face was wet with tears when I kissed it. I held him close to me, kissing him, saying his name. The night of

Martha's funeral, when he and I walked down to the church in the cold, I had offered myself to him and he had refused me, seen it as a joke. Now he was naked beside me, and everything was redeemed. I was a sorceress. I could foretell the future; I could change the past. My powers awed me: my control, my brilliant lies like spells, my ability to make time compress itself, and return, and become its own mirror. He pushed the hair back from my face and looked at me with tenderness, maybe with love, and said, "Thank you." I felt low, and evil. I whispered to him, "Oh, God, Will, you make me so happy."

Later he said that if he'd known for sure that Martha hadn't committed suicide he never would have married Cindy. "It was as if she knew about Martha and used it against me," he said. "What a dope I was. And it wasn't just Cindy I married, it was her whole damn family. Me against the establishment. You know?" His laugh was awkward, as if he wasn't used to talking in those terms. Then in the dimness I saw his face soften. "Of course, if I hadn't married Cindy I wouldn't have Freddie."

Freddie. All I could think of was Fred, my old cat, who had died of kidney failure two winters before. Will told long, fond, rambling stories about Freddie, his son. The kid was precocious, eccentric, beautiful, adored. He sounded like a handful to me, a problem child who'd kept both his parents in a state of servitude and anxiety. Will told me that one afternoon he sang "Pop Goes the Weasel" to Freddie sixty-seven times in a row. Another time he drove him around in his car seat for more than an hour so he'd fall asleep. I tried to picture Will doing this: Will as doting father. "He sounds like a great kid," I said—not insincerely. If Will said so, I believed it. "You'll get him. Don't give up."

"I can't give up, Anna," he said. "He's been the only good thing in my life." I kissed him then, to remind him that now, if he wanted me, he had me in his life—his comfort, his necessity, his sorceress.

Toward morning, groggy from beer, I told him things I hadn't meant to, the small silly details of my long passion for him: the fantasies I wove in Latin class, and the pictures of him I hoarded, and the plastic angel I'd treasured for years because he had held it and because it reminded me of him. He was amazed, and touched: he'd had no idea of how I felt. The nuns used to say, "Mr. Westenberg, could you please inhabit the same universe as the rest of us for just a few minutes?" Once, Sister Elizabeth made him stand at the blackboard during history class and write fifty times, "I will stay in touch with reality."

"How could you not know?" I asked him. "Everyone knew. I made a fool of myself over you."

"You?" he said. "You were never a fool."

"I'm probably a fool now," I said. "To come here with you."

He whispered, "No."

"Why are we here?" I asked him. As soon as I spoke, I was afraid I'd made a false move: walking on eggs, I had tripped and made a mess. But I pursued it. I needed more than kisses, smiles, vague whispers. "Really, Will. Why did you ask me to come here? Why are we in bed together after all these years?"

"It's not very complicated," he said, smiling. "I wanted to be with you."

"But why?"

"I don't know, Anna." He frowned, and I prayed that I hadn't turned him off with my questions. But I saw that he was thinking. I had to learn that he took his time, he liked to get things straight before he spoke. He said, finally, "I didn't know you had such a crush on me when we were kids, but I always knew I could turn to you, somehow. I can't explain it, but I've wanted to talk to you so many times over the years. I can't say I thought about you all the time. It wouldn't be true. But I did think about you some-times. I was aware of you."

He paused again. *Sometimes,* he said. *Aware. So many times.* What did those words mean? What did they imply in terms of minutes, hours? How did they compare with my obsessed reveries and the bits of paper in my pockets bearing his phone number and the photograph I'd purloined from a dead girl's room? I wanted to force declarations from him. I wanted to batter him with questions: *Do you think I'm too fat? Do you like my hair? Do you like me in bed?*

I said, fishing for something, anything, "I'm glad you didn't forget me completely after you left town."

He gave a short laugh and said, "I'm beginning to wonder if maybe I was as crazy about you all that time as you were about me, and I just didn't know it. What do you think? Was I?"

I wanted to say yes, to test my powers. Could they extend that far? Could I really erase the past and write it again from scratch? Martha died accidentally, Duncan was never important to me,

Will was in love with me forever. But he spoke again before I could answer.

"I don't know about the good old days, Anna, but I feel pretty crazy about you now."

Yes: everything was redeemed. I put my arms around him. I whispered into his neck, "I've never stopped loving you, Will. I've thought about you every day, every hour. I've dreamed about you." This is the central truth of my life, I thought. I ran my hands down his body—his hard little nipples, his flat stomach framed in sharp bones, the crisp hair, his soft penis hardening under my touch, the tight muscles of his long thighs. The body of an angel. "I never got over it," I said. "I never will get over it."

He said, "That makes me feel like a lucky kind of guy. It's a weird feeling. I've never been lucky before in my life, but you make me think that's going to change now."

"It is," I assured him. I pulled him on top of me. I stroked his long, smooth back. "Everything is going to change now, Will."

"I think I love you, Anna," he murmured, and when he entered me again I cried out with a rapture that had nothing to do with sex.

When we finally got out of bed it was past noon. I had slept briefly, dreaming shadowy, panicky dreams in which Will and I fought over some silly misunderstanding, or lost each other in a crowd. I dreamed that I left his side and went downstairs in the dark and looked out a window. There was no sound, not a cricket, not a car, and I could see nothing but utter blackness, a void that wiped out my existence, and Will's, and the cabin—a black hole that terrified me so much I ran up the stairs back to him, and found him gone.

There was no shower and no hot water, but we took cold baths in the dingy little bathroom, and then I cooked eggs for breakfast. There was no coffeepot, so I made coffee in a pan, and I put the toast in the oven. The stove was covered with years of gleaming brown grease; the edges of the plates were crusted with ancient bits of food; the wood floor hadn't been washed in years; the windows were mottled with gray filth, curtained in stained gingham.

I said, "It wouldn't be so bad if it were fixed up and cleaned. It could be really cute."

279

"Johnny likes it this way," Will said. "'He figures that if he fixed the place up it'd just be vandalized. As it is, there's nothing to steal, nothing to break in for." He looked around the grungy room. "It's okay here. I kind of like it."

"Have you come up here much?"

"Couple of times." He hesitated. "Twice, three times."

From the way he said it, I knew he'd been to the cabin with a woman before. I couldn't bear the thought. I would allow him the dreadful Cindy with her underhand manipulations. I knew he hated her, she hated him. Cindy was safe. And Martha, who was dead—safer yet. But there must have been others. Women liked him, I knew that. There must have been hordes of them, vast armies of horny women—long-haired babes in love beads, college girls who tried to get him to read books, waitresses and dental hygienists and customers at his wife's father's grocery store, women at the place where they had the Shirelles on the jukebox. I stood there pushing the eggs around in the pan and imagined the numbers of women who must have been after him all these years. It made me dizzy. Lack of sleep, no food, too much beer, all those women . . .

He startled me with a question. "Do you ever smoke pot?"

I turned to look at him and laughed. "Everyone smokes pot, for heaven's sake. Don't they?"

"Yeah, I guess so." He shrugged. "I just wondered."

"Why? Did you bring some stuff?"

"No," he said. "I didn't bring any." He looked wounded, the way he used to get when the nuns made fun of him. "I wouldn't know where to get it if I wanted it." He was blushing, not looking at me, fussing with the paint under his nail.

"Well, I'm glad," I said hastily. "Personally, I'm feeling a little strung out. I don't think I'm in the mood."

I thought this would be the right thing to say, but it only seemed to increase his embarrassment—the big-city sophisticate scorning something that was still exotic to him, still hard to get.

He said, "Don't forget what a hick I am, Anna. I haven't exactly been around much."

With his words, the flush on his cheek, the uneasy little silence that fell between us, dividing us, I could see a glimmer of the truth about what his life since high school had been like: stunted and small and mean, not rich and complex and full of armies of wild women but tangled with money worries and stupid jobs and nowhere towns and a whole list of fears and limitations I couldn't even conceive of. He'd told me his life had been hell, and until that moment I hadn't known what he'd meant. No wonder he said Freddie was all he had. No wonder—I thought humbly—no wonder he had wanted me to come up here with him. He had nothing—God, not even a marijuana cigarette—to take his mind off it.

I wanted to put my arms around him and tell him I could change his life if he would let me. I looked at his hands that I loved so much, the strong, thin, sensitive fingers and bony wrists, the hands of a craftsman or a musician—hands that could create. I imagined him as my piano player, Will in a white dinner jacket on the stage of the Cantabile . . .

I set his eggs in front of him and bent over to kiss him. "I wish you'd brought your guitar," I said.

He looked up at me, still chagrined, his face full of comic surprise. "Why? Do you play?"

"Very funny." I sat down opposite him. "So you could play for me, of course. We could sing. We could make music together."

"I'm no good. I mean—I'm okay, good enough for a bunch of nursery-school kids, but I'm not *good*. I picked it up fast, but I haven't really improved much since I began."

"You need a teacher."

"Oh—yeah." He laughed ruefully, and started in on his eggs. "A guitar teacher. I also need a car and a place to live and some decent clothes."

"But you should at least think about it," I said. "Your guitar—music—those things are important, Will. You have so much talent."

"Right." He smirked at me, chewing, and took a gulp of coffee. "Just call me Duane Eddy."

"I mean it. I *know* you've got it. I knew it when you were fourteen years old." Our knees touched under the table; the rough fabric of his jeans against my bare skin quickened the current of desire that was always there, always ready and waiting. I said, "I wish you could come back to Boston with me, Will. I know so many musicians, so many people I think you'd really like and get along with. And teachers. I could hook you up with some really good people."

"Right. Then I'd get shown up for the musician I ain't."

He ate quickly, mopping up egg with pieces of toast and

swilling coffee—concentrating on the food, I felt, as a way of denying that what I proposed meant anything to him. I had a sense that I was pushing him too far, too fast. I was a hunter, clumsy, crashing through the underbrush, and my quarry was scared, was slipping away.

I said, "I'd just be afraid that you'd meet all these fascinating people and forget about me." I took his cup and filled it with muddy coffee from the pan on the stove. "Okay. Here's a better idea. Let's move in for the summer. Just the two of us."

"Move in? Where?"

"Here." I set his coffee in front of him. "Johnny's little Adirondack crash pad. Wouldn't it be cozy? Just us and the mice."

I was standing by his chair. I wore his plaid shirt and my spare underpants. He pushed up the shirt and pressed his lips to my stomach. "Cozy is one way of putting it," he said. I leaned down to him, my lips against his hair. The tension between us dissolved. I would gladly have let the eggs get cold, gladly have gone upstairs to the mattress again. I would never have enough of him, I thought, not if we stayed in bed the whole summer. But he said, "Mmm," hugged me tight, and let me go. "It would be fantastic," he said.

I sat down again opposite him. "Would Johnny mind? You said he hardly ever comes up here. Maybe not the whole summer but a couple of weeks. We could take a vacation. We could even climb a couple of these mountains." I laughed. "I suppose there *are* other things to do up here besides what we've been doing."

He smiled over at me. "I'd love it," he said. He took a bite of egg, a bite of toast. "God, I'd love it. But I've got to be back in Indiana by Thursday. I've got a job interview at a place out there. An old friend came through for me. I'm leaving Wednesday morning."

I put down my fork. "You're leaving?"

He nodded. "Greyhound. The bus leaves at eight A.M."

"You mean—Wednesday, like day after day after tomorrow?"

"Grace Hill gets out Tuesday," he said. "I couldn't leave until I finished out the year. But now I'm going to go out to Richmond and establish myself once and for all. This time I'm going to do everything right." He wiped his mouth primly with a paper napkin; for a minute, in the gray light of the dingy kitchen, he looked like no one I knew—a skinny bearded man with hard little eyes. "Just like we said, everything is going to change. No more screwing up. I'm going to get a good job and a decent apartment, lay off the booze, do nothing but work and save. Do what my lawyer tells me. The next hearing is a year from October, and you'd better believe I'm going to impress that judge."

What has that got to do with me? What do I care about any fucking judge? For a horrible second I thought I had actually said those words, but he was still looking at me earnestly, forgetting to eat, going on about his son, his wife's father's lawyer, his own lawyer, the Indiana custody law, his old friend Claudia who was going to help him out. *Claudia. Who is Claudia?* I felt faint. I said, "Let me just get this straight. You're leaving for good this coming Wednesday."

"I haven't got a choice, Anna. I wish to hell I did. I wish I didn't have to go through this."

"I'll come out there and see you," I said. "Soon."

He reached for my hand, laid his on top of it. "I would love to see you. That would be so great. I can't believe how much I'm going to miss you. But—" He paused, looked down at his plate.

"But what? I could fly out every couple of weekends, Will. I wouldn't mind. I could afford it. I do pretty well, between the Cantabile and the bookstore. How much could it cost to fly to Indiana?"

"I can't risk it."

"Risk it?"

"They watch me—my wife's family. Ex-wife. They'd hold it against me at the hearing. That I had women in."

"I'm not *women*. Am I?"

"Shh. Anna. Obviously you're not, to me. I'm just talking about how it's going to look to them. I've got to be straight-arrow."

"Until a year from October? Sixteen months?"

"Anna, I can't screw up!" He was getting irritable. I wondered if he was crazy, paranoid, if the trials of these seven years had made him into a madman. We're a good pair, then, I thought. I clutched his hand. *I can be as crazy as you, I can be twice as crazy, crazier than Cinderella with her mop, crazy as a saint.* A poor Madame Butterfly with her pathetic hopes. *Moriar propter te.* I said, "What about you coming to Boston, Will? I'd send you the money."

"You've got to understand. I can't. I can't take any chances. I've got to be good old dull, boring Will. He goes to work, he goes home, he watches television or whatever, he plays his guitar, he fixes up the place—you know? He's devoted to his son, nothing else matters to him." He began to stroke my hand. "Do you understand, Anna? It's not that I don't want to see you. It's not that I won't think about you all the time."

"Can I call you? Can I write?"

"Of course," he said. "Call—yes. Write—well—I'd have to say I think that would be kind of risky."

"Risky! How? Do you think they're going to steal letters out of your mailbox? God, Will." I stared at him, his apologetic half-smile, his furrowed brow. "I think you're getting a little nutty on the subject."

He dropped my hand on the tabletop and went back to his eggs. "You've never had a kid, so you don't know a goddamn thing about it," he said coldly.

"Oh, Jesus." I put my head in my hands and began to cry, stiff little sobs that I had tried but failed to hold back. I said, "I'm sorry," and my voice came out in a dismal, sniveling wail that horrified me, and that I assumed would alienate him forever. I said, "I'm sorry, I'm sorry, I don't know what I'm saying. You can't imagine what this does to me. After all this time—and now you're just—you're leaving me, you're going away—"

I sat there crying, listening to him finish his breakfast. The egg on my plate stared up at me, shiny with grease. I watched him slice into egg white and spread margarine on toast. I watched him use his knife to load up his fork. He put pepper on everything. His silverware clinked. He cleaned his plate, every crumb, and used a piece of toast to sop up the last of the egg, and then he got himself another cup of the disgusting coffee. I couldn't stop crying, thinking of all the women in the world who were happy on this summer Sunday, who were having breakfast with men who loved them, trading bits of the newspaper, planning picnics and trips to the hardware store, talking about the kids and the dog and whom to have over for dinner. I decided that if he didn't speak to me by the count of ten I would go out the door, walk into town in my underpants, and hitch a ride somewhere, anywhere, as far away as possible. One, two—

He finished his coffee and said, "Anna?"

I just looked at him. I couldn't speak; my voice would be thick with sobs. I imagined how I looked—red-eyed, red-nosed, no makeup. The tears kept running down.

He said, "Anna, you know how I feel about you." I shook my head. Upstairs in the bedroom I had thought he loved me, but maybe he hadn't said that at all. Maybe I'd been having one of my fantasies. "Anna?" He laughed a little, reached over to touch my wet face. "I love you. You know I do."

I managed to say, "Most people want to be with the people they love."

"It's not that I don't want to be with you." He sighed, took his hand away, went to the refrigerator and took out a beer, opened it, drank. "Think of it as a hitch in the army or something," he said. "It's temporary, Anna. Just until I get this legal crap straightened out and get my kid back."

"We could have other kids," I said.

I didn't mean to say it aloud, and as soon as I did I saw it was a mistake. He stared at me, biting his lip. "You still don't get it," he said. "Freddie is the important thing in my life. Compared to him, nothing else matters. There isn't anything else. You have to understand that."

Or else what? He took a long swallow of beer, and I reached over and grabbed the can away from him. The beer slopped over his plate and onto his khakis. I threw the can across the room. It landed on a pile of ancient newspapers, and beer dripped down in a puddle on the filthy linoleum floor. Anger filled me. He was Duncan all over again, only instead of suffering humanity it was bratty little Freddie. I wanted to hit him, I wanted to throw the plates and forks and cups, overturn the table, kick holes in the walls. The beer can rolled down the pile of papers and hit the floor with a clank.

"That was not a cool thing to do," he said.

"How can you drink that stuff with breakfast, for Christ's sake?"

"I told you I've got a drinking problem." He went to the refrigerator for another beer and took it out on the porch.

I sat at the table, refusing to cry, refusing to apologize. I could see him through the screen door, leaning shirtless against a post, looking out toward the gray mountains in the distance. The morning had started out sunny, but it became overcast as we sat at the table, and now it was raining lightly. We had intended to hike a little before we drove back. I'd had visions of making love one last time on a mountaintop or beside a clear stream in a woods. Now my visions were all of disaster: Will walking down the porch steps, carrying his beer can, and vanishing around the curve in the road. Will, drunk, crashing the car into a tree on the way

home. Will coming back in to tell me to get out of his life, to leave
him the fuck alone. I was thinking that he had nothing, but I was
wrong. He had beer. Let that be his salvation—not me.

He turned and looked at me through the screen. "Anna?
Come out here? Please?"

I took my time. I sat there staring back at him, and then I got
up slowly and took the dishes to the sink. I ran water on the plates.
I stood at the sink looking at the accumulated scuzz of the ages:
rust stains, ragged gray dishcloth, cracked linoleum on the counter
tops, filth-filmed window. I dropped a rag on the puddle of beer
on the floor. I splashed water on my face and dried it on my
shirttail. Then I went to the door and stood there.

"Come on," Will said. "Sit down."

We sat beside each other and watched the rain come down.
He said, "I'm sorry, Anna."

I whispered, "I just love you so much."

"I know that. Listen to me. I don't mean to be paranoid about
the goddamn Petraskis. I just need to be careful. You know? But
we'll see each other. We can work it out. I'll be in Albany to see my
sisters and my mother. Christmas, Thanksgiving. We could meet
then. Maybe you could drive over from Boston, or I could come
up there. Money will be tight, but what the hell. We can see each
other sometimes. As often as we can."

He turned his head to look at me, but I kept staring straight
ahead at the slanting rain because if I looked at him I'd be on my
knees at his feet, I'd be crying, I'd be acting like a woman I didn't
want to seem to be.

"Okay, Anna? All right?"

It would be like the old days, when I used to collect my little
rosary of glances and words. The times he borrowed my homework, the day he delivered the angel, the night Martha and I
changed partners and he danced with me. Now it would be a
couple of nights in a couple of motels, a few letters, an occasional
phone call. But it was only time, and time would pass, the months
would dwindle away, and at the end of them would be Will. Meanwhile, I would take what I could get. Five months until Thanksgiving: it was fitting, how often we met at Thanksgiving.

"Okay," I said. "That will help."

"I don't want you to be unhappy."

"I won't be."

"What about Duncan?"

Duncan who? "I don't know."

"Don't know what? You're not going to keep living with him, are you?"

"You don't want me to?"

"Want you to? What are you talking about? You think I want you living with some other guy?"

I looked at him then. "You would really care?"

"Anna, for Christ's sake."

I took a deep breath. I smiled at him. I snuggled into his plaid shirt in the cool air. I wondered if I could forget to give it back so I could sleep with it until a year from October, trying to find in it the faint Will odor of paint and soap and sweat. I said, "Of course I'm not going to keep living with him. I wish I never had to see him again."

"Will it be messy?"

Would it? If it weren't for the cold spot on the other side of the bed, would Duncan even notice I was gone? "I don't know. Yes, I guess it'll be messy." I thought of Duncan hunched over his bass fiddle, nodding his head to the rhythm, his glasses glinting in the Cantabile lights. "I don't give a flying fuck," I said, to make him laugh.

We didn't talk much more. We had done all our talking. Will went inside and put on a sweat shirt and got himself another beer, and we sat there on the cold porch watching the rain for a while, hoping it would let up, but it got heavier. From somewhere, down the road or over the mountains, maybe somebody's radio, came the sound of harmonica music, thick and sweet and mournful. I thought about going home to Duncan and telling him he had to leave. I thought about meeting Will in a hotel somewhere in Albany at Thanksgiving. I thought about going on a diet, about getting a slinky black nightgown at the lingerie shop on Newbury Street. I went over in my mind the two times he had said he loved me, his indignation about Duncan, his desire that I not be unhappy.

The rain came down harder. The front yard was mud and weeds. Across the road was an empty field of scrubby bushes and small trees. Some wild flowers I didn't recognize, some kind of early lily, a hundred shades of green. In the distance, the hazy tops of mountains against the pale sky. It was absurd, sitting there doing nothing while the rain splashed down, but I didn't want to leave. I had only my life to leave for—what passed for my life: the bookstore and the Cantabile and the scenes with Duncan. I looked at my feet up on the porch railing, my bare toes next to Will's. Our feet were wet and bluish from the cold drizzle. Our joined hands swung back and forth in the space between our chairs. Whatever happened, my real life would be back here in this cabin. My real life would be this plaid shirt, and letters from Indiana, and waiting for Thanksgiving.

Will stood up and went to the edge of the porch, looking into the rain. He said, "Anna? I need to ask you a favor."

"Anything."

"It's a little embarrassing." He turned to face me, his mouth set into a line. "I hate to ask you."

"Will, really," I said. "You can ask me anything, you know that."

"I do know that, and that's why I don't like to. But—" He looked down at the Budweiser can in his hands. "I wondered if you could lend me some money. I mean—you were talking about sending me plane fare and everything, I wondered if I could borrow a couple of hundred."

When he looked at me again, his face was full of pain. I imagined how hard this must be for him, but for some reason I didn't interrupt, I made him go on.

"Just until I get settled," he said. "I've got this lawyer's bill, and I'll have to put down a security deposit on an apartment. I've saved every cent I could, but Grace Hill doesn't exactly pay much. I hate to ask you, Anna, and I wouldn't have if you hadn't said that about the plane fare, but it would really help me a lot, and I promise you'd get it back. And I'd never forget it, Anna, I'd—"

Suddenly I couldn't bear it anymore. I got up, ashamed of myself, and stood beside him. "Shh, Will," I said. "Of course you can have it. God, you know I'd give you my last dime if I thought it would help."

It was terrible, it was degrading, but just standing by his side like that, our arms touching, I felt lust for him rise up in me like some living thing, a wild animal that inhabited me and would never be tamed. I thought, *I'll pay you for it, let's go upstairs, I'll give you whatever you want . . .*

He said, "I feel like a jerk asking you for money—"

"Don't say any more, please, Will." I kissed his neck, I kissed his sweat shirt, I lifted my head to kiss his face, his lips. "I should have realized," I said. "I should have offered. You shouldn't have had to ask me. I'll write you a check when we get back."

He said, "Thank you." He finished the beer and threw the can across the road, into the trees, and put his arms around me.

I said, "I'm glad there's something I can give you." I wanted him so much I trembled. His body was tense against mine, his fists pressed into my back. He tried to draw away, but I wouldn't let him, I held him tight. When would I hold him again? I thought: I have never lived before this weekend, never really lived the way people are meant to live. It's my own life that has been stunted and small and incomplete.

He relaxed against me and said, "Oh, God, Anna, I'm not worth all this. I'm a drunk, I don't have a job, I'm obsessed with my kid, I'm going to be—what?—a thousand miles away. You should stick with that guy Duncan, go back to Boston and pick up where you left off. I don't think I'm worth this much devotion."

I pulled back from him then so I could look at him, at how beautiful he was in the gray daylight. I wished I had brought my camera, the Pentax Duncan had given me for Christmas, to photograph him there against the weathered siding of the porch. I said, "This probably sounds crazy, but at this point I think I know you better than you know yourself. Really, Will. I do. Your whole life is ahead of you. You haven't even begun to live it. That's why you're saying these things. But I believe in you. I want you to know that. I believe that you're worth anything, everything."

He said, "Anna," and closed his eyes. I could see my sorcery working on him again—my power. How could he do without me for sixteen months? I imagined him as I used to, sitting at a window out in Indiana, looking east. Now he would sit there in his lonely apartment and think of me. When we met at Thanksgiving, I'd wear his plaid shirt over the slinky black, and he would laugh, and he would take me in his arms. . . .

I said, "Will, in sixteen lousy months we can be together. That's not so long. And you'll have Freddie, too. That's going to work out. Everything is going to work out. We're going to be happy, Will."

He just stood there with his eyes shut. Was he picturing himself and Freddie and me in a little house together? In a Boston apartment? Out in Indiana? I pictured cornfields, long empty roads, the banks of the Wabash. Jean's prophecy. *Believe it, Will,* I instructed him silently. *Believe it, it's real.* I touched his arm and he opened his eyes.

He said, "It sounds like a dream."

"It is a dream," I said. "But dreams come true. This weekend is living proof."

I didn't see him the next day—Monday. He had to work at the nursery school all day and he was spending the evening with his family. I sat most of the day with my father at the hospital. He would be coming home at the end of the week. I told him I'd better drive back to Boston on the weekend.

"You miss Duncan?" my father asked me. Duncan, his favorite. His eyes twinkled at the mere mention of his name.

I said, "Duncan and I aren't getting along all that well."

"I guess I should have figured that," he said. "Or you would have been just a little more enthusiastic about getting back to him." He was propped on pillows. The IV was out of his arm. He'd shaved and had a haircut that morning. He looked thin and dapper and restless and concerned. I wondered what Jean had said to him. "I worry about you, Anna. I'd like to see you settle down."

I laughed. "You! Don't you think I'd like to see me settle down?"

"Well, then," he said. "What's going on with you and Duncan? You seem like a pretty steady couple. He's been your whatever-you-call-it—roommate?—for six months now. When's he going to make an honest woman of you?"

"Live-in, Daddy. He's called my live-in. And it's a lot more honest to live together than to marry someone you don't love just because you want to go to bed with him."

There was a complicated pause, full of the Catholic morality my father and I were both brought up on, and his concern for my welfare, and the fact that the world he read about in *Time* magazine every week was full of free love and flower children and dope-smoking. Then my father sighed, and looked sad. He'd picked the important point out of my statement. "You don't love him?" he asked.

"I love someone else."

"All right," my father said. "I'll quit butting in. I hope it works out this time."

"If it doesn't work out this time, I'll give up," I said, and he looked at me, startled.

"What do you mean by that?"

"I'll enter a nunnery. I'll become a missionary or something."

My father smiled. He reached over to his bedside stand and

poured some ice water into a glass—proud, I saw, that he could do it. A week ago he'd been flat on his back, hooked up to tubes, dying. He raised the glass to me before he drank. "I wouldn't put it past you," he said.

That night I called Johnny Tenaro. He'd heard about my father's illness, wondered if I was in town, meant to call but hadn't gotten around to it. He told me about his new girlfriend, a guidance counselor at the school where he taught chemistry. "I'll bring her up to Boston one of these days," he said. "I'd like to catch your act again."

"I may be giving that up," I told him. I hadn't realized it until that moment, that when I broke up with Duncan the act would fall apart. "I've been having a little trouble with my band. And I think I'm getting burned out."

"So what are you going to do?"

"I don't know. I was going to be a singer on a cruise ship but that fell through. Go around the world. Maybe I'll do something like that." I knew I wouldn't. I had to be close to Albany. Five months until Thanksgiving, but he'd need me before that. Wouldn't he? Would he?

I told Johnny I'd been to the cabin with Will.

He let out an explosive snicker, as if I'd told him a dirty joke. "So you got your hooks into him at last. All *right*!"

I said, "Oh, grow up, Johnny," but I kept my voice amiable. "We're not in high school anymore."

"You don't have to tell me that. I haven't seen a nun in seven years except in the penguin cage at Burnet Park Zoo." He laughed, and took his time calming down. I remembered how all the girls used to pretend to find him hilarous. He stopped laughing finally and said, "No kidding. Seriously, Annie. I'm glad to hear about you and Will. Glad he's come to his senses. Christ—the crush you used to have on that guy. I still remember graduation night. Goddamn Trevor Finch. He's still in town, the slimy little bastard. I run into him every once in a while when I can't avoid it."

I interrupted him. The last person on earth I wanted to hear about was Trevor Finch. "Johnny, who's Claudia?" I asked him. "Do you know some friend of Will's named Claudia?"

"Claudia. Nope. I know Dorcas, but I don't know any Claudia. Why?"

I leaned against the wall. I was upstairs on the hall phone. From down in the kitchen I could hear Patty's voice, and the television on, and then Jonathan beginning to scream—the long, whiny cry that meant Patty was tormenting him. I was supposed to be watching them while Jean was at the hospital.

I said, "Who is Dorcas?"

"From the nursery school. She's the director or something. She's a nice girl—sweet, but kind of—oh, I don't know. She's older than Willie. Kind of—what would you say? Uptight?"

"He was dating her?"

"For a while last spring. I don't think it worked out real well. It always seemed to me that she liked him a lot more than he liked her."

Sounds familiar. "But he works with her every day." Sweet Dorcas, surrounded by little Freddies. The way to his heart. "You're sure they're not still involved?"

"Sure I'm sure," Johnny said. "He brought her up to the cabin twice, three times maybe, I don't remember. But after that it was kaput."

"But Claudia." I put my hand over the mouthpiece and yelled down the stairs, "Patty! Leave him alone! And turn that television down."

"It's my shovel!" Patty screamed back. "Give it back, you dummy!" On television someone sang, "I wish I were an Oscar Mayer wiener . . ."

"But you've never heard of any Claudia?" I said into the phone."

Johnny laughed at me. "Give it a rest, Annie. She's probably an old drinking buddy, a neighbor—nobody. I would have heard of her if she was important. Will and I had some long talks this winter. You know—I like him. He's all right. I don't know why everybody hated him so much back in school. What was it about him?"

"Everybody didn't hate him."

"Well, *you* didn't."

"People didn't *hate* him, Johnny. I think they found him hard to get to know. He kept to himself."

"Hey—you don't have to defend him, honey. It's all water over the dam. Under the dam? Whatever. Relax."

He asked me if I wanted to go out for a drink but I told him I was baby-sitting, and then I had to hang up because Jonathan's screams intensified. When I got downstairs Patty was holding the shovel high in the air out of his reach, Jonathan's diaper was soggy, the TV picture had gone out of whack and was jumping up and down, a glass of juice had spilled all over the floor. Jonathan's wails changed to whimpers when he saw me. I calmed them down and cleaned them up and put them to bed. I thought until my head spun. *Where is he now? Who is Claudia? Where is he tonight?* I considered calling his house to see if he was there. If he was there I could hear his voice. If he wasn't I would have learned something. But I didn't let myself do it. I sat waiting for Jean, trying to distract myself with little pleasures: I ate some sliced roast beef for my supper. I had a cup of good coffee with cream. I poured myself a glass of the Courvoisier left over from Christmas. I put on my father's recording of Maria Callas singing *Carmen.*

Around nine o'clock Duncan called to tell me Jack Sparks was way ahead according to the *Globe*'s telephone survey.

"I'm glad, Duncan. That's wonderful." I spoke with more warmth than I had in a long time because I knew the survey was important to him and I'd forgotten all about it.

"I know the election is four and a half months away," Duncan said. "But it's not too early to gauge people's attitudes. The conventional wisdom is that people don't really change their minds that much as the election approaches, not if they know the issues and can kind of get a handle on the candidate's image. And that's what we were trying to find out, just how much they're actually aware of Jack. And it looks good. Hey—I miss you," he said. "When are you coming back?"

How simple it would have been if I loved him. Duncan sitting up late at his card table, surrounded by books, papers, the paraphernalia of other people's problems, humanity's woes. Duncan in his suspenders, his soft brown socks, his little gold glasses. If I could just go back to him, put my arms around him, fall asleep to the sound of his voice on the phone with Jack Sparks. If I could erase this weekend, erase half my life, teach myself to want less.

"It feels like you've been gone for ten years," Duncan said.

"Oh, Duncan," I said, and wanted to cry. On the stereo, Carmen was turning over the cards, finding only *la mort, la mort.* "It feels like twenty years. A lifetime."

"Come home, baby," he said.

I saw Will the next night—his last. We went to Danzer's and drank beer side by side in a booth. He told me more about the job possibility in Richmond—something with the Parks Department, working with children on the playgrounds. If he could afford it

293

he'd try to take some courses, maybe go for a degree; the city had a plan where they might pay half his tuition. He didn't say a word about his friend Claudia, and I didn't ask. God help me, I was sick of the thought of Claudia, sick of the details of his leaving, sick of drinking beer. All I could think of was going somewhere with him where we could make love.

We left, finally. We went to a secluded corner of some park or other and held each other on the rough, patchy grass. Looking up, I could see above us the black hole of the night. He pulled my T-shirt off, and my jeans. Everything had to go, he said. He wanted me naked. Like graduation night, I remembered: the same scratch of grass on my back. His mouth was on me, his soft furry beard, his tongue, his beautiful hands. I opened my legs to him and we made love quickly, nervously, once and then again. At Thanksgiving, he said. In some motel. The things I will do to you. My beautiful Anna. I lay there with my clothes off, his head between my breasts, and I thought, *I can't let you go,* but I didn't say it. I didn't say anything. I just lay there on my back, stroking his hair, looking up at the fearful black sky.

The next morning I went out early in Jean's car and parked on a side street across from the bus terminal. I saw Will's mother drop him off in the old Plymouth. I heard him tell her not to come in. Thanks for everything, Mom, I'll write. I saw him lean down to the window to peck her on the cheek. Then he walked into the building, carrying a small suitcase and a shopping bag. He was wearing brown pants and a white knit shirt with a collar. I saw the door swing shut behind him, catching a sharp glint of sun that made him, for a moment, invisible. Then he went around a corner, out of my sight. I waited. At five after eight a bus nosed out from behind the building. BUFFALO, it said in front. I knew he was going to have to change buses in Buffalo. I couldn't make out his face through any of the windows. The bus pulled out onto Erie Boulevard and stopped for the light, then it roared down toward the highway, and then he was gone.

THANKSGIVING

1

W e kept the Cantabile act: Anna Nolan and the Duncan Maguire Trio. "I don't care," Eric said when I suggested that, since Duncan and I were breaking up, maybe I should find a new group or he should find a new singer. "You guys are good together. You can't keep doing this to me, Annie. Why don't you get involved with a dentist or somebody? A plumber with a tin ear. Lay off the goddamn musicians."

He talked to Duncan, and Duncan agreed to keep the group together if it was okay with me. I said it was. What else could I do? I didn't want to be a villain, and we *were* good together, Duncan and Mart and Wally and me. And so the show went on, not much different from before. You'd think the old magic would be gone, the old sexy pizzazz, but if anything we got better. At any rate, we got more popular. Largely because of us, Eric closed the place for six weeks late in the summer so he could expand—a whirlwind renovation job that moved the Cantabile upstairs into a Chinese restaurant that had gone bankrupt. It seated a hundred fifty instead of fifty, and when we reopened in October the place was packed.

All that autumn, we played to sellout crowds. Tourists loved us, and parents in town for football weekends, and the young professional types from Back Bay and the suburbs. We got another review in *Boston After Dark*, a bad one this time, claiming we were irrelevant, irresponsible, and decadent, and comparing us to the Busby Berkeley comedies of the Depression: "perversely committed to frivolous fiddling while the world goes up in flames around them." But there were a surprising number of letters to the editor defending us and accusing the paper of losing its sense of humor, so in the end the review probably did us more good than harm. And then *The New York Times* mentioned us favorably in an article on Boston nightlife, and the *Globe* said we were the best thing in town. And, decadent or not, the Cantabile was jammed every Saturday night.

Eric was in heaven. He had gotten fatter and more flamboyant over the years. His graying hair was shoulder length, and his newest suit was a sort of Edwardian thing, very Carnaby Street, lined in paisley and worn with a matching tie and hanky. We laughed at his clothes and his teenage girlfriends and his self-importance, but we were all fond of him, and he paid us well. There was another raise when the new Cantabile opened. Eric offered it to us with tears in his eyes. "No, no," he said when we tried to thank him. "You put me on the map." He hugged us, weeping into his paisley hanky and enveloping us fondly in the nautical scent of his cologne.

And then a month later, after Jack Sparks was defeated in the election and I'd finally heard from Will, Duncan and I told him we'd be leaving town after the first of the year. We were getting married and moving to New Haven, where Duncan had a job—a real job, no more volunteer work—at New Haven Legal Assistance.

Surprisingly, Eric took it well. He was a practical businessman. "I knew this day would come," he said. "I hate to say this, but I've even got myself kind of geared up for it. I can move Wanda in there with Wally and Mart and it'll take a while but I think it'll go. Now that you guys have laid the groundwork."

There were more emotional, aromatic hugs. He even told us we should have the wedding at the Cantabile, and we considered it—cocktails, soft jazz, and the bride in a red dress singing "O Promise Me" to wild applause. But in the end we got married at St. Elizabeth's, and the choir that I'd soloed in for three years sang Bach for us. My father and Jean and the kids were there, and my aunts and uncles, satisfied at last, and my cousin Roseanne and her husband and baby, and Mart and Wally and Alice and Lydia and Jack Sparks and Duncan's law-school crowd and all our musician friends—everyone I loved except Will Westenberg, whom I knew I would never see again.

I suppose I married Duncan partly because of Will—the cool little note I had received from him in November, enclosing two fifty-dollar bills and leaving an empty corner on the envelope where the return address goes. If it had been the letter I'd been expecting all summer, if there had been a word of love in it besides a nearly illegible "Love, Will" at the end, I would have gone on waiting—waited forever. Duncan knew that. I told him everything during that six weeks when the Cantabile was closed, and Duncan had passed the bar exam, and the heat of August and September had Boston by the throat, and Jack's campaign got off the rails and never got back on. During that six weeks, we talked.

But first Duncan moved out, into a rooming house in Brookline. He went willingly—humbly, even. I was touched by his reaction, and by something I'd never seen in him before—a kind of sad capitulation to a force he didn't understand but desperately wanted to. I hadn't realized before his leaving that what Alice had told me, and what I'd claimed to be aware of, was literally, simply, and profoundly true: Duncan loved me.

When he and his clothes and books and papers were gone, I spent some time sifting through my belongings, sorting and throwing out as if I were saying good-bye to more than Duncan. I couldn't bear to get rid of the letters from George or the few notes I had from Hal or my little hoard of newspaper clippings in varying shades of yellow, but I dumped piles of old opera magazines and playbills, alumni mailings from the conservatory, letters from ex-roommates, scribbles from Patty and Jonathan, old birthday cards and Christmas cards and bills and press releases.

Sweating in the muggy heat, I went to work in the evenings like a maddened hausfrau. I cleaned out drawers that hadn't been touched in years. I scrubbed shelves and cupboards, terrifying the roaches and spiders. I washed windows and bought a new bookcase for the bedroom. I went through the muddle in my wire-enclosed basement storeroom—a rusty bicycle that had belonged to Hal, a suitcase limp with rot, schoolbooks stinking of mildew and chewed by mice. Alice came over to watch me, bringing beer. "Next thing, you'll scrub the front stoop," she said. "You'll clean the inside of the piano with Lysol. You'll put doilies under the beer cans."

I told her it was a distraction, it kept me busy, and finally, one night after she'd helped me lug grocery bags full of old magazines down to the Dumpster, I told her about Will. She said I was crazy, that I was living my life as if it were an opera—all the things Hal used to say. "Donizetti," she said. "Some opera where the heroine goes mad. *Lucia?* Or one of those wild Bellini ones. Something all wrong for your voice." But when I broke down in tears she brought me a cold washcloth and a fresh beer and said, "Jesus, honey, if it's really that bad, call him, send him a telegram, fly out to Indiana and drag him back east by the hair."

Her enthusiasm infected me. I washed my face and drank a long swallow of beer and said, "I don't have his phone number or his address."

She dialed Information in Richmond, Indiana, but there was no number listed. Then she made me try Johnny Tenaro, but his amused voice said sorry, he hadn't heard from Will. I called Mrs. Westenberg's number: it was no longer in service; I'd forgotten she'd moved to Albany with Ruth, whom I had no way of finding. Alice's final brainstorm was Cindy, Will's ex-wife, out in Indiana. She got her number from Information and I dialed it before I could think twice: a blurry recording, vaguely female, said, "At the sound of the tone, please leave a message."

"Go ahead," Alice advised me. "Tell her to call you back. She must have his phone number or the name of his lawyer or something you could use to get in touch with him."

But the sound of Cindy's voice sobered me, and I hung up, appalled at what I was doing: this was Will's life, for him to fit me into or not. The revelation I'd had in the car with him returned to me, that he was a complete person, independent of my daydreams. The voice on the phone was the mother of his child. He and I were two books on a shelf, side by side but with separate plots and casts of characters. I tried to explain this to Alice, to convince her that even if I had his number I shouldn't call him, or fly to Indiana and throw myself into his arms. "It's his move," I said.

"Screw that. What is this, a chess game? Do you love this guy or not? I mean, he just sounds like the kind of wimpy type that if you want him you've got to take action. You know?"

As we sat there together on my front steps in the dusty Boston afternoon, I tried to imagine Alice handling the situation, but it was impossible. Alice wouldn't have let it develop. She would have either married Will years ago or forgotten him. I wished sometimes that I were Alice, who faced adversity by laughing at it and going on to something else. She was tall and skinny, her hair cut as short as boys used to wear it. She wore the tiniest skirts in Boston and suede sandals that laced nearly to her knees. She was a fantastic violinist, a great cook, a talented calligrapher, and she beat me regularly at Scrabble.

"What the hell," she said. "Let's borrow Mart's car and drive out to Indiana and look for him. Just comb the streets until we find him."

I said, "You're serious, aren't you?"

"Perfectly."

"How can anyone so beautiful and smart hand out such bad advice?"

She looked indignant. "Why is it bad? I think you're crazy—you know that. I think Duncan's the one for you. But if you want this Will person, go get him."

I said, "God, Alice, I may not have much at this point, but I do have a little pride left."

"Did Lucia have pride?" Alice asked me. "Elvira? Norma?"

I got irritable—told her to quit joking, quit making fun of me, and she apologized hastily. "I'm just trying to cheer you up," she said. She was on her way out the door to meet Mart—or to escape my craziness. "Quit worrying. He'll call. Or write. You'll probably get a letter tomorrow."

I didn't get a letter. I heard nothing. August slid into September, September settled in. The leaves turned gold on the maple tree behind my apartment building—the one I could glimpse from my bathroom window. The geraniums and petunias in the Public Garden gave way to orange and brown chrysanthemums, the renovations at the Cantabile were nearly done, I bought a new dress for opening night—dark blue this time, with sequins and a plunging back—and I continued to clean and organize and throw things out.

I had Jean send me all the junk from the attic—two large cardboard boxes filled with old report cards and yearbooks and snapshots and letters and prom favors. I found a picture of Roger Gable and me sitting on the fender of the old Nash Rambler in which he had deflowered me, and one of a pigtailed Martha Finch, wearing a pleated plaid skirt and kneesocks, dated 1953. Both of them made me cry. All my old Will-mementos were there, intact. The photograph from Martha's room, the fifth-grade snapshot of the two of us in the Thanksgiving pageant, the angel with its tissue paper, my diaries, a Latin test of his that I'd filched in tenth grade, the scratched 45 r.p.m. recording of "My Baby Left Me." When I gathered them together, reverently, into an old Bonwit's box, they seemed a scruffy little collection, a heap of worthless junk distinguished only by the extravagant and worn-out associations they had for me: my pathetic adolescence, closed up in a box. I gazed into Will's teenage eyes in the photograph (its frame now cracked neatly across), I studied the errors and misspellings on his Latin test and my romantic, overheated diary entries, I played the whiny Elvis record, and I think I began to understand even then—even before I'd officially given up hope—that the silly dreams I'd lived on for so long were finally, irreparably, definitively doomed. That we were no Elvira and Arturo. That life was not an opera or a fairy tale. That my baby left me, never said a word.

Meanwhile, Duncan and I talked. I told him how I felt about his involvement in every life but mine, his commitment to the world's problems at the expense of ours. And I told him about Will. Duncan used to meet me after work once or twice a week and we'd go around the corner to a diner on Massachusetts Avenue for a cheap dinner and good coffee. Or we'd go for long, cool evening drives in his old Volvo. Once we drove up to Marblehead and ate clams and walked through the quaint town down to the water to watch the sailboats in the setting sun, and Duncan asked me if we could get a motel room and stay the night and I said no. On his birthday, I invited him over for a candlelight dinner of beef stroganoff and cheap champagne and apple pie, and Duncan told me that if I couldn't make it work out with Will he would be waiting, he would try to change, he loved me.

I had thought it would be therapeutic to tell people about Will, but the long talk with Alice, and the continuing saga I told to Duncan on our nights together, had a strange effect on me. It was as if I were telling someone else's story. I found myself becoming detached and analytical and, finally, slightly bored. It was only when I was home in bed alone, with Will's old plaid shirt tucked around my pillow, on nights when the heat kept me awake, that I would remember Will as a real person and our weekend together and all the years before as real moments, as times that mattered and cut deep. I would recall the way his hands felt on my body, and the way he had looked on the porch in the rain, and his clinging to me when we talked about Martha, and, like the picture of the bottomless cup of coffee in the diner where Duncan and I hung out after work, I would be filled again with hope.

The letter from Will came in early November. It said, "Sorry this is all I can send at this time. Won't forget I still owe you, and not just money. Things are looking good at this end. Theirs no way I'm giving up. Love, Will." That and two fifties. I looked at it for a long time, the cheap paper, the hasty scribble, the misspelling, the lack of a return address, the perfunctory love, the crisp bills. It kept reminding me of something, and finally I had it: Martha's suicide note, and the five twenties tucked into the pink envelope.

I mailed the two fifties to the Back Bay Peace Council. Then I burned Will's note in the kitchen sink and took his shirt and the Bonwit's box downstairs to the Dumpster and heaved it up over the side. When I calmed down, I called Duncan.

2

Two days after we were married, Duncan drove to New Haven in a U-Haul truck and I followed in the Volvo. It was a bright January morning, and as I drove down the Mass. Pike to Route 91 the sun on the snow was blinding. I squinted into the light until I got a headache, going over and over in my mind all the promises Duncan and I had made—not the big, easy promises to love and honor, et cetera, that came with the marriage ceremony, but the tough little details we had worked out on our own. Duncan promised not to get so caught up in his work that he had no time for me. I promised to understand when the pressure of events forced this to happen. He promised to allow it to happen only occasionally and temporarily, and to keep weekends free. I promised not to get silently hostile when something bothered me but to talk it out: no more long resentful walks. We both promised to arrange our schedules to allow for frequent visits to my father and Jean, to get up to Boston regularly to see Mart and Wally and Wanda at the Cantabile, and to keep things neater around the house.

Moving, frankly, terrified me more than marriage. I could work things out with Duncan, we could discuss our differences and make resolutions, but a new city was not something you could negotiate with. Nor did I have to leave one husband for another as I had to leave Boston for New Haven. I was leaving behind the streets I loved, the dear shabby apartment, the Cantabile where I'd been a fixture for four years, the voice teacher I'd had for nearly that long, the bookstore, the Mexican restaurant where I used to eat with Hal, the parks and the shops and the filthy glittering river.

"It's a whole life," I said to Duncan.

302

"You're so melodramatic," Duncan said. "You're not dying, Anna. You still have a life. You're just moving. People do it every day."

"Won't you miss it, though?" I pressed him. I resented the ease with which he made transitions as much as he resented my difficulty. "Doesn't it kill you, in a way, to leave things behind?"

"I'm used to it," Duncan said.

I followed the orange truck west through Massachusetts and then south into Connecticut, terrified that I'd lose it in the traffic. The route was simple enough—"a right angle, zip, zip, superhighway all the way," Duncan had said—but I'm not good with unfamiliar roads. I get singing or thinking or listening to the radio and I forget the turnoffs and miss the exit numbers. I followed Duncan doggedly, nervously, frowning into the glare. I wished he would stop on the road to pee or eat lunch, but I knew he wouldn't; he wasn't the type. The Volvo shook violently if I pushed it past fifty, and around Springfield the heater began to work only intermittently. When we pulled into New Haven early in the afternoon, and I followed Duncan through town to our apartment, I was tired, hungry, freezing, and depressed.

New Haven seemed a grungy, charmless little city, plagued by the misty rain that had begun as soon as we crossed the Connecticut border. I had never really been there before—just that one quick trip for a job interview with a firm Duncan considered insufficiently committed to social change. Then, when the opportunity in Legal Aid came along, Duncan had gone down to New Haven and spent several days talking to the people he'd be working for and finding us an apartment. In his efficient, well-adjusted way, he already liked the city. He liked the job and the people he'd met, he liked the presence of Yale, and he liked the neat New Haven green with its churches.

"It's a manageable city," he said—a remark that had stayed in my mind throughout my long drive. *Manageable:* his highest accolade. No wonder he'd never be a great bass player.

When I pulled into the driveway behind him, he bounded out of the truck, beaming at me. I hated the mood I was in, but I didn't have the energy to fight it. I really felt, as I sat sulking in the Volvo, that my life was falling apart, that the last thing I wanted was this manageable little life in this tacky little city with a man who would never understand me.

He saw that I wasn't getting out of the car, and he came up

to the window and said, "What's the matter?" The way he said it managed to suggest not concern but criticism: what's the matter with you *now*? His bouncy good mood was gone, and that at least gave me a certain satisfaction. I rolled down the window.

"I'm cold and it's raining and I hate this damned car, that's what's the matter." I banged my fist on the steering wheel as if the car were New Haven and marriage and Duncan instead of a 1955 Volvo badly in need of a wheel alignment and a new heating coil.

Duncan wasn't sympathetic. Mist filmed his glasses and stuck his hair down against his high, bald forehead, giving him a maniacal, alienated appearance, like a character in *Dr. Strangelove*. He said, "You're so negative, Anna." It was his new thing, part of our promise to be frank and open with each other. You're so this, you're so that, Anna: moody, demanding, melodramatic, negative. "And you're so tied to your little comforts. God—loosen up. You're here, we've got work to do. Everything's not perfect but you've got to make the best of it."

"Who says I do?"

"Oh, for Christ's sake, Anna."

"Who says I can't get on a train and head back to Boston right now if I want to?" A taut, charged pause followed my words, and I had the feeling that they were lit up in fire, they were crucial words in the history of our life together. At the same time I knew that they were cosmically stupid, and I had a mad urge to laugh.

Duncan said, "If that's what you want, I won't stand in your way."

We glared at each other for a few seconds, and then I said, "Oh, the hell with it," and got out of the car.

Barely speaking, we unloaded the truck in the rain. There wasn't a lot—mostly small pieces of furniture and cartons of books. An armchair, a mattress and box spring, the heavy oak dining table. Piles of clothes. Duncan's bass. Some leftover groceries. We had pared down our lives as much as possible before the move. My piano was one of the possessions that had to go; it was too big and difficult and expensive to move, and we sold it for practically nothing to the couple who rented my apartment. I didn't know when I'd have a piano again. I wasn't a pianist. I played only for fun and to accompany myself, and I knew a piano was too frivolous a thing to spend our meager hoard of money on. But it was one more thing I had against New Haven: for this dreary little place, I'd sacrificed my piano.

I cheered up, though, as we unpacked the truck. The rain was not unpleasant, and the air was actually warm. It was like a spring day. Our apartment, a second floor on Orange Street, was large and freshly painted, everything white, with elaborate moldings around the doors and windows and a tiny screened back porch. I wanted to compliment Duncan on his choice—I wanted, actually, to put my arms around him and apologize, he was so hard-working and patient, carrying all the heavy things, holding the door for me, making two trips for every one of mine. But I didn't know how to take back my words, to break the mood of quiet and almost contented hostility that we'd settled into, and so I said nothing, and we hauled and carried and arranged furniture and opened cartons in an absurd, exaggerated silence that kept striking me as comical.

Finally he sighed, got up from the floor where he'd been unpacking books, rubbed his back, and stretched, making the soft grunting noise he made sometimes in bed, and I jumped up impulsively and went to him. He was my husband; this was no way to live. We held each other tiredly in the middle of the chaotic living room, and then we made our apologies and collapsed together on the bare mattress, while the misty rain dribbled against the windows and the people in the apartment downstairs played *Nashville Skyline* at top volume on their record player.

3

A lot of things improved after that first day. "No place to go but up, man," Duncan said, grinning, imitating Mart. We moved in on a Monday, and by Friday, except for cartons full of Duncan's junk, the apartment was settled. The weather became impossibly warm and sunny; snow melted into mud in our back-yard. We met our downstairs neighbors—three Chinese graduate students in biology, nice young men in glasses and bow ties with Oxford accents and a fascination with American music, which they played, loud, whenever they were home. Once, when they came upstairs for a beer, I did my Barbra Streisand imitation, and they were charmed. After that they called me Barbra, and were always begging for a song. "Please, Barbra, just a small bit of 'People,' just a few beautiful notes for your fervent fans."

Duncan got me a piano as a surprise. The doorbell rang one morning while I was in the shower. I threw on Duncan's old woolen bathrobe and found two men at the door and a truck in the driveway. My hair dripping, I signed a delivery slip and watched them maneuver a turn-of-the-century claw-footed up-right—blood brother to Mamie's old war-horse—up our narrow stairs and into the space I cleared between the windows in the living room. The ease with which they performed this feat was what impressed me as I stood there shivering. It was only when they had left—sweating, rushed, heedless of my blissful exclama-tions—that I took it in properly: Duncan had bought me a piano. Before I dried my hair or got dressed, I called him at the office.

"I stopped into this place on Whitney Avenue the other day," he said. "The secretary here told me about it. They had a cellar full of them. It was like the warehouse of some Victorian mad-man. God, all that *carving*!" He was trying to be modest and off-

306

hand, but I knew he was pleased that his surprise had made me happy.

"I love the carving. I love the whole beautiful thing. And Duncan, Duncan, I love you, too," I said.

I found the box with my music in it, and then I sat down and played, badly, some Bach and the first movement of a Mozart sonata and finally, rather better, a little Gershwin, some Noël Coward. The piano needed tuning but it had a sweet, rich tone. It sounded the way it looked—like caramel. It reminded me of Mamie. I played "I Dreamt I Dwelt in Marble Halls" and "Danny Boy," admiring the way the morning light fell across the old ivory keys, and I swore I would never again fail to appreciate Duncan, never argue with him, never wish he was something he wasn't.

I look back on those first couple of weeks as perfect. They could go on record as part of a chronicle of ideal marriages. Duncan had to work hard, right from the beginning, but his work with Legal Aid was fascinating to us both. I loved it when he came home and we drank a glass of wine together before dinner and he talked about his cases and then asked me, smiling his wonderful smile, touching my hair, pulling me over to sit on his lap, "And how was your day?"

My only complaint was that I invariably had to answer Duncan's question with bad news. I was spending my time looking for both a job and a good voice teacher, and I'd managed to find neither. Lydia had given me two names of teachers, and I went to see them both, but one—a sweet old man with wild white hair who called me Madame Maguire—was about to retire, and the other was a large Wagnerian woman in a gray suit and an ascot stuck with a huge, dangerous-looking jeweled pin who said I'd have to unlearn everything I knew and she hoped it wasn't too late.

I called all the colleges in the area, told them what I was looking for and left my name, but no one called me back. I knew I should have been vocalising every day, continuing the work I'd done with Lydia, but when it was time to practice I'd find myself noodling around on the piano with pop music, singing Gilbert and Sullivan and my old Cantabile repertoire, and looking out the window at the house next door where the window facing ours was full of potted plants and bits of stained glass and fancy colored bottles. Looking at all that color and light I'd go into a little daze and slump down on the piano bench and wish spring would come.

Job hunting went no better. I had a fantastic letter of recommendation from Reed, but none of the bookstores needed help, and though I put in applications at the Yale Employment Office and a few other places, no one gave me much hope. I had no skills except singing and shelving books. The man at Yale looked over my résumé and said, "It looks to me like you really should be singing," but no one could tell me how to get a singing job. There were a couple of coffeehouses in New Haven, folk-music places, but nothing like the Cantabile. I walked downtown every day hoping vaguely for something to happen, but I couldn't imagine what it could be. I went to employment offices and an-swered a couple of ads in the newspaper. I walked regularly past the Yale School of Music. Even in winter, with the windows closed, I could often hear someone vocalising, or the sound of a violin. Once, I heard "Vissi d'arte" being poured out so beautifully, so unexpectedly, into the icy gray air, I stopped in the cold and listened to the whole thing with tears in my eyes.

"You should be there," my father said when I talked to him on the phone. "Get yourself a degree. Do something with your talent, Anna." It was the same advice he'd been giving me since I left the conservatory, but it didn't scare me so much anymore. Maybe I didn't have the voice to be a great singer, to give recitals and sing in concerts in a serious way instead of belting out pop music in piano bars, but it wouldn't hurt to try. All I could do was fail.

"There are worse things than failure," my father said. "Don't waste your life." It was a theme that came often into his conver-sation since his illness and reprieve—like poor old George with his *Vive ta vie!* "And you know we'd help out with the money," he added.

I allowed myself to fantasize: on my walks over to the School of Music I imagined going in the massive front door instead of standing outside in that symbolic cold. I'd run upstairs to the studio where my voice teacher waited—a motherly, well-uphol-stered woman with an unspecified accent. "Anna!" she would cry. "You are late, my dollink! If you are goink to be ready for your Carnegie Hall recital, we must verk! verk! verk!"

But I was nearly twenty-six, married, supposed to be self-sufficient: I couldn't ask my father for money. Nor could I bring it up with Duncan. Our financial position confused me. I knew that Duncan had a little money—that after he settled his parents' estate there was some left over—but I had no idea how much. He had struggled to put himself through law school, first by taking night courses and working days, finally with a hefty scholarship so he could study full time, so I assumed the money wasn't much. And yet it bought him cashmere and good wool and leather. It had, I assumed, bought me the piano. But money wasn't one of the things we discussed, and though I knew we had more than the pittance in our savings account, and the joint checking account into which we deposited Duncan's paychecks, there was something proper and old-fashioned about Duncan that made it seem like prying to ask for the vulgar details. Besides, the roles we had assumed with each other made it impossible: I was the carefree Bohemian, the artiste who rose above such mundane matters; he was the practical one. When I tried to rev myself up to ask him, I imagined him saying, "Don't worry your pretty little head about it," like some awful television husband.

Once, ashamed of myself, I went through the cartons of his junk that still lived, unsorted, in a corner of the bedroom, looking for stock certificates or bank statements, but it was a curiously sterile, impersonal collection, nothing but old *Law Reviews* and textbooks and yellow pads full of jotted notes. I wondered if the absence of records meant that Duncan didn't like to think about his money, if in Duncan's mind every dollar in the bank or the stock market was one more small contribution to the sum of misery in the world. Maybe even Duncan couldn't really eradicate guilt in six sessions with a therapist.

The Legal Aid office where Duncan worked was downtown, on Church Street, across from the green. I used to pass by it sometimes on my walks, but I seldom went in. I used to imagine Duncan in there, hunched over a brief or a book like a character out of *Bleak House,* his glasses slipping down his nose, and I would envy him because he was busy and happy and useful, and I was walking the slushy New Haven streets with music going around in my head.

Duncan's boss, Dave Brady, had hired Duncan on a provisional basis—Duncan would have to pass the Connecticut bar exam in February—so in addition to working full time he was taking a private cram course two nights a week at the Yale Law School, a situation he kept apologizing for. But he often managed to be home in the evenings, and he kept his weekends immaculately free, as promised. We went to movies and concerts and to a folk-music place called The Space, and we went skating a couple of times with our Chinese neighbors—they were fantastic skaters—at the Edgewood Park rink. One sunny Saturday Duncan and I walked from one end of New Haven to the other, holding hands, and we bought matching red mittens at the Yale Co-op.

Soon after we got to town, we were invited to dinner by Dave Brady and his wife, Valerie. They had three small children and they rented a large, shabby, messy house on Elm Street. There was a crowd at the party, all lawyers and their wives and a few children brought by people who couldn't afford sitters—babies sleeping among the coats on the Bradys' double bed, a couple of toddlers running around in pajamas. The men were all from Legal Aid—a room full of Duncans. The women were nervous and intense, many of them involved in the arts—painters, poets, a dancer, a couple of musicians. There was plenty of cheap wine, plenty of joints being passed around, plenty of potato chips and onion-soup dip, but dinner was minimal—watery stew from a big pot on the stove and long loaves of Italian bread set out on a board on the kitchen table. Chipped ceramic bowls. Margarine in the wrapper. Carrot and celery sticks. Black olives. Loud music on the record player. No one ate much; people drank and smoked and shouted above the music while the stew congealed and the bread got hard and the kids grabbed the olives and carrot sticks.

All that winter, Duncan and I went to parties like this almost every weekend—Saturday night bashes which were, it became clear, the only occasions on which the lawyers we were married to could wind down and relax. Everyone was poor, but there was always enough money for wine and dope, and there were a lot of Saturday night drunks and weekend potheads.

At the parties, I tended to smoke a little and drink hardly at all, and it was a long time before I felt comfortable with Duncan's friends—or even with their wives, whose almost universal tendency to minimize their own talents and maximize their husbands' made me uncomfortable. I was used to artists who took their work seriously, but these women laughed when they talked about what they did—nervous, fluttery little laughs, as if the words *chamber group* or *watercolor* were either funny or obscene. I sensed an unspoken but unmistakable agreement that the men's work was important, the women's frivolous, but what bound everyone together was the us-against-the-system feeling that, in those days, in that crowd, underlay everything, even a simple act like making soup or buying wine—a sense of specialness that was prominently in the air at those parties, as pungent and inebriating as marijuana smoke, a feeling that we were there, at that point in history, for a purpose. Boiled down, it was a belief that we could change the world—the *we* a vague collective pronoun that really meant the brilliant, dedicated men we were married to who had turned down lucrative jobs with big law firms to work selflessly for the betterment of mankind.

Often, while Duncan (in the forest-green sweater and elegant camel-hair trousers he was wearing that winter) stood in a noisy group of men talking shop, I would curl up somewhere and listen to the music—Janis, the Stones, and, almost always, Dylan, his lonesome harmonica a painful reminder of the porch of Johnny's cabin and the sound of harmonica music coming suddenly from nowhere through the rain. I would sit there alone, too shy to talk much to anyone, and give in to the pain of it almost with pleasure. At times like that, if I concentrated, I could make the miserable memory of that rainy Sunday, the mountains in the distance, the lilies in the lot across the road, Will's hand in mine, into the only important thing in my life. And yet, of course, I knew all the time that the memory was unimportant, peripheral, even destructive, and that this party, these lawyers and their artist-wives, this talk and laughter, were the vital facts of my existence—were my life now with Duncan.

Gradually, I became less of an outsider. I found friends, and Duncan and I began to throw our own parties. All that winter—the tenacious, wet southern Connecticut winter—Duncan and I worked at being happy together, and for a long time we were precariously successful.

We had to learn to be careful with each other. We were often angry, but we devised rituals for expressing it that were as meticulous and extravagant as the carving on my piano. We became adept at wordless apologies and symbolic gestures of affection. After one of our courteous, controlled arguments, I would find a note from Duncan in my coffee mug, or he would bring me a present—a book, a scarf, a bunch of daffodils. I kept the apartment clean and organized. I packed him delicious little lunches. I made sure there was always fresh orange juice—his passion—in the refrigerator. I ironed his shirts the way he liked them. And in bed we made love in ways we never had before—like married people with a long-term, secure, passionate commitment. In bed the commitment seemed genuine and worth fighting for; back in the real world, I had doubts that I knew Duncan shared.

But we didn't let up. We were like students working hard in a demanding and valuable course they were in danger of flunking. We said marriage isn't easy, nothing worthwhile is easy, and we admitted that we had to rethink some of our ideas. Legal Aid was still a fairly new phenomenon; until it got off the ground, there wasn't going to be much togetherness: that was our main adjustment, and it was an easier one than I'd expected—so easy that it scared me. As winter gave way to a muddy spring, and Duncan had less and less time for me, I saw myself pass from desperate need to cooperative acceptance to something close to indifference. I began to like having the neat white apartment to myself, without the tension of Duncan's presence. When I heard the Volvo pull into the driveway and the tired clomp-clomp on the back stairs, my first reaction was a mild disgruntlement, and although I could shake it off and meet him at the door with a kiss, I couldn't banish it permanently.

Once he passed the bar exam, his working day got longer instead of shorter. His clients began calling him at home on weekends, often the same people over and over, with the same old problems or new ones—horrible, unimaginable problems: midnight evictions, welfare checks that didn't arrive, women beaten up by their husbands, landlords who turned off the heat—and Duncan would dash down to the office. Or he'd have to go out to a tenants' rights group, or a meeting of the Board of Aldermen, or over to Dave's to talk strategy.

Very quickly, I began to lose the conviction that the world was being changed. I'd transferred my cartoon collection from the Boston bathroom to the New Haven one. Every time I brushed my teeth I saw THE WORLD IS ROOLED BY DOPS, and it seemed truer than ever. It seemed to me that Duncan was pouring out his blood to feed some monster that always demanded more, more—that would stay on your back if you let it, and weigh you down until you were broken. I couldn't see how all those gifted young men could bring themselves to go to work every day and deal with the forlorn faces and the hopeless bureaucratic knots and the jangling phones and the eternal running around without giving in to despair.

When I broached this with Duncan—tentatively, because I

knew it wasn't a question he'd like—he said it didn't make a damn bit of difference whether what he was doing had any ultimate worth, the important thing was to do it anyway. Despair, he said, was a luxury he didn't have time for, and if I'd participate in things instead of analyzing them to death I'd be a lot better off and so would everyone else.

My old, futile Boston guilt returned—futile because I knew I was never going to do what he did. I wasn't going to devote my life to humanity. I wasn't even going to make what Duncan always called "some little gesture," like tutoring kids in the ghetto or teaching music in a day-care center or learning just enough to help out with the paralegal stuff down at the office. When I said I was too untrained, too inexperienced, too confused in this new city, this new life, to barge into things the way he did, he raised his eyebrows, shrugged, gave up, changed the subject. Nor did he want to hear about my fear of the ghetto itself, the Hill section and the slums around Dixwell Avenue—even the bleak, scruffy streets behind the Legal Aid office—where there were men with knives and guns and grudges, women who would despise me, street-smart children making faces behind my back. When I said I didn't see what good I could do, what difference I could make, his reply was, "If you're not part of the solution you're part of the problem," said with an ironic little smile because it was such a cliché and because he didn't really mean it. But I knew he did mean it, that he saw me as a kind of lovable parasite. I stopped talking about music, how much I missed singing and studying—it sounded so trivial. The despair Duncan didn't have time for settled snugly into my daily routine along with the job interviews and the walks and the ironing.

Once he said to me, half joking, "Maybe it was a mistake, Anna—getting married so fast." It was a shocking statement. We sat staring at each other as if the room had suddenly burst into flames, but in the midst of my shock was a crazy kind of peace. I wanted to embrace his words, I wanted to consume them, wrap them around me. I thought: *Yes, a mistake, this is. it, this is the moment, say it again.* But the moment passed. Duncan held me in his arms and apologized, took it back, said he'd been so harassed lately, so distracted, he was so tired, he was sorry, sorry. I leaned against him and cried as if I'd lost something precious.

Valerie Brady and I became friendly. Although she had three children, she was only a year older than I—an amazing woman who managed a house, kids, her own small career as a painter, and Dave: a big, loud, difficult man who tended to hit her when he got drunk. I came to dislike him intensely, maybe because Duncan idolized him, maybe because Dave ignored me almost entirely. What Valerie told me didn't help.

"He hits his wife," I told Duncan once when he was telling me about Dave's latest achievement, a class action that had forced the state to raise welfare benefits. Duncan and I were eating dinner— *fricassée de poulet à l'Indienne* from the Julia Child cookbook Jean had given me for Christmas. Duncan was shoveling it in as if it were Chef Boy-ar-dee. I spent a lot of time trying not to resent anything so petty. "I think it's wonderful that he's responsible for that, Duncan, but he's given Val two black eyes in the past year. He hits his children. Val told me he even hit the baby the other day."

"He's under a lot of pressure," Duncan said. "You've got to show some understanding. I'm sure he can be a son of a bitch at home. There are times when he's a son of a bitch at work. I don't expect you to agree with me, but Dave is kind of a special case." Valerie had said the same thing; she always laughed dismissively when she told me about Dave's little cruelties, as if, like her painting, they didn't really matter much. I found her enthusiasm and support for her brutish husband disgusting. It was as if Dave and his work were a cult that Valerie had been hypnotized into supporting—or like my father's hospital roommate Ed Kreiger's blind, fanatical devotion to Richard Nixon. Duncan said, "Do you know how hard Dave works? He never eats, he never sleeps, and he has single-handedly improved the standard of living of thousands of welfare mothers—thousands of children all over the state. I mean, he's put food in their stomachs!"

"Duncan, that baby is seven months old!"

Duncan began to suck the inside of his cheek, nodding slightly, looking down at his plate—signs that I was pushing him too far. He said, "I'm not saying it's right to take out your frustrations on your wife and kids. Obviously." His voice became very patient and guarded—his keeper-in-the-asylum voice. "I'm not saying Dave's an ideal person, Anna. I'm just saying you've got to keep some perspective—make some allowances for human weakness."

"What's weaker than a seven-month-old baby?"

"Christ!" He threw down his fork and gazed helplessly around the kitchen as if for assistance, or escape. "Your gift for distortion and exaggeration is truly incredible. It's too bad you can't market it."

"They put people in jail for that kind of thing," I said. "Knocking their kids around." I was getting worked up. Was the man a criminal? Should he be in jail? I tried to remember exactly what Val had said—something about giving the baby a good whack. Probably meant nothing. It was the chicken that was making me push it—that and the old story: I was wrong, I was always wrong, he wouldn't even consider that I might have a point. I tried to stay calm and rational and not like the mental incompetent I knew Duncan periodically considered me to be. I said, "I'm sorry, but even making allowances for human weakness I think he's a bit of a monster."

Duncan turned to me with what looked like hatred. "Jesus! Loosen up a little! You're always so goddamn rigid!"

"Maybe I'm rigid," I persisted. "But at least I don't defend child beaters." Duncan banged his coffee mug down on the table and clenched his fists. "Go ahead," I said. "Hit me. It's all the rage." I almost wished he would. I could see myself walking out on him then, my black eye or dislocated jaw convincing even Alice, even my father, all the people who adored him, that I had a legitimate gripe at last.

But he didn't hit me. He did what I knew he would do: he grabbed his mohair coat and slammed out the door and worked at the office until midnight.

I didn't blame him for hating me. I didn't even care, except at odd moments. Once, I saw him standing in the bedroom doorway looking at his bass fiddle, closed up in its case in the corner, with a look of such loss on his face that I ached with love for him. Sometimes he fell asleep on the couch on a Sunday afternoon and, with his eyes closed, his mouth a little open, his face relaxed and young, he looked like a person one could deal with, a person with all the normal needs and vulnerabilities. Watching him sleep, I loved him as I used to on the stage at the Cantabile.

But when we battled, I hated him, too. The fights we were having—the perverse result of our mutual pledge to bring things out in the open and talk out our problems—lost their polite, almost loving character and became full of a mean, dangerous excitement. We often fought at dinner because it was almost the only time we were alone together. We would begin with a harmless enough disagreement that would escalate quickly into a full-fledged battle in which we deliberately baited each other, hatred suddenly between us like a vicious animal that had been crouched, waiting, under the old metal kitchen table. Then we would start yelling at each other, and it would end in a way I found so curiously satisfying that I began to suspect myself of engineering it: Duncan would storm out of the apartment and go down to the office to work, leaving me alone to spend a peaceful evening doing the dishes and listening to music and then reading in bed late into the night.

I was reading Anthony Trollope. His calm, measured voice brought a kind of composure into my life. I wanted nothing more than to narrow my attention down to Lily Dale's rejection of Johnny Eames, Phineas Finn's struggles in Parliament, the suicide of Augustus Melmotte. I walked to the public library on Elm Street for the lovely little dark-blue books, each one with its silky ribbon bookmark. I took them out one at a time and went through them compulsively. I read for long stretches during the day when I should have been vocalising or job hunting or examining my soul—doing something useful, as I knew Duncan would say if he had been aware of the hours I put in with Trollope.

When I read late at night, it was partly to keep myself awake until Duncan came home. Our sex life went quickly from sublime—or at least interesting—to dismal. He was always tired, and if, in the mornings, we woke up in each other's arms, half the time Duncan would look at the clock, say "Oh shit, I'm late," and have to dash out the door. I considered it my duty—I did try to do my duty—to wait up for him in case he was in the mood to make love. He hardly ever was. Sometimes he was too tired or preoccupied to talk to me, much less touch me, and there were times when weeks would go by without sex, without even much affection.

In the mornings after Duncan left for work, I used to sit over coffee—the prototype of the disaffected, aimless, bathrobed housewife—and try to figure it out: How could a marriage go bad so fast? How could such noble intentions so quickly become good for nothing? Was it right to keep trying to work within the system, or should we blast the whole thing apart and separate? I would sit there at our old metal kitchen table, drinking coffee until I felt sick, thinking until my brain rebelled, and then I would turn to Trollope, or call Valerie, or take one of my wistful walks down to the School of Music.

Besides Val, my other good friend was Susan Marshall, one of the Legal Aid secretaries. There were two of them, Susan and May—overworked, dedicated women who were intimately involved in the tensions at the office but who worked for a salary that made Duncan's measly paycheck look princely. May was a smart, sour widow in her fifties who should have been a lawyer herself. Susan was twenty-two and looked fifteen—plump and apple-cheeked, with her hair in a thick blond braid down her back. She looked like a farm girl, but she was from Pennsylvania, a Bryn Mawr dropout who liked being in the thick of things. An old boyfriend of hers was one of the Harvard students who had held a Dow Chemical recruiter hostage for seven hours: she told this immediately to everyone she met. She herself sent a portion of her paycheck every week to the Berrigan brothers. The first time we had lunch together she told me she wanted to be the first woman president, and she meant it.

"Just don't appoint Duncan your attorney general," I said. "Please. Do me a favor."

She laughed tolerantly. "Duncan's too *busy* to be a cabinet member. He's too fanatical."

Susan was sweet-natured and fearless. She lived right downtown, in the middle of things, and though she hadn't been in New Haven much longer than I had, she knew the city and its resources like a native. She sang alto in the New Haven Chorale, and got me an audition even though rehearsals were just about to begin for the spring event—the Berlioz *Requiem*. I passed the audition—"Well, my God, of *course*," Susan said, but I had had no such certainty. It seemed a long time since I'd been a singer, and when I found out I was in, I went around all day dopey with gratitude. At the chorale rehearsals on Tuesday nights, I felt myself becoming valid again, authentic, myself.

Susan also found me a voice teacher, a man named Jerome Peverel, who, oddly enough, had been on the faculty at the conservatory. He had led the chorus my first year, when we sang the Haydn *Lord Nelson Mass* in Jordan Hall. I remembered him vaguely as a dapper little moustachioed tenor about whom rumors circulated. When he left the conservatory for a year at L'Accademia di Santa Cecilia in Rome, the story was that he was either chasing some contessa or escaping an entanglement with a student he'd knocked up. I was dubious about singing for him—the name Jerome Peverel was such a diabolical blast from the past—but when I went to see him I liked him immediately. He didn't remember me at all, and the man I recalled as dashing and romantic was an aging little fellow with dyed black hair and bright eyes. It was impossible to imagine him chasing contessas over half the world, or impregnating anyone. He seemed as sexless as an elf, or as my neutered old black cat Fred, whom he resembled.

Jerome was ecstatic over my audition for him—or maybe he just needed students. He told me I should be more ambitious, I should be pushing my voice further, I should be preparing for a serious career, I should be singing Mimì and Gilda and Marguerite and Violetta, I should be putting together a solo recital. I wasn't a pop singer, I should be serious. It was what I wanted to hear, and so I began studying with Jerome.

He had obviously come down in the world, from the New England Conservatory faculty to a shabby apartment/studio on College Street, but as I got to know him I discovered that he had designed this life for himself and was perfectly happy with it. He had few students but they were all, he told me, great: great singers but, more important, great souls. He lived simply and ate some kind of health-food diet of grains, nuts, and fruit juices that he squeezed himself in a huge, noisy machine that dominated his tiny kitchen. After my lessons, we drank a cup of herbal tea together while Jerome talked about his philosophy of purification. Purify the body, Jerome said, and you purify the spirit. The solution to the woes of the world was natural, unadulterated food. It was his belief that if Nixon ate cracked wheat and almonds and grated apple for dinner instead of steak with ketchup on it, he would find himself inevitably drawn toward a negotiated peace in Vietnam. He said that if the Black Panthers had been given oatmeal and wheat germ for breakfast when they were little, instead of Sugar Pops and white bread, they would be promoting a spiritual revolution instead of a violent anarchy that threatened the fabric of society. He liked Pierre Trudeau because he had read somewhere that Trudeau and his wife were fond of whole-grain bread.

Duncan thought Jerome was a little crazy, and I suppose I did too, but he was a wonderful teacher. He had complete faith in me, and he said Lydia had spoiled me and not taken me seriously. It was time, Jerome said sternly, to quit goofing off. It was also time to give up meat and coffee and refined sugar. After my first session with him, he gave me a little brown bottle of zinc tablets and told me to take one with my morning papaya juice.

Susan, who had met him over a barrel of brown rice in the health-food store on Whalley Avenue, thought his food theories were brilliant. She tried hard to follow Jerome's diet, but she had a weakness for what she called capitalist-pig food—pizza, especially. She and I used to meet for lunch sometimes at the pizza joint near the office and share a medium-sized pepperoni-and-onion while she told told me the latest Legal Aid gossip.

It was obvious that Susan was fond of Duncan, with an Alice-like blindness to his flaws. "He's so decent," she told me. "He has such a hard time ordering me around. He looks guilty every time he asks me to bring him a file or something. And he spoke to Dave about the crummy salaries the secretaries get—he told him we should be paid the same as the attorneys because we work just as hard."

"And what did Dave say to that?" I asked her. Duncan hadn't told me this—a further sign, if I needed one, of the increasing divergence of our lives. I hadn't told him that Jerome had had the flu or that Thomas Chan, from downstairs, had tried to kiss me when we met in the back hall or that Jean had called to say my cousin Roseanne was pregnant again.

"Oh, God—Dave," said Susan. "I think you could hear him laughing all the way over to Elm Street. But Anna—" Her big blue eyes glistened with sincerity. "He's so *good,* Duncan is. I respect him tremendously. He's really—of all the lawyers—he's the best human being, I think—the most tolerant, the most humane."

It was impossible to talk to Susan about my troubles with Duncan, but I used to talk to Valerie sometimes, although I never found her grin-and-bear-it approach very helpful.

"We might as well not have gotten married, Val," I would say. "I feel like I'm living alone."

"It will pass," she'd tell me soothingly. Sometimes she patted my hand, or held it, or took me by the shoulders as if she wanted to shake some sense into me. Val was very physical. She told me once that she and Dave had sex almost every day, a fact that, as Duncan and I settled into a phlegmatic sexlessness, continued to amaze me.

Val and I used to sit in her living room, on the broken-down couch with its homemade corduroy slipcover. There were milk stains on the corduroy, and the floor was littered with headless dolls and pieces of games and plastic trucks without wheels. April would be on Val's lap, usually nursing. Sebastian would be standing beside the couch, thumb in mouth, clinging to Val's skirt, occasionally leaving temporarily to get down on the floor with Emily, who was given to violent, single-minded games that involved crashing trucks into dolls. All three of the children needed frequent attention—noses wiped, disputes settled, sweaters put on or taken off, cookies supplied. Val would tend to them with affectionate, absentminded efficiency, talking, talking, all the time, advising me, giving me her theories about marriage and child-raising and people and life.

"This is like Duncan's apprenticeship," she told me once. "These guys just need to get organized. And of course it would help if our society weren't so sick. I mean, a little less tax money for the war and a little more for social programs would improve the quality of life for a lot of people, and not just the clients at Legal Aid. Am I right?"

I said she was right. She dislodged her breast from April, tucked it back into her nursing bra, and slung the baby up on her shoulder for a burp. "Give it time, Anna. You had nuns, didn't you? *Patientia virtus est,* or something like that. Those old broads were usually right, if you think about it—except about the evils of sex." April produced a loud belch, and Val grinned. "Here," she said, and handed her to me. "One of the evils of sex. Hang on to her for a minute, will you?"

"But our lives are slipping by." I held April while Val got down on the rug to change Sebastian's diaper. "This is my youth, and I'm spending it waiting for my husband to come home."

"In five years you'll be glad you did it," Val said. "Five years from now you'll be doing the whole middle-class bit—nine to five, house in the suburbs—if that's what you want." She looked up at me when she said this, a pin in her mouth. I had the feeling that, because I kept the apartment neat and took Duncan's clothes to the cleaners, Valerie saw me as a closet bourgeoise. I used to imagine her as Dave's secret agent, sniffing out signs of disaffection among the wives. *Anna's sick of it, she wants a Chrysler, she wants a house in Woodbridge . . .*

"All I want," I protested to Valerie, "is some time with my husband." I didn't tell her how complicated this desire had become—how often it was no longer true. "A companion, Val. Somebody to talk to, somebody who's not always running out the door or talking on the phone or snapping at me."

Val released Sebastian and took April back. "Have a baby," she said.

I scoffed at this advice, told her a kitten or a puppy would do just as well. I didn't want to admit that having a baby had been at the back of my mind since Duncan and I decided to get married. When I sat in the mornings over my coffee pondering that decision, it seemed to me more and more that, among our complex tangle of reasons for getting married, each of us had had a practical, unspoken, ulterior motive: marriage made Duncan more immune from the draft, and marriage would provide me with children. Could it be that our bellicose, sterile union was based on peace and procreation?

We'd talked about children, of course—but always *in potentia*. One night over a bottle of wine we'd even thought up names for them—joking names like Legal Aïda (a tribute to us both) and Duncanette and (for twins) Roseola and Rubella. "When we have kids," one of us would sometimes begin a sentence. "When we have a family . . ." Once, when I was holding Emily Brady on my lap, I caught Duncan looking at us with a bemused, fatuous, fatherly smile.

Not long after my talk with Val I brought the subject up with him again. It seemed to me a chancy thing to do. I never knew what would make Duncan mad. He reminded me of little Emily's game with her trucks: crash! and another unsuspecting doll would be flat on her back, run over. But Duncan and I had been getting along better. He had not only come to Woolsey Hall to hear the Berlioz, he had taken the following Saturday off so that we could hike up Sleeping Giant Mountain. And we were talking about going to Boston for Memorial Day weekend.

I approached him during dinner, another Julia Child effort—*bifteck à la Russe*. "I don't necessarily think we're ready now for a baby, Duncan," I said. "I'm still trying to have some kind of career, and I know you'd have trouble squeezing in fatherhood along with everything else. I just think we should start considering it. Work out some kind of timetable. What do you think?"

I spoke diffidently, afraid to sound too committed. But Duncan surprised me: he smiled—a wistful little smile that made his eyes greener. I smiled back, feeling hope. It was all of a piece: the hike up Sleeping Giant, the plans for Memorial Day. Maybe Duncan had been thinking about a baby, too. Val was right. Patience is a virtue, things do get better.

"Look at it this way," I said. "It would freak out your draft board."

"I'd love to have a kid." His voice was very gentle. I imagined him as a daddy, explaining to little Duncanette that no, she couldn't have a lollipop before dinner. I thought of the sweet, domestic coziness of Jean's prophecy: settle down with some nice man and have a wonderful family, a good life . . . "I'd really love it," Duncan said. "But we'd have to be crazy."

"Why?" I asked him, my heart sinking. Probably not with Duncan, Jean had amended. "What's so crazy, Duncan?" In spite of everything, I didn't want to hear him say we should separate.

"We can't afford luxuries like babies," he said. "Are you kidding? Our expenses are incredible. If we tried to feed a third person we'd have to live on the kind of crap Jerome eats."

"You mean—it's just money? We can't afford it?" What I meant was: *That's all? Money? Not me? Not my moral failings?*

"Just money! Jesus Christ!" Duncan threw down his fork. In two seconds he went from calm to anger, and I saw that he had been holding it all back, the gentleness had been forced. He would, I knew, eat no more *bifteck*. (When Duncan was upset he lost his appetite; when I was, I'd bake a batch of cookies and eat a dozen.) "Just money!" he kept saying. "Jesus Christ, Anna, do you know how little we've got to live on? Do you know what a sacrifice it is some months just to pay the rent? Plus all our little luxuries. The wine in this sauce, for example. And asparagus! Not to mention stuff like your lessons with Jerome."

I sat silent, shocked. From downstairs, Janis on the record player begged me to take another little piece of her heart. The smells of the food on my plate seemed to fill the kitchen: beef, wine, asparagus. I'd gone to the annual shirt sale at the co-op that morning and charged two new shirts for Duncan and a blouse for myself. It was a beautiful spring day. On the way home, I stopped in the Orange Market and saw asparagus tied into little bundles. "First of the season," they told me. "A bargain." A woman in line behind me said that it never seemed like spring to her until she had some asparagus vinaigrette. I bought half a pound for us and half a pound as a present for Jerome because he was still recovering from the flu.

I said, "I'm sorry, Duncan. I didn't know."

"I'm not complaining," he said, calmer. "I'm just asking you to face facts." He smiled again, tightly. "Babies don't grow on trees, you know. They cost."

I said, "I didn't know you resented the money for Jerome. I mean, he's so cheap, and I keep expecting to find a job. I still look, you know." I said this a little guiltily because I hadn't been looking very hard, and I'd turned down a job in a clothing boutique because the manager told me that the first thing I should do was lose five pounds and rethink my makeup scheme.

Duncan said, "Well," and then he shrugged and added, "What the hell." His smile went away again, and he sat with his arms folded, staring down at the remains of his meal. I put down my own fork, folded my arms, and said, "What else do you resent about me, Duncan?"

I expected him either to ignore the question as too vast for a proper answer or to tell me to quit bugging him and stomp out the door, but he looked up and said, "Do you really want to know?"

I said, "Yes, I would, I'd just utterly, totally adore it," in my best sarcastic voice, but I meant it, I did want to know: what, out of my array of faults and inadequacies and weaknesses, annoyed him most?

He said, "I'll tell you," and paused, looking at me thoughtfully. I looked back at him, straight in the eye. Whatever he said—parasite, moral coward, lazy reader of trivial books—I wouldn't flinch. He said, "I resent the fact that you contributed to Jack's losing the election."

I thought I had heard him wrong; maybe Janis had distorted what he said. "What?"

"I mean it. God, Anna, I was so distracted last summer, you and I were so tuned in on what was going on between us, that I lost touch with the campaign right when Jack needed me. I mean, the guy lost by a hair. And not only did you never help—never volunteer one minute of your time to hand out leaflets or make a couple of phone calls—not only that, but you hit me with this bombshell right in the middle of everything, so that I'm spending my time listening to you pour out the details of your grand passion for some alcoholic bozo and trying to convince you to switch it over to me." He snorted, half a laugh.

"I don't believe I'm hearing this," I said. "You're blaming me because Jack Sparks got creamed in the election?"

"When I think of the sleepless nights in that flophouse I was living in, when I think of the hours we spent in that diner on Mass. Ave.—"

"Duncan!"

He stood up, went to the refrigerator, and poured himself a glass of orange juice. Automatically I thought, Good thing I stocked up. He stood with his back to me, drinking. "Don't you care about me at all?" I asked.

He turned, leaning against the refrigerator, holding the glass in front of his chest. He looked handsome and distinguished standing there, like a man in a TV commercial—tweedy-brown sweater, camel slacks, pale-blue shirt, little gold-rimmed glasses; even the bright slash of orange in the glass was exactly right. It was the thing about him that always dazzled me, how wonderful he could look. He said, "Well, I guess I did last summer or I wouldn't have screwed things up for Jack."

"That was last summer."

"Yeah, it was," he said. We looked at each other for a couple of seconds, and then he drained his glass and said that if I didn't mind he thought he'd go down to the office and do a little work.

4

That spring, I began giving piano lessons to Linette Beaumont.

The Beaumonts lived in Susan's apartment building, a roach palace on lower Chapel Street squeezed between a bicycle repair shop and a Laundromat. Dina, Linette's mother, was one of Duncan's clients—pregnant and on welfare. She was separated from her husband; she had perennial troubles with him, and with her landlord, her welfare worker, her neighbors. Duncan had helped her with all these problems, and he was handling her divorce. Dina was lazy and argumentative and promiscuous, according to Susan, but basically not a bad person. Susan sometimes stayed with Linette when Dina was out late. Linette was eight years old and musical, Susan told me. It would be so great if someone could teach her a little something—anything! The kid was starving for music.

I went over there one evening with Susan. Before Dina let us in, Susan practically had to shout her life story through the door. "It's Susan, from downstairs. Susan! We had a cup of coffee the other day? The apartment with the pink walls in the living room? We were talking about Linette, the way she plays the piano at your church?"

Dina unlocked the door. God knows who she was afraid it was—her husband, a welfare worker, a thief/rapist/killer. Maybe the Board of Health, Susan and I said later to each other. The place was a hole—dirty, messy, crammed with dusty knickknacks, stinking of food and urine and cats and Raid.

"I've brought my friend Anna," Susan said when Dina opened up. "The one I told you about, who plays the piano."

"Not really well," I said quickly. "I mean, I've played all my life, and I've studied the piano periodically, but mainly I'm a singer."

But I saw that Dina didn't want to hear the details of my musical career. She said, "Can you teach a kid who's not very smart to play?"

We were still standing in the doorway. Susan said, "Maybe we could sit down and talk about it for a minute, Dina."

Dina said sure, okay, and we all went into the living room— a small, filthy, junky space that made Johnny Tenaro's cabin look like a Mr. Clean commercial. The room seemed full of cats—fat, sleepy animals draped over the furniture. They all looked up when we came in, and yawned simultaneously. In the middle of the floor, like a venerable old landmark persisting in the slums, was a dainty and immaculate dollhouse, a Victorian mansion painted bright blue—four feet high, at least, with a turret and a wraparound porch and fish-scaling on the dormers.

"Don't mind my cats," Dina said, removing a white one from a chair and settling it on her shoulder. "Or my dream house." She gave the dollhouse an affectionate pat. "That's mine, by the way— not Linette's. Look but don't touch, I tell her. You got your toys, I got mine."

The radio was on, loud, playing songs from *Hair,* and Dina turned it down but not off. She was a fat blonde with delicate features and mushroom-colored skin. She looked as if she had never been outside in her whole life. She wore a red maternity top over black bell-bottoms, and her hair was skinned back into a pony tail. I got the feeling she had fixed herself up for our visit, though she had apparently given up long ago on the apartment. The rug was stained and filthy, the sparse furniture was falling apart, and there was junk everywhere—incongruous, unexpected things like the hose from a hair dryer and a chipped ceramic peacock and, on the couch, a paper grocery bag stuffed with what appeared to be empty tin cans.

Dina removed the bag of cans, and Susan and I sat down on the couch. Dina took a rickety maple rocking chair facing us. We sat grouped around the dollhouse as if it were an altar. The white cat jumped from Dina to the floor, stretched, and leaped to my lap.

"He likes you," she said. "That's Ferdinand."

I petted Ferdinand dutifully. "So your daughter wants piano lessons," I said to Dina.

"She needs them," Dina corrected me. "The kid just bangs away, it's disgusting. Crash, crash! Every Sunday after Bible school down in the church basement. They can't get her to stop, and Mr. Kendall, the minister, finally says to me, he says, 'Dina, why don't you get that child some training?' And my husband, Lee—my ex—practically my ex, anyway, and it can't be too soon for me—" She paused to roll her eyes and rake her fingers back through her hair, as if no words, only these desperate gestures, could suggest the hideous nature of her husband. *"He* says she's got a talent. Not that he knows anything."

"But you did say he's a musician," Susan prompted.

"Used to be." Dina laughed, exposing crooked teeth in front and a space where one was missing on the side. She covered her mouth immediately with her hand. "He used to be a lot of things. Now he's just a plain rat bastard."

No one said anything for a minute. A commercial for Seven-Up blasted into the room. Ferdinand, as I petted him, began an enraptured purr. I had just cleared my throat, preparing to say something businesslike, when Dina yelled, "Linette, get out here, and let the lady have a look at you."

A little girl came through a door at the side of the room, hanging back shyly, a cat in her arms. "That's Linette," Dina said. "Come on over here, you, and say hello."

Linette put the cat down and came over. She was a tall, fat child with plump pink lips and a huge puff of light-brown hair. Looking at her, I saw instantly that her father, the rat bastard, must be black—a fact Susan had neglected to tell me. (She made a point of never describing people in terms of their race.) Susan said hi to her, and Linette said hi back, and then she held out her hand for me to shake, an old-fashioned gesture that must, I thought, come from her father; it certainly wasn't Dina's style. Linette's hands were moist and pudgy—unpromising, I thought. Up close, her skin was a uniform pale brown, and she had her mother's delicate nose and hazel eyes. When she let go of my hand, she twined her fingers together and stood awkwardly between her mother and me. Her fat knees stuck out from under a blue dress with a sweater over it. She wore filthy white socks and no shoes. The look on her face expressed amiable patience and nothing else. I wondered what Dina had meant by not very smart.

"I hear you want to play the piano," I said. Linette nodded wordlessly, staring down at the dollhouse. "Maybe you could come over to my apartment sometime and play for me, and we could decide what to do. Would you like that?"

Linette shrugged, and Dina said, "Where?"—suspiciously, as if she feared I lived in an opium den.

"I live over on Orange Street. Not that far from here. Right down the street from the Orange Market."

"I know where that is," Linette said, then put her hands over her ears and giggled.

"Quit that," Dina said to Linette, then to me, "She could go over after school. What about tomorrow?"

I wanted to respond to Dina's high-handedness by objecting, saying tomorrow was no good, how about a week from Thursday. But I thought, What the hell, and said, "Great. What do you think, Linette? Tomorrow? Do you think you can find number five-ninety-two? It's a big gray house and you ring the middle doorbell."

I tried to sound enthusiastic, but my heart wasn't in it. I couldn't imagine that Linette had any talent or even interest, and I didn't like Dina at all—why should I do her a favor? But I thought how pleased Duncan would be. Here was my gesture toward easing the lot of humanity. Here's where I quit being a parasite.

"Write it down," Dina said. "She'll never remember it."

I dislodged the cat—my black skirt had become a nest of white fur—and found paper and pen in my purse. I wrote, very carefully in caps, "592 Orange Street, block after Orange Market, gray house with red front door, ring the middle doorbell." I gave it to Linette. She stood open-mouthed, staring at it, and Dina took it from her. "I'll hang on to it until tomorrow," she said. "She'll just lose it."

I wondered again if the child was retarded. "What grade is she in?" I asked.

"Third," Dina said. I waited for details, for the words *remedial* or *special school*, but nothing came. Dina sat looking at my note, then she glanced up at Linette with a sharp, annoyed look, as if she despaired of the child ever making sense of it.

Susan said, vaguely, "Well, good. That's that." She and I stood up, and Dina hoisted herself to her feet, heavily, one hand on her stomach, one on her back. It was the classic pregnant woman's gesture—though she wasn't yet all that far along—and it was accompanied by a massive grunt. I caught on that we were supposed to feel sorry for her.

"How have you been feeling?" Susan asked her.

"Still got the back aches," Dina said with a sigh. "Still got the swollen feet."

We stood there a minute looking sympathetic, saying oh dear, shaking our heads, while some of the cats rubbed around our legs, and then Susan said, "We'll be getting along, then, Dina." We headed toward the door, but Dina came up to us and took me by the arm.

"Wait." She went back into the room. "Watch this. You've got to see it."

Linette clapped her hands, and Dina turned out the overhead light and the floor lamp that had been lit in a far corner of the living room. Then she went over to the dollhouse and pressed a switch. From inside it, lights glowed. There were curtains at the windows, pulled back to reveal bits of furniture—a plush red Victorian loveseat, the post of a brass bed, a shelf full of tiny books. With darkness all around it, the house was magical, an oasis of order and beauty in the stinking chaos of the apartment.

We stood looking at it, the four of us and a couple of cats, until the Fifth Dimension finished singing "Aquarius." Then Dina put the overhead light back on and it was just a garish plywood-and-balsa dollhouse taking up too much floor space. "I won it at the church bazaar," Dina said. "The only thing I've ever won in my life."

"It's beautiful," Susan said. "You're lucky." Dina looked pleased for the first time since we'd arrived.

At the door I looked back at Linette, to say good-bye. She was still gazing raptly at the dollhouse, a cat in her arms, her cloud of hair glowing golden-brown in the light. She was smiling. "I'll see you tomorrow, then, Linette," I said to her, and she turned toward me vaguely, in a trance, and slowly nodded.

"She'll be there," Dina said grimly. "Or I'll know the reason why."

Linette showed up at three-thirty. She was wearing jeans and sneakers and a long-sleeved T-shirt that was too short and showed her stomach. Her cloud of hair had been confined in five or six frizzy ponytails that stuck out all over her head—a hairdo, I suspected, of her own devising. I had made oatmeal cookies, and I asked her, "Do you want a snack, Linette, or do you want to play the piano first?"

It was obvious that she wanted both, simultaneously, and so

it took her a minute to decide. I doubted that she was often forced to choose between two desirable alternatives. The plate of cookies was on a platter on the coffee table. She stood looking at the cookies, and then she looked over and saw the piano and said, "Piano, please."

Away from her mother and the oppressive confusion of their apartment, she seemed more alert.

"How was school today?" I asked her.

She thought for a second, narrowing her eyes but keeping them on the piano. "I got ninety-six on an arithmetic test," she said.

"Well, *that's* good, Linette. That's *wonderful!*" I gushed because I was relieved: if she could do arithmetic, maybe there was hope. Maybe she was, truly, a prodigy. My little Mozart, my discovery. Fantasizing, I felt fonder of her.

I pulled the bench out for her, and she sat down, her feet just touching the floor. I drew up a chair beside her. "Do you want to play for me a little?" I asked her. "Show me what you do when you fool around on the piano at church?" Linette put her hands over her ears—that odd gesture—and giggled. I said, "Go ahead, Linette. Play anything you want." I kept urging her and she kept giggling, until I was beginning to think the project was impossible. Then finally, without warning, as if she'd given herself some kind of mental kick, she removed her hands from her ears, put them on the keys, and began to play.

She played for a couple of minutes, and I didn't know what to make of it. She did bang away. She seemed to have no idea that you could get music from the piano without playing as loud as possible. And at first, what she played seemed very strange and formless—crash, crash, as Dina had said, but after a while I thought I could begin to deduce a rhythm and a purpose. She was playing bits of popular songs and improvising around them as a jazz musician would, taking a phrase (I recognized part of "Lady Madonna") and embroidering it with what I realized were her own harmonies—bizarre but consistent combinations of notes, as if some celestial musical system played in her head and she was trying to bring it to earth for the first time. She played with ferocious concentration, bending down over the keys with her face only inches away from her hands, then raising her head again to stare unblinkingly into space. The music was weird and harsh, but not unpleasant, certainly not boring—an amazing sound coming from a fat, shy little girl with no musical training.

After a while, in what sounded to me like the middle of everything, she stopped, as suddenly as she'd begun, and sat with her hands folded in her lap. She looked down at the keys for a minute, and then she lifted her eyes to mine. "That's how I like to play," she said. "But I want to learn to play right, too."

It was the longest statement I'd heard from her, and she said it with pride and determination. It was as if playing the piano had suddenly matured her: no more giggling little girl. Even her eyes looked more serious, the look in them more adult, the brown skin of her face somehow darker, shinier, taut with what I could now see was intelligence.

I said, "I'm not sure I'm the right teacher for you, Linette."

"You're all I got," she said, and I knew that was true. It would do me no good to refer Linette to a real teacher, someone who could teach her jazz theory and improvisation techniques. Dina obviously couldn't afford such a luxury, although Susan had pointed out that if she didn't have to feed all those cats she could afford to send the kid to Juilliard.

I said to Linette, "I wish I could teach you jazz, Linette. Do you know what jazz is? It's the name for the kind of music you play—at least, it's the closest thing I can think of. But it's usually not written down. I'd have to teach you written-down music. Like this."

She shoved over, and I sat beside her on the bench and played the beginning of a Bach minuet.

"Do you like it?"

"It's not written down," she said.

"What? Oh—it is, but I've memorized it. I used to play it when I was your age."

"Does it come in notes?"

"All this kind of music comes in notes."

There was a book of Chopin mazurkas on the stand, and I opened it to show her. She pointed to a note. "This is a note, and it means one of those piano keys. Right?"

"Right," I said, groaning inwardly, thinking what zero we would have to start from.

"So what note is this?" Linette asked, pointing.

"It's D." I played it.

Linette played it herself. "What's this one called?" She banged out the A. I told her, and we went through them all. I knew it was a half-assed way to give a first piano lesson, but she absorbed what

331

I told her instantly, effortlessly, even the complicated idea that the black keys could be called either sharps or flats. She went up and down the keyboard playing the keys and calling them by name as if they were her friends.

When I suggested, after a while, that we take a break, she kept her fingers on the keys, frowning. I said, "I'll show you how to play a real tune if you'll sit down with me and have a cookie and a glass of milk."

"I already can play real tunes. I can play that one you just did."

"We'll take a break and then we'll see," I said firmly, and pulled the bench away from the piano so she could hop off it.

I had to make her chocolate milk; she shuddered at the thought of plain as if I'd offered her rat poison. While she ate, I asked her about school, about what she liked to do in her spare time, about her friends. I wanted to figure her out, get to know her better, but I didn't progress very far. She had no friends, she said. She liked school okay. She did okay in reading. At home she watched TV with her mother and played with her dolls. Sometimes her father took her out on Saturdays, and they went to his girlfriend's house and washed the car or listened to records. His girlfriend's name was Rochelle. She was nice. Her mother was expecting a baby in August. She hoped it would be a girl. She didn't like boys.

She told me all this unwillingly, answering what I asked her but volunteering nothing. She ate cookies steadily and kept her gaze implacably on the piano. The conversation obviously didn't interest her. Nor, I soon realized, did it interest me. The Linette who went to school and watched TV with her mother had little in common with the Linette who wanted to learn the names of notes. Finally, when she had eaten maybe half a dozen cookies and gulped down the milk—there was a dark-brown milk moustache against her toast-colored skin—I said, "Maybe we should get back to the lesson."

Her eyes gleamed. "Is this a lesson?"

"Well—sort of."

She smiled shyly and went back to the piano. "I'll bet I can play that tune," she said. "That one you played."

She sat down and began her crashing chords, and in the midst of them I could hear, like a captive animal in a dense forest, the main theme of the Minuet in G struggling to emerge.

When she was finished, she again sat with her hands in her lap. "That's the way I play it," she said after a second.

"What else can you play?" I asked her. She smiled at the keys, silent, then drew her mouth down and gave a gentle shrug. Anything, it meant. I said, "Suppose I play something, and then you do it your way."

I played "The Happy Farmer," and she played it after me, banging out harmonies that would have driven Schumann up the wall—or maybe not. Her playing was very appealing, and strangely assured, and though she never hesitated, never fumbled for a note, there was an exploratory quality to what she did, as if she knew what she wanted but wasn't sure how to get it. She would play variations on her variations, pounding at the keys with an empty, expectant look on her face, and her fat little hands against the ivory looked exactly right, with the combination of tension and ease that some pianists (me, for example) struggle for all their lives.

I looked for the pattern in what she was doing. Sometimes it seemed to me that her searches were random, shots in the dark to see what would turn up, but sometimes I was sure that I was simply missing something: my ear wasn't as good as hers. I wished, suddenly, that Hal were there. Hal would know what to do, he could teach her things I couldn't, he would understand the structure, if there was one, behind the violent chords and the densely packed notes.

She worked her spells on "The Happy Farmer" for quite a while. When she stopped, and after the pause to collect herself which I now saw was customary and necessary, I took her fat little hands in mine and said, "Linette, you are an amazing piano player. You're fantastic. You're very talented. I don't know what I can teach you, but if you really want to learn to play, I'll be happy to do whatever I can."

She stared at me, and then she took her hands away, put them over her ears, and giggled.

Linette came over regularly once a week, on Wednesday afternoons. Dina was supposed to pay me fifty cents a lesson. "Charge her something," Susan had advised. "Otherwise she won't take it seriously." I didn't like to accept even that small amount—although when, after a couple of weeks, Dina stopped paying, I began to feel ripped off and resentful. But I didn't complain about the mother because the daughter was a joy to teach. She was no Mozart, but she was quick and willing. She learned speedily to read music—she seemed to have an instinctive knowledge of musical notation, as if she had learned it in another life—and by the middle of the summer she could play everything in the basic beginners' book I had bought her. Her playing was invariably, uncannily correct, but she was content to play each piece with competence, without fire or feeling, as if playing the piano were a game, or an arithmetic problem.

"Isn't that the way all gifted kids play?" Duncan asked. "All technique and no soul?"

"But she does have soul," I insisted—or something, some inner music that came out only in her improvisations and that I couldn't define or explain to anyone. She loved the pieces in her book, the little minuets and folk songs and marches; "Au Clair de la Lune" moved her almost to tears. She even played scales with enthusiasm, and with a secure sturdiness that I knew would delight a real piano teacher. But no matter how hard she worked at what she called the note pieces, I always sensed in her a carefully controlled impatience for the second half of the lesson, when I would let her improvise and she would sit there tirelessly for another half hour or so, sometimes much longer, completely absorbed in the freakish variations she performed on her pieces.

Her only real technical problem was with dynamics; she played everything loud, and I spent a lot of time trying to get her to control the pressure of her fingers, to play softly when soft was called for, to work up to crescendos instead of letting loose as soon as she saw one coming—and to understand why it was important to play that way instead of the whacking and thumping she preferred.

Oddly enough, though, it was in her own improvisations—the second half of the lesson—that her dynamic control improved. Her music also became more intelligible, a phenomenon that worried me. Maybe it was simply that I was getting used to her style, but it seemed to me that the melody emerged more easily and strongly the more she spent with me, and her harmonies were less startling and bizarre. I didn't know if that was a positive development, or if I was having a deadening influence on her genius. I didn't know if it *was* genius, or what I was supposed to do with it besides insisting that she get the dynamics right when she played Bach.

I became fond of Linette. Duncan and I didn't talk about

having babies anymore—it was too volatile a subject—and Val said Linette was my baby substitute. If she was, she was a mighty big baby. Linette got visibly taller over that spring and summer, and fatter—a large beige lump of a girl with a dreadful mother, no friends, and music in her blood. When school let out, she began coming over an extra day a week, to practice or just to hang around. We went to the library a couple of times and I picked out books for her, the girls' books of my own youth: *Anne of Green Gables, Sensible Kate, The Secret Garden, Little Women.* Sometimes she stayed with me for hours, reading or, more often, playing the piano, drowning out the noises from the street and the records played by our neighbors downstairs. Her music became as familiar to me as the sound of my own voice; it came into my head at odd moments, crowding out the Puccini arias I was singing that summer.

While she was practicing, I'd occasionally go out to the store or for a walk, and as I returned up Orange Street I'd hear the sound of the piano—she played louder when I wasn't there to bug her about it—and be carried back to my youth and the sound of Mamie at the piano. In fact, Linette often reminded me of Mamie—the passion for the piano, the aggressive music, the strong will, even Mamie's fearless eccentricity, all were part of Linette, and made me love her more.

I was in the mood to love people in general. After the baby argument, I think Duncan and I both realized the immensity of the danger we were on the brink of, and we drew back in silent accord. He was pleased that I was giving lessons to Linette, whom he called "the Pudgy Prodigy," and pleased when I finally found a job—part time, mornings only, as a summer replacement in a bookstore. At least until Labor Day, I could pay Jerome out of my own pocket. Duncan's accusations about Jack Sparks and the election preyed on my mind, but when I got up the nerve to ask him about them again he only said, "I have a bad habit of mouthing off about things I don't really mean." Forgive him, he said, pay no attention—so that I had no idea how he really felt.

But our hateful arguments stopped, and we returned, deliberately at first, and then naturally, gladly, to the tenderness of the first months of our marriage. Duncan started bringing work home and sitting with it, evenings, at the kitchen table the way he used to back in Boston. I appreciated the gesture, grateful for what I had complained to Alice about in the old days. Our sex life revived with the warm weather. One Saturday we drove out to the beach in Madison and spent the whole day lying together on a blanket, kissing like teenagers, rubbing suntan oil on each other's backs. We began to forego the Saturday night parties and stay home together to spend long, hot, sleepy nights in bed with a bottle of wine or watching the Red Sox games together. When I heard Duncan's step on the back stairs, I ran to meet him, and we stood in the middle of the kitchen floor with our arms around each other while he told me the news from the office and then asked, "And how was your day?"

Late in the summer, Dina had her baby. It was a boy, which upset Linette—who was already upset because her mother was so preoccupied. She stayed with her father and Rochelle while Dina was in the hospital, and she remained with them even when Dina came home. Dina said all her energy went into struggling to cope with the baby, she didn't have a minute for Linette. Duncan was trying to get Dina some help from the city health services, but so far he hadn't succeeded, and Susan and I were both over at the apartment a lot trying to help out.

The baby—Zane, for some reason—was difficult, a cryer, hungry and demanding. He was also white, and obviously not Lee's child; he looked exactly like Dina—same lank hair, same tiny nose—and he seemed to have inherited her bad temper. Dina was having trouble breast-feeding him, she was irritable from lack of sleep, and, when I was over there one boiling-hot day, she got mad at me because I began cleaning up the place—accusing me of lording it over her, looking down on her because she was poor and fat. I kept doggedly scrubbing the kitchen floor over her protests, and we yelled back and forth at each other from room to room, over Zane's squalling and the eternal rock 'n' roll blasting from the radio. When Susan arrived, I escaped, leaving behind a clean kitchen, Dina in tears, the cats underfoot, and Susan looking after me reproachfully as I fled down the stairs.

I walked home, the sidewalk burning through the soles of my shoes. Sweat dripped down my back. Our apartment had been closed up all day, and when I got home it was airless and oppressive; it seemed not merely empty but deserted, bereft. Duncan was going to be late, and I missed him. I wanted to put my arms around him. I wanted someone to bitch about Dina to. I was tired—I'd worked at the bookstore in the morning and been with Dina the rest of the day—and I still felt bad about my argument with her. I had to admit to myself that what she had said was true: I did look down on her, I thought she was a lazy, improvident slob to an extent that poverty was no excuse for, I thought she provided an unwholesome environment for Linette, and I had washed all her dishes and scrubbed years of dirt and crud and cat shit off her linoleum because I wanted her to be grateful to me and to see the error of her ways, not because I truly wanted to help out. I was going through the apartment, opening windows and putting fans in them, thinking what a terrible person Dina was, what an even worse person I was, when the phone rang, and it was Johnny Tenaro.

I had called him soon after Duncan and I were married, but we hadn't communicated since. "I've got news," he said, and immediately I thought he was going to tell me something about Will—something horrible that jibed with the rotten day I'd just put in: he's dead, he's married again, he's in jail. I steeled myself for it, but the news had nothing to do with Will. Johnny was getting married, in November, to the woman he'd been seeing for over a year. Her name was Julia. They wanted me to come to the wedding.

"You'll be getting a real-live invitation in the mail, the whole engraved bit, but I wanted to invite you in person," Johnny said. "It's Thanksgiving weekend, on the Saturday. So everybody should be in town. We'll have a little class reunion—selective, of course. Bring your husband. It'll be a blast, I promise. Like old times."

I told him we'd come, and then he asked about me—Duncan, New Haven, my father and Jean, my singing. As we talked, as Johnny made his worn-out jokes, as I passed on the small details of my life, a desperate impatience boiled up in me. Having once thought of Will—Will in jail, Will dying alone in some hospital, Will with his hands on other women—I could think of nothing else, and finally, when there was a pause in the conversation, I asked Johnny if he'd heard from him. There was the obligatory condescending chuckle: good old Willie, a rare bird. Yes, indeed, Willie boy had been in town a while back, visiting his sister. He was getting along okay out in Indiana, working for the city doing something, Johnny couldn't remember what—coordinating programs for kids? Some real low-key thing. Out in the fresh air a lot. Anyway, he liked it. Seemed happier than he'd been in years. Wasn't drinking much. Waiting for the custody hearing. Hopeful. What else? He'd let his hair grow, looked kinda skuzzy. Johnny'd had his cut, at Julia's insistence. She'd see at the wedding: he looked like a preppy asshole. But what the hell, all for love. Don't forget—November 29. See you then. *Did he ask about me? Is he coming to the wedding?* I couldn't get the words out. See you then.

Happier than he'd been in years. When Duncan came home I was still crying, and he blamed it on Dina, told me enough was enough, I didn't have to sacrifice myself to her and her blasted baby. The Visiting Nurse Association was sending someone over there the next day, I should forget Dina, put my feet up, slow down.

He brought me dinner on a tray. We watched a Yankee–Red Sox game together. I sat next to Duncan on the couch, the fan blowing on us, and I counted up my blessings, carefully, precisely, beginning with Duncan and ending with the ball game: the Red Sox creamed the Yankees, 7–1. During the night I woke sweating from a dream whose details I couldn't recall. Vivid in my mind was the Bonwit box full of relics that I'd thrown in the Dumpster back in Boston: my old diary, the photograph with its cracked glass, the plastic angel, the Elvis record. I wondered where they were, ground to bits in a dump somewhere, burned and melted and buried, but—I squeezed my eyes shut, kept my hand over my mouth so I wouldn't sob aloud—never, never forgotten. I lay awake beside Duncan for a long while, listening to his soft snoring, watching dawn sneak into the room around the corners of the window shades, and feeling the tears run down my hands, my hot cheeks, and soak into the pillow.

5

The Beaumonts' divorce became final that summer, and though Dina had custody, Linette for the time being continued to stay with her father. I'd stopped spending time at Dina's; Susan told me Zane was no easier but Dina was coping better with the help of a nurse. Linette began coming less regularly for lessons. Sometimes she simply wouldn't show up, but usually Lee would call and explain that Linette just couldn't make it. He never said why.

I met him a few times when he came to drive her home. He always shook my hand when he arrived and when he left, and once he brought me a box of Italian pastries from Marzullo's. He was a tall, handsome black man, usually in a khaki uniform; he worked as a security guard at Winchester. When he wasn't working, he wore his shirts unbuttoned and a chain around his neck. He'd stand talking to me, or waiting for Linette to finish playing—he was never in a hurry—and his presence would fill the apartment and make it seem small and plain. Meeting Lee, I could see where Linette's exuberant music came from. He was sexy, charming, always laughing. I couldn't imagine why he had married the dour Dina. He obviously adored Linette—said he was glad Dina had had her little white bastard so he could spend some time with his daughter. I believed that Dina loved her, and Linette had told me that, for reasons I couldn't fathom, she missed her mother badly. But when Linette was with Lee she was a different child—less shy, sillier, and full of all his courteous habits. Once, when leaving, she made a deep curtsy to me, and Lee roared with laughter. Quite a compliment, he said. Rochelle had taught her to do that in case she ever got introduced to a queen.

Lee insisted on paying me two dollars for Linette's lessons.

Dina's fifty cents was a joke, he said. I didn't tell him that Dina never paid me, anyway. Lee thought it was great that Linette could study piano, he'd always wanted a career as a musician himself, but things just didn't work out that way. He'd never had a lesson, but he'd played for a while in a jazz band when he was in high school and he still did a gig now and then, for a party or a friend's wedding.

"What instrument?" I asked him, thinking that if he said bass—he looked to me like a bass player—I'd drag Duncan's old neglected fiddle out of the back room and get him to play, and I'd ask Duncan to give him a few lessons. In a flash I had a vision of this happening, of a kind of paradise in which a laughing Lee maneuvered his fingers up and down the strings, Duncan got involved in music again, Linette and her father played jazz together and I sang, and the Chinese boys downstairs came up to drink beer and applaud—all of us one big happy integrated family.

"Saxophone," Lee said. "Another Coltrane, that's me, ha ha," and he caught Linette up in a violent, joyful hug.

Jerome began grooming me for the fall tryouts of the New Haven Opera Company, a group that used local talent, working with the New Haven Symphony and the Connecticut Ballet, to present grand opera on a small scale, accessible to the community—singing in hospitals and nursing homes, giving workshops in the schools, encouraging gifted amateurs to sing in the chorus and play in the orchestra.

"But it's all on a very high level, musically," Jerome assured me—as if I were Joan Sutherland slumming.

"I don't care what level it's on, Jerome," I told him. "It sounds great, I want to do it. God—just to get up on a stage again and sing!"

The fall production was *La Bohème*. I wanted to try out for Musetta—I could sing "Musetta's Waltz" standing on my head—but Jerome insisted I go for Mimì. He said, "We haven't worked all these months so you can play a two-bit part with a two-bit opera company." He also wanted me to eat only grains and fruit for the month before the auditions. I did try, at least when Duncan wasn't around, and as a result I lost a few pounds, which pleased Jerome. "You'll sing even better thinner," he said, and slammed his own flat stomach with the palm of one hand. "Here! The meat goes straight down here and compresses the voice. It squeezes everything shut. It's a myth that fat people make great singers."

Whether that was true or not, I felt that I was singing well. Jerome was a wonderful teacher, at least for me, because his confidence never faltered for a second. He said it was all crap, what I'd been told at the conservatory and what I'd told myself all those years, that my voice was limited, too light, too insignificant and plain, somehow, to sing great music.

"You have a gift," he said. "It's there. It just has to be drawn out of you." He spoke in the same convinced, emphatic way in which Sister Cecilia had once told me I'd inherited my grandmother's blessed voice, and his certainty wasn't something I wanted to quarrel with. I worked on "Sì, mi chiamano Mimì" all summer. "You study with me," he said, "and you sing with NHOC for a year, and then we'll get you into Yale if that's what you want. Or a recital, if you want to go that route."

I didn't know what route I wanted. It seemed to me that I should want something—I *did* want something—but when I tried to figure out what it was, it was like listening to Linette's searches at the piano: there was a pattern, but I couldn't quite grasp it. I no longer took my long, wistful walks past the School of Music, but I thought about it sometimes, and I pictured myself studying there, and going on to sing in New York, in Rome, in London, to teach, to make recordings. I would brighten my father's old age, make Duncan proud of me, and earn vast sums of money which I would donate to worthy causes, among them Linette's education, a start in a musical career for Lee, some job training for Dina to make up for all my evil thoughts about her, and big bucks, given anonymously, for secretaries' salaries at New Haven Legal Assistance.

And then I didn't get the part. I sang badly, as I tend to at auditions; with no real audience, singing is a clinical thing, like a practice session—I can't connect with the music. And I had warmed up too long because I was nervous, so that the aria sounded thin and tired and mechanical; I had to force the high notes, and it showed.

Halfway through I wanted to stop, but I pushed through to the end, and when I finished I was shaking.

My competition was a powerhouse soprano, a local legend named Vanessa Sinclair. She was a Juilliard graduate who'd given up a career to be a housewife to her Yale-professor husband, and her voice was a miracle. Next to her, I sounded like—what? I sounded like a cabaret singer. Her singing brought tears to my eyes, and not only because all my hopes were effectively dashed. Worst of all, she was nice to me.

"You have a beautiful, beautiful voice," she trilled at me when it was over, pretending she hadn't seen my tears. "You are going to be a great success. And look at you—" She touched my cheek. "You're lovely. So young—and so thin! You must look wonderful onstage."

"We'll call you," the music director said to us both, and Vanessa hugged me and swept out on his arm. I was offered a part in the chorus, but Jerome advised me not to take it. He said it would just distract me from the work I was doing with him, and it would do my career no good.

"What career, Jerome?" I asked him. "I'm not going to have a career."

"Don't say that, you're just upset. These things happen, it's no reflection on you."

I tried to tell him the truth—that I didn't feel upset, I felt unburdened. "I've been living in a dream world," I said. "I'm not a real singer, Jerome. I'm never going to sing Tosca, for Christ's sake. I'm no Mimì, I'm no Violetta. I don't want to try for it anymore."

"You haven't tried at all," he insisted. "One lousy audition that was probably rigged."

"Jerome." We were sitting in his studio drinking rose-hip tea. He had cursed the New Haven Opera Company, its music director, and poor Vanessa Sinclair with every foul word in his vocabulary. "Please, Jerome," I said. "Let's do some Gilbert and Sullivan. Let me sing a little Gershwin for you. A couple of show tunes. That's what I'm good at."

He snorted scornfully and took a long swig of tea as if it were whiskey. "Show tunes," he said. "Spare me."

I felt sorry for him. I knew I was the best of his students, his best hope. "Oh, come on, Jerome," I said. "Let's have some fun. Let me just sing 'September Song' for you. Come on. I'll make you cry."

He sighed massively and gave a what-the-hell shrug, and we went over to the piano. I sang, and he cried.

That fall, three things happened: Dave knocked Val down the stairs, and she broke two ribs and her left arm; Lee and Rochelle disappeared, taking Linette with them; and Duncan made a pass at Susan.

I suppose all three events were connected. Duncan and I had a violent argument about Dave and Val. Dave insisted it had been an accident, and Duncan took his side. He said Val must be exaggerating, or telling an outright lie. She was staying at her mother's in Hartford with the children. I drove up to visit her, I saw the bruises and the cast on her arm, I heard her story. "Why would she lie?" I asked Duncan. "Why would she make such an appalling statement if it weren't true?"

"Who knows?" Duncan said. "I only know what Dave tells me. He's devastated by this. He doesn't understand why she blames him for something he didn't do, then takes off with the kids. His theory is she wants a divorce and this way she can really soak him for alimony."

"And you believe that?"

"Why shouldn't I? You believe Val."

"Duncan, Dave's got a history of this kind of thing. You know what he's like! He's got a violent temper, he's been knocking Val around for years."

"Let her try and prove it in court."

"I've seen her black eyes, Duncan. I've heard her versions of all this stuff. If she needs someone to testify for her, I will."

"You would do that?" He glared at me, his eyes hot and alienated like they were the time he took LSD. I thought: I will never understand this man. "You would really do that," he said—as if it were some sort of personal betrayal.

I said, "Duncan, this is a woman in trouble! This is my friend! Of course I'd do it, if it would help."

He quit speaking to me then, and the next day Dina called me with the news about Linette, and I was so agitated I didn't even try to make things up with Duncan. Dina said Lee must have been planning this move for a long time. He and Rochelle had given the landlord a month's notice, Lee had formally quit his job, he'd even told Linette's teacher she might be moving away. But he'd told Dina nothing, and he'd left no forwarding address anywhere.

"He's probably gone to his people down in Virginia," Dina said. "Or maybe to those no-good friends of Rochelle's in New York. I'm going to make inquiries, let me tell you. That son of a bitch isn't going to get away with this, kidnapping my little girl away from me."

In the background, I could hear Zane crying and the radio

playing. I'd been over there a few days before—stopped in on impulse on my way home from an interview for an office job I knew I wouldn't get. Dina's kitchen had reverted to its filthy state—maybe worse—and the deluxe illuminated dollhouse in that squalid place, the poor pale-faced baby crying in his crib, the blasting radio and the hungry cats, all made me so angry I had to leave almost as soon as I arrived. Linette was well out of it, I couldn't help thinking, but as I stood there listening to Dina's whiny voice over the phone, I realized with a kind of outrage that she would do nothing to retrieve Linette. She didn't really want her back; under the phony indignation and the pleas for sympathy, there was a shallow pool of indifference and selfishness. Linette had been with Lee for over a month, and Dina hadn't complained, except to abuse Lee in general terms. She raved on, said she'd get Duncan to track him down, she'd get the cops after him. I stood there with the phone in my hand, and when she stopped for breath I said, "Go to hell, Dina," and hung up.

I knew that one of the things that bothered me was Lee's failure to tell me he was taking Linette away. I'd thought he was, in some way, a friend; I'd thought I'd sensed a small, unspoken magnetism between us. I felt foolish and betrayed, I grieved for Linette and her music, for the little person who sprawled on my living-room floor eating cookies and reading *Anne of Green Gables,* and when Duncan came home I took the whole thing out on him. We had another fight, and he stormed out of the house and went to the office.

It was maybe a month later that Susan and I had lunch together and she looked earnestly at me across an anchovy pizza and said, "I want to tell you something, Anna. I think it's important that you know this."

I knew already. I guessed from the way she looked at me, with the pitying affection you feel for a victim. Her big blue eyes were shiny with unshed tears and a kind of excitement. She said Duncan tried to kiss her one night when they were both at the office late. She didn't think it meant anything, they were both tired, they'd worked so hard, trying to bring that landlord to court—did I remember the Willis case? Really, it wasn't important, but she thought I should know. Maybe I hadn't been paying Duncan enough attention lately—she knew I was still upset about Linette, and she knew Duncan and I never did see eye to eye on the Dave and Valerie thing. Maybe we should take a vacation somewhere; Duncan had been working himself to death.

I sat in silence, barely listening to Susan's advice on how to save my marriage. The more she talked, the more convinced I became that it wasn't just a case of Duncan trying to kiss her. She'd kissed him back—I could see it on her pale lips, in her shining eyes. And maybe not just kisses. For all I knew, they'd been having an affair for months. I thought of Thomas Chan last summer, bending his lips to mine on the back stairs, my grocery bag between us. When I pushed him away, he said, with his Oxford accent, "Oh, Barbra, forgive me, but sometimes I'm overcome by how beautiful you are." He followed me upstairs, and I sang "Happy Days Are Here Again" for him in my Streisand screech, but when he tried to cuddle up beside me on the piano bench, I said, "Really, Thomas, you have to remember that I'm a married woman." I sat watching Susan make her little speech, thinking that I should have done it. I liked Thomas. He had a kind heart, he appreciated me, he was trim and healthy and smart and his straight black bangs touched the tops of his horn-rimmed glasses. I could imagine him asking me, "And how was your day, my beautiful Barbra?"—really wanting to know.

Susan said, "He's so incredibly dedicated, I know it wouldn't be easy to get him to take time off, but he needs a break, Anna, he really does, he's under such a strain all the time—I don't think he's himself lately, Anna, you have to forgive him. I don't want you to think this means anything."

"You can stop talking, Susan," I said finally. "Because I really don't care what you and Duncan do together."

"But we didn't do anything, Anna! Please believe that. It was just a moment of madness, a crazy impulse that didn't mean a thing!"

I reached across the table to lay my hand on hers. "You can have him if you want him, Susan. Please. Take him," I said, and then I walked out, leaving her with the cold pizza and the check.

I began to feel as if someone had taken a tuck in my life and snipped away the new good parts, leaving me back where I'd started. Linette—my pudgy prodigy, my baby substitute—was gone, my summer job had come to an end, Duncan and I were back to being mere roommates, winter was returning to New Haven, and I was singing Gershwin again. I'd even had an audition with the manager of the cocktail lounge at the new Park Plaza

Hotel. They had a little combo and wanted to add a singer. If life were a movie, I said to Val, I'd walk out on it: this is where I came in.

Val and Dave were back together and seeing a marriage counselor. Val didn't want to talk about it. She said she was stuck. "Three kids, no skills, no money. What else is there to say?"

So we talked about me instead. Val said she was sure Susan and Duncan weren't having an affair. "If they were, I'd be aware of it, believe me," she said. "I've been picking up vibes from that place for so long that they can't sharpen a pencil without my knowing." I thought she was probably right. I even called Susan and apologized for overreacting. It was everything, I explained: the audition, Linette, Val and Dave, my period—probably the lack of the proper grains in my diet, who could say? Susan and I had an expiatory lunch during which we exchanged chorale gossip (we were rehearsing the Bach B Minor Mass), and she told me about Harold, the cat she'd adopted from Dina. We went through a medium pizza, two root beers, and a hunk of strawberry cheesecake, and we didn't mention Duncan's name once.

When I talked about it with Valerie, she said, "Your problem is that although Duncan's not screwing Susan, he's not screwing you, either. Am I right?"

I said, "Oh, Valerie, everything doesn't always come down to sex." But she got me to admit (Valerie would have made a formidable trial lawyer) that our sex life had deteriorated again—disappeared, in fact.

"I can't make myself want to go to bed with someone I hardly ever talk to," I said. "Someone I go around being polite to all the time."

Valerie said that was ridiculous. She insisted that her passion for Dave, his for her, never let up, even in the worst of their troubles. "It's just organs, for heaven's sake, Anna," she said to me. "Think of yourself as one vast vagina—not all day, of course, but when Duncan gets home at night. Think of Duncan as nothing but a penis."

"It's hard to think of someone as a penis when he's sound asleep," I said. "I never heard of a snoring penis. And what good would it do anyway? What good is sex with nothing to back it up? No feeling?"

"It'll come," she said. "Reconciliation through reproduction. Flush your birth-control pills down the toilet and seduce him.

Duncan thinks he doesn't want a baby, but when he's faced with the little bugger he'll change his mind."

"Is that what you did with Dave?"

"Only the first one," she said, smiling. "After that it was a piece of cake."

"Oh, right," I said. She still had the cast on her arm, still gasped when she stood up because of the broken ribs. "Some piece of cake, Val."

She didn't stop smiling. "We're not going to talk about that—remember? But let me give you a tip. Sex with a cast on your arm can be really kinky."

Duncan didn't go home with me at Thanksgiving. I begged him to come. "You promised," I pleaded. "You said this wouldn't happen."

"Anna, I tried," he said. His voice didn't sound as if he'd tried very hard. "I said it wouldn't happen if I could help it, and I couldn't help it. I'm right in the middle of a dozen things that are really critical. I can't just walk out on it."

"Duncan." I sat down beside him on the couch and took his hand. We hadn't touched, deliberately, in so long that he felt strange, foreign, the skin of his hand rough and hot. His grandfather's gold watch said quarter past ten. I matched my hand to his, finger to finger. I said, "Duncan, I think we've got a problem."

"A problem?" His voice was polite, even amicable—the voice of an interviewer on a news program. But I'd become adept at sniffing out Duncan's real mood beneath his impersonal cheerfulness and good-natured bustling around, and I sensed hostility. He started to take his hand away, then thought better of it. "What kind of a problem?"

I couldn't immediately answer. In that moment, when his hand tensed and half withdrew from mine, I had one of my visions, a flash of insight that I knew was true no matter what Val's vibes told her, or what Susan said—or what Duncan himself would have said if I'd asked him. He was seeing Susan—if not Susan, then someone else, but I would have put money on Susan. I don't know why I became so sure at that moment, why that slight hesitation of his hand should tell me this. But I did become sure. As sure as big George's picture is on the almighty dollar bill, as Eric Silver used to say.

I said, "We have a problem with the sink in the bathroom." I disentangled my hand from his. "It leaks around the housing for the faucet. What does that mean? We need a washer? Or some

347

kind of packing? Don't say a new faucet, we'll never get Grossman to put it in."

He stared at me. "That's the problem?"

"Don't laugh. It's driving me crazy. It drips, too."

He shrugged. "Hell, I don't know how to fix it. Call Grossman. Ask one of the guys downstairs. They know about that stuff." I'll ask Thomas to come up and look at it, I thought: Thomas Chan, who thinks I'm beautiful. "Or Val," Duncan suggested. He stood up, yawning. "Val knows everything."

I had the vision again: Duncan and Susan together on the broken-down old couch in the back storeroom at the Legal Aid office. Susan's pink, pink lips and blue, blue eyes. Duncan taking of his Shetland sweater, his new blue shirt, his camel pants, his grandfather's watch. "I don't think Val knows quite everything," I said.

"No kidding." We smiled at each other. It was okay to disagree about Dave and Valerie now that they were back together, now that everything was fine. They had become a joke, like a sitcom on TV: catch the Bradys, those wacky battling lovebirds!

"I'm really sorry about Thanksgiving, Anna," Duncan said. His smile disappeared, but I could see he was keeping it ready. "If it were just a day or two I could swing it, but not this four-day weekend. Not Thanksgiving dinner plus the wedding."

"I understand," I said. "If it weren't for Johnny's wedding I'd stay here with you."

"No—no, you need to be with your family—see your old friends. It'll be good for you. I'll survive."

"What will you do for Thanksgiving dinner?"

He laughed. "Assuming I have time to eat one, I'll probably get together with some of the other lame ducks around here and go out for a pizza or something."

He was heading for the bathroom. He would brush his teeth, I knew, and wash his face, and pee, and put on the clean pajamas I'd ironed for him that afternoon, and be asleep half a minute after his head hit the pillow.

"That doesn't sound so bad," I said.

"Could be worse." He turned at the bathroom door to look at me with an enigmatic smile. "I won't have that much to be thankful for, anyway."

6

My cousin Roseanne and I were exactly the same age, but we were never great pals. For as long as I could remember, we had trouble thinking of anything to say to each other, and if we were thrown together at a family gathering we always ended up playing crazy eights or Monopoly. She was a pale, skinny little girl with mosquito bites all up and down her legs, famous for her collection of Trixie Belden books. Then she became a nervous, pimply high school girl who longed, she told me, to be a cheerleader—then a psychology major at a Catholic women's college in Albany, talking about the vernacular mass and IQ testing.

Now she was, as she said, nine and a half months pregnant, so huge she couldn't sit properly at the table—she had to lean back in her chair like a seal on a beach, sipping at Uncle Phil's pink wine, unable to eat more than a few nibbles of turkey. Ronnie, her husband, was kept busy minding their first child (a quiet, red-headed two-year-old named Nicole) and tending to Roseanne—bringing her another cushion, filling her wineglass, massaging her shoulders. "I just wish this kid would hurry up," Roseanne said at one point. "I know I look awful," and she burst into tears.

She did look awful, and it was obvious that she didn't feel so great, either. Her temper was precarious. Her life had dwindled down to nothing but a long, tedious wait. Her husband was one of the most unengaging men I'd ever met. I knew for a fact that she couldn't carry a tune. But, sitting across from her at my father's table that Thanksgiving, I envied her so profoundly that it ruined the dinner for me. I sat there inattentive to turkey, relatives, wine, pondering the mystery of why boring old Roseanne should be this visible, strident, almost embarrassing personification of fecundity and family life while I remained loveless, childless, mateless.

"So where's your husband this weekend, Anna?" my aunt Gert wanted to know. *Your husband:* they weren't well enough acquainted with him to call him by his name; for all I knew, they'd forgotten it.

"Working," I said, in a cheerful, resigned, groaning kind of voice that was meant to imply all sorts of things about my husband's dedication to toiling on behalf of a better world and to supporting me in style.

Aunt Gert wasn't impressed. "Somebody ought to tell him that work isn't everything," she said. "There's family."

I sat next to Patty and cut her turkey for her. In his high chair at the end of the table, Jonathan munched on a celery stalk. "He seems to be a natural vegetarian," Jean said. "Give him a piece of meat and all he can say is yuck."

"Yuck," Jonathan said, and banged his fist down on the highchair tray. "More!"

"Jonathan is turning into a complete brat," Patty said to me.

"A complete brat?" my father asked her. "Complete? No redeeming characteristics?" Patty shook her head firmly. My father chuckled and said, "Good Lord, will you look at the two of them? Have you ever seen such a resemblance?"

He meant Patty and me. Jean had a photograph of Patty, age five, on her first day of kindergarten. She wore a plaid dress and white socks; in between were her chubby knees. Her hair was in braids tied with ribbons. Her smile showed a missing tooth. Jean put it into a hinged frame alongside an old snapshot of me—same occasion, same hairdo, same knees, same gappy smile. Except for some indefinable mossy aura that dated my picture at approximately 1948, the two of us in our little ovals looked like the same person.

"Two peas in a pod," said my aunt Nancy, not entirely approvingly. We had all sat patiently for half an hour before dinner while Patty played the piano, sang "I'm a Little Teapot," and showed us her ballet routine.

"The sourpuss twins," said Uncle Ralph. "Smile, girls! What have you two got to be so down about?"

"Jonathan," said Patty, with a world-weary air that made everyone laugh.

After the pumpkin pie, the coffee, the Courvoisier I brought and pretended was a present from Duncan, Jean and I did the dishes. "Tell me about this new job," she said. "Is it going to be great? Are you going to be the toast of New Haven like you were the toast of Boston?"

I wasn't sure what I thought of my new job. I would be opening on New Year's Eve at the Park Plaza. I'd had one rehearsal so far with the pianist and bassist, two peppy, briskly professional black men named Forrest and Chuck. They knew everyone, they'd played with all the big names. In addition, Forrest taught jazz improvisation at Yale, and Chuck was a composer who was writing a song cycle for Leontyne Price.

Jerome claimed it was my big break. "If this is what you want," he told me, "these guys are the way to get it." Chuck said after our first number, "Hey—this girl can *sing*," and they gave me huge hugs and noisy, friendly good-byes when the rehearsal was over, but I didn't believe any of it. I had a feeling they saw me as naïve and small-time, a bit of a loser, that the Park Plaza job was a very minor part of their lives, and that when I wasn't actually with them, performing, they would forget I existed.

"It's a job in a hotel lounge where I sing mostly to tired businessmen who need to kill an evening," I told Jean. "Jerome says it can lead to all kinds of things—concerts, recitals, jobs in New York. But I don't know—I guess I'll always be homesick for the good old Cantabile."

"And no more opera auditions? What about that Hartford thing?" I smiled at her; she was so conscientious, such a good stepmother, remembering all the little details of my life and being sure to ask about them. "What about that competition Jerome wanted you to enter?"

"Ow—it ain't for the loiks o' me," I said in the Cockney accent that always made her laugh, and then I changed the subject—told her the latest Jerome stories. He had become quite fond of pop music and was trying to get his other prize student, a massive baritone with big ambitions, to sing Gershwin duets with me.

"But how's Duncan?" she asked. "Your father was so sorry he didn't come. We haven't seen him since the wedding."

"Oh, God," I said. "Duncan." The sound of his name made me feel tired and defeated. Duncan, who was probably with Susan Marshall at that very moment. Eating Thanksgiving pizza. Or would she make him a cozy domestic feast—turkey and champagne? Or would they skip dinner altogether and get right to it?

From the living room, I heard my father's voice raised for the punch line of some story, my uncle Phil's loud guffaw,

Roseanne's giggle. The familiar hominess of those noises, those people, the smells of turkey and coffee that lingered in the air, my mother's old dishes sudsy in the sink—all those things seemed hopelessly melancholy all of a sudden, frail bulwarks against the futility of everything. Eighteen months ago, Jean and I had sat in this kitchen drinking gin and discussing Duncan's faults. A week later I was with Will. Now I was married to Duncan, Patty was taking piano lessons, Jean and I were washing dishes, I had a new singing job that scared me to death, my cousin was grossly pregnant, Duncan was banging Susan on her waterbed, Will was out in Indiana with his son, and none of it—nothing—mattered. Everything was hopeless, pointless, and sad. It was like having mono, but I didn't have anything, I was perfectly healthy: it was only my life that was sick.

"He really had to work on Thanksgiving?" Jean asked.

"Oh—I don't know, Jean. He said he did."

For a while, I washed and she dried in silence. I could tell Jean wanted me to confide. She had never asked me why I had decided to marry Duncan after all—why I was binding myself to a man I had told her I hated. I sometimes felt I owed her an explanation—but how to explain such a thing? *I changed my mind, I didn't care what I did, he pressured me, my heart was broken . . .*

"What's troubling you, Annie?" Jean asked me all of a sudden, and I said, without thinking, "I'm so jealous of that cow Roseanne I could kill her!"

We both laughed, and then Jean sighed and said, "Oh, Annie." She put her arm across my shoulders. I began to cry. In the sink, under my agitated hands, I felt one of the old flowered dessert plates crack in two.

The next afternoon, I took my ritual walk. For the first time, I didn't enjoy it, and not only because the day was cold and damp and overcast. There must have been children on vacation playing in their yards; there must have been people walking and raking leaves and throwing Frisbees. But all I remember from that day is desolation. The graffiti on the fence by Northside High told me to eat shit, fuck war, fuck myself. The old neighborhood struck me as seedy: shabby houses, bare brown yards, tacky little stores. At the corner of Court and Carbon streets, there was a shaggy black dog lying in the gutter, looking asleep but really stone dead. Our old house on Spring was ludicrously small, a house for gnomes.

How had we survived there all those years, plagued with my mother's illnesses and not much money and the cold winter wind invading the place through a million cracks? The memory of Mamie's music ringing out from that house into the cold air seemed unreal, like something from an idealized children's book.

I walked by the Westenbergs' place. The green paint was still bright, and someone had put up a picket fence. On the porch was an arrangement of cornstalks and pumpkins. There were drapes at the windows, and through one I could glimpse an ornate gold lamp. In the backyard was a metal swing set. I stood there a long time, looking at the house, imagining the happy family that lived there, thinking of Will reunited with his little Freddie, of Linette in Virginia or New York with Lee and Rochelle, of Roseanne with her big stomach and cute daughter and attentive husband, until my hands and toes were numb and I was so depressed I would almost have welcomed a slow death by freezing.

Johnny's wedding was Saturday afternoon at St. Joseph's. It was a sunny day, for once—wedding weather, in spite of the cold. To cheer myself up, I wore the most flamboyant outfit I owned: a black velvet miniskirt, lacy black stockings, a gold sequined tunic, and my black-fox–collared coat. I tied up my hair with a gold ribbon, making a few ringlets with a curling iron and letting them hang in my face—very Jean Shrimpton. I put on black eye makeup and white lipstick and gold dangling earrings. When I was leaving, my father said, "You're going to *church* in that getup? You're going to a nuptial mass?"

I grinned at him. "Got to impress the old gang, pop. Besides, Julia's not a Catholic so there's no mass. Just your basic wedding."

"Well, you look—" He groped for the right word. "You look like some kind of a sexpot."

"Good," I said. "That's the general idea."

"You look beautiful," Jean said. She tucked a pair of gloves into the pocket of my coat. "But they're predicting snow. You're going to freeze in that outfit."

"That's the price a sexpot's gotta pay," I said.

It wasn't until I pulled into the parking lot in the ancient Volvo that I realized that, in spite of my gold sequins and my satin shoes trimmed with rosettes, I was going to look bad because I was there without Duncan.

He absolute had to work, he has this wonderful job, really, the work he's doing is so important and challenging and he's so dedicated, he's so selfless, he even gave up Thanksgiving with my family whom he adores, I mean it just kills him when he and I have to be separated for even one night, but he had no choice whatsoever, he's working on this absolutely crucial case, human misery doesn't take time out for holidays . . .

I parked the car and sat in it for a few minutes, rehearsing my lines and watching people approach the church. I saw no one I recognized—not, at least, from a distance and bundled up in hats and scarves and fur coats. Everyone seemed to be in couples—women hanging on to the arms of their men, men bending protectively to shield their mates from the wind. The spring after we were married, Duncan and I had gone to the wedding of one of his colleagues, and we had held hands all through the ceremony, smiling at each other misty-eyed when Jack and Cheryl said their vows. For a brief, irrational moment, before I remembered Susan Marshall's waterbed, I missed Duncan fiercely.

Without the heater, the car turned cold, and I got out and went up the steps of the church, my teeth chattering. The clean gray stone shone in the sun like a vision of heaven. The steps were worn shallowly away in the middle by years of the footsteps of the faithful—mine among them, faithless though I had been. They were lined with tubs of white chrysanthemums whose bright heads whipped around when the wind hit them. In my finery, I felt cold and conspicuous and unloved: some sexpot.

I was late. The ushers were standing around looking restless. One of them snapped to attention, glad to have a customer, and approached me—a young man I'd never seen before who had a vague, probably cousinly, resemblance to Johnny. He was resplendent in pale-blue and white, a wildly unseasonable outfit that reminded me of George Sullivan's rented tux for the senior ball. This one, though, was bell-bottomed and tight-jacketed, and the usher's brown eyes peeped out through masses of curly hair, moustache, beard. Trotting into the church with my gloved hand on his dutifully crooked arm, I felt like an aging groupie with Ringo Starr, or a modern-dress Musetta off for an evening at the Café Momus.

Inside, there was organ music, and white lilies on the altar, and a smell of incense and humanity and the heating system and something else I couldn't define: sanctity? nostalgia? All of a sudden, my knees felt weak.

"I don't want to sit near the front," I told the usher.

He looked at me in dismay, as if my appearance warranted a front-row seat. "Don't be shy," he said, and gave my arm a reassuring squeeze.

But I dropped his elbow and hustled quickly into one of the last pews. I sat back, my heart pounding. It was an unexpectedly overwhelming experience to be in St. Joseph's again. I hadn't set foot in the place since my grandmother's funeral, but sitting there in the shadow of one of the massive pillars, with the stained-glass window of St. Francis and the birds casting colored shapes on the seat in front of me, I was reminded not of Mamie but of all the Sundays of my distant youth spent in that church—the long hours of kneeling and standing, belting out the hymns, enduring the sermons, and praying for the love of Will Westenberg.

I calmed down and looked around for people I knew. Several pews ahead of me I saw Marie Barshak and some man—presumably her husband. Behind them I thought I recognized the broad back of Bobby Horgan. Could he be so unchanged? Still fat, and wearing a loud plaid sport jacket that I could have sworn he had worn in high school? He turned, saw me, and raised a hand in greeting. He nudged the woman by his side, and she turned and waved too. It was Maureen Roesch, valedictorian, composer of Martha Finch's eulogy, class goody-goody. How did she end up with fat Bobby Horgan? I was still absorbing this when Joey McCoy hurried in with a tiny pregnant woman in a fur toque, and then his sister Kathy on the arm of an older man with silver hair and a camel topcoat like Duncan's. Kathy was in a massive cape that looked like mink. They didn't see me, but Arlene Nuncio and Art Brewer said, "Hey! Annie!" as they went by. I'd heard they were married. Arlene hissed, "Dig you later!"

The organist stopped noodling around. There was a silence, and then a woman I recognized as Johnny's sister Cynthia was escorted to the front by my wild-haired usher. Johnny's father walked down with some female relative. The organ lit enthusiastically into Gounod, and the bridesmaids, in pink velvet, started their peculiar hesitating march down the aisle.

I sat there close to tears, surprised by a powerful emotion I didn't recognize and couldn't at first pinpoint the cause of. It wasn't the music, with all its associations, and it wasn't the church full of old friends and the overwhelming presence of the place iself and the memories it brought back. I closed my eyes and tried to think, and when the organ wound up the wedding march and was silent again, I realized that what I was feeling was loss—the familiar, dismal letdown that was so much a part of this church and these people and this city: I had been waiting for Will.

Knowledge flooded me, as if I'd taken a drug that brought everything into focus, clear as diamonds. *Will:* it was because of Will that my knees had gone weak. It was for Will that I had needed so urgently to sit in the back—to have a clear view of everyone present, to search out his familiar head and shoulders in the crowd, to stare at him across a sea of people just as I used to every Sunday morning of my youth at the ten o'clock mass. It was for that possibility that I had dressed in these outrageous clothes. It was why I was here in the first place, why I'd left Duncan in the clutches of Susan, why my heart had beaten so hard when I came in. Because I might see him.

It was like the night I sat in the bar with Trevor, knowing I was there for news of Will. Knowing that it was Will I organized my life around: that it was Will I loved. Still loved. It devastated me. I opened my eyes. The front of the church was a frieze of pink and blue, bridesmaids and ushers in their symmetrical lines. A fluff of white that was the bride, standing beside Johnny at the altar. Some priest I didn't recognize, smiling over his little book, talking about the sanctity of the marriage bond. It seemed, all of it, unbearable. The air was overheated and suffocating, and the congregation, all in pairs—bride and groom, bridesmaid and usher, Art and Arlene, Bobby and Maureen—seemed depressingly gullible, sitting there so perky and attentive, so sentimentally pleased by the sad, false words of the marriage ceremony.

I couldn't keep myself from looking behind me to see if he was lurking back there in the last pew—shy Will. But he wasn't, and I immediately hated myself for checking, for the way my heart lifted and then dropped. I slumped in my seat sweating, wanting to cry, wanting to leave. The church was full of him and of my trivial, desperately hoarded memories—like the Sunday he sat directly in front of me and I spent the entire mass looking at his sharp shoulder blades moving under his shirt and listening to his voice singing the hymns. And the times I lingered in church on Saturday afternoons waiting for him to come in and go to confession, a vigil rewarded exactly once, when he walked down the aisle, entered the confessional, left it, and walked out, right by me, without a nod of recognition. And the day after Martha's death when he cried in my arms. I ran through all his offenses again: indifference, insensitivity, cruelty, lies, abandonments. But the only thing that was clear in my mind was the intensity of my disappointment. It was as if I had some debilitating illness, some undiagnosed miliary tuberculosis of the spirit, a chronic fever curable only by massive doses of Will—my streptomycin, my ethambutol. I didn't care if he drank, if he despised me, if his spelling was atrocious, if he was a thousand miles away with some Claudia or Dorcas. I didn't care about anything. I just wanted him.

Johnny and Julia said their vows, both of them loudly, so that I heard every painful word. I sat there burning up with my fever, restless, longing. I watched the wavering colored pebbles scattered by St. Francis on the empty seat in front of me. I took the wedding band off my left hand and switched it to my right, then back again, wondering why I wore it at all. I got a mirror out of my purse and furtively inspected my makeup. I noted the new red cushions on the kneelers, replacing the dull brown ones of my childhood. I watched Bobby Horgan and Maureen Roesch smile at each other when Johnny and Julia were pronounced husband and wife. And, like a persistent migraine, his name kept beating in my head—*Will, Will, Will*—as if I were sixteen again, as if I hadn't progressed an inch since I was a teenager scribbling in her diary. As if life were nothing but a stale old joke, digging its one groove indelibly into your soul so that you're condemned to stumble along it forever.

Things were better at the reception. It was cocktail-party style, with unlimited New York State champagne, and it was held in the Apple Blossom Room at the Hotel Syracuse, the scene of our Senior Banquet the year I graduated from St. Joseph's. Will hadn't attended the banquet, and so the room, with its French windows and red carpeting, held no associations for me. I remembered only the reading of the mildly raunchy class prophecy, which predicted that George Sullivan would invent a vaccine to prevent hickeys and I would become a rock 'n' roll star with a gold record called "Let George Do It." That and the bottle of J & B that was passed around, wrapped in Arlene Nuncio's lacy white shawl.

Now the Apple Blossom Room was filled with many of those same people, diligently rounded up by Johnny from all over—faces I'd never expected to see again, never even thought of once I'd left town. People who had disliked each other heartily, who had stolen each other's boyfriends and ridiculed each other's clothes and hurled insults at each other after too much beer at parties, hugged each other with screams and tears. I was greeted like a prodigal daughter, but one who'd made good in the big city and come home gilded, a heroine. They'd all heard about my career—mostly through Johnny, but a couple of people had read about me in the *Times*.

"Oh, my God," Arlene screeched. "I thought, I *know* that girl! I said to Art, 'Look at this, honey, it's Annie Nolan, can you believe it?' "

"We were going to come up to Boston and see you," Art said. "Then Johnny told us you moved to New Haven."

"I want to hear about this husband of yours," Arlene said. "I ran into your stepmother at the Victory Market and she said he's a real dreamboat."

She showed me a picture of her children and told me all about Art's promotion—how he almost didn't get it, how the next in command had it in for Art because Art worked so much harder than anybody else—her face as she talked full of honest indignation and wifely pride. I thought of her and Art in high school, how shocking they were, famous for being horny and indiscreet, frantically screwing every chance they got, doing it in cars and on lawns and on people's living-room sofas—and now here they were, this noisy mom with a tummy, and Art managing a sewing-machine store in North Syracuse. It seemed a shame, all their wildness come to this: a Sears wallet-size photo of three little girls in smocked dresses.

"What about you?" Arlene asked. "Anything in the oven? Or are you going to be a career girl for a while longer?"

I smiled enigmatically and sipped champagne. "Who knows?" I murmured, and told everyone my lies: Duncan was dying to come, he's called me twice a day, he made me promise to leave for home early in the morning, he has tomorrow off and he wants to take me out to dinner . . .

Lying cheered me up and gave me confidence. Johnny introduced me to Julia, a tiny blonde who hung on his arm as if she couldn't stand up on her own, and when she said, "Johnny's told me so much about you, we wondered if you might sing something later with the band," I told her I'd love to, I'd be honored. I spoke automatically but I was perfectly sincere. I'd been hoping, in fact, to be asked—to impress these people, many of whom had seen me

last in tears, with blood all over my dress, at the party where
Trevor Finch punched Will Westenberg in the nose.

I talked to Joey McCoy—still a clown—and his tiny pregnant
wife. "This is our third effort," Joey said, patting Tricia's huge
belly. "The first two look just like me, and we're going to keep
trying until we get one who looks like a human being."

Tricia whipped out the pictures. "Don't listen to him," she
said. "Aren't they dolls?"

Joey's sister Kathy introduced me to her silver-haired husband. "We flew in from New York this morning," Kathy said,
fingering her necklace. "Selwin is a producer with NBC." The
necklace looked like diamonds, and she wore matching earrings.
She kept the mink slung over her shoulder.

"Ex-nun makes good," Joey said, and Kathy said, "Oh, Joey,
lay off," exactly as she might have in 1960, and we all laughed,
except Selwin, who stared off into space and emptied his champagne glass at a gulp.

Marie Barshak and I had a tearful reunion. We poured out
our vital statistics (a veterinarian husband, three kids, and a litter
of Weimaraners for her; my two half-siblings, the Park Plaza job,
and the rehearsed litany of Duncan's virtues for me) and then
stood there smiling at each other, nothing left to say. "I think of
Martha so often," Marie said finally. "I'll never forget that night.
I'll always miss her."

"And George," someone said. "Jesus, poor old George." The
crowd around us murmured sadly. No one mentioned Will.

I danced with Johnny, with Art Brewer, with Paul the long-
haired usher, with Kathy's Selwin (who described to me in slow,
scrupulous detail their trip to Copenhagen to buy the mink), with
Bobby Horgan. Bobby told me how he'd run into Maureen last
spring at a sales conference in Cincinnati. Pure coincidence. They
couldn't believe it, after seven years. They were both swept away.
They were married two months ago, and Maureen was already
expecting.

"You're looking at a happy guy," Bobby said. He spoke decisively, as if he wanted me to know that it was no longer important that he'd once liked me more than I liked him. I couldn't stop
looking at his jowls—he was a frisky dancer, and they shook when
he bobbed his head to the music—and I remembered how I had
recoiled in horror when he tried to corner me at parties. I gave his
hand a penitent squeeze.

"I hear you're married to a hot-shot lawyer," he said, and I said that I wished Duncan could have come and met everyone, I would have loved to show him off, he was so wonderful, so really, really wonderful. . . .

"Hey, you sound like a newlywed," Bobby said. "Pretty good advertisement for marriage after almost a year."

"I still feel like one," I said. "I just never get used to how fabulous it is."

"Gee, I'm glad you lucked out, Annie," Bobby said. He tightened his grip on my waist. "Isn't it great to see everyone so happy?"

Johnny took me over to the bandstand and introduced me. The band was a Syracuse institution—Eddie and the Busboys. They had played at the hotel when my parents were young. Eddie was obviously second-generation—young, sideburned, and energetic—but the rest of the band was composed of tough, wizened old guys who played like robots, strictly for schmaltz, every song coming out the same.

"Anna's the singer I told you about," Johnny said. "She says she'd be glad to sing a couple of numbers."

Eddie looked unenthusiastic. The saxophone player stared, frowning, at my black lace legs. The drummer puffed at a joint behind his hand. "Sure," Eddie said. "We'll be taking a break in a couple of minutes. You come on up and tell me what you do, and we'll see if we can put something together." He shrugged. "What the heck."

Johnny and Julia had a request: would I sing "People"? I said I would, and suggested that and two others to Eddie: "Love Me Tender" and "Our Love Is Here to Stay."

Eddie said, "Okay by me, lady. Nice wedding music. Nice love songs." The drummer protested that they were all the same tempo, all a bit slow, and suggested we put "Our Love Is Here to Stay" in the middle and accelerate the tempo. "Okay by me," Eddie said. "We'll jazz it up a little."

During the break I drank champagne and pondered what Eddie could mean by jazzing it up. But I was prepared for anything. I wanted to sing. At the prospect, I felt as I had on Cantabile nights: invigorated, eager, happy.

"I haven't sung for an audience in a long time," I said to Johnny.

He misunderstood me. "Don't be nervous," he said. "We're all friends here."

We sat down together with a bottle of champagne. Without his shoulder-length curls, Johnny looked no different than he had in high school. Senior year, he and I had gone to the Mistletoe Dance together. All night long I had tried to talk myself into the inevitable—kissing him good-night when he took me home—and then he hadn't even tried, a puzzling circumstance that Martha Finch and I discussed on the phone the next day: was Johnny a homo or not?

"You look like your senior picture in that haircut," I told him.

"Well, *you* don't!" He patted my black lace knee. "You looked pretty good then, but you look like a million dollars now."

"My father didn't approve of my outfit."

"Who can blame him?" Johnny said, grinning. "I wouldn't let a daughter of mine out of the house in that rig." He gave my knee a good squeeze. "Speaking of daughters," he said, "are you going to tell me that you're the only woman at this reception who isn't pregnant except my great-aunt Delma?"

"And Julia, I assume."

Johnny winked at me. "Who knows?"

It was time, I sensed, for a lie. "I just wish Duncan could be here to meet everybody."

"Maybe at Christmas," Johnny said.

"We'll definitely have to get together," I said, wondering if Duncan and I would still be together by Christmas. It seemed impossible that we could travel peaceably to Syracuse, wrap presents for each other, have a night out with Johnny and Julia like normal people. And yet what was different? Nothing tangible had changed. Even the affair with Susan could be my imagination. Even the way I had felt in church, the sudden, sick awareness of my need for Will—that was nothing new, after all; it was older than anything else in my life.

I took a deep breath and said, quickly, before Johnny could drift away to talk to someone else, "I thought Will might be here."

"Oh, Christ," he said. He filled his glass again and drank. "I was afraid you were going to ask me about that. Old Willie—Jesus. Don't think I didn't invite him. I gave him a personal invitation."

I put my own glass down, unsteadied by a return of the desolation that had come over me in church. Why did I ask? Why did I think I wanted to know that he was invited and he didn't come?

Johnny said, "In fact—oh, hell, I don't know if I should tell you this, I told him I wouldn't spill the beans to anyone, and I have no idea if I did the right thing or not." He gazed out at the snow while I waited, thinking: He was invited, he didn't come, and there is a secret to be kept even from me. Even if Johnny didn't say another word, I had that to add to my collection of griefs.

"You can tell me," I said.

Johnny gave his knowing little laugh, but broke it off quickly. He put his hand on my shoulder, looked at me a moment, took his hand away. "He came through town again last month—no, early this month. Couple of weeks ago. He showed up late one night on my doorstep. Driving a beat-up old car. Half loaded."

He paused, staring into his glass and swirling the champagne around, and I knew in that instant that the secret was something terrible: something terrible to me. "And?"

"This is the part I promised not to tell."

"Promised not to tell *who*, Johnny?"

"Anybody." Johnny looked at me again. I could see him deciding on brutal frankness—the way Dr. Greifinger had probably looked when he told Jean my father's chances were small. The truth isn't pleasant, but it's better to know. "He didn't mention you," Johnny said.

Some kind of hope had been building in me, fluttering around the desolation. *I'm in love with Anna Nolan,* he could have said. *Don't tell anybody. I know she's married but I'm really hung up on her.*

Johnny said, "Hey! Don't look so down." He took a cocktail napkin and dabbed at my eyes. "I don't believe it," he said. "You never did get over him, did you?"

I laughed. "Johnny, it's not a question of getting over something." I took the napkin from him and blew my nose. "I'm married to someone else, for heaven's sake. It's just that I thought he and I were friends, and I haven't heard from him. I just feel bad that he didn't mention me." I balled up the napkin in my hand and threw it accurately into a trash container beside the bar.

"I'm sure he still thinks of you as a friend," Johnny said—not, I could tell, entirely fooled. "It's just that he's going through a bad time, is all, and when he comes out on the other side of it I'm sure he'll—you know—get in touch and all that."

We were silent a moment. Johnny waved at someone across

the room. I picked up my glass again and sipped, but my throat closed up when I tried to swallow, and I had to concentrate to make it go down. Finally I said, "So what's the big secret?"

Johnny sighed. "So he shows up on my doorstep and says he wants me to do him a favor and promise not to tell anyone about it."

"What favor?"

"He was in bad shape," Johnny said. "I don't know when I've seen him so bad." He stared into his champagne again as if debating whether to drink it, remembering Will's condition. "Not just drunk," he said, and decided to drain his glass. "I mean, this guy was a basket case. He could hardly communicate. Remember how he used to be in high school? Mr. Inarticulate? Stuttering when he tried to answer in Latin class? This was worse. I mean, talk about depressed."

I thought, *Don't tell me, I don't want to hear it.* I had an urgent, overwhelming impulse to get up from my chair and run—out of that room, the hotel, away from the bad music and the clinking of forks against plates and Johnny's hesitant story that I knew I didn't want to be burdened with. It would stay with me forever, whatever it was. It would be part of what I thought about every night before I fell asleep.

I looked toward the tall draped windows. Outside, lit by floodlights, the snow was coming down hard in large, lazy flakes. To be out in it, away from this heat, this fever.

"Depressed about what?"

"He lost his kid."

"Freddie?"

"Four years old, Will said. His old lady got married again and moved to—where did he say? I forget—someplace far, anyway. He wasn't very clear. Vancouver? Someplace out there. I'm not even sure he knows. But she got full custody, I guess, and moved to East Jesus or wherever with the kid to spite him. Or so he says."

I remember his paranoia, his fear that Cindy would do something like that to cut him out forever. I remembered that he had once sung "Pop Goes the Weasel" to Freddie sixty-odd times in a row.

I said, "Oh, God, Johnny, he lived for that kid. He told me—" I picked up another napkin and held it to my eyes. Freddie was the only good thing in his life, he had said, and he couldn't expect me to understand because I'd never had a child. I thought of my sorrow over Linette, my envy of my cousin Roseanne: multiply that by a million, a trillion. I said, "Freddie was everything to him."

"Yeah. There's no justice—you know what I mean? God forbid somebody like Willie should try to buck the system. It's always the little guy that gets kicked in the teeth."

We sat there silently for a minute, Johnny drinking, me dabbing at my eyes. I couldn't believe it. How had he failed? Was it all for nothing, then—our separation? I might as well have returned to Indiana with him and shacked up in his apartment.

"But what happened, Johnny? You told me last summer that he had a good job, he was happy, he wasn't drinking."

"Who knows?" Johnny said. "He was up against big bucks. And let's face it. Our Willie doesn't know the first thing about surviving in the real world."

Eddie and the Busboys began straggling back to the bandstand, and I saw Eddie, seated at the piano, looking around for me.

I said, "Just tell me quickly, Johnny. What else?"

"So he asked me if he could hole up in my cabin for a while. He said he needed to be alone, needed to think and all that. He said he had nowhere to go. He was flat broke, spent everything on lawyers, and the lawyers let him down. So I said sure—what else could I say? Nobody uses the place in the winter—I wouldn't ski if you put a gun to my head. Lucky to get up there a couple of times a summer. I said, 'Hey buddy, you know where the key is, there's a shed out back full of wood, be my guest.' You know? How could I refuse him?"

I thought of Will drunk, poking the fire, sparks flying, flames shooting up against the leafless trees. I said, "He shouldn't be alone up there."

Johnny shrugged. "I told him the cabin isn't insulated or anything—hell of a place in the winter. No hot water, no phone. But he said just for a couple of weeks, maybe till Christmas. By then he'd get his ass in gear, probably head down to Albany and stay with his family there, look for a job. I advised him to stock up on groceries in case he gets snowed in. If I know Will, he'll stock up on booze and drink himself into a stupor. Not that I blame the guy."

"I can't stand to think of him up there like that," I said.

"Don't worry about old Willie," Johnny said. He drained his

glass again with an air of winding things up. "He always lands on his feet. Hey—come on. You've got to do a little singing."

"I could save him," I said abruptly.

Johnny gave me a sharp look, half-amused. "Save him? What in hell does that mean?"

"You know what that means. I could bring him back to the world. I could save him from himself, all his demons."

"Oh Annie, Annie." Johnny set down his glass and put his hands on my shoulders. "Honey. Forget him. Do me a favor. Forget old Willie."

"But I could save him," I insisted. Johnny stood up and pulled me with him into a hug, and I stood there stiffly, with my head against the shiny lapel of his tuxedo. "That summer, Johnny—that weekend we spent in your cabin—we were so close, you can't imagine how close we were. I don't mean just sex. We talked and talked, he told me everything, and he said he needed me, he said I was his salvation."

Johnny held me away from him and smoothed back my hair with a look of such sympathy that I began again to cry. What was I doing? How could I reveal these things to someone who called him old Willie?

"I could save him, Johnny," I said. "Really."

"Annie," he said. "Just one minute here. I want to give you some serious advice. Okay? This is Uncle John talking. Listen to me."

"But I *could*, Johnny." I felt something coming over me—hysteria, maybe. Anger. Despair. "I know him," I said. "I know how to handle him. He can't just be abandoned."

"Ssh. Listen. Annie. Forget him. Please? As a favor to me? Don't you think this has gone on long enough? This little crush?"

"It's not a crush!" I jerked my head away from his hand. "God, Johnny—a little crush. I wish it were that simple."

"Okay," he said, very patient. "All right. Call it whatever you like. But Annie—" He took me by the shoulders again and looked me in the eye. Not sympathy, I saw, but pity. "I don't think he wants saving. I don't think there's a damn thing anyone can do for him—guys like Will. Just leave him alone. He's a grown-up. Let him get through this his own way."

"His way is to drink himself to death," I said, and pulled away again. "You don't have to pity me, Johnny," I told him. "I have to get through things, too. It doesn't help to just trivialize everything. It doesn't do a damn bit of good to pretend things aren't the way they are. *Guys like Will*—what's that supposed to mean?"

"Honey, I like Willie a lot, but let's face it—he's an alcoholic, he's a bum."

"He's not!" My voice rose. I imagined people staring over at us, talking about me, but when I looked out across the room I saw only calm, laughing wedding guests, and Eddie sitting patiently at the piano smoking a cigarette.

Johnny shrugged again, conciliatory. "All right, already. What do I know? I'm just a humble chemistry teacher who's waiting for his favorite old girlfriend to sing on his wedding day."

I apologized. All my anger drained away. I felt exhausted, suddenly, as if a major argument had taken place and a life decision taken. I said, "Forgive me, Johnny. I just had to know, I needed to find out about him. I'm sorry if I'm being a bitch. I always have this impulse to defend him. I think he's been underappreciated all his life."

"He'd be glad to know he's got a friend like you," Johnny said.

"That's what I've been saying all along," I told him. But his comment hadn't been serious; it was meant as an exit line. He smiled vaguely, gave me a fast peck on the cheek, and took me by the hand.

"Here she is, folks," he said to the room at large, and Eddie and the Busboys perked up. There was a little drum roll. I walked unsteadily to the bandstand and faced the crowd. Someone started applauding, and as the noise grew my exhaustion disappeared and the talk with Johnny became a cold gray shadow at the back of my mind. I would forget it while I sang—like singing with a headache, or with the knowledge that your best friend has just drowned. I smiled into the crowd, the band lit into a predictably syrupy introduction to "Love Me Tender," and I began to sing.

The Busboys played better with a singer. They quit doing the show-off, crowd-pleasing stuff that they weren't good at and concentrated on backing me up. The jazzy Gershwin came across pretty well, and after the sax player put in a nice, restrained little solo riff at the end of "People," Eddie signaled me to sing it again. I threw in my Streisand imitation, and the crowd loved it. When we were done they yelled for an encore, and I sang "The Man I Love," and a revved-up version of "Summertime," and then at Eddie's suggestion, "Till There Was You."

The applause was tremendous. Joey McCoy got up on a table and whistled, yelling for more, and Bobby and Maureen came up and asked me to sing "Never My Love"—their song. But I didn't want to take over Johnny's wedding or alienate Eddie. I said thank you, thank you all, this has been wonderful, isn't it fun, isn't this a great party, let's have a round of applause for the bride and groom, and then I stepped down from the stage.

Johnny took my arm and led me back. "One more song," he said firmly. "Just one more itty-bitty song." He went over to talk to Eddie, and then he turned to the crowd and said, "I went to see Anna last year in Boston when she was singing at a little nightclub there—great little place, I'd remember the name of it if I hadn't had so much champagne. Anyway, she closed her act with an old song that her grandmother used to sing, and that if I'm not mistaken Anna sang at one of those memorable glee-club concerts back at good old St. Joseph's Academy." Joey whistled again, and there was scattered applause, but Johnny held up his hand again and said, "A lot of you are going to recognize this song, and all of you are going to love it. My band, unfortunately, doesn't know it—" The drummer played another brisk little roll, and Eddie scratched his head, looking confused, which made everyone laugh. "But hey—Anna can live without them for a couple of minutes," Johnny said. "What do you call it, Annie? Acapulco? No—wait— a cappella. Which is Italian for who needs these bozos, anyway? So here it is, folks. 'Marble Halls.' Great song, great singer." There was applause, then silence. I looked at Eddie and he nodded, and I started to sing.

The song was all wrong: too serious, too operatic, a bad choice for a wedding reception, and slightly absurd sung a cappella. But I pressed on, singing into all those upturned, attentive, champagne-drinking faces until halfway through the song something happened to me that had never happened before: tears began to roll down my face. I couldn't stop them, I had nothing to wipe them with. I stood there singing, crying, feeling like a fool. And I began to sing badly, worse than at the *Bohème* audition. My throat closed up, I forgot the audience, I sang nothing but words, and each word was painful. I kept thinking of Will, alone in Johnny's cabin, drinking, depressed, defeated, while I stood on a stage looking like a tart, singing to him, in a room full of people who never gave him a thought, who would laugh at him and call him old Willie if they did.

I had riches too great to count,
Could boast of a high ancestral name . . .

He had smiled at me, his cheeks red from the cold. He had handed me a tissue-wrapped package containing a plastic angel, and there had been an understanding between us, even then. And nearly twenty years later he had told me I was his salvation.

But I also dreamt, which pleased me most,
That you loved me, still the same,
That you loved me,
You loved me still the same . . .

They all applauded, of course. What else could they do? I stood there with Eddie holding one hand and Johnny the other while the applause went on, and then I stepped off the stage and dried my eyes with a napkin, blew my nose, laughed with people about my tears, accepted their congratulations. And all the while I was thinking: If I don't see him I will die.

The band began to play. Johnny came up to me and said, "You're not worrying about what I told you, are you, Annie? He's all right. I wouldn't have let him use the place if I thought he wasn't. You know that, don't you?"

I said sure, yes, of course, and then Paul the usher backed me into a corner, told me I'd been fantastic, and asked me to dance, but I excused myself and went quickly out, through the double doors and down the hall to the women's room. It was empty. In the mirror I saw that my eyes were red, my mascara was smeared, the gold ribbon was loose in my hair. I stood there staring at myself, full of belated mortification. How could I have confessed all that to Johnny, how could I have sung that song and cried? I imagined him telling Julia all about it while they danced: *She's really pathetic, this has gone on for years, the guy's a complete loser, he's what she was crying about . . .*

But my embarrassment petered out as I stood looking at myself. I tried to see in the mirror the pitiable victim of a ridiculous crush, but I could only remember what Will had said, that I was his salvation. I saw again his golden body, the body of an angel, coming into the room, kneeling at my side. I wanted to be with you, he had said. I'm falling in love with you. If I wasn't crazy about you then, I am now. I remembered my power over him: I could make him sad or happy, hopeful or despairing. I could transform his past and make the future into something good, something wonderful.

With effort, as if it were a scene from a book I'd read long, long ago, I turned my mind to Duncan and Susan on the waterbed, on the couch in the back room at the office, on the brass bed in the Orange Street apartment. It didn't matter. I didn't care if at that very moment they were fucking their brains out in any of those places, if they'd spent the whole weekend bouncing from one bed to another, screwing like rabbits. How could I ever have thought it mattered?

I heard someone coming in and scuttled into one of the stalls. I couldn't imagine talking to anyone. What could I say? More lies about Duncan, more false enthusiasm for other people's children, more funny remarks about my own singing making me cry, ha ha. My ancient love sealed me off from my old friends, from such humdrum activities as dancing and eating and talking, as thoroughly as if I were from another planet.

I sat there on the toilet listening while two women I didn't know peed and touched up their hair and had a conversation about breast-feeding. I put my head in my hands and waited, and when they were gone I came out and fixed my makeup. How easy everything was, after all. That morning, I had thought of my long, difficult love as an illness. But it could just as plausibly be seen as a sign of health—something vital. How else could it persist all these years, undiminished? How else could it be that he was still my angel, my only desire, my one necessity?

I left the women's room and, down the hall, gave my ticket to the hatcheck girl; she handed back my black-fox number. There was no one else around. From the Apple Blossom Room I could hear a drum roll, shouting, cheers: Julia must have thrown her bouquet—a good time to sneak out, everyone preoccupied, some young cousin catching the bouquet, Julia and Johnny saying their farewells. Then the door opened and, in a rush of snow and laughter, three people came in, a woman and two men. They stood there stamping off the snow, and then one of them turned and I saw that it was Trevor Finch.

He was wearing a huge tweed overcoat. His wet hair hung limply in his face, and he had the beginnings of a patchy beard. "Oh, my God, will you look who's on the premises," he said to no one in particular, and gave me an ostentatious hug. "The famous Anna Nolan in one of her rare appearances in the old hometown."

I pushed away from him. He smelled of booze and halitosis and wet wool. "Hello, Trevor," I said. "I was just leaving."

"Wait. Meet my old pal Mack, here," he said. A short, slick-haired man said he was pleased to meet me; he looked like someone disguised, for a joke, as a gangster: black shirt, yellow tie, dark suit, thin moustache. "And my new pal, Marge," Trevor said, and took the arm of the woman he'd come in with. Marge smiled—a tough-looking blonde in a red pantsuit and pearls and no coat. Her shoulders sparkled with drops of melted snow. "Anna Nolan," Trevor said. "Old girlfriend of mine. I knew her when, if you know what I mean."

"How do you do," said Marge. She took a pack of Marlboros from her jacket pocket and lit one. "How's the party? I hope we didn't miss anything good. We're a little late—got sidetracked." She grinned at me as if, as an old flame, I knew all about how Trevor could get sidetracked.

"I was just leaving." I drew my coat around me. "Nice to meet you. Nice to see you, Trevor."

"So soon?" Trevor took a cigarette from Marge and stuck it between his lips. He lit it, squinting at me. In his beard, he was like some evil little animal with the mange. "What's the matter?" he asked me. "Tenaro's reception a drag? Loverboy Westenberg not there? Or is he passed out somewhere already?"

I said, "I'd just love to stay and chat, Trevor, but I'm afraid I can't. What a fucking pity."

He swayed toward me and put his arm around my shoulders. The smoke from his cigarette drifted into my eyes. "Marge," he said. "This may sound crazy to you, but this girl could have had me and instead she went for the town asshole. Can you believe it?" I broke free and went toward the door. Trevor said, "Look at her in those lace stockings. Thinks she's hot stuff. All prettied up for Mr. Wonderful. He might be the town asshole but good old Anna stays true blue to the end."

I turned back to him and said, "Shut up, Trevor, you jerk, you filthy drunken shit."

"Hey, now," said Mack. "Just a minute here."

Trevor said, "Aw, Annie, come on, I didn't mean it." He came toward me again with his sly, wobbling smile. All I could think of was his mouth on mine that night at the Green Horseshoe, and the hate in his eyes when he told me he loved me. "Come on, let's be friends. We go back a long way." Behind him,

Marge and the hatcheck girl looked at each other and shrugged, and Marge took a long, bored drag on her Marlboro. "Hey, Annie," Trevor said. "Come on back to the party. Dance with me. I'm glad to see you, I really am."

"Don't you come near me, Trevor, you stinking son of a bitch," I said, and pushed through the door to the outside. Behind me, I could hear Trevor curse and Marge laugh, and from back in the Apple Blossom Room trickled the faint clamor that was poor old Eddie and the Busboys mangling "Julia" from the "White Album."

Outside, it was snowing gently, and the air was sharp as a knife. I took several deep breaths—a singer's breaths, from the diaphragm, from deeper than that: "Breathe from your gut," Lydia used to say; "Breathe with your balls," Jerome told his male students. I looked back. Trevor and his pals were gone. Only the hatcheck girl was there, leaning back in her chair, half asleep. I filled my lungs with air, inhaling the fresh smell of snow, and the big flakes fell on my face and down the neck of my coat. I forgot Trevor, and my blurted confessions to Johnny, and my bad, tearful singing. The air made me feel cleansed, strong, free. I walked across the parking lot in the snow, alone in my cold dark as Will must have been alone in his.

When I got back, my father's house was quiet, everyone asleep. I got silently into my flannel nightgown, brushed my teeth, washed off my makeup. The radiator in the bathroom made the whooshing, banging noises it had been making for years. I wasn't sleepy. My attic room eventually collected all the heat in the house: it was too warm, bad for sleeping. I went downstairs again, pausing in Jonathan's room to check him as he slept. He lay peacefully, thumb in mouth, and when I touched his soft cheek with the back of my hand, he said "mum-mum-mum" without waking up. I stood there a long time listening to him breathe, and then I wandered down to the kitchen, made myself a cup of instant coffee, and ate a piece of leftover pumpkin pie. It occurred to me that I should drive home, in the middle of the night, and catch Duncan and Susan in bed together. I imagined Susan fleeing in her nightgown into the snow. I would offer Duncan my forgiveness on the condition that we have a baby. Someone to care for. And once I was pregnant I would banish Duncan forever.

Duncan: I tried to bring him into my mind, get a serious grip on who he was and what he meant to me, but he was a foreign language, a whole other alphabet and vocabulary. Once, I had told Will that Duncan was nothing to me, and I'd felt guilty for it, and unsure if it was true. Now I knew it had been true for a long time. I thought again of Will in Johnny's cabin. I tried to picture him there, at that moment. Half an hour until midnight, in the middle of a snowstorm. Would he be awake? Asleep? Would the fire have gone out? Would he be cold, hungry, lonely? Would he be thinking of me? Or would I be in his dreams, a shadow from the past who lay down beside him, put her arms around him, and said "I believe in you"? True blue to the end.

I went back to my attic room and got dressed—jeans, sweater, heavy socks. Downstairs, I found my boots and jacket in the hall closet, purse and keys on a chair by the front door, mittens knitted by Jean stuffed in my pockets. I left a note on the phone pad: "Driving home tonight. Don't worry. I'll call in the morning. Love." Silently, I let myself out the front door and closed it behind me. I stood on the porch, trying to think, but my mind was blank, I couldn't settle it to anything. I watched the snow coming down, a shower of gold in the cone-shaped yellow glow from the streetlight. The sidewalk, the bushes, the road, looked beautiful, a clean white moonscape made of stone. When I walked out into it, my brain cleared and focused.

In the hour or since I'd been inside, a skin of snow had accumulated on the Volvo. I brushed it off, and then I got in the car and started it. The engine caught right away—a rarity—but the heat always took a few minutes to come on, and while I waited I looked out the window, watching my footprints on the front walk fill up again with snow. In an hour there would be no trace of my presence. Outside the illumination from the streetlight, everything was cold velvet-black, even the snow. I turned on the radio and heard the end of "Proud Mary," then a weather report: a storm was moving down from Canada.

By then the car warmed up. I turned it around in my father's driveway, and then I headed down the street and took a left onto the main drag—not south toward home, but north, into the storm.